The High Tide Club

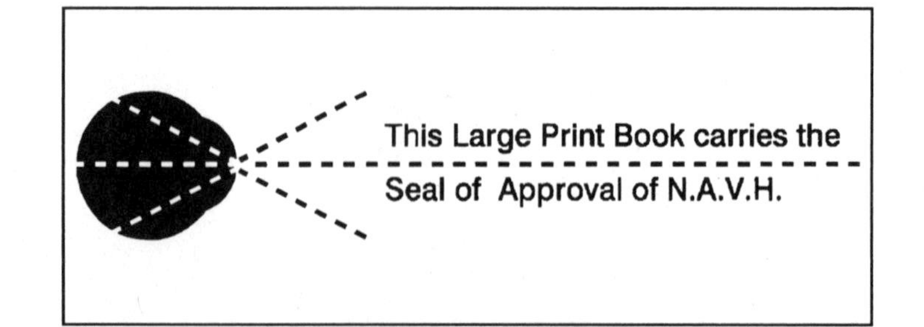
This Large Print Book carries the
Seal of Approval of N.A.V.H.

The High Tide Club

Mary Kay Andrews

WHEELER PUBLISHING
A part of Gale, a Cengage Company

Farmington Hills, Mich • San Francisco • New York • Waterville, Maine
Meriden, Conn • Mason, Ohio • Chicago

Wheeler Publishing, a part of Gale, a Cengage Company.

Wheeler Publishing Large Print Hardcover.
The text of this Large Print edition is unabridged.
Other aspects of the book may vary from the original edition.
Set in 16 pt. Plantin.

**LIBRARY OF CONGRESS CIP DATA ON FILE.
CATALOGUING IN PUBLICATION FOR THIS BOOK
IS AVAILABLE FROM THE LIBRARY OF CONGRESS.**

ISBN-13: 978-1-4328-5202-3 (hardcover)

Published in 2018 by arrangement with Macmillan Publishing Group, LLC/St. Martin's Press

Printed in the United States of America
1 2 3 4 5 6 7 22 21 20 19 18

This one's dedicated with love to
Andrew Rivers Trocheck,
whose love of Georgia's wild places
inspire me.

ACKNOWLEDGMENTS

The setting for this novel is entirely fictional. Inspired by the beautiful and fragile Georgia coast, I created a barrier island called Talisa, a county called Carter, and its county seat, St. Ann's, and inserted them into the real geography of the Georgia coast, just north of Cumberland Island, but South of Sapelo Island. I can't offer enough thanks to Blaine and Jenna Tyler for sharing their love of that island.

It's always foolhardy to create a character whose work you know nothing about, but it's a very good idea to have experts who are willing to share their knowledge. Many thanks go to Robert Waller, Sharon Stokes, Beth Fleishman, Mary Balent Long, and Kathryn Zickert for their legal expertise. Any misstatements of fact are due to my own ignorance and not the excellence of their advice.

Savannah friends who contributed their knowledge of local history include Polly Powers Stramm and especially Jacky Blatner Yglesias.

As always, my community of author friends lent their ears and advice during the process of brainstorming and writing *The High Tide Club.* The members of The Weymouth Seven: Diane Chamberlain, Margaret Maron, Katy Munger, Sarah Shaber, Alex Sokoloff, and Bren Witchger, were as always, essential to my process. Special thanks to my favorite low country ladies, Patti Callahan Henry and Mary Alice Monroe for their brilliant suggestions.

I couldn't do what I do without my dream publishing team: the best agent in the whole damn world, Stuart Krichevsky, and the gang at SKLA, marketing genius Meg Walker at Tandem Literary, and of course, my publishing house, St. Martin's Press. There aren't enough words to express my gratitude for editor extraordinaire Jen Enderlin, capo di tutti capi Sally Richardson, and the team who make it all happen: Brant Janeway, Erica Martirano, Jessica Lawrence, and Tracey Guest. Thanks again, Mike Storrings, for yet another gorgeous cover.

I may wander far and wide in search of the next story, but at the end of every quest I'm blessed enough to have the love and support of my family, who know enough about me to leave me alone when necessary, and reel me back home to reality at just the right time.

All my love goes to Katie and Mark Abel, Andy Trocheck, my darling grands Molly and Griffin, and most of all, best of all, my starter husband of forty-one years — and counting, Tom.

Prologue

October 1941

The three young women stared down at the hole they'd just dug. Their gauzy pastel dresses were rumpled and slightly damp, and the heels of their dainty sandals made them teeter precariously on the rounded oyster shell mound. Their faces were flushed and shiny with perspiration. The fourth in the circle was a girl of only fourteen, dressed in a hand-me-down set of boy's overalls and a pair of worn leather shoes, her eyes wide with terror in a smooth, toffee-colored face. The first shafts of sunlight shone softly through the thick intertwined branches of moss-hung live oaks.

"Give me the shovel," the tallest one said, and the girl handed it over.

The blade of the shovel sliced into the crushed shells and sand, and she dumped the material onto the form at the bottom of the hole, then wordlessly handed the tool to the redhead standing beside her. The redhead shrugged, then did the same, being careful to distribute the shells and sand over the dead man's face. She turned to her friend, a pretty blonde who now had both hands clamped over her mouth.

"I'm gonna be sick," the young woman managed, just before she leaned over and retched violently.

Her friend offered a handkerchief, and the blonde dabbed her lips with it. "Sorry," she whispered. "I've never seen a dead man before."

"You think we have?" the tall one snapped. "Come on, let's get it done. We have to get back to the big house before we're missed."

"What about him?" The redhead nodded toward the body. "When he doesn't come to breakfast, won't people start asking questions?"

"We'll say he talked about going fishing. He went out yesterday too, remember? Before dawn. Millie can say she heard him leave his room. His gun is right here, so that makes sense. Anything could have happened to him. He could have gotten lost in the dark and wandered into one of the creeks."

"There's gators in the creeks," said the young girl in the overalls. "Big ones."

"And there are snakes too," the tall one volunteered. "Rattlesnakes, cottonmouths, coral snakes. And wild hogs. They run in packs, and if they get you . . ."

"Good heavens," the redhead said. "If I'd known that, I never would have snuck out in the dark last night. Snakes and gators?" She shuddered. "And wild hogs? Terrifying."

"We don't know anything," the tall one said emphatically. She searched the others' faces carefully. "Agreed?"

A tiny sob escaped from the blonde's lips. "Oh my God. What if somebody finds out?"

"Nobody's going to find out," the redhead said. "We swore, didn't we?"

"They won't. Nobody ever comes here. They don't even know it exists. Right, Varina?"

The fourteen-year-old looked down at her dusty shoes. "I guess."

"They don't," the tall one said. "Gardiner and I found it by accident, when we were little kids. It's supposedly an Indian mound."

The blond girl's brown eyes widened. "You mean a burial mound? We're standing on dead people?"

"Who knows?" A single drop of water splashed onto the tall one's face, and she glanced up, through the treetops, where the clouds had suddenly darkened. "And now it's starting to rain. Come on, we've got to finish this and get back to the house before we all get soaked and ruin our shoes and have to answer a lot of questions about where we've been and what we've been doing."

Tears welled up in the blond girl's eyes,

and she unconsciously rubbed her bruised, bare arms. She was weeping softly. "We're all going to hell. We never should have gone swimming last night. What if somebody finds out what's happened? They'll think it was us. They'll think it was me!"

The redhead, whose name was Ruth, was thoughtful. "It doesn't matter who killed him. Any one of us could have done this. He was a terrible man. He's the one going to hell for what he did. You never should have agreed to marry him, Millie."

"She did, though. And what's done is done," said their leader. "There will be a lot of questions, girls, when he turns up missing. There's bound to be a search, and I'm sure my papa will call the sheriff. But we don't know anything, do we?"

The blonde looked at the redhead, who looked at the tall one, who looked expectantly at the young girl, who nodded dutifully. "We don't know nuthin'."

1

Rooke Trappnell rarely bothered to answer her office phone, especially when the caller ID registered "unknown number" because said caller was usually selling something she either didn't need or couldn't afford. But it was a slow day, and the office number actually was the one listed on her business cards, so just this once, she made an exception.

"Trappnell and Associates," she said crisply.

"I'd like to speak to Miss Trappnell, please." She was an older woman, with a high, quavery voice, and only a hint of the thick Southern accents that prevailed on this part of the Georgia coast.

"This is she." Brooke grabbed a pen and a yellow legal pad, just in case she had a potential real, live client on the other end.

"Oh." The woman seemed disappointed. Or maybe disoriented. "I see. Well, this is Josephine Warrick."

The name sounded vaguely familiar, but Brooke didn't know why. She quickly typed it into the search engine on her computer.

"Josephine Warrick on Talisa Island," the woman said impatiently, as though that should mean something to Brooke.

"I see. What can I do for you today, Mrs. Warrick?" Brooke glanced at the computer screen and clicked on a four-year-old *Southern Living* magazine story with a headline that said "Josephine Bettendorf Warrick and Her Battle to Save Talisa Island." She stared at the color photograph of a woman with a mane of wild white hair, standing defiantly in front of what looked like a pink wedding cake of a mansion. The woman wore a full-length fur coat and high-top sneakers and had a double-barreled shotgun tucked in the crook of her right arm.

"I'd like you to come over here and see me," Mrs. Warrick said. "I can have my boat pick you up at the municipal marina at 11:00 A.M. tomorrow. All right?"

"Well, um, can you tell me what you'd like to talk to me about? Is this a legal matter?"

"Of course it's a legal matter. You are a lawyer, are you not? Licensed to practice in the state of Georgia?"

"Yes, but —"

"It's too complicated to go into on the phone. Be at the marina right at eleven, you hear? C. D. will pick you up. Don't worry about lunch. We'll find something for you to eat."

"But —"

Her caller didn't hear her objections because she'd already disconnected. And now Brooke had another call coming in.

She winced when she glanced at the caller ID. Dr. Himali Patel. Was the pediatric orthopedist already calling to dun her for Henry's ruinous medical bills?

"Hello?"

"Hello, Brooke. It's Dr. Patel. Just following up to see how Henry's physical therapy is coming."

"He's fine, thanks. His last appointment was this week."

"I'm so glad," Dr. Patel said. Dr. Himali Patel was the soft-spoken Indian American doctor who'd treated Henry's broken arm. Brooke shuddered when she thought about the thousands she still owed for the surgery. She'd rolled the dice on an "affordable," high-deductible health insurance policy and came up snake eyes when Henry fell from the jungle gym at the park and landed awkwardly on his arm, leading to a trip to the emergency room, surgery, and weeks' worth of physical therapy.

"If he has any pain or his range of motion starts to seem limited, bring him back into the office. Other than that, he's good to go."

"Thanks, Doctor." Good to go. Easy for her to say. Brooke still needed to call the hospital's billing department to set up a payment plan.

The *Southern Living* magazine article was timed to coincide with Josephine Warrick's ninety-fifth birthday. Which would make her ninety-nine now. Brooke reached for the glass of iced tea and the peanut butter and jelly sandwich she'd brought from home and read the article, and half a dozen others she'd found online, catching up with the colorful life and times of Josephine Bettendorf Warrick.

She already knew a little about Talisa, dating back to a brief, ill-fated Girl Scout camping expedition nearly twenty-five years earlier. Her memory of the place was hazy, because she'd gotten seasick on the boat ride across the river on the way to the island and then managed to get stung by a jellyfish *and* hike through a patch of poison ivy. The assistant troop leader had to arrange for a boat to take her back to the mainland a day early to await pickup by her parents, who were two hours away in Savannah. It had been Brooke's first and last camping trip. The name *Talisa* called up memories of calamine lotion, burned marshmallows, and her sight line, from the backseat of the Cadillac, of her father's neck, pink with barely suppressed anger at having to miss his Saturday golf game.

Brooke jotted notes as she read and chewed her sandwich. Talisa, she learned, was a twelve-thousand–acre barrier island a thirty-minute ferry ride from where she now lived in St. Ann's, Georgia. It had been purchased as a winter retreat in 1912 by Samuel G. Bettendorf and two cousins, all of whom were in the shipping business together in Boston. In 1919, Samuel Bettendorf and his wife, Elsie, had built themselves a fifteen-room Mediterranean revival mansion, which they named Shellhaven.

In 1978, the cousins had sold their interest in Talisa to the State of Georgia for a wildlife refuge, which explained how Brooke's Girl Scout troop had been allowed to camp there. Samuel Bettendorf had retained his property, which was on the southeast side of the island, facing the ocean.

And Samuel's daughter and only living heir, Josephine Bettendorf Warrick, had been engaged in a lengthy court battle with the state, which had been trying, in vain, to buy up the remainder of the island for the past twenty years.

Was this why Mrs. Warrick wanted to see her? Brooke frowned. She'd spent the first three years of her career working at a white-shoe Savannah law firm, doing mostly corporate and civil work. But since fleeing to the coast as a runaway bride, she'd hung out a shingle as a solo practitioner. The *and Associates* part of Trappnell and Associates was pure fiction. There were no associates and only a very-part-time receptionist working in the one-story, wood-shingled office she rented downtown on Front Street. It was just thirty-four-year-old Brooke Marie Trappnell. In life, and in law, come to think of it. She did some divorce work, DUI, personal injury, and the occasional petty civil or criminal work. But she knew next to nothing about the highly specialized area of eminent domain law.

Which was what she'd tell Josephine Bettendorf Warrick. Tomorrow. And why not? She had a 9:00 A.M. appointment to see a client who'd been locked up for assault and battery in the Carter County Jail for a week, following a run-in with a clerk at the local KwikMart who'd tried to charge her ninety-nine cents for a cup of crushed ice. But the rest of her calendar was open. Not an unusual occurrence these days.

There were, by her count, nearly three dozen other attorneys practicing law in St. Ann's, all of them long-term, well-established good ol' boys, who gobbled up whatever lucrative legal work was to be done in this town of seventeen thousand souls. Brooke counted herself lucky to pick up whatever crumbs the big boys didn't want.

If the weather app on her phone was to be trusted, tomorrow would be another sunny, breezy spring day. Why not take a boat ride to reacquaint herself with Talisa on her own terms and meet the legendary Josephine Warrick?

2

She heard the music blaring from within the office as soon as she parked the Volvo out front on Friday morning. Twangy guitar, heavy drumbeats, some kind of party-hearty country music. Brooke dug a can of Mace from her purse and quietly moved toward the door, which was slightly ajar.

She eased the door open with her foot and cautiously poked her head inside.

The intruder was so intent on her task, she never even looked up. She was seated with her bare feet propped up on the receptionist's deck, her head bobbing, singing along with the radio. "Play it again, play it again, play it again," she repeated, drumming the desktop for emphasis.

Brooke reached down and tapped the wireless speaker sitting atop the file cabinet.

The girl, startled, jerked upright.

"Jesus, Brooke!" she exclaimed, reaching for the bottle of nail polish she'd been applying to her toenails. "You scared the shit out of me!"

"And you almost gave me a heart attack when I drove up and heard that music and saw the door standing open," Brooke said. She held up the can of Mace. "You're lucky I didn't spray first and ask questions later."

"What are you doing here, anyway? I thought you were supposed to go see Brittni in the jailhouse this morning," Farrah said, glancing at the clock that hung over the office's sole bank of file cabinets.

"And I thought you were supposed to be in second-period English."

Farrah Miles was a high school senior who also doubled as Henry's babysitter. Brooke and Farrah had met in September after Brooke had given a career-day talk about law at the local high school. Most of the teenagers had napped or stared at their phones during her talk. But the next day, Farrah, a petite blonde with a tiny gold nostril stud, blue-green streaks in her hair, and a penchant for cowboy boots and supershort cutoff jeans, showed up at her office and proclaimed herself interested in the law and a job.

The girl was smart and efficient — when she wanted to be — so they'd struck a deal that Farrah would work five days a week after school and pinch-hit as a babysitter for three-year-old Henry, as needed.

Farrah sat down and resumed her pedicure,

dabbing a bit of purple polish on her big toenail. "Mr. Barnhart's a prick. We've only got two more weeks of class before graduation, and I've already got a solid A, but he still won't exempt me from taking the final exam like my other teachers."

"So you're cutting class? Farrah, he could still flunk you. I thought we talked about this. You've got to keep your grades up if you want to get into Georgia."

The girl scowled. "They wait-listed me, Brooke. I'm not gonna get in. I'll just go to Community College like everybody else. It's no biggie."

Brooke rolled her desk chair over to Farrah's desk and sat inches away from her. The girl lowered her head, pretending to concentrate on her toes. Brooke reached out and tilted Farrah's chin, lifting it until they were eye to eye.

"Listen to me, Farrah Michele Miles. You still have a really good chance. You aced your SATs and your ACTs. You've got a solid 3.9 grade point average in mostly advanced placement classes, and plenty of extracurricular activities. You wrote amazing essays, and your teachers wrote you great recommendation letters. Do not screw this up. Please?"

"I'm not screwing anything up." Farrah changed the subject. "So what happened this morning with Brittni?"

"I went over to the jail. Her stepfather still won't post bail, and her court date's not 'til next week, so there's not much I could say except hang tight and try not to get in any more fights."

Farrah shook her head. "I know she's my cousin, but she is such a dumb bitch. She shoulda just paid the ninety-nine cents for the damn cup of ice. It's not like she was broke!"

"I told her the same thing," Brooke said, "but she says the KwikMart cashier was some kind of high school frenemy who thinks Brittni stole her boyfriend."

"Right. That's Kelsy Cotterell, and she hates Britt because she totes did steal Kelsy's boyfriend. And also because Brittni had his name tattooed right across her chest, which is not even hot, despite that boob job of hers," Farrah said. "She thinks because she used to be a cheerleader the whole world owes her something. Mama says she gets that and her lard butt from Aunt Charla."

Brooke pressed her lips together to keep from laughing at Farrah's dead-on assessment of her client and her client's mother. "Okay. Enough about Brittni. As long as you're here, you might as well get some work done. I need you to go online and do some research. See what you can find out about *State of Georgia v. Josephine Warrick*. Print out what you get and start a file."

"Josephine Warrick? Is that the old lady who owns Talisa? What's up with her?"

"She called me yesterday, wouldn't say what it's about. Just that she wants to see me about an unspecified legal matter. I'm headed over there in a few minutes."

"Awesome. A new client. So that's why you're all dressed up today. You look nice, by the way."

"Thanks," Brooke said. "I kinda like that nail polish of yours too. What's it called?"

"Violet Femmes," Farrah said. She held up the bottle. "Want a hit?"

"No, thanks. I'll stay with my Bubble Bath. Gotta look conservative in my line of business."

Shunning her usual casual office attire, Brooke had reached to the back of her closet and brought out an expensive tailored navy pantsuit, which she wore with a white silk shell, pearl earrings, and a pair of black lizard-skin Tod's loafers, throwbacks from her Savannah wardrobe, which rarely saw the light of day in St. Ann's.

"That old lady's, like, filthy rich, you know," Farrah said.

"I doubt that she'll end up hiring me. I don't practice the kind of law it sounds like she needs."

"You're a lawyer, right? Why wouldn't she hire you?"

"I'm a general practitioner, remember?

From the little research I've done, it sounds like she needs somebody who does eminent domain law. But she seems like quite a character, so I'm gonna go see her anyway."

"Text me some pictures of the house, okay? I've never actually been inside. Jaxson and I used to ride over to the island on his brother's boat last summer to party at the top of that old lighthouse, but I hear she's got an armed security guy roaming around now."

"Talisa is private property. You and your friends had best stay away from there," Brooke said, trying to look severe. "Unless you want to share a jail cell with your cousin."

"Whatevs." Farrah set the bottle of nail polish aside and turned the music on again.

Brooke promptly turned down the volume. "Who is that, anyway?"

The girl's eyes widened. "You're kidding, right? Seriously? You never heard Luke Bryan before?"

"These days my playlist mostly consists of Kidz Bop and the Wiggles," Brooke replied.

"Girrrrrl, you need to get in the now," Farrah said condescendingly, reeling off her current favorite country music acts before stopping abruptly. "Hey, I almost forgot to tell you the good news."

"What's that?"

"I might have gotten us a new client. Jaxson's mom left his dad again this week, and she swears this time it's for good. So I gave her your card. If she hires you for the divorce, do I get, like, a finder's fee or something?"

Brooke laughed. "We've got to find a way to get you into UGA, kid. Someday, you're gonna make somebody a hell of a lawyer."

The municipal marina was quiet at midday. The tide was dead low, and most of the serious fishermen had set out earlier in the morning. Seagulls screeched and swooped for fiddler crabs scuttling across the exposed gray pluff mud of the riverbank. A couple of derelict-looking shrimp boats creaked at their moorings at the end of the wharf, along with a handful of the open, shallow-hulled center-console boats favored by local crabbers. There were seven or eight shiny new cabin cruisers and three sailboats scattered along the wharf too, but most of the larger, more expensive boats were to be found up the coast, on St. Simon's Island, which was where really wealthy boaters congregated.

Brooke gazed along the length of the long wharf, wondering which of the boats belonged to Josephine Warrick.

She heard a sharp whistle and swung around to see who it was meant for.

Finally, she spotted a modest, faded-yellow craft bobbing at its mooring at the end of the dock. A lone man stood on the bow, waving at her. He cupped his hands around his mouth and called to her.

"Are you Brooke?"

She nodded and hurried toward the boat.

He was skinny, with thinning hair bound into a scraggly gray braid that hung down his neck, bow-legged and sun-bronzed, wearing an ancient green army fatigue shirt with the sleeves hacked off and unbuttoned to his bare bony chest, and cutoff jeans that had seen better days. Clipped to the belt of his shorts was a holster with a large pistol. Brooke wasn't good with guns, but she was pretty sure it was a 9 mm.

His face was shaded by a sweat-stained ball cap, and his eyes were hidden behind cheap aviator sunglasses, but she felt the intensity of his stare.

"Are you C. D.? From Talisa?"

"That's me," he said, offering her a hand. "C. D. Anthony, in the flesh. Come aboard."

He motioned for her to sit atop a cushioned bench at the stern and busied himself untying the boat.

"All set?" he asked, and without waiting for her reply, he gunned the motor and expertly backed the boat away from the wharf.

The man turned to look at her as the boat putted quietly through the marina's no-wake zone.

"Nice day for a boat ride," he said abruptly. "You ever been over to the island before?"

"A long time ago," Brooke said.

"I don't reckon it's changed much, no matter how long ago it was," he said. "You a friend of Miss Josephine's?"

"Not really," Brooke said.

"She don't get a lot of visitors. So I reckon maybe you've got business over there?"

Brooke found herself squirming a little under his stare. "Something like that."

He was sizing her up. "You a lawyer? You look like a lawyer to me."

"Good guess," Brooke said, keeping it light. "How about you? I assume you work for Mrs. Warrick? In what capacity?"

"Whatever needs doin', I do," C. D. said. "Run the boat, work on the vehicles a little. Fetch groceries and supplies from the mainland. Like that."

"How nice."

"She ain't in real good health. Took her to the doctors over in Jacksonville last month. She don't say a lot, but I reckon they gave her bad news. Louette, she's kinda the housekeeper, she says Josephine don't eat much. Makes sense. She was pretty stout when I met her, but lately, she's gotten real skinny. Eat up with cancer probably."

Brooke wondered how Josephine Warrick would feel about one of her employees gossiping about her health with a total stranger.

"If that's true, I'm sorry to hear it," Brooke said politely.

She pivoted sideways, signaling their discussion was over, gazing back toward the mainland. She knew it was a five-mile crossing to Talisa, and she didn't care to spend the trip chatting with this unnerving cornpone Popeye.

He took the hint and gunned the boat's motor the minute they passed the last piling marking the no-wake zone. She gripped the seat with both hands and within minutes found herself being drenched with sea spray every time the small vessel crested one wave and bounced back into the water.

Eventually, Brooke saw a green swath appear on the horizon, and ten minutes after that, C. D. slowed the boat down and they glided into a narrow tidal creek. At the creek's widening, she spotted a long dock jutting into the water. A sturdy black man stood at the end of the dock, his arms crossed over his chest. A child of about eight or nine sat at the edge of the dock, holding a cane fishing pole. Long, bead-wrapped dreadlocks reached to his shoulders.

"Hey, Lionel," C.D. called. "Catching anything?"

The kid looked up and waved. "Ain't no fish biting today. You take me for a boat ride?"

"Sorry, pal, maybe another time."

As they approached the dock, C. D. put the boat in neutral, and the black man tossed them a thick line, which the captain knotted to a cleat on the bow.

"Hey," the man said quietly, nodding politely at Brooke.

"This here's Shug," C. D. said. "He'll drive you up to the house." He busied himself fiddling with something on the boat's console.

Shug bent down and gripped Brooke's arm at the elbow, helping her make the two-foot leap from the boat's deck to the dock.

"You okay?" Shug asked solicitously. "Got everything?"

"Oh," Brooke said, pointing toward the bench on the stern. "Oh no. I left my briefcase."

C. D. grunted, picked up the briefcase, and slung it in the general direction of the dock. Shug reached out and snagged it, midair, before it could hit the water.

"You have a nice visit now, you hear?" C. D. said. "I'll be around when you're ready to go back."

An ancient, rusted seafoam-green Ford pickup truck was parked at the end of the dock among a motley-looking assortment of junker cars.

Brooke patted the rounded front hood. "Wow. How old is this thing?"

"Mmm, I think it's from around the late fifties," Shug said, opening the passenger-side door. "I do know that Mr. Preiss Warrick bought it new way back when. He's been gone a long time, but Miss Josephine, she don't like to part with nothin' that was his. Likes to keep everything just like it was before he passed."

He turned the key in the ignition and pumped the gas pedal. The truck's motor whined, then stalled. He shook his head, repeated the same motion twice before the engine finally caught. Moments later, they were bumping along the narrow crushed-shell roadway. Brooke poked her head halfway out the open window, marveling at the scenery.

Gnarled, moss-draped live oaks on both sides of the road met in the middle to form a dense, nearly impenetrable canopy of green overhead. Thick stands of palmetto, swamp myrtle, pines, and cedars were festooned with blossoming jasmine, whose heavy scent perfumed the air. As they rounded a bend in the road, she spotted a pair of blue herons intent on fishing for their lunch in a shallow ditch. Another turn revealed an expanse of marsh where patches of sun-bleached driftwood and cypress knees were host to dozens of large, brown nesting birds.

"Wood storks," Shug said, pointing. He gave her a smile. He was a thickly built man, in his fifties, she guessed, with heavily muscled arms. He wore neatly pressed blue jeans and a short-sleeved blue work shirt. "We got lots of birds over here. Famous for it, I guess. Is this your first trip to Talisa?"

"Sort of," Brooke said. "I was here for a

Girl Scout campout years ago. It didn't end well."

"You must have been on the other end of the island," Shug said. "Whole different world over here."

"It's beautiful," Brooke said. "So . . . wild. And peaceful. Do you live on the island full-time?"

"We do now. Louette, that's my wife, she was born and raised here. We moved to Brunswick a long time ago for work, but then our kids got grown and moved away, and I got laid off my job at the port. Right around that time, Louette's sister, who still lives here, said Miss Josephine was looking for some help. We come over and talked to her, and we been here ever since. Eleven or twelve years now, I guess."

"I didn't realize anybody but the Bettendorfs or Warricks lived here," Brooke said.

"Oh yeah. There's a bunch of black folks been living at Oyster Bluff, since right after the Civil War. The whole island was part of a plantation that got burned down by the Yankees, because they thought the owners were blockade-runners. Later on, the government gave all these former slaves a little piece of land up at Oyster Bluff. Nobody else wanted it, because it was swampy and they were afraid of yellow fever. Those folks, they stayed and scratched out a living, farming and fishing and hunting. They're what are called

Geechee. Louette's people, they're all Geechee."

"And do they still own their own land?" Brooke asked, fascinated by this chapter of Georgia history she knew so little about.

"Nope," Shug said. "People moved off and sold their land to the Bettendorfs, or they had so many kids, and none of them wanted to stay here, so they just abandoned the houses. There's not but ten or twelve families still living at Oyster Bluff now, and Miss Josephine owns all that land. She's nice and all, don't charge hardly anything for rent, but it's still not the same thing as owning your own place, you know?"

"I know all too well," she said wistfully, thinking of the modest two-bedroom concrete block cottage she rented at St. Ann's, as opposed to the restored Italianate three-story town house in Savannah's historic district that she'd walked away from when she broke her engagement to Harris Strayhorn.

The truck rounded another curve, and suddenly, a blanket of bright green lawn spread out before them. The grass was patchy and spotted with clumps of dandelions, wild garlic, and silver-dollar weed. Overgrown formal beds of bedraggled-looking azaleas and camellias were planted in tiers on the gently sloping lawn, and a line of palm trees announced that they were approaching the Bettendorf family compound.

"We're here," Shug said, slowing the truck to a stop so she could get out and take a look.

3

Situated at the top of the gentle slope was an astonishing pale pink wedding cake of a mansion, consisting of a two-story central block bristling with vaguely Moorish-looking arches, a pair of peak-roofed turrets, and a crenelated balcony projecting over a porte cochere. This was flanked on either side by wings of only a slightly more modest design. Each was marked by a towering sentinel palm tree. The roof consisted of pale-green fired-clay barrel tiles that reminded Brooke of the frosting on a gingerbread house. The place bristled with leaded glass windows, wrought iron Juliet balconies, heavy plaster bas-relief flourishes, and curlicued ornaments. A thick green curtain of ivy crept across the façade of the house, and crimson bougainvillea traced the outline of the porte cochere.

"Wow."

"Mmm-hmm," Shug agreed. He started the truck again, and as they drew closer, she could see that the curving concrete driveway leading up to the mansion was buckled and potholed, the pink stucco on the house was cracked and faded, and the roof sported great gaps of broken or missing tiles.

Shellhaven was slowly, inexorably crumbling as surely as a century-old layer cake.

"It don't look like it ought to," Shug said, his voice sorrowful. "I keep after it the best I can, but it's only me now. Time was, half a dozen hands worked on the grounds here. One man, his whole job was taking care of the roses. There was a tractor kept the grass cut and a grove with the prettiest oranges and lemons and grapefruit you ever seen. Peach trees and pecan trees, of course. A greenhouse too, just to grow flowers and orchids for the house. All gone now. A pine fell on the greenhouse, and some kind of blight killed all the fruit trees. Just as well, 'cause these days, you can't find nobody wants to live way over here and do an honest day's work. Plus, Miss Josephine, she's pretty tight with a dollar."

If Josephine Warrick was as rich as local legend had it, Brooke wondered why she'd allowed her home to deteriorate to this extent.

"I'm sure you do the best you can, and she's probably very grateful to have you," Brooke said tactfully.

He pulled the truck beneath the porte cochere and pointed to the heavily carved arched double doors. "Go ahead on inside.

Louette's waiting to take you to see her."

She pushed the door open and stepped inside timidly, momentarily blinded while her eyes adjusted from the harsh sunlight to the near darkness of the entry hall.

The naked bulb of a tarnished brass wall sconce dimly revealed a high-ceilinged room with black-and-white checkerboard tile floors, cracked plaster walls, and age-darkened wooden beams overhead. The crystal chandelier hanging from an ornate plaster medallion was caked with dust and cobwebs. The air was oppressively hot and damp.

"Hello?" Her voice echoed in the empty room.

"I'll be right there," a woman's voice called from the darkness. A moment later, a woman she guessed was Louette bustled into the room. She looked younger than her husband, with close-cropped graying hair and a freckle-flecked, caramel-colored complexion two shades lighter than his. She had the comfortable thickness and heavy bosom of solid middle age and was dressed in a white synthetic-blend uniform.

"Miss Brooke? I'm Louette. You got here okay? That C. D. didn't ride you too hard coming across the river today?" Her pleasant accent had a distinct singsong lilt.

"It was bumpy, but I'm here in one piece," Brooke said.

"Well, we don't get a lot of company these days, and Miss Josephine's got herself all worked up waiting to see you, so I guess I'd best take you back there."

She gestured for Brooke to follow her down a wide hallway. They passed arched entryways into what looked like twin parlors, furnished with overstuffed sofas and chairs and heavily carved tables and chests.

Louette paused outside a closed door at the end of the hall. "This used to be the library, but she can't make the stairs no more, so me and Shug fixed her up a bedroom in here. She don't hear so good, so you got to speak up when you talk, and she's been pretty sick lately, so you need to make sure she don't tire herself out. But don't go thinking because she's nearly a hundred years old she's weak-minded or something. No, ma'am! Not Miss Josephine. She don't miss a trick."

She rapped loudly on the door, waited a moment, then poked her head inside. "Miss Josephine? You ready to see your company?"

"Is that the lawyer I sent for? Bring her in, Louette."

The library at Shellhaven had been a grand room once. But now the dark mahogany paneling was dull, the draperies at the windows faded and tattered. Three walls of the room were lined with bookshelves, crammed with books and rows and rows of the distinctive bright yellow spines of *National Geographic* magazines. Every flat surface was littered with items; birds' nests, sun-bleached seashells, chunks of coral, even a huge set of yellowed shark jaws. A stuffed bobcat sat on a pedestal near the window, muzzle open in mid-snarl, his molting yellow fur drifting onto the dark pine floor. A five-foot-long intact skeleton of an alligator stretched across the top of one of the built-in bookcases, and tall apothecary bottles were filled with sharks' teeth, sea glass, and what appeared to be tiny bird skulls.

A hospital bed had been set up in the far corner of the room, partially hidden by an ornate three-panel chinoiserie screen.

A box fan whirred in one of the two open windows, doing little to dispel the heat or the scent of antiseptic soap.

The lady of the house was ensconced in a brown vinyl recliner. Brooke had been expecting a slightly diminished version of the defiant mink-wrapped, shotgun-toting heiress she'd seen in *Southern Living,* but the passing of years had been as cruel to Josephine Warrick as it had been to her home.

The flowing white mane was gone, replaced by a navy-blue baseball cap that did little to conceal the nearly bald head beneath it. Pale skin blotched with vivid brown liver spots stretched over skeletal cheekbones and a pointed chin. Her lips were thin and bloodless. But a pair of bushy white eyebrows arched over large, dark eyes behind oversized yellow-tinted glasses that carefully studied Brooke as though she were another museum specimen.

In the quick research she'd done, Brooke had seen dozens of photos of Josephine Warrick. She'd been a striking — if not beautiful — woman, a slender, serious-faced debutante with the short, wavy hair of the period, then a dewy-faced bride in the fifties, turned into a rangy, imposing force to be reckoned with in later years. The society pages of the newspapers in Savannah, Atlanta, and Palm Beach showed her dressed in golf togs, tennis wear, and expensive designer gowns, as well as hunting gear, standing with one foot atop a massive buck.

The woman sitting in the cracked vinyl recliner weighed less than ninety pounds and was wrapped in layers of knitted afghans and throws. An oxygen tank stood beside the chair, and a pair of thin plastic cannulas snaked toward the transparent breathing apparatus on her face.

"Hello, Mrs. Warrick," Brooke said, after the momentary shock of the old lady's appearance had worn off. "I'm Brooke Trappnell." She took a step toward the chair, then stopped abruptly.

"Grrrrrr."

She hadn't noticed the dogs, they were so

small, and nearly the same beige as the afghan.

"Grrrr."

A pair of miniature Chihuahuas sprang into defense mode; the fur on their necks bristling, teeth bared.

"Hush, Teeny. Hush, Tiny." The old woman stroked their backs, patted their heads. "Don't mind the girls," she told Brooke. "They won't bite. Unless I tell them to. Sit down over here," she said, pointing to a faded chintz wing chair. "And you needn't call me Mrs. Warrick. Josephine will do just fine, and I'll call you Brooke, if I may. The doctors keep saying I'm going deaf, but I'm not really. It's just that people these days mumble and fail to enunciate properly." She gave Brooke a sharp look. "You're not one of those types, are you? I can't abide a mumbler."

Brooke sat down in the chair and balanced her briefcase across her lap. "No, ma'am," she said loudly. "I've got a lot of faults, but that's not one of them."

"You didn't tell anybody why you were coming over here today, did you?"

"No, because you never actually explained why you wanted to see me."

The old lady chuckled. "But you were curious about me and this island, so you decided to come anyway. Is that correct?"

"Something like that."

"Then we'd better get to it, hadn't we? As

you can tell by my wretched appearance, I don't have a lot of time these days for social niceties."

"Your housekeeper mentioned you'd been ill. I'm sorry to hear that."

"Louette likes to fuss. I smoked too much and for too long, and I've had COPD for several years, but it's lung cancer now, and that's a different matter. I did the radiation, but I draw the line at chemo. So that's that. Let's talk about something else, shall we?"

"Of course."

"Do you know anything about this island, Brooke?"

"I did some reading after your call, and I was here briefly as a child, on a campout."

"On the other end of the island, which my wretched cousins' heirs sold to the State of Georgia in 1978 for pennies on the dollar," Josephine said. She shook her head. "If they'd offered me the same deal, I would have bought it myself."

"Why didn't they?"

"Bad blood. We'd had boundary disputes over the years, silly feuds over water rights, that type of thing." She shrugged. "Also, from what I heard, they needed the money. As you may know, my father, Samuel Bettendorf, along with two cousins, bought Talisa in 1912."

She nodded toward the bookshelves. "Somewhere I have a copy of the original bill of sale. They each chipped in $10,000, which doesn't sound like a lot of money now, but back then, it was the equivalent of $2.4 million apiece. My mother hated the cold Boston winters, so Father bought the island and eventually built this house. His cousins' wives had no interest in spending time in a place as wild and remote as this, so they eventually partitioned the land, with my father retaining this end of the island. His cousins had more acreage, which was all they were interested in, but Father bought most of their holdings and kept what really mattered — this tract, which has ocean frontage, high ground, and the only freshwater source on the island."

"Clever man," Brooke said.

"He was brilliant, really," Josephine said. "He made his money in the family shipping business, but Father was interested in everything — natural science, the law, literature, the arts. He was the one who insisted I go to college, which was not the norm for girls at that time."

She sighed. "He loved it here. He loved the climate, the wildlife, the peacefulness. That's why I have to preserve his legacy here." She gestured around the room. "Saving Talisa, studying it, understanding its beauty was his life's work. And then after I married Preiss, it was our work."

Josephine's voice grew raspy. "Which is why I've fought so hard all these years to keep the state from taking my land."

Brooke opened her briefcase and took out a yellow legal pad and pen. "I didn't have time to do much research, but I do know from what I've read that your Atlanta lawyers have been fending off the state's offers."

"The state built the campsite you stayed at, they paved roads, and then they cut down some of the oldest trees on the island to build another campground, cabins, and a ten-thousand–square-foot 'conference center.' Can you tell me why Talisa needs a conference center?"

"Maybe as meeting space?" Brooke guessed.

"That ferry of theirs runs four times a day," Josephine rasped. "Hundreds of people tromping around, leaving their fast-food wrappers and beer cans and dirty diapers. It's deplorable. They're deplorable!"

"How do things stand with the state currently?" Brooke asked.

"Their last offer, made five years ago, was for the same amount they paid my cousins nearly forty years ago," Josephine said bitterly. "It's an insult. When I refused, the state filed notice that they'll take my land by condemnation. For the public good." Her lips twisted in disgust. "The public hasn't got any right to traipse across this land. I won't let them."

"What is it you think I can do to prevent

that?" Brooke asked. "You already have the best law firm in Atlanta representing you."

"I want you," Josephine said.

"But why? You don't even know me."

"I've been following your career in the newspapers. You've got spunk. And I need somebody with spunk. Besides, you sued the National Park Service, didn't you?"

"And lost," Brooke said calmly.

"But you fought them tooth and nail for three years. You wore the bastards down."

"Not really. You of all people know what that's like. The Park Service decided that Loblolly, my family's house on Cumberland Island, was 'nonconforming,' so they knocked it down. And we're not allowed to build anything to replace it."

"Which is precisely why I need you to fight my last battle," Josephine said. "I won't be around that much longer. I've seen their secret preliminary master plan. The first thing the state will do is to tear this house down. And I can't have that. I can't die knowing they'll ruin everything. All our years of work."

"Tear down Shellhaven? Why would the state do that?"

"You've seen the condition it's in. It would take millions to preserve it. Much cheaper for them to knock it down and build more cabins and conference centers. They'd build a big marina where my dock is — we've got the only deepwater boat access on this end of the island."

Brooke looked down at the few lines of notes she'd taken. "Josephine, I just don't think I can help you. It's true I'm a lawyer, but this is not my area of expertise at all."

"Word is out that I'm sick," Josephine said, ignoring her. "They've already come over here, sniffing around. C. D. ran off a boatload of 'em a couple of weeks ago. Survey crew, they said they were. They'd tied up at our dock, just as C. D. was coming back from the mainland with a load of groceries. He fired a couple of warning shots across the bow of their boat, and they took off like a pack of scalded dogs, but they'll be back."

Brooke shook her head in alarm. "I'm not sure that's such a good idea."

"They were trespassing. As long as I'm alive, this is still private property. They've got no business sniffing around over here. I want this thing settled before I get too sick to fight anymore."

"And how do you propose to do that?" Brooke asked.

"I want my land and this house protected, put in a trust or something, so that nobody, and I mean *nobody,* can develop this end of the island or tear down this house."

"Who'd be the beneficiary of such a trust?" Brooke asked. "Do you have family?"

The old lady put her head back and closed her eyes. "Not really. My brother, Gardiner, was killed in World War Two. Preiss and I never had children." She smiled, briefly. "Never wanted any, either. I didn't marry until I was in my thirties. He was six years younger than me. Bet you didn't know that. No, there's somebody else. My friends. My oldest, dearest friends. The High Tide Club girls."

4

JOSEPHINE

April 1932

It was Ruth's idea to "borrow" my papa's Packard to go exploring on the island. At thirteen, she was the oldest, and the bossiest. I was still twelve, and Millie, whose birthday wasn't until the last week of August, was the baby of the group. That was the night the High Tide Club was born.

We were on spring break from boarding school, having taken the train down from Boston a good five days before the rest of the family would join us.

With the run of the house mostly to ourselves and largely unsupervised, we'd spent the week listening to the radio, playing endless hands of canasta, and taking turns reading aloud from the naughty parts of *Lady Chatterley's Lover,* which we'd found hidden in my mother's lingerie drawer.

It was the night before my parents and Gardiner were to arrive.

"I'm bored. Let's go for a drive." Ruth jumped up and ran down the stairs with Millie and me trailing along behind. We followed her out to the barn, which had once held racehorses but now housed Papa's "island cars" — a disreputable-looking collection of automobiles that had outlived their useful lives back at home in Boston but were still well suited for life on Talisa.

Ruth jumped into the front seat of the Packard. Once, when it had been Mama's favorite car for shopping jaunts, it had been shiny and black with gleaming chrome trim and soft leather upholstery. But now the windshield was missing, along with the bumpers. The leather was cracked, and the chrome was pitted from exposure to the salt air.

"What do you think you're doing?" I stood in front of the Packard's blazing headlamps, my hands on my hips. Somehow, Ruth had managed to start the motor. And now, she blasted the car's horn so loudly Millie and I both jumped, and a chicken, who'd been roosting up in the rafters of the barn, squawked and flapped down onto the sawdust-covered floor.

"Let's go!" Ruth said, tapping on the horn again.

"But . . . but . . . ," Millie sputtered. "You can't drive. You're not old enough."

"I'm plenty old enough," Ruth retorted.

"I've been driving for ages and ages. My sister, Rose, taught me how."

That was good enough for me. I opened the door and swung onto the front seat.

Millie stared at the two of us, trying to make us be sensible. "What if somebody finds out? We could get in a lot of trouble."

Ruth was rummaging around in the glove box, but she looked up, annoyed. "*Pffft.* Who's going to tell on us? We have the whole island all to ourselves."

"That's not true," Millie said stubbornly. "Mrs. Dorris is here, and the rest of the servants, and the colored people who run the commissary, and the man who brought us over on the boat . . ."

"Mrs. Dorris goes to bed at seven o'clock, and the rest of the servants had better mind their own business or I'll tell Papa to fire them," I said, which I never would have done, and Papa wouldn't have fired anybody on my say-so anyway, but Millie didn't know that.

"Lookie here!" Ruth cried. She was holding up a clear pint bottle with a brownish liquid. "Hooch!"

"Ruth Mattingly, don't you dare," Millie said.

So of course, Ruth uncapped the bottle, sniffed, and took a chug. She coughed and gagged, then wiped her mouth with the back of her hand, and handed the bottle to me. I pretended to drink, then tucked it under the seat for safekeeping.

"Are you coming or not?" Ruth asked. "Scaredy-cat!"

Millie barely had one foot in the Packard before Ruth jammed the car into reverse, stomped on the gas, and shot us backward out of the barn.

"Slow down!" Millie pleaded as the Packard lurched forward over the narrow asphalt road the islanders called Dixie Highway. But Ruth just laughed and sped up, and soon the wind was whipping our hair, and the headlamps shone yellow white in the inky darkness.

"Where shall we go?" Ruth turned to me for directions. It was only her second time on Talisa, but I'd been coming to the island my whole life.

That's when I had the brilliant idea. I pointed ahead, toward a huge three-trunked live oak tree that marked a split in the road. "Take a left, just up there. We'll go down to Mermaid Beach."

Without slowing down, Ruth veered so sharply left we almost left the road, and as it was, a low-hanging limb from the tree scraped the Packard's roof and right side, in the process depositing a long, lacy strand of spanish moss in Millie's lap.

"Hey!" I protested. "You almost put us in a ditch."

But Ruth just cackled with that demonic laugh of hers.

Millie planted both hands on the dashboard to brace herself. "Look! There's something up ahead, in the road."

Ruth slammed on the brakes, and the three of us watched as a five-foot-long alligator, its eyes glowing yellow orange, ran across the road.

Millie's screech echoed in the thick night air, but Ruth soon resumed driving.

The asphalt gave out without warning, and then we were in the wildest part of our wild island. The road was a narrow, haphazard trail of crushed shells, and wax myrtles, palmettos, and oak trees crowded against the side of the Packard, the palm fronds slashing at the sides of the car.

"Where are we?" Millie asked. She clutched my hand, and I clutched hers back, trying to act braver than I felt, partly because I had never been to Mermaid Beach at night but mostly because my thirteen-year-old best friend was driving my papa's Packard, at night, in the dark.

"It's not far now," I said, pointing toward the place a hundred yards ahead where the road seemed to disappear in a green curtain of underbrush.

"Stop here," I told Ruth. "We'll have to walk the rest of the way."

But she didn't stop until the Packard was ensnared in a tangle of wisteria and morning glory vines.

Leaves and twigs rained down on our heads as we gingerly stepped out of the car.

"I don't like this," Millie said, gripping the door handle. "I'm staying right here."

"Okay. Fine by me." Ruth set out ahead of us, stabbing at the underbrush with a thick branch she'd picked up. "Go away, snakes!"

"Come on," I urged Millie, grabbing her hand. "It's not that much farther."

The thick, humid air closed in on us, and as we pushed through the vines, we stirred up clouds of stinging, swarming mosquitoes.

"Aaaggghhh!" Millie cried.

The skeeters were in our hair, our mouths, our noses.

"Let's run," I urged. So we did, lunging through the green curtain toward a clearing I prayed was right where it had been during my last trip here, in the daytime, with my brother, Gardiner.

Ruth stopped short at the point where the tunnel opened up to a shimmering platinum world.

She flung her arms wide as though to embrace the spectacle and make it her own.

"Wow," she breathed.

Millie and I stood beside her, breathless from the run.

The wide sandy beach ran down to the Atlantic Ocean, and a huge full moon shone down from a black velvet sky. It was high tide, and the silver-streaked rollers broke just inches from our feet.

"What is this magic place?" Ruth asked, slipping out of her shoes and digging her toes into the cool white sand.

"We call it Mermaid Beach," I said, plopping down on the sand to untie my shoelaces.

"It's wonderful," Millie said. She tilted her head back and gazed up at the sky. "Have you ever seen a moon so big and beautiful?"

"It's called the king moon," I told my friends, feeling important at possessing such knowledge. "I think it only happens once or twice a year."

I glanced at Ruth, expecting her to ridicule or contradict me, but to my astonishment, she was busily unbuttoning her cotton blouse. She dropped it onto the sand and unfastened the gingham skirt she'd dressed in that morning, and soon it joined the blouse.

"What are you doing?" I asked.

"I'm going swimming," she said, leaning forward to unfasten the brassiere she'd just begun wearing earlier that spring.

"But you don't have a swimsuit," Millie said.

"I don't need a swimsuit. I've got my birthday suit." Ruth dropped the brassiere, and next came her panties. She danced toward the waves, wiggling her bare bottom the way we'd seen the sideshow hootchy-kootchy girls do when the carnival came to town. She glanced back at us, over her shoulder. "Come on, you prissy-pants!"

I was hot and sweaty, and I could feel itchy mosquito-bite welts on my face and arms. I pulled my dress over my head and kicked off my cotton panties and the icky cotton undershirt Mama insisted on making me wear. A moment later I was as naked as a jaybird, the breeze ruffling my hair. I glanced over at Millie, who'd averted her eyes out of modesty.

"Come on, Millie," I begged. "It feels great."

"I can't," she whispered.

Ruth was leaping and diving into the waves. She pulled the pins from her long red hair and let it cascade, dripping down her knobby breasts. "Look, Josie. Look, Millie. I'm a mermaid!" She dove backward into the water, kicking her feet at the last minute.

"I'm coming in," I announced, and I made a running leap into the surf. I'd never felt so daring or so free. The ocean was as warm as bathwater. I floated on my back, staring up at the velvet sky, pricked with millions of stars and that low-hanging king moon. The tide carried me back toward the shore, and when my bare bottom scraped the sand, I flipped over and looked toward the beach. Millie was crouched on the sand, her knees pulled up tightly against her chest, looking thoroughly miserable.

"If you don't get in here right now, I'm

never speaking to you again," I called.

"And I'll tell you-know-who that you have a crush on him." Ruth ran forward and began splashing Millie.

"Ruth, stop!"

I joined in, and within minutes, Millie was soaked and laughing despite her protests.

"Oh, all right," she said finally. Gritting her teeth, she pulled off her dress and ran shrieking into the waves, dressed only in underclothes similar to mine.

"No fair," Ruth said, splashing Millie again. "It's not skinny-dipping unless you're naked."

"That's right," I agreed. "You can't be in the club unless you are tee-totally stitch-stark naked."

Millie sank down into the water until only her head and shoulders were exposed. "This is stupid," she grumbled. A moment later, she stood and tossed her remaining clothes onto the beach.

"See? Doesn't it feel wonderful?" Ruth asked.

Millie ducked down under the water and popped back up again, spouting a stream of water from pursed lips, like the fountain in the garden back at school. She shook her head, raining droplets on both of us. "Yes! All right. Yes, it feels marvelous!"

After that, we laughed and splashed and floated and swam until our arms and legs were so tired we could barely drag ourselves onto the beach. Finally, we lay flat on our backs in the sand, our fingertips barely touching, while we gazed up at the moon.

"You said there's a club," Millie said, sitting up and looking around for her clothes. "And now you have to let me be in it, because I skinny-dipped too. What's it called?"

"Hmm." Ruth found Millie's wadded-up dress and tossed it at her.

"It's the High Tide Club," I announced.

"Yes!" Ruth proclaimed. She found her skirt and pulled a packet from the pocket, tapping out a cigarette and a book of matches.

"Ruth Mattingly! I didn't know you smoked," Millie said, wide-eyed.

"Oh, sure," Ruth said carelessly. She held out the package. "Want one?"

"No, thanks," Millie said.

I shook my head. Ruth shrugged, lit the cigarette, inhaled, then tilted her head back and blew a series of perfect smoke rings.

"What should we have for rules?" Millie asked as she began to dress.

"Well, skinny-dipping, for starters," Ruth said. She flicked ashes onto the sand, took another puff on the cigarette, and handed it over to me. I hesitated and took a tiny puff. My lungs burned, and I coughed and passed the cigarette back.

"But only when there's a full moon," Millie said. "It's so much more glamorous."

"And a high tide," I added between coughs.

"Next meeting, this summer," Ruth said. "You're all invited to my house at Newport." She waved her cigarette in our faces. "And don't forget your birthday suits."

5

Josephine closed her eyes. Her chin sagged, and a moment later, she was softly snoring, the Chihuahuas each nesting with their snouts in the opposing crooks of her elbows. Brooke waited tactfully. Should she leave?

Remembering Louette's warning about overtiring Josephine, Brooke quietly stashed her notes in her briefcase and began to tiptoe toward the door.

Josephine's eyes opened. "Where do you think you're going?"

The Chihuahuas scrambled to alert, yawning, their huge eyes staring expectantly at the intruder.

"Um, I thought maybe you needed some rest," Brooke said.

"I'll let you know when I need some rest. Now, where was I?"

Brooke sat down again. "Well, I asked you who would be the beneficiary of your trust, and you said something about the girls of the high tide? Was that sort of a youth organization? Like Pioneer Girls maybe?"

"I've never heard of that organization, so why would I leave my island to them?"

"Sorry," Brooke said. "Maybe I misunderstood. The High Tide Club?"

"For heaven's sake. Keep up, will you? I just told you, these were my oldest, dearest friends in the world."

"Oh."

"It was all so long ago," Josephine said drowsily. "Sometimes, I almost wonder if I dreamed them. Dreamed the times we had together."

Brooke shifted uncomfortably in her chair. "Um, just how long ago did you have these friends?"

Josephine waved her hand dismissively. "We were just girls. Millie and I were in kindergarten together. Ruth, oh, I don't know. I suppose I met Ruth my first year at boarding school. We were both so terribly homesick. We hated our roommates. So we tricked them into ditching us so that we could room together. Oh, that Ruth. She was the most delicious fun! Sweet Millie, well, she had such a soft heart, the other girls would take advantage of her. So we had to take her under our wing, didn't we? We were peas in a pod. We made our debut together . . ."

Josephine's eyelids fluttered, and Brooke feared she was falling asleep again. Should she leave?

"I want you to find them for me," Josephine said suddenly, fully awake again. "I . . . it was a long, long time ago, but it's begun to eat at me. I'm not sleeping. I want to make amends. Before I go."

"Make amends with these women? Your old friends?"

Josephine gave her a withering look. "Are you always this slow? Have you heard anything I've said so far?"

Brooke wondered what she was missing here. Josephine Bettendorf Warrick was inching up on the century mark. What was the likelihood that these girlhood friends would also still be alive?

"It's just that, well, if these friends were your age, I was wondering . . ."

"If they're dead?"

"I was trying to be tactful," Brooke said.

"We don't have time for tact, dear. Just say what you mean. I find that's the best policy."

"All right. When was the last time you were in touch with these friends?"

Josephine looked down at the dogs in her lap. She stroked their ears, scratched their noses. "Too long," she said softly. "Much too long. Maybe it's too late. Probably it is, but I have to know. I have to try."

"Well," Brooke said. "With computer databases, it's usually not that difficult to track people down these days."

"Computers?" she sniffed. "Never had any

use for one. And unfortunately, I have no idea where to start looking." She turned to a small mahogany end table that stood beside the recliner. Sliding the drawer open, she reached in and took out a yellowing envelope.

Brooke leaned in, trying to get a better look at it. Three names were scrawled on the envelope in fading blue ink.

The old lady's hands shook violently, but she managed to unseal the flap. "Put out your hand," she said.

Brooke obeyed, and the old lady shook a small item into Brooke's palm, quickly returning the envelope to the drawer it had come from.

It was no more than half an inch high, a tiny gold-and-enamel brooch depicting the slender silhouette of a girl in a jackknife dive. The girl was nude, and a diamond chip twinkled in the position where her nipple would have been.

"What's this?" Brooke asked.

"We called ourselves the High Tide Club." Josephine's lips curved into a smile. "You see, we had a ritual. Whenever we were together, the four of us, and there was a high tide and a full moon, we'd go skinny-dipping. At Newport, at Ruth's family's home there, or Nantucket, at my grandmother's house, and at Palm Beach, back when Millie's family had a winter home there, before her father lost everything in the crash. Of course, Varina was only with us when we skinny-dipped here, on Talisa. You're shocked, I imagine."

"Not at all. My friends and I used to skinny-dip off the dock at my cousin's house, on the bluff, at Isle of Hope in Savannah." Brooke held the pin up to the light to admire it. "It's lovely."

"Millie had them made for us. As bridesmaids' gifts. For the wedding that never was."

"When was the last time you spoke to your friends?"

Josephine shrugged. "Sometime right after the war, I suppose. Maybe Ruth's wedding? But I don't think Millie was there. It's such a long time ago, I really can't recall."

"You said there were four members of the club? You, Ruth, and Millie? Who was the fourth?"

"Varina." Josephine held out her hand for the pin, which Brooke surrendered.

"And why didn't Varina join you at those other places, Newport and Palm Beach?"

The old lady stared at her as though she were daft. "Varina? Don't be absurd."

"Did your friends come to your wedding?"

"No," Josephine said. "We were . . . estranged." She looked out the window, which was nearly covered by a thick green vine whose tendrils had crept through the window screen. "They're probably all long dead by now. All but Varina. She was younger than the rest of us. She comes to see me, still, although it's harder, because she's getting on in years now. Like me."

"This really isn't the kind of work I usually do," Brooke said. "Have you considered hiring a private detective to find your friends?"

Josephine looked her over carefully. "If I didn't know any better, I'd think you didn't need money."

Brooke felt her face flushing. "What do you know about my finances?"

"I've asked around," Josephine said. "You left a top law firm in Savannah after you broke off your engagement a few years ago, isn't that right?"

"Yes."

"You're a bit of an ambulance chaser these days, aren't you? And representing drunk drivers and shoplifters, between divorces and debt collection?"

Brooke said nothing. Because it was true. She'd take just about any legal, ethical work thrown her way these days. There were bills to be paid. Hospital bills. She couldn't afford pride. Any more than she could afford cable television, dinners out, or a set of new tires for her eight-year-old Volvo. Her car needed work. She needed work.

"And I believe you're an unwed mother? Oh, wait. I beg your pardon. Nowadays women like you are called *single mothers,* isn't that right?"

Brooke felt her jaw clench and unclench. "I

have a son, yes, and I'm not married."

Josephine yawned widely. "What do your people think about your having a child? Out of wedlock?"

She considered ignoring the question. But why? Henry's existence was no secret. Except to his father.

"My father and stepmother are scandalized. Dad definitely does not approve. He and Patricia have only seen their grandson once or twice. My mother, at first, was worried, but once she held Henry in her arms, she fell madly in love. She comes down from Savannah to see him as often as she can."

"Your mother is a lovely person. I'm sorry I can't say the same about that unfortunate woman your father left her for. How is your dear mother, by the way?"

"She's, uh, fine."

"I imagine that divorce knocked the wind out of her sails."

"She was devastated," Brooke said truthfully. "She never saw it coming. Nobody did. But I think she's finally come to terms with her new life. So you know my parents?"

Josephine waved the question away. "Savannah's not that big a town, my dear. Everybody knows everybody else. Except for the nobodies that nobody cares about anyway."

"Exactly how do you know my family?" Brooke persisted.

"If you must know, your grandmother was

a dear, dear friend of mine."

"You were friends with Georgette?" Brooke asked, confused.

"Good heavens, no! Not your father's mother. I'm sorry to say this, but Georgette Trappnell was truly a horrible woman."

Brooke wouldn't argue that point. Georgette Trappnell had been a dragon. A selfish, self-centered terror whose acid tongue could peel the paint off a wall. Not unlike Josephine Warrick.

"I meant your mother's late mother," Josephine said sadly. "Dear, darling Mildred."

"Wait. Your friend Millie was my granny? The friend you went skinny-dipping with?"

"Yes," Josephine said. She changed the subject abruptly again. "What about your son's father? Do you know who he is?"

Brooke shot to her feet, nearly knocking the chair backward. "I think I'd better be going. I don't need money badly enough to be insulted this way." She reached for her briefcase and her pocketbook. "I suggest you find somebody else for this particular assignment."

Teeny and Tiny, sensing her hostility, went on the offensive, jumping down to the floor, bracing themselves on either side of their mistress's chair, yapping loudly.

"Don't be foolish," Josephine snapped. "I didn't mean to wound your pride. I just wanted to learn more about you."

Brooke's face was hot. "I don't appreciate your insinuation that I'm some sort of harlot." She would have said more, but she hadn't been raised to disrespect her elders. Even elders who were as loathsome as Josephine Bettendorf Warrick.

"That's not what I meant to insinuate at all," Josephine said. She scooped the dogs back up into her lap, stroking their heads soothingly. "I just wondered if your son's father is part of your life — that is, does he provide financial support? Does he see the boy?"

"He doesn't need to be part of our lives," Brooke said. "Henry and I do just fine without him."

"Is this man even aware that he has a child?"

The smaller of the two dogs arched her neck and began licking Josephine's chin.

"No." Brooke still had no idea why she was submitting to this deeply personal line of questioning. Maybe it was because she'd become immune to the intrusive questions asked by strangers who all seemed to feel entitled to ask questions about Henry's absent father.

"Do you think that's fair? To your little boy? Doesn't he wonder where his papa is?"

Brooke sighed. How often had both her parents asked that same question? "Henry's only three. I'm all he knows. Anyway, times have changed, Mrs. Warrick. There's no longer any real stigma to being a single parent. Now that we've established that I'm broke and unmarried, is there anything else, before I catch the boat back to St. Ann's?"

"I really must insist you call me Josephine," the old lady said. "And I've already told you what I want. Two things. I want you to keep the state from taking my island away from me. From ruining all of it. Whatever it takes, that's what I want from you. And I want you to help me make things right by those women I told you about."

She coughed again, then reached for a thick, leather-bound book on the table beside the chair. Opening it, she took out an envelope and extended it toward Brooke.

"That's your retainer. It's a certified check. I'm assuming $25,000 is sufficient for you to get started?"

"I'm sorry," Brooke said. "As I've tried to explain, based on the little you've told me, I really don't think I can help you."

The old lady's eyes were closed again.

"And remember," Josephine said. "Strictly confidential. Not a word to anybody about what we discussed today."

Josephine nodded off once more, leaving Brooke wondering again if she should go or stay. She still smarted from the intrusive questions about Henry's paternity and whether his father knew of the boy's existence.

Henry had straight dark hair, a high forehead, and a short nose like her own. His moods changed moment to moment. One minute he was climbing into Brooke's lap and smothering her face with kisses while she was trying to work at the kitchen table, and the next thing she knew he was scowling and howling, "Bad Mommy!" Strangers stopped her at the grocery store to comment that he was a carbon copy of his mama. But sometimes, when the tantrum clouds passed, and he gave her that full-faced impish smile, all she could see was Pete. He had Pete Haynes's smile, Pete's square jaw, long, Bambi-like lashes, stormy blue eyes, and smooth olive skin. Even the faint sprinkle of freckles across Henry's nose and cheeks were Pete's.

He was his father's son, a son Pete knew nothing about.

6

JOSEPHINE

October 1941

"Such a lovely party." Everybody kept saying it, and it was true. Papa and I wanted everything perfect for Millie's engagement party.

The ballroom floor had been waxed and polished until it shone like a mirror. The orchestra, brought all the way down from Atlanta — ten pieces — played all the most popular songs from that year. Caterers had been brought in too. A steamship round of roast beef, silver trays piled high with cracked lobster tails, steamed shrimp and oysters mounded on beds of crushed ice, poached quails' eggs, and the cleverest little pink cakes. Flowers everywhere. Orchids from the greenhouse, huge vases of peonies and roses and lilies, their perfume scenting the gentle breeze blowing in from the open doors to the veranda.

Thank goodness for that breeze! October could still be oppressively warm on Talisa, but even the weather cooperated that evening, with a full moon shining down on the loveliest party that I'd ever seen.

My gown was pale blue silk, with elegant beading and a plunging neckline. Millie was fairy-tale pretty in pink organza, the gown a surprisingly generous gift from her miserly grandmother, and Ruth, in seafoam-green satin to complement her copper hair. "You girls look like a rainbow," Papa had said, nodding in approval.

A hundred people filled the ballroom at Shellhaven that night. Or was it two hundred? Such a pretty, perfect night.

Until Russell strolled back into the ballroom from the veranda. He'd been drinking steadily all night, supplementing the champagne punch from the silver flask stuck carelessly in the breast pocket of his dinner jacket. Poor Millie had been on edge all night, fluttering around, too nervous to do more than nibble at the edges of the plate of food Ruth had tried to coerce her into eating.

"He hasn't danced with her once tonight," Ruth had hissed in my ear, glaring in Russell's direction.

"Too busy drinking and talking sports and smoking cigars with his fraternity brothers," I'd agreed, following her gaze.

Russell Strickland stood by the French doors, holding the stub of a still-lit cigar in his hand, coolly surveying the room. The dance floor was a crush of color and movement because right at that moment the orchestra was playing Glenn Miller.

Ruth slipped her arm around my waist, and we both hummed along and swayed to the rhythm. "Moonlight Serenade." A perfect song for a perfect night.

"What's he staring at?" I muttered.

Russell's eyes were narrowed, his jaw tight with anger.

"Oh Lord," Ruth said. "It's Millie. She's dancing with another man."

"Where?" I craned my neck to see through the crowd.

"Over there, near the punch bowl."

Finally, I spotted Millie's gauzy pink dress. She was in the arms of a lanky man with a white dinner jacket and a deep tan. "Oh, for heaven's sake. It's only Gardiner. He's just being nice. Papa probably made him ask Millie."

"Maybe your brother is just doing the gentlemanly thing, asking his little sister's best friend to dance, but I doubt Russell sees it like that," Ruth said. "He is holding her awfully close."

"Because every single living person in the room is on that dance floor," I said, laughing. "You and I are the only ones who aren't dancing."

"Russell isn't dancing. And he doesn't look at all happy at the way his fiancée is looking right now."

Ruth was right.

"Should we do something?" I asked. "Maybe try to distract him?"

"And how would we do that?" Ruth's dark green eyes crinkled in amusement. "Strip naked? Faint at his feet? Offer him some cake?"

"Or another flask of whiskey. I've got a better idea, though. You could ask him to dance."

"You ask him. You're the hostess."

"Should I?" My stomach did a little flip. Russell Strickland had always been perfectly polite to me, but there was something intimidating about him. And not just his football-player size. Everything about him was outsized and intense.

"Never mind now. The song's almost over. I think you and I should warn Millie . . ."

But it was too late. The music had ended, and Russell was steaming across the room, shouldering his way through the throng of partygoers until he'd reached the spot where Millie was standing.

She'd been talking to Gardiner, her cheeks pink with excitement. A moment later, Russell clamped his hand around her bare upper arm. She turned, and her eyes widened in surprise. Russell said something to Gardiner, who took a step backward, shaking his head in disgust.

The next moment, Russell was towing

Millie toward the ballroom door, not really holding her hand but nearly dragging her. Luckily, most of our other guests didn't notice. The music started again, and Ruth and I stood rooted to the spot where we'd been standing.

"Should we do something?" I asked. "Should we tell my father?"

Ruth thought about it, then shrugged. "Maybe not. It would just make Russell madder. And he'd probably take it out on poor Millie and spoil your wonderful engagement party."

"Poor Millie," I whispered.

"Are you going to help me or not?"

"I want to help you," Brooke said. "But I'm still not clear on what you think I can accomplish. Besides, you never finished telling me about these friends of yours. Or how you plan to make amends with them."

"I certainly did," Josephine snapped. "I told you about Millie. And Ruth. And Varina."

"You told me that Varina is still living and that your friend Millie was my grandmother," Brooke said. "But what about Ruth? And why do you need to make amends with these women?"

"Oh." Josephine looked down at the Chihuahuas, who were dozing on her lap. "Sometimes I do get a little forgetful. And sleepy."

Brooke laughed. "Sometimes I dream of

sleeping 'til noon. My son creeps into my room two or three times a night. I don't think I've gotten more than four uninterrupted hours of sleep since he was born."

"Why don't you just lock him in his room? Or lock your own door, for that matter?"

Brooke tried not to show her shock. "You're joking, right? Lock a three-year-old in his room? What if there was a fire? Or he really needed me in the middle of the night?"

"Oh, well, I didn't think of that," Josephine said with a shrug. "That's why Preiss and I never had children of our own. I don't think I would have made a good mother."

Brooke silently agreed with that assessment. "Anyway, it's time for Henry to transition to a big-boy bed. Maybe then he'll let me sleep in peace."

"Is Henry a family name?"

"Yes. He's named for my grandfather. Millie's husband. I suppose you knew him too?"

"I regret now that I never met him. But Ruth said he was a good man, and I heard he was good to Millie."

"Mama was only sixteen when he died, and she was devastated. I think he was much older than Granny," Brooke said.

"I believe that's what I heard." Josephine nodded. "Thank goodness he left Millie well fixed. You know, Millie's father — he'd be your great-grandfather — lost everything in the crash of '29. If it hadn't been for her grandparents, they would have been penniless."

Brooke gazed at the pin fastened to Josephine's chest. "I'm a little confused. Earlier, you said my grandmother had those pins made for her bridesmaids. But you just told me you never met my grandfather."

Josephine ran a bony finger over the pin. "Millie was engaged to someone else. His name was Russell . . . something." She looked up at Brooke. "Can you believe I've forgotten his last name? That's the wedding I was to have been in. But it never came off. Later, Millie married your Henry. Ruth said he was very distinguished. Some type of educator, I believe?"

"He was an English professor at Kenyon College, in Ohio," Brooke said. "His first wife died in one of the influenza epidemics, and Mama said he'd been a widower for years before he met Granny at a party in Boston. They got married a month later. Can you imagine doing that now?"

"Quite the whirlwind courtship," Josephine said, her tone acerbic. "But dear Ruth said the wedding was a lovely, intimate affair."

"You were going to tell me more about Ruth," Brooke prompted.

"She had the loveliest red curls," Josephine said. "And a temper to go along with them. A spitfire, we called her. But she had a tender heart. And she was such an animal lover. She'd find an abandoned kitten behind the dining hall at school and rescue it. Sneak it into our room, feed it milk with a medicine dropper. She hated any kind of injustice, hated cruelty. Ruth was a crusader."

"Whatever happened to her?"

Josephine shrugged. "We . . . had a disagreement. I suppose it came to a head with the '72 election. Ruth despised Nixon. She was what Preiss called a limousine liberal. Came by it honestly. Her mother was a suffragette."

Brooke shrugged. "Was that so awful? She sounds pretty amazing to me."

"You wouldn't understand," Josephine said. "It was a different time. Ruth was so . . . preachy. So damn certain about everything. Now? I see that our quarrel was silly. She and Millie were wonderful friends. We were like sisters. Closer than sisters."

"I know what you mean about missing your oldest friends," Brooke said wistfully. "My best friend, back in Savannah? Holly? She was Harris's sister."

"The man you jilted," Josephine said.

"She was supposed to be my maid of honor. But I ran away the night of the bachelorette party," Brooke confessed. "I was scared and confused. Afterward, I was too ashamed of the way I'd acted to reach out and apologize. It's been nearly four years, and we still haven't spoken."

"Foolish pride," Josephine said, shaking her head. "Foolish, foolish pride."

7

"So, Ruth and Millie. They were your best friends from boarding school? What about Varina, the woman you mentioned yesterday?" Brooke asked.

"Ah, Varina. Of course she didn't go to school with us. She was black! And much younger than we were. Only fourteen. Her father was Geechee, and her family worked for my father here on the island. Do you know about the Geechees?"

"They're the descendants of slaves, right? From the Gullah tribe in West Africa? Who stayed here on the coast of Georgia after the Civil War and emancipation?"

"That's right. Harley — he was Varina's father — was a Shaddix. The little church graveyard at Oyster Bluff is full of Shaddix headstones. Harley's people were slaves who worked at the plantation that once stood right where Shellhaven now stands. Harley and his wife, Sally, came to work for my papa before he'd even finished building this house. Poor

Sally, she was from the mainland, and I don't think she ever got used to living over here. Sally died, leaving Harley to raise their four children. Varina was still a baby, and the only girl."

Josephine fiddled with the trim on the afghan draped loosely around her shoulders. "I'm afraid the Shaddix boys took after their daddy. They were hard workers, and capable enough, but I don't think any of them ever went to school beyond sixth grade."

"But Varina was different?"

"Oh yes. She was the prettiest little thing, and bright as a new penny. After Sally died, Harley's sister, Margie, came to work here, and she'd bring Varina up here to Shellhaven with her most days. She was reading before first grade and had such a thirst for learning. She knew every inch of this island and loved to show us all her secret places."

The old lady's face shone as she spoke of Varina's accomplishments. "At first, Papa didn't think it was right — her spending so much time here. He was a free thinker for that day and time, but even he worried that people would wonder about a little colored girl getting big ideas."

Brooke winced at the term *colored girl.* She'd lived in the South her whole life but had never gotten used to the lingering vestiges of racism.

"But Varina became a friend?" Brooke asked.

"We all doted on her. We gave her clothes and shoes, treated her to gifts — candy, new books, things like that. Harley had diabetes, and the doctor had to amputate his right foot, and then he really couldn't work anymore, so he took up preaching, and the boys all quit school to help out. The Shaddixes never had enough to go around. Varina was like our little sister."

"If your little sister happened to be a colored girl," Brooke said.

The old lady's eyes flared. "You're very rude, you know that? I never called Varina a colored girl. That was Papa. And he didn't mean it in a derogatory way. He never, ever used the N-word, which most people did back then. It was a different time."

"You said Varina is still alive?" Brooke asked, interrupting. "And you've kept in touch all these years?"

"Of course. After the war, Varina worked in Jacksonville. For the railroad. But she missed Talisa and her family. Her brothers were all married, with a dozen children between them, and eventually she moved back here."

"Here? To Shellhaven?"

"Part of the time. She worked here for me after Preiss's death. It was lonely, you know? I never imagined he would die first. He was six years younger than I was. I still can't get over it. I'll never get over his death."

"I'm sorry for your loss," Brooke said. She'd noticed that Josephine's breathing was growing labored, her narrow shoulders hunched, and her voice raspy.

She leaned forward and touched the old lady's hand gently. "Are you feeling all right? Is there anything I can get you? Some water?"

Josephine's cough rattled, and she abruptly yanked her hand back, as though she'd been burned. "I've taken my pills, and there's nothing more to be done."

"I can leave and come back later, maybe when you're feeling better?" Brooke offered.

"I'm not going to feel better," Josephine snapped. "My time is short, so I'd really prefer it if we could get down to business."

"All right. Tell me more about Varina. Does she still live on the island?"

"No. One of her great-nieces — Felicia, I believe is the girl's name — took it upon herself to move Varina to Jacksonville, supposedly to take care of her. Felicia is Homer's granddaughter, or maybe great-granddaughter. He died back in February. Varina has been living with Felicia three or four years now. They tell me the girl is some kind of professor at a college down there, but I don't know where or what she teaches."

"And you've had no contact with Varina since then?"

"I didn't say that," Josephine retorted.

"Varina came back here for Homer's funeral, and that girl brought her here to see me then."

"Why is a great-niece caring for her?" Brooke asked. "What about her own children?"

"Varina never married," Josephine said. "Bad luck and bad decisions have haunted that family. There were three brothers, and all of them had their problems. Drinking, gambling, bad women, and of course, the damn diabetes. It killed Omar and Otis before they turned fifty. Varina helped raise her brothers' children and then their grandchildren. Oh yes, they all love their auntie Vee, as they call her."

"And you're on good terms with her?"

Josephine coughed violently, startling the sleeping dogs, who jumped down from her lap.

Brooke waited.

"That pushy Felicia has put all kinds of wild ideas in Varina's head," Josephine said, dabbing at her lips with a sodden handkerchief. "When she came to see me, back in February, I assumed it was strictly a social call. But I was sadly mistaken. Shocked, really."

"What did Varina want?"

"Varina never would have thought of it on her own," Josephine said. "That girl — Felicia — she's just like all the rest of this generation. Think they're owed something. Always looking for a handout."

Brooke waited.

"Can you imagine? She wanted me to deed over Oyster Bluff to the families living there. Just give it to them! Land I bought and paid for. And paid a fair price, I might add, when I could just have easily waited and bought it for next to nothing on the courthouse steps for back taxes."

Josephine's indignation sparked another alarming spasm of coughing. Brooke glanced toward the door. Should she call Louette?

A minute or two later, after the coughing subsided, Josephine's face remained pink with remembered outrage.

"What was your answer?" Brooke asked, her face deadpan.

"I refused! And I let Varina know I was disappointed that she would ask such a thing of me, considering all I've done for that family over the years."

"I thought the land at Oyster Bluff originally belonged to those Geechee families after the Civil War. Wasn't the land given to the freedmen by the government?"

"It was, but as I said, the Shaddixes and the others chose to sell their land. In fact, they came right to this house and begged me to buy, because they needed the money. Nobody made them sell it, and I paid a very fair price."

I'll just bet, Brooke thought. "How much land are we talking about?"

"A little over twenty acres. When Papa was alive, it was a nice little community, with a schoolhouse, a commissary, and a church, but then, over the years, all the young folks moved off, and the families that stayed are either too shiftless or sorry to keep up with their property."

"Don't Shug and Louette live at Oyster Bluff?" Brooke asked. "Do they rent from you?"

"I wasn't referring to them," Josephine said. "What I mean is the others."

"How did Varina take it, when you refused to deed the property to the residents of Oyster Bluff? Did you quarrel?"

"What could she say? She was embarrassed. I tell you, that pushy niece put her up to it. Varina never would have been bold enough to ask such a thing, in the light of our friendship over the years, which is what I told Felicia, right to her face, when she tried to pick a fight with me that day."

"Did you fight?"

Josephine drew herself up as best she could in the sagging recliner. "We had words. She called me some very unpleasant names and accused me of taking advantage of Varina and their family. Can you imagine? Finally, I'd had enough. I told her to leave. And I haven't seen or heard from Varina since that day. It makes me very sad, but what could I do?"

"It seems to me you could have done as Varina asked, if you cared as much about her as you say. It's only twenty acres — and you have what? Twelve thousand? It's not like you need that land. Or what little income you derive from the rent," Brooke said earnestly. "Think of it, Josephine. Varina's people were slaves. Abducted from their homes in Africa, then shipped here where they were bought and sold and worked and treated with less regard than mules or chickens. The government meant for them and their heirs to have that land as restitution. Why not give it back to them?"

"*My* family never owned slaves," Josephine shot back. "Anyway, it's the principle of the thing that I object to. Felicia has no right to make demands of me. That girl has no sense of gratitude, no idea of propriety. I'm afraid she's poisoned Varina against me." The old lady's hands shook in her lap.

"You told me earlier you want to keep the state from taking your land and to make amends with your friends, including Varina, isn't that right? So why not go ahead and deed Oyster Bluff over to the heirs of the original Geechee families, including the Shaddixes? Wouldn't that go a long way toward repairing your relationship with your old friend?"

Josephine brooded over the suggestion,

shaking her head. "I resent being backed into a corner like this. It makes me furious."

"Don't think of it like that, then," Brooke suggested. "For one thing, if you deed the land over to those families, you'll reduce your own tax burden. Right?"

"I suppose."

"And you'd be doing a really good thing. You're fond of Louette and Shug, aren't you? Think of what it would mean to them — to own their own home again."

Brooke paused, then reached out again and touched Josephine's hand. This time the old woman sighed loudly but did not shake her off.

"Look, Josephine. You called me over here because you said you want to make things right, because you're not sleeping. You said yourself, you don't have much time left. If that's true, why not start by returning Oyster Bluff to those families who still live there?"

"It'll be a big mess," Josephine grumbled. "Lots of paperwork."

"That's why you have me," Brooke said. "I can get started on it right away, if you'll get me a list of your tenants. My assistant can look everything up in the county tax office."

"Fine," Josephine said, throwing up her hands in surrender.

"Do you have contact information for Varina's niece in Jacksonville?" Brooke asked.

Josephine motioned to the corner of the

room, in the general direction of a huge antique mahogany Chinese Chippendale secretary. "There's an address book in the top drawer of the desk. It has a blue leather cover. I might still have the last birthday card Varina sent me tucked in there somewhere."

"What about a phone number for Felicia?"

"I don't know. Just look in the address book."

"While we're on the subject, if I'm going to try to track down your friend Ruth's family, I'm going to need whatever information you have. Old correspondence, anything like that with her last known address."

Josephine's eyelids drooped, first one, then the other, and she leaned her head against the back of the recliner. "Dear Ruth. She always had the cleverest Christmas cards. She was a wonderful writer, Ruth was. That was one of the things I missed, after our quarrel. Those damn Christmas cards."

"Josephine?"

Brooke leaned forward. Her client was perfectly motionless. She gingerly touched her bony wrist. Her skin was cool, the skin dry as paper and brown-splotched. Brooke wrapped her fingers around the old lady's wrist, watching her face for any reaction. There was a surprisingly strong pulse.

Josephine snored softly. Not dead. Just napping.

Brooke stood and walked over to the secretary. She might as well start trying to find contact information for Ruth's heirs and for Varina. She yawned involuntarily. What she wouldn't give for a few stolen hours of sleep. Her son had climbed into bed with her sometime after midnight, nestling against her back, his sweet, warm breath close against her neck. And sometime after that, he'd wet the bed, and they'd both ended up sleeping on the lumpy sofa in the living room.

She heard a hesitant knock at the door, and Louette entered, carrying a silver tray with a plate of sandwiches, a bowl of potato chips, and a silver pitcher beaded with condensation. She cleared some magazines from a tabletop and set the tray down, glancing over at her employer.

"I was hoping she'd eat something," Louette said, shaking her head. "The doctor says she needs to gain weight, but I can't hardly get her to eat anything. I made her favorite — egg salad on toast, and there's a pitcher of iced coffee too. Does that sound okay? I could fix something else if you want."

"Actually, that sounds perfect. My son was a little fussy this morning, so I didn't have time to grab breakfast and I'm starving."

"You need anything else before I run down to the dock to meet Shug? He's bringing our groceries, and I don't want my milk to sour in this heat."

"No, thanks. I'm going to eat this lunch,

then go through Josephine's address book for some folks she wants me to contact."

Louette nodded and started to leave the room, but then she turned and came back. "I'm not trying to pry into Miss Josephine's business," she said, her voice low. "But I do know she's not sleeping well or eating, and she's all upset about those state folks coming around, trying to make her sell the island to them. Is that why she wanted to see you?"

Brooke hesitated. "I'm sorry. My business with Josephine is confidential. She specifically asked me not to tell anybody about our discussion."

"Okay," Louette said. "I figured you couldn't say anything. It's just, Shug and me and the rest of us, we're worried about what will happen. You know . . . after." Her dark eyes rested on Josephine, asleep in her chair. She smoothed her hands over her hips. "If the state takes the rest of Talisa, what'll happen to Oyster Bluff? Where'll we go? Shug wasn't crazy about moving over here, at first, but now, he's turned into a real Geechee. He hates the idea of going back to the city. And so do I."

"I don't blame you," Brooke said. "This island. There's something special about it that I can't describe. It's like the last wild place."

"It is that," Louette said. "You know, when I was coming up, I couldn't wait to get off this island. The day I got done with high school, I told my mama I was getting me a job in town and finding me a man from away, and then I wasn't ever coming back here again."

"I felt the same way about Savannah, where I grew up," Brooke agreed. "I didn't even want to go to college in Georgia. And then I ended up moving right back home after law school. So what did your mother say when you told her you never planned on coming back here?"

"She just laughed and told me to go on and get all that running around out of my system," Louette said. "But she always said she knew someday I'd end up right back here on Talisa. And she was right. My mama was nobody's fool."

8

The secretary was enormous, with seeded glass doors behind elaborate fretwork, and a drop-front desk with a dozen small cubbies and drawers. Each slot was crammed with yellowing stationery, envelopes, pencil stubs, and notebooks. Behind the glass doors, leather-bound books with stamped gold lettering were shoved up against Chinese export blue-and-white porcelain vases and bowls. The top shelf of the bookcase held a turtle shell, an old mayonnaise jar full of beach glass, and a stuffed squirrel with lifeless brown glass eyes and a tail that seemed to have lost most of its fur.

Brooke tried to open the top drawer. Stuck.

Finally, after prolonged jiggling, one side of the drawer loosened, and as she inched it open, she could see stacks of papers and notebooks inside. She worked on the other side, and after five minutes of tugging and cussing, the whole drawer pulled free of the cabinet, landing on the rug with a dull thud.

"Damn," she whispered.

The drawer was about eighteen inches deep and was as crammed with papers as the bookcase above it. There were stacks of rubber band–bound canceled checks and bills, spiral-bound notebooks and black-and-white composition books, and bundles of letters and cards tied together with faded blue ribbons.

Brooke dug around in the drawer until her fingers closed on something that felt like leather. As she lifted the address book from the drawer, shards of the palest pink rose petals showered down on the faded rug, releasing their faint, musky scent.

She sat cross-legged on the floor and lifted out a rubber band–wrapped bundle of likely looking correspondence, each with the same handwriting on the envelope. Opening one, she saw that it was an anniversary card.

"To My One True Love" was written in thick gold script on the outside of the card, beneath an image of red roses. The inside right side of the card had a treacly Hallmark verse, beneath which the sender had written in a strong, slanting script: "My darling Jo, with love from Preiss." On the opposite side, the sender had copied a poem called "Always Marry an April Girl."

Praise the spells and bless the charms,
I found April in my arms.
April golden, April cloudy,
Gracious, cruel, tender, rowdy;
April soft in flowered languor,
April cold with sudden anger.
Ever changing, ever true —
I love April, I love you.

— OGDEN NASH

"Ohhh." Brooke let out a long, involuntary sigh and looked again at her would-be employer, her crepe-like eyelids closed, nearly bald head slumped sideways, a tiny bead of saliva trickling from narrow, colorless lips. Of course, Josephine Warrick had been young once, with slender limbs and a laughing smile. She had won the love of a much-younger man, this Preiss Warrick, who called her his April Girl.

9

An hour later, she'd finished her sandwich and chips and made what she thought was a decent start on completing the old woman's assignment.

"Well?" Josephine was awake again. Her dark eyes glared accusingly. "What did you find?"

Brooke looked down at the notes she'd scrawled on her yellow legal pad. She'd drawn circles around the names *Varina Shaddix* and *Ruth Quinlan.*

"Josephine, if I find Ruth's relatives and Varina, what do you want me to tell them?"

"*When* you find them, I want them to come to Talisa," Josephine said. "I want to see them. Your mother too, of course. She was Millie's only child, wasn't she?"

"Yes," Brooke said cautiously. "And what will you tell them — if they agree to come here to see you?"

"I want to leave this island to them — in a trust," Josephine said promptly. "And I want you to set up the trust and administer it."

"But that's impossible," Brooke said quickly. "If my mother is to be included in the trust, that would present a clear conflict of interest." She shook her head sadly. "I wish you'd told me that from the beginning. I can't represent you, Josephine. It's a matter of ethics."

"Ridiculous," the old lady snapped. "I can hire whomever I want to help me dispose of my property."

"You can, but that person cannot legally benefit in any way from such a relationship," Brooke said. She was already thinking of the $25,000 check. She was going to have to give it back.

So, goodbye to paying down her Amex bill. Goodbye to replacing the bald tires on the Volvo, and goodbye to making a dent in Henry's hospital bills.

"If you really don't trust your Atlanta lawyers, I can help you find an attorney to set up the trust, and contact the others in the High Tide Club," Brooke offered. "It would probably be better anyway, since I have absolutely no experience with estate law."

"You're not listening," Josephine said. "I want you. Only you. Millie's granddaughter."

"That's a lovely sentiment, but I can't ethically do the job," Brooke said. "It's not just a whim of mine. It's the law."

"There must be a way around that kind of

thing. A work-around, Preiss would have called it. There's always a work-around."

"Not this time," Brooke said. "I'm sorry, Josephine. I really am. I'm willing to track down Ruth's relatives and Varina, and I'll let my mother know you'd like to meet with her, but that's the extent of the services I'm legally able to offer you. Of course, I'll be returning your retainer."

"I don't want my money back," Josephine fumed. "And I don't need any more damn lawyers complicating what's left of my life." She shoved the sandwich plate aside. "Go on, then. Take your so-called ethics and get out."

Brooke had been standing under the shade of the porte cochere for at least ten minutes, staring down at her cell phone, which still had no service. So she was thrilled and relieved when Shug pulled up in the pickup truck.

Louette leaned out the passenger-side window, a look of alarm on her face. "What's wrong? Where's Josephine?"

"Nothing's wrong," Brooke said quickly. "She just woke up, and she's in a foul mood."

"Sounds about right," Shug said.

"You're leaving already?" Louette asked, climbing down and grabbing two canvas totes of supplies.

"I've got to get back to my son," Brooke

said. "Anyway, I've told Josephine I can't represent her in the matter she raised. So there's not much more I can do here." She looked over at Shug. "I hate to ask, but can you or C. D. take me back across to the mainland?"

"No bother," Shug said. "It'll have to be me, 'cause C. D.'s off this afternoon. No telling where he's got to."

She sat in the bow of the boat as they crossed the river. It was hot and sunny, and the water was dead calm. A pair of dolphins skimmed along in the boat's wake, and Brooke felt grateful for the slight breeze.

"So . . . you won't be coming back over to the island after this?" Shug asked, his face impassive behind his sunglasses.

"Probably not," Brooke said.

"Too bad. Louette said Miss Josephine was all excited about whatever it was she wanted you to do for her. She's been kinda low since the last time she went to the doctor. Seems like she perked right up since she got the idea to call you. Even started eating a little bit again."

"I'll help her as much as I can," Brooke said, already feeling guilty. "But there are . . . technicalities that prevent me from providing the services she needs."

"I got ya," Shug said.

He steered the boat toward the first available slip in the marina, and once they were tied up, he jumped onto the dock and helped her off. "You need a ride?" he asked, looking around the crowded complex of boat slips, launch ramps, and bait shop. "We keep a truck over here. It ain't got no air-conditioning, but it runs all right, and I can take you wherever you need to go."

"I'm parked right over there under that oak tree," she said, extending a hand to shake his. "And thanks again."

He smiled and gripped her hand with both of his. "My pleasure. You take care now."

"You too," she said.

He turned to go back to the boat, and she felt a sudden stab of guilt.

"Wait a minute, Shug," she called.

He stopped and walked back to her.

Brooke dug in her purse and handed him her business card. She'd ordered a box of a thousand after setting up practice three years earlier and had barely made a dent in her supply.

"Take this," she said impulsively. "It's illegal as hell for me to discuss this with you, but, well, Louette mentioned that y'all are worried about what will happen at Oyster Bluff once Josephine is gone. Maybe there's something I can do to help."

He looked down at the card and then up at her and frowned. "We got no expectations. And Louette, she shouldn't have said anything to you about that. We can take care of ourselves. Always have."

"I'm sure you can," Brooke said quickly. Had she insulted his pride?

10

Brooke eyed the stack of bills on her desk. She'd gone over her budget one more time looking for something else to cut, and turning the pages of her legal pad, she found the notes she'd jotted during her visit with Josephine Warrick.

That seemed like a lifetime ago. She tapped her pencil on the check Josephine had given her. On the boat ride back from Talisa, she'd made up her mind to return the check.

Was there any way, ethically, she could keep Josephine's money? She chewed the end of her pencil for a moment, then opened her laptop and her favorite search engine.

It took less than five minutes to discover the whereabouts of Josephine's oldest friend, Ruth.

The obituary ran in *The Boston Globe* on October 16, 2008.

Ruth Mattingly Quinlan, formerly of Boston, died October 12 at Hospice Care of Palm Beach, Florida, after a short illness. She was 89. Born in 1919 to Frederick Eustis Mattingly and the former Prudence Patterson, Mrs. Quinlan attended the Grosvernor School and Smith College, from which she graduated in 1942. In 1946, she married Robert Hudson Quinlan of Highland Park, Illinois. Mr. Quinlan, a former pharmacist, was a successful businessman who owned a chain of midwestern drugstores, which he later sold to Walgreens in the 1970s.

Mr. and Mrs. Quinlan made their home in Winnetka, where Mrs. Quinlan became active in civic and charitable circles in between raising the couple's two children: Robert Hudson Quinlan Jr., born in 1949, and Diana, born in 1951.

A devoted mother and advocate for liberal causes, Mrs. Quinlan became involved in the civil rights movement in the early 1960s, joining the Rev. Martin Luther King's Washington peace march in 1963. She was a delegate to the 1972 Democratic National Convention and was also a key organizer for Walter Mondale's 1984 presidential bid.

Following the death of her husband in 1996, Mrs. Quinlan became a full-time resident of Palm Beach, Florida, where she resumed fundraising for favorite charities and causes. In August, she served as the oldest Florida delegate to the Democratic National Convention, where she cast her state's ballot nominating Barack Obama for president.

Ruth Mattingly Quinlan was predeceased by her daughter, Diana Quinlan, who died in 1968. Survivors include her son, Robert H. Quinlan Jr., of Orlando, Florida, and one granddaughter, Ruth Elizabeth Quinlan, of Los Angeles, California.

No services are planned. At Mrs. Quinlan's request, memorials may be made to the American Civil Liberties Union or Planned Parenthood.

Brooke chuckled at the last line of the obituary. Ruth Quinlan sounded like the lefty liberal Josephine had described. And like someone Brooke would have loved to have met. According to the newspaper, Ruth was survived by a son and a granddaughter. She typed the name *Robert Hudson Quinlan Jr.* into the search engine.

The first hit she got was for an article in the *Orlando Sentinel.* A Robert Quinlan had been arrested in 2009 for breaking and entering, assault on a peace officer, and public intoxication.

She found two more published police reports concerning minor legal skirmishes for the man she assumed was the same Robert Quinlan, another in 2011, and a third in

2012. She found a white pages listing for R. H. Quinlan, in Oviedo, Florida, and called the number, but got a recorded message saying the number had been disconnected. Maybe Quinlan was currently residing in a local jail or prison?

Next she typed the name *Ruth Elizabeth Quinlan* into the search engine and was thrilled to see a list of more than a dozen hits. Clicking on each citation, Brooke learned that R. Elizabeth Quinlan was a somewhat prolific, if not wildly successful freelance journalist.

She wrote for obscure trade journals like *American Hardware Retailer* and *The Journal of Lawn Care Professionals.* She'd penned a handful of travel stories for regional airline magazines, and her most prestigious byline, as far as Brooke could tell, was for a series of stories about midlife dating for the online version of *Glamour* magazine.

Brooke bookmarked the articles to read later. Right now, what she really needed was to locate Ruth Elizabeth Quinlan. She couldn't find a telephone listing for the woman, but after clicking around, she did find a website for R. Elizabeth Quinlan, freelance journalist. Which led her to R. Elizabeth's private Facebook page.

Brooke clicked on the private message button and typed in a missive to Ruth Elizabeth

Quinlan, one she hoped would be intriguing enough to elicit a reply.

Hi. I'm an attorney in Georgia, and my client was a lifelong friend of Ruth Mattingly Quinlan, whom I believe was your grandmother. If that is the case, my client would very much like to contact you. Please call or reply to this message at your earliest convenience.

Almost immediately after she'd sent the message, she received a reply.

This is Lizzie Quinlan. My grandmother has been dead nearly ten years. I don't know anybody in Georgia. What does your client want? If this is some kind of a scam and you're looking for money, you're out of luck, because I don't have any.

That made Brooke laugh out loud, and she quickly typed a reply.

Welcome to my world. I'm broke too. I can assure you that this is not a scam. My client was an old classmate of your grandmother's. She is a widow and never had children. She lives alone on a barrier island off the coast of Georgia, and I'm sorry to say that she is terminally ill. She lost contact with your grandmother some years ago, and now she would like to meet and make amends to Mrs. Quinlan's heirs.

Lizzie Quinlan's reply took less than a minute.

Yeah, sure. And I'm the crown princess of Istanbul. Who is this really?

Brooke sighed. It was late, and she was exhausted and in no mood to play games.

My name is Brooke Trappnell. I'm a member in good standing of the Georgia bar. Feel free to check me out. In the meantime, I'm going to bed. If you want to talk further, contact me tomorrow, after 8:00 Eastern time.

Brooke closed her laptop and looked at her phone again. Too late now to call her mother and ask for a loan. Maybe tomorrow she'd call. Maybe tomorrow things would look better.

11

October 1941

Millie's head spun. She'd had three glasses of champagne, which was two too many. She was dizzy but strangely happy. She knew Gardiner Bettendorf had asked her to dance out of pity — he felt sorry for her because her oafish fiancé had been ignoring her all evening. But she didn't care.

She let her chin rest on his shoulder and relaxed as Gardiner guided her around the polished dance floor, his hand resting lightly at the waist of her new gown.

In the next instant, Russell was there, wrenching her away from Gardiner. His fingers dug into the flesh of her bare upper arm, and his breath stank of cigars and whiskey as he confronted her dance partner.

"What the hell do you think you're doing with my girl, Bettendorf?"

"Hey, fella," Gardiner said, taking a step backward. "Take it easy. We were just dancing."

"Fuck off," Russell said. "I'll deal with you later."

Without another word, he dragged Millie through the crowded room and out the French doors and onto the veranda.

"Russell," Millie said breathlessly. "Russell, stop. Let go. You're hurting me."

He released his hold on her arm. "But it's okay when that clown Bettendorf grabs you, right?"

"Gardiner didn't grab me," Millie said, trying to keep her tone light. It was always best to keep things light when Russell was drinking. "He didn't even really want to dance. He only asked me because Josephine asked him to."

"And why would she ask her brother to dance with you? What business is it of hers?"

"She's our hostess," Millie said. "You weren't around, and I guess she felt sorry for me because I was sort of a wallflower. She was just being polite."

Russell edged her into the shade of a huge magnolia tree that towered over the slate-floored veranda. The full moon spilled light onto the other end, where a group of young men laughed and joked, passing a silver flask among themselves. Fireflies flitted in the treetops, and Millie could see the glowing tips of the men's lit cigars.

It was like a scene from a movie, Millie thought. Or a book. The creamy magnolia blossoms were the size of dinner plates, and they contrasted brilliantly against the glossy dark leaves. Their perfume filled the night air.

Russell's dinner jacket was white too, although his tie was slightly askew, and his face had a fine sheen of perspiration.

"You weren't a wallflower. You're the prettiest girl here. I was just out here having a smoke with some of the fellas." He looped his arm around her shoulders and pulled her closer. His mustache tickled her ear, and he flicked his tongue just behind her earlobe. "Don't tell me you missed me." His words were only slightly slurred.

Millie shivered, despite the warmth of the evening. "Just a little," she said. "You haven't danced with me all night. And it's our engagement party."

"Too many people around," Russell groused. "You know how I hate crowds and big parties. Too much small talk. Small drinks, small food, small people." He nuzzled her neck and slid his hands around beneath her breasts, pushing them upward until they spilled from the neckline of her dress.

"Russell, please behave," Millie whispered, blushing in the dark. "Somebody will see us."

"Aw, who cares? We're engaged, aren't we?" He pulled her closer.

"I care," Millie said indignantly. "My mother is here. And my grandmother. What if they stepped out here and saw us like this?"

"Your mother is inside, flirting with old man Bettendorf. And your grandmother is blind as a bat. She just asked a hat rack in the foyer if he'd get her a cup of punch. Anyway, if she did see us, that could be good. Maybe your grandmother would have a heart attack and leave all her money to us."

Millie giggled despite herself. She really should not have had that third glass of champagne. Unlike Josephine and Ruth, she wasn't much of a drinker. "That's a terrible thing to say. You're terrible."

"I'll show you just how terrible I am."

Russell's teeth shone white in the darkness. "Come on. Let's get out of here. They've got me staying in the guesthouse, out by the pool. It's way more private there." He tugged her by the hand, but Millie stood her ground.

"But these are our friends. Josephine and her family have been so wonderfully generous to throw us this party, Russell. It would be rude to leave now."

"Who cares? They won't even notice."

"You know I can't go to your room alone. What if somebody saw me? What would they say?"

"I said, let's go," Russell said hoarsely. He grabbed her arm and started towing her toward the walkway that led around the edge of the house, through the gardens to the pool. The walk was narrow and closed in on either side by tall boxwood hedges.

"Russell, no," Millie said, her voice rising. She stumbled along behind him, catching her heel on one of the cobblestones and nearly tripping before he roughly pulled her upright.

"What is wrong with you tonight?" he snarled. He shoved her up against the trunk of another magnolia tree and pressed himself into her until she felt the rough bark scraping against the flesh of her bare shoulders. He forced a knee between her legs and pushed her dress up until it was nearly at her waist. "That's better," he breathed in her ear. "No more games."

She flailed helplessly against his hands, but they were everywhere, tearing at the neckline of her gown, fumbling with the snaps of her garter belt. He thrust his tongue into her mouth, and a moment later, he was unbuckling his belt and unzipping the fly of his pants.

"Stop it!" Millie cried. She pushed against his chest with both hands, but he was stronger, a head taller, and she was pinned there, half-naked, exposed to the world. She felt panicky. She was no virgin — Russell had seen to that — but this . . .

"Just relax, baby," Russell said, chuckling. "Let me just —"

"No! Stop it!"

"Millie?" A man's voice.

She heard the rapid clatter of hard-soled shoes on the cobblestones.

He stopped, a few feet away. It was Gardiner Bettendorf. "Millie? Are you all right?"

Russell kept her pinned, right where she was. "Get lost," he said calmly, not even bothering to turn around. "The lady and I were just admiring the moonlight."

"That's not what it sounded like to me," Gardiner said. "Millie, would you like to go back to the house?" He stepped closer, peering at them.

She squirmed under the weight of Russell's body, mortified at her appearance, desperately trying to cover herself. She took a deep breath, willing herself to sound normal.

"Um, yes. We were just about to come back to the party. But you go on ahead and we'll catch up."

"I think I'll just walk back with you, if you don't mind," Gardiner said. His tone was light, affable.

"I said get lost!" Russell yelled. He whirled around and without warning threw a punch at Gardiner's nose, just barely grazing it. He swung again and connected solidly this time.

"Stop it!" Millie screamed.

Russell was bigger, but Gardiner was faster, and now he swung hard, landing a solid blow to Russell's jaw and then to his gut.

The big man staggered two steps backward, a look of astonishment on his face. "I'll kill you."

A thin stream of blood trickled from Gardiner's nose and onto the spotless starched collar of his white dress shirt. "Enough, all right?" He nodded at Millie. "Why don't you go on back to the party now?"

12

Brooke's cell phone rang at precisely 8:01 A.M. She grabbed the phone, hoping the loud ring wouldn't awaken her son.

"Hello? Is this Brooke Trappnell? This is Lizzie Quinlan."

"Oh, hi."

Brooke glanced over at the crib mattress on the floor by her bed, momentarily reassured that Henry was still asleep, his favorite blue-and-white quilt wrapped around him, burrito-style. She took the phone and walked into the kitchen.

"Who's your client?" Lizzie asked.

"Excuse me?"

"His name. You said your client was a dear friend of my late grandmother's. So I'd like to know his name, since you know mine."

Brooke hesitated. Josephine hadn't told her not to reveal her identity, and she couldn't really think of a legitimate reason not to disclose it.

"*Her* name is Josephine Bettendorf Warrick.

Does that name ring a bell at all?"

"Never heard of her," Lizzie said. "Spell it for me, okay? So I can Google it?"

Brooke spelled out her client's name. "While you're at it, you might want to do a search for Talisa; that's the island Josephine owns, and it's off the Georgia coast."

"Got it," Lizzie said. "My Wi-Fi is slow as hell, so if you would, fill me in on the details while I wait. Like, what's the deal with this Josephine? And what does she want with me?"

"It's complicated." Brooke took a deep breath.

"You'd be surprised at the depth of my ability to handle complicated issues, Mrs. Trappnell."

"It's Ms. Trappnell, but call me Brooke."

"Okay, Brooke. I'm listening."

"I know there are gaping holes in this story, but what you have to realize is that Josephine is ninety-nine and critically ill. I met her just a few days ago, so she's been feeding me the details in tiny little spoonfuls," Brooke said. "Your grandmother Ruth and Josephine were lifelong friends. They were roommates in boarding school and made their debuts together."

"I never knew Granny was a debutante," Lizzie said, chuckling. "That's just crazy! She was a card-carrying liberal."

"Which Josephine decidedly is not," Brooke

volunteered. “Anyway, Josephine and Ruth were also best friends with Mildred Updegraff, who, by the way, was my grandmother. They had another friend, who was much younger, named Varina. The four girls had a little club, sort of a secret society, which they called the High Tide Club.”

“Cute, but what’s the point?” Lizzie said.

“Sometime after the war — World War II, that is — Josephine had a falling-out with my grandmother Millie and later, your grandmother Ruth. Over the years, she lost contact with everyone except for Varina. Josephine is hazy on the details, but that’s it in a nutshell. Now she’s got terminal cancer. She wants to reconnect with her old friends’ heirs and ‘make amends’ as she says. I should add that Josephine has been a widow for many years and never had children.”

Brooke heard the tapping of keys from the other end of the line.

“Holy shit,” Lizzie said. “I’m just reading an article about Josephine Warrick. This says that Talisa is twelve thousand acres. Is that true?”

“Yes. A small portion of the island was owned by distant cousins, who sold it to the State of Georgia for a park in 1978, but Josephine retains ownership of the rest of Talisa, and she’s determined not to let the state take her land. That’s how I got involved.”

“I’m looking at a photo of some gorgeous

pink mansion. It looks like a frickin' castle!" Lizzie exclaimed.

"That's Shellhaven. It was built in the twenties by Josephine's father, who was a shipping magnate. It's in pretty bad shape these days, but Josephine is also adamant that the house should be preserved. She wants her land and house transferred intact to her beneficiaries," Brooke said.

"Are you telling me a woman I never met, never even heard of until today, wants me to inherit a twelve thousand–acre island in Georgia?"

"Not exactly," Brooke said. "I mean, maybe. It's not really clear. And yes, I understand how insane this all sounds to you, because it sounds insane to me too, and unlike you, I've met her, and I've been to Talisa."

"This is totally, totally nuts," Lizzie said.

"Agreed. So here's the thing. Josephine wants to meet you. You and your brother. I've been trying to find a way to contact him too, but I'm sort of at a dead end."

There was a long pause on the other end of the line.

"Bobby's dead," Lizzie said.

"Oh. I'm sorry to hear that," Brooke said.

"Don't be. My brother had what we journalists like me call 'a checkered criminal career.' We hadn't talked in years. I only found out Bobby was dead when his landlord called me up to ask for his last three months of back rent. Turns out he'd listed me as next of kin on his apartment application."

Brooke was at a loss for words.

"So you were saying?" Lizzie prompted.

"Josephine would like to meet you. In person. On Talisa. To be honest, I don't know what happens after that. She's old and ornery, and she's dying."

"Is she rich?" Lizzie asked bluntly. "Because if she's not, I have no interest in flying out to Georgia to meet some eccentric old crackpot. I'm on deadline for a crappy magazine story right now, and I can't really afford to take time away from that, not to mention the cost of a plane ticket. So you tell her that. Tell her I'll come if she'll pay my way. All expenses, including airfare, meals, and hotel."

"I'll tell her, but there's no hotel on Talisa. There's hardly even cell phone service," Brooke warned.

"Sounds dreamy," Lizzie said.

Henry pounded on the plastic tray of the high chair with his sippy cup. "Milk! Milk! Milk!"

"Milk, *please,*" Brooke said.

"Milk, please, milk, please, milk, please," he chanted.

She refilled the cup and called her mother.

Marie answered on the second ring. "Hi, sweetie. Is everything okay?"

"Of course. Why wouldn't it be?" Brooke asked.

"Don't be so sensitive," Marie said. "You usually don't call on weekdays while you're working."

"Actually, I am calling you about work. I need to ask you something about my new client."

"Is it somebody I know?"

"Well, she seems to think she knows *you.* It's Josephine Bettendorf Warrick."

"You're kidding."

"I'm not. Do you know her?"

"In a roundabout way. She was your granny's oldest friend. Does she still live down there in that creepy old mansion on that island?"

"Yep."

"Good heavens. I had no idea she was even still alive. Let's see. She must be in her nineties, right?"

"She turned ninety-nine in April," Brooke said.

"How did you get mixed up with her?"

"She called me. Out of the blue. She'd seen those old newspaper stories about me trying to sue the Park Service, and she wants me to keep the state from condemning Talisa and taking it for a park. And that's not all. She wants me to find the heirs of her oldest friends. I've already contacted one granddaughter, who lives in California. I'm trying to track down another woman and her niece. And that just leaves you."

"Me? What's she want with me? Or those other women?"

"She wants to meet with you. And then, if she likes what she sees, I think she intends for the three of you to inherit the island. And the mansion."

"Really? Josephine Warrick hardly knows me. Why would she do something like that?"

"She says she wants to make it up to her oldest, dearest friends. But she hasn't really told me what she's trying to apologize for. It's all pretty sketchy, to tell you the truth. I tried to talk her out of hiring me, but she's absolutely adamant that she wants me and nobody else."

Marie mulled that over for a moment. "You say she's ninety-nine? Are you sure she's not suffering from dementia?"

"Josephine is sharp as a tack. Most of the time. But she's been diagnosed with lung cancer, so she tires easily. I gather she was a pretty heavy smoker for most of her life."

"Funny you should mention that," Marie said, "because that's what I remember about her. Your father and I were at a party, years and years ago, at the Oglethorpe Club, and she was there too, and what I remember about her was that she had this long, jeweled cigarette holder, like something out of *Breakfast at Tiffany's,* you know? I thought she was quite exotic."

"Did she speak to you?"

"Only briefly. I was in the ladies' lounge, fixing my hair, and she came up and introduced herself and said how sorry she was about Granny. She went on and on about what a dear friend Millie was. Which I thought was very odd, since she didn't go to Granny's funeral or send a sympathy card or anything."

"That sounds like Josephine," Brooke said. "And you'd never met her before that?"

"Not that I can recall," Marie said.

"Do you remember Granny ever talking about the High Tide Club?"

"Say that again?" Marie asked.

"The High Tide Club. Did Granny ever mention it to you?"

"Granny wasn't much of a club woman. I think she did Junior League because her mother and grandmother did it . . ."

"This was a different kind of club," Brooke said. "According to Josephine, it was just her, another friend named Ruth, Granny, and a young black girl, Varina, who worked for the Bettendorfs and grew up on the island."

Marie gave that some thought. "I remember Granny talking about Ruth and Jo and the scrapes they got into in boarding school. And the name *Varina* sounds vaguely familiar, but what you have to remember is this was all a long time ago. Granny's been gone almost thirty years now."

"Twenty-eight," Brooke said promptly. "She

died when I was six."

"Has it really been that long?" Marie said, her voice wistful. "I do miss her, Brooke. And I wish she'd lived long enough to enjoy you and, of course, our sweet Henry."

Brooke glanced over at sweet Henry, who at that precise moment was in the process of trying to climb out of his high chair. He had one chubby leg over the tray, and the chair was starting to tilt.

"Henry, no!" Brooke yelled. "Sorry, Mom. Gotta go."

13

Farrah was on the phone when Brooke arrived at the office, talking in what the young assistant liked to refer to as her "takin'-names-and-kickin'-ass voice."

"Hi, Mr. Mabry," she said, the model of crisp efficiency. "This is Ms. Miles, the office manager at Trappnell and Associates."

Farrah frowned and looked up at Brooke in amazement. "He hung up on me! The douchebag hung up as soon as I said your name."

"Was that Steve Mabry, the long-haul trucker who owes me $5,000 for handling his DUI case back in January?" Brooke asked with a sigh. "Forget it. He's a bona fide deadbeat. I'll have to file against him in small claims court, and it's probably not worth my time."

"No way," Farrah said. "He's gonna pay, and I'm gonna make it happen." She picked up her phone and redialed.

"Hi. Steve Mabry? Dude, don't hang up. I

mean it. Look. You owe our firm $5,000 for representation on that DUI charge from way back last winter."

Farrah listened, tapping long violet fingertips on the desktop and shaking her head. "Yeah, I am aware that the judge revoked your driver's license. I'm also aware that it was your third DUI in the past five years, and if it hadn't been for my boss, or 'that bitch Brooke Trappnell,' as you just referred to her, your sorry tail would be sitting in the county jail right now."

Farrah's eyes narrowed as she listened to the diatribe on the other end of the line. "Let me get this straight," she interrupted. "You're telling me you have no intention of paying your legal fee, 'cause you don't have a job, 'cause you're not allowed to drive? Then how come you delivered a pizza to my boyfriend's house last night? Yeah, that's right. I was there, and I also took a picture of you behind the wheel of your pickup. Which I'm fixin' to email over to Judge Waller's office unless you deliver the money you owe this firm, in person. Like, today."

Brooke gasped in horror, but Farrah smiled smugly. "That's great. And hey, don't bother bringing a check. We're gonna need either cash or a money order. And if I were you, dude, I'd ask your mama to give you a ride."

She disconnected and gave her boss an angelic smile. "He says he'll be right over."

"Did you really get a photo of him driving last night?"

"Nope. It was way too dark."

Brooke tried to look stern. "Blackmail is against the law, you know."

Farrah shrugged. "So if that douchebag gets me arrested, I'll hire a good lawyer. Know any? I gotta go to class now. Don't forget to give him a receipt when he shows up."

There was a light tapping at her office door. A moment later, it swung open, and a black woman in her midthirties stepped inside. "Come on in, Auntie," she said, grasping the arm of a tiny white-haired woman with a walker.

"Hi," Brooke said, standing. "I'm Brooke Trappnell. Can I help you?"

"This is a nice office," the elderly woman said, looking around. "You reckon this is the right place?" She gave Brooke a warm smile. "We're looking for a lady lawyer."

"I'm a lady lawyer," Brooke said.

"See, Auntie Vee? It is her."

"Wait," Brooke said, startled. "Auntie Vee. Is your aunt Varina Shaddix?"

"That's right. And I'm her great-niece Felicia Shaddix. My aunt's cousin Louette called this week and said you might be in contact. We were coming up from Jacksonville today anyway, to see about a headstone for my great-uncle, and I just decided to drop in and see what you wanted with my aunt."

"This is great," Brooke said, still surprised. She pulled two chairs up to her desk. "Won't you sit down? I'm glad Louette called, although I wasn't aware Josephine had let her know I was looking for your aunt."

Felicia Shaddix got her aunt seated and then sat down in the other chair. She was tall and willowy, with short-cropped hair that had been peroxided nearly white. Her skin was a shade darker than her aunt's. Half a dozen gold-and-ivory bangle bracelets jangled from her left wrist. Her dark, almond-shaped eyes were outlined with kohl, and she wore a form-fitting black tank top, white jeans, and cork-soled gold sandals.

"What's that old bird want from my aunt now?" Felicia said, crossing her legs.

Brooke found herself momentarily at a loss for words. Had she told Louette she wanted to contact Varina — and her niece? Had Josephine Warrick asked Louette to reach out to the two women?

"Um," she said, stalling. "I didn't know Louette was related to your great-aunt."

Felicia gave a wave of her jangling wrist. "Everybody who ever lived at Oyster Bluff is somehow related to everybody else. Except Shug, of course, and he married into the family."

"Right." Brooke took a deep breath. "I'm sorry. You really did take me by surprise. I spoke to Josephine last week about trying to track you and your aunt down. In fact, that was my plan for today. And now you've showed up."

"Josephine wasn't very nice to us last time, was she?" Varina said, looking from Felicia to Brooke. Her skin was surprisingly smooth for a woman in her nineties, Brooke thought. Varina Shaddix seemed swallowed up in the wooden office chair. She wore a neatly pressed pink floral cotton dress, loosely belted at the waist, of a style Brooke hadn't seen since her own grandmother was alive, with pin tucks on the button-front bodice. Varina had undoubtedly made the dress herself. A large white patent-leather pocketbook dangled from her bony wrist. Her rubber-soled, white lace-up shoes were spotless, and her snowy white hair was parted down the middle, braided in a series of cornrows, and fastened with pink plastic barrettes. A tiny silver cross nested in the hollow of her throat, and a pearl brooch was pinned to the collar of her dress.

"Josephine was Josephine," Felicia said, shrugging. "She's only nice when she wants something from you, Auntie Vee." Now she turned again to Brooke. "So what is it she wants this time, and why now?"

"She's been diagnosed with terminal lung cancer," Brooke said. "And she wants to make amends with her oldest friends and their heirs. She's hired me to try to make that happen."

"Make things right how?"

Brooke sighed. "Nothing is in writing yet, but as you know, Josephine has no living heirs. She wants to leave Talisa, and Shellhaven, to her friends and their heirs. And that includes your great-aunt."

"What's that?" Varina leaned in.

"Josephine is dying," Felicia said loudly. She sat back in her chair and crossed her arms defiantly over her chest. "Serves her right, for all the things she and her family did to all of us. Now she wants to make things right by you, Auntie Vee."

Varina blinked rapidly. "Is that right?" she asked, her voice quavering, eyes welling up with tears. "Josephine is dying?"

14

October 1941

Just as fast as Varina finished washing a load of plates and glasses in the big kitchen at Shellhaven, one of the waiters who'd been brought in special for the party from Atlanta toted in a tray with another load of dirty dishes. She had been standing at the big cast-iron sink for three hours with her arms plunged up to her elbows in soapy water, and still it seemed the dishes kept coming.

The back door was propped open with a big electric fan, but it barely made a dent in the heat of the kitchen. It might be October in the rest of the world, but summer lingered on in this part of the Georgia coast. Sweat dripped down her face and her back. Her calves ached.

Whenever the swinging door from the butler's pantry opened, she could hear the strains of music coming from the ballroom. At one point in the evening, she'd been allowed to put on a frilly white apron and take a tray of sandwiches and drinks out to the men in the orchestra while they took a break from playing, but other than that, she'd been cooped up right here in this kitchen.

The ballroom was so crowded she hadn't even seen her friends, but that was just as well, considering how ugly she looked.

She had a brand-new dress store-bought, special for the party, that Josephine had given her. It was her first grown-up dress, a light pinky-orange color with beautiful embroidery and no baby-looking puffy sleeves or silly bows or sashes like her mama used to make her wear. She had almost-new shoes too, which Ruth had brought her, all the way from Boston.

They were pink. Pink shoes! With sassy ankle straps that fastened with rhinestone buckles. Rhinestones! And a little heel, and they were as far from her scuffed-up hand-me-down brown leather brogans as a pair of shoes could be. They looked just like the shoes in the fashion magazines Millie brought her every time she came to the island, and they were almost too perfect to wear.

The biggest mirror they had at home at Oyster Bluff was the one on the bureau in Daddy's room. She'd snuck in there, before leaving for the party, and tilted the mirror just the right way so she could admire how the shoes looked.

Everybody said she was small for her age.

She had light skin and good hair, which her auntie said came from her mama's people, who were from away and part Indian. Her brothers called her Skinnystick, and her daddy was always saying she needed "some meat on her bones," because she was not built like the rest of the Shaddixes. Just this year, her bosoms had started to come in, and Auntie gave her a brassiere, which she'd bought from the Sears Roebuck store in Jacksonville, and which was Varina's most treasured possession, if you didn't count her white leatherette Bible.

Looking in the mirror at herself, Varina thought she looked real fine. She had no stockings, but she'd used some lotion Ruth had given her on her legs, and they looked smooth and silky, like the models in the fashion magazines.

She wrapped up the new shoes in a flour sack and carried them on the walk to Shellhaven. After she got to the house, she used the flour sack to wipe her feet off, then put the shoes on and reported to work.

Mrs. Dorris, the white boss lady, took one look at Varina and pitched a fit.

"Girl, what do you think you are doing sashaying in here in that fancy dress and silly shoes? You ain't getting paid to look pretty, and you sure can't work like that."

Varina's face fell. "I can wear an apron so it won't get all messed up."

"No, ma'am," Mrs. Dorris said. She rummaged around in the broom closet until she found one of her own faded cotton housedresses hanging from a nail and tossed it to Varina. "Go put this on, and be quick about it." A moment later, she managed a rare smile. "But first, go find Miss Josephine and her friends so they can see how nice you look. And then you get your tail back in here and start washing those dishes."

Varina had run up the back stairway and managed to catch Josephine just as she and Ruth were walking out of Josephine's bedroom heading toward the guest bedroom where Millie was staying for the week of the engagement party.

"Look here, Jo," Ruth had said, when she caught sight of Varina. "It's a fairy princess!"

"Oh, Varina!" Josephine had exclaimed. "Turn around. Let me see!"

The soles of the shoes were slippery, so Varina did a slow pirouette, her arms poked stiffly out from her sides.

"You look so pretty," Ruth said, touching the sleeve of the silk dress. "Jo, this color is perfect for her. And what a cute figure you have too." She caught Varina's hand in hers. "Come on, let's show Millie how beautiful you look for her party."

Varina glanced at the grandfather clock in the hallway. "I have to get back downstairs. Mrs. Dorris needs me."

"If Dorris fusses, you just tell her I needed you upstairs for a few minutes," Josephine said.

Josephine rapped lightly on Millie's door. "Come on out, bride-to-be," she called gaily. "We have a surprise for you."

Millie opened the door and stepped into the hallway. Her blond hair was tied up in soft rag curlers, and she still wore a bathrobe. There were dark circles under her eyes, but when she caught sight of Varina, her face lit up with a smile.

"Who is this gorgeous creature?" Millie asked.

"It's me," Varina said, suddenly shy.

"And I'm furious at her, because she is much prettier than all three of us put together," Josephine teased. "No boy at this party will want to dance with us after they see Varina."

Varina blushed furiously. "Y'all know I can't really come to the party. Mrs. Dorris only let me come upstairs to see y'all for a minute. She says I got to get back and change out of this dress and shoes so I can work."

"Well, I think I'm just going to sneak you downstairs and into the ballroom for a few minutes so that Papa and Gardiner can see how nice you look," Josephine said.

"Oh no," Varina said quickly.

"Varina's right, Jo," Ruth said. "We don't want to get her in trouble."

Millie gave the girl a quick hug. "Go on back downstairs, then, Cinderella. Before your coach turns into a pumpkin."

"Huh?" Varina gave her a puzzled look.

"Don't tell me you never read the fairy tale about Cinderella and her wicked stepsisters," Ruth said. "With the pumpkin that turned into a coach?"

"And the rats that turned into coachmen, or were they footmen?" Millie asked.

Varina looked from one of the girls to the other. "Are y'all my wicked stepsisters?"

The girls all laughed.

"No, silly girl," Josephine said. "We're more like your fairy godmothers."

"Okay," Varina said. "I'd better go back now, before Mrs. Dorris comes looking for me."

"Wait just a minute, Varina," Millie said. She darted into the bedroom and came back a moment later.

"Josephine gave you this dress, and Ruth gave you the shoes. Now I want you to have something from me. Mama gave me this pearl pin for my sixteenth birthday. You're almost sixteen, aren't you?"

"Not for another year and a half," Varina said. "But I can't take this, Miss Millie. This must've cost a lot of money."

"It really didn't," Millie said, fastening the pin to the collar of Varina's dress. "Anyway, it's a gift. And it's bad manners not to accept a gift from a friend, isn't it, girls?"

"It certainly is," Ruth said solemnly.

It was ten o'clock before she'd worked her way through the mountains of dirty glasses and plates. Finally, Mrs. Dorris took the dishtowel from Varina's hand.

"Go on home now, girl. Those fancy waiters can finish up in here once the party's over." She fished in the pocket of her apron and handed Varina two crisp dollar bills. "Miss Josephine said this was to be your pay for tonight. I told her that's way too much, but she insisted."

Varina stared down at the dollars. "You sure?"

"I'm sure," Mrs. Dorris said. She peered out the back door. "It's mighty dark out there. Is one of your brothers coming over to walk you home?"

"No, ma'am," Varina said, untying her apron. "It's not that dark. There's a full moon tonight, and anyway, I could walk to Oyster Bluff with my eyes closed." She headed for the broom closet, where she changed out of the ugly housedress and back into her own beautiful dress.

"Girl!" Mrs. Dorris was laughing at her. "You are bound and determined to wear that dress tonight, aren't you?"

"It's the prettiest thing I ever owned," Varina said.

"Well, I can't say I blame you. If I were as young and skinny as you, I guess I'd do the same thing. Just be careful and don't get nothin' on it. That's real silk, you know."

Varina knew she should have gone right home, but she just wanted to get one more peek at the party before it was all over. She cut around the side of the house and positioned herself at the edge of the veranda behind a tall camellia bush. The French doors were open, and when she poked her head around the camellia, she caught glimpses of ladies in their beautiful party dresses and the men in their stylish white dinner jackets. She closed her eyes and hummed a little of the song the orchestra was playing. Josephine brought a record of the song when she came down from Boston, and she said it was called "Moonlight Serenade." She and the girls played it all the time in the days before the party, and they'd even shown Varina how to do a dance called the foxtrot.

At one point, she thought she saw Josephine dance past the doors with a short, stout man with a shock of gray hair, who looked like Mr. Bettendorf. She saw Ruth too, beautiful in a seafoam-green dress with white flowers tucked into her shining red hair.

Suddenly, a huge man in a white dinner jacket burst through the French doors. He had a woman by the arm, dragging her along like a puppy on a short rope.

It was Millie! She recognized the dress, and then a moment later, Millie's voice.

"Russell, stop. Let go. You're hurting me."

Russell. That was the man Millie was fixing to marry. Josephine said he was richer than King Midas. It looked to Varina like they were fighting.

They stopped for a moment, just a few feet away. Varina shrank back behind the bush and held her breath, certain they would see her there.

They were talking now, but their voices were lower, and she couldn't make out what they were saying. She heard Millie's soft laugh and relaxed a little.

Now the man was on the move again, and he was dragging Millie after him. They went a little ways down the walkway, out of sight and earshot. Curious, Varina slipped out from the bush and tiptoed down the walkway, being sure to stay in the shadows.

The moon was so bright that night, she was afraid she'd be seen, but she darted across the cobblestone walk and crept closer.

Millie was crying! Varina tensed. She ducked behind a huge ball-shaped bush and craned her neck to try to see.

The crying was coming from beneath the deep shade of the big old magnolia tree that towered over that part of the garden. Varina could see the white of Russell's dinner jacket, but not much more.

"No! Stop it!" Millie cried. It sounded like he was hurting her. Varina took a deep breath. She had to do something to stop that man. She took a step sideways but then heard footsteps coming from the direction of the veranda, and she slunk back to her hiding place.

Gardiner Bettendorf, Josephine's big brother, hurried past. Mr. Gardiner had just about quit coming to Talisa, ever since Mrs. Bettendorf died. Josephine said her brother hated to come here because it reminded him of his dead mama, and anyway, he'd been in college and started law school, but now, Josephine said, he had dropped out of that and was getting ready to go to Canada to sign up to be a pilot and bomb the hell out of the Germans.

"Millie?" Gardiner called.

Russell said something that Varina couldn't quite make out, and the next thing she knew, he was right there, standing under the magnolia tree, and things were starting to get ugly.

Then Millie screamed, and Varina heard bone meeting flesh. Millie screamed again.

And then it was over. Millie rushed past Varina's hiding place. Her dress was torn at the bodice, and she was crying so hard she never even saw Varina standing there, wondering what to do.

Varina knew she should go too, but she just

had to see what would happen next. She darted across the walkway and into the shadows on the other side of the walk. As she crept closer, she could hear the familiar sounds of two men fighting, which she knew well, having older brothers who regularly "tussled," as her daddy called it, sometimes in fun, but mostly out of anger.

"Uuunhhh," would be followed by a low groan, then another blow.

Their voices echoed in the night air, cursing — she knew those words too from her brothers, who mostly did it only when their preacher daddy was not within earshot.

Finally, Gardiner staggered onto the walkway. In the moonlight, she could see one of his eyes was swollen, his lip and nose bloodied, his white dinner jacket spotted with more blood.

"Enough!" he shouted. "We're through here. In the morning, if you're not on the first boat off this island, my father and I will contact the sheriff, and I'll tell him exactly what you did to Millie."

Russell stepped into the moonlight too. A gash above his eye leaked blood, as did one on his jaw. "Charges? What kind of charges? Millie is my fiancée, and what I do to her or with her is none of your goddamn business."

"She's not your property yet," Gardiner said, his voice low. "Now, get out of my sight. And I warn you, if you lay hands on her or try to force yourself on her again that way, I'll leave the law out of it and take care of you the way people down here handle things."

"You don't have the balls," Russell taunted.

Gardiner turned and walked away. Varina shrank back into the shrubbery and watched as he skirted the house and the veranda. She glanced up at the sky. Clouds rolled past and obscured the moon. The temperature had dropped, and the wind had picked up. Rain was coming. She needed to hurry home or her dress and shoes would be ruined. She would have to leave the way Gardiner had gone. But quietly.

She took a step in that direction, and her shoe landed squarely on a dried twig that snapped loudly.

"Who's there?" Russell called.

Varina scurried back into the boxwood hedge and stepped on another twig.

The big man was at her side in an instant, reaching through the tangle of underbrush, grabbing her by the arm. Thorns snagged on her silk dress, scratching the bare skin on her arms and legs. Varina clung helplessly to a branch of the shrub, but it broke off in her hand, and a moment later, he'd hauled her onto the walkway.

"Who are you? Were you spying on us just now?"

She was so terrified she was unable to speak. He slapped her face so hard she felt her ears ringing.

"Damn it, girl, who are you?"

"N-n-nobody," she stammered. "I didn't see anything. I was just walking home."

"What are you doing up here?" he demanded.

"I was working at the party," Varina whispered. "In the kitchen. Mrs. Dorris, she said I could go home, so that's what I was doing."

His eyes narrowed as he looked her over, up and down, the way you'd look at a horse or a mule you were sizing up to buy.

"Where'd a servant girl get an expensive dress like this?" He ran his hand down her shoulder and over her chest, right over her breast. He flicked the pearl pin with one finger.

"I know this pin. It belongs to my fiancée. Did you sneak upstairs in the house and steal this pin? And that dress? What else did you steal, girl?"

At first, Varina was too terrified to speak.

"Nothin'," she finally managed. "I didn't steal nothin', I swear. Miss Josephine gave me this dress as a present. And Miss Millie gave me the pin."

"Liar," he spat. He pinched her nipple so hard she screamed, and he clamped his hand over her mouth.

"Millie never gave jewelry to a colored girl. You stole these things. I know you did. That's why you were hiding out here. Like a thief."

Varina couldn't breathe. She couldn't speak. Finally, he moved his hand. She exhaled and began sobbing.

"I'm not a thief. You can ask Miss Josephine. I'm not. I was just going home. I got to get home now. My daddy will be looking for me."

"Your daddy will just have to wait," Russell said. He jerked her arm so hard she thought it would pull from its socket. "You're coming with me. I think the two of us will have our own private party."

15

Felicia Shaddix leaned in close to Varina. "Now, Auntie, you knew that old lady had cancer. Louette told you. I told you."

Varina nodded and dabbed at her eyes with a crochet-edged handkerchief. "Cancer, yes. But nobody said nothin' about dying." She looked over at Brooke. "You sure you got that right?"

"Josephine told me herself."

"I should go see her. Take her some of my soup. She always loved my beef consommé. Mrs. Dorris showed me how to make it so that it was clear as could be. You could see the bottom of the bowl," Varina said. She turned to Felicia. "I used to make that consommé for all you children when you were sick. Remember?"

"We were your family," Felicia said coldly. "You took care of all of us, Auntie. And now I'm taking care of you. But Josephine Warrick is not your family. What did she ever give you besides some old clothes she didn't want anymore?"

"Josephine is my friend," Varina said. "She's got her ways, that's true. But she is my friend. I told you she would do right by us, didn't I? And that's what this lady lawyer is going to see about." She gave Brooke a warm smile. "Isn't that right?"

"Yes," Brooke said.

"We'll see." Felicia looked around the office at the stained, fraying carpet, secondhand furniture, and single bank of file cabinets. She stared at Brooke's framed college degrees.

"Emory Law, huh?"

"That's right," Brooke said.

"Felicia went to Emory University too," Varina said proudly. "They gave her a full scholarship. And she graduated first in her class."

"Undergrad," Felicia said. She turned back to Brooke, crossed and recrossed her slender legs. "You know, my aunt asked Josephine, only a few months ago, if she would consider deeding over the land at Oyster Bluff to our family. And Josephine refused. Threw us out. It was really ugly."

"So I heard," Brooke said. "If it's any consolation, I think she now regrets the way that meeting ended. And that's why I wanted to talk to your aunt. Josephine has authorized me to start the process of returning the property at Oyster Bluff to the people who live there."

"See there?" Varina said. "I knew she'd make things right. Didn't I tell you?"

"I'll believe it when I see it," Felicia said. "Louette told me the state wants to make Josephine sell them all the rest of Talisa, for the state park. How's she going to give twenty acres to our people with the state breathing down her neck? How would that work?"

"I'm not sure yet," Brooke admitted. "I was just hired last week, and I haven't had time to start my research. I can tell you that Josephine intends to fight the state to prevent them from taking her land. And in the meantime, she'd like to immediately begin the process of deeding over Oyster Bluff to the families who still live there."

"About time," Felicia said. "You know what she paid for my folks' house over there? Did she tell you? If not, I will. She paid my widowed mother $1,500. For the house and more than an acre of land. I think Louette's daddy got even less than that when he sold to her."

"Now, Felicia, honey," Varina said gently. "You know as well as I do those houses was in bad shape. Josephine fixed your mama's house up real nice for her after your daddy passed. And Louette's daddy, well, he was my cousin, and I don't like to speak ill of the dead, but Gerald was bad to drink and didn't care nothin' about patching a leaky roof or painting a porch. That house of his wasn't fit for chickens by the time he died."

Felicia rolled her eyes but didn't argue with her great-aunt.

Brooke sighed. "I can't speak to the fairness of the real estate transactions. It's my job, now, to get a list of the surviving Oyster Bluff families who sold their land to Josephine. My assistant can do some of that research in the courthouse, but it would be great if you and your aunt could give me names and addresses."

"We can do that," Felicia said. "Right, Auntie?"

"She's really gonna give back Oyster Bluff?" Varina said. "All of it? The church too? The graveyard where my mama and daddy and brothers are buried?"

"Yes," Brooke said. "All of it."

"Praise Jesus," Varina said. She dabbed at her eyes again and sniffed. "I guess we can go on home now, Felicia."

Felicia stood up and helped the old woman from her chair. She looked around the room again. "Auntie, would you like to visit the bathroom before we get on the road back to Jacksonville?"

"That would be real nice."

After she'd helped her aunt into the bathroom and closed the door, Felicia turned back to Brooke with a stern expression.

"I didn't want to say anything more in front

of my aunt, Ms. Trappnell, because she doesn't like to 'fuss,' as she calls it, but I think it's best you know who you're dealing with here. My aunt is an amazing woman. First in her family to finish high school, and then to leave the island to take business classes and work for the railroad. You have no idea what an accomplishment that was in the forties, and in the Jim Crow South. She is the matriarch of this family, and she has been doing for others her whole life. But she still very much suffers from a plantation mentality. She's grateful for whatever stale crumbs Josephine Warrick throws her way."

Felicia crossed her arms over her chest. "But that's not me. In case you're interested, after I finished Emory, I got a master's in American history and a PhD in African American studies at Northwestern, but I'm currently my aunt's caregiver."

"That's very admirable of you, giving up a career for your great-aunt," Brooke said.

"Please don't patronize me," Felicia said. "Auntie Vee is the one who did without to buy me a secondhand car to take to college. A month didn't go by that I didn't get a card with a little check in it from her. I didn't give up my career. I'm teaching online classes through the University of North Florida and working on a book proposal. All of this is just to let you know — I don't intend to let Josephine continue exploiting my aunt or the rest of my family."

Brooke was startled by Felicia's intensity. "I know it's late in the day, but I honestly do believe Josephine wants to make things right by your aunt and by the others living at Oyster Bluff."

"Do you know anything at all about my people? About the Geechee and how long we've lived on these coastal islands?" Felicia asked.

"Only a little," Brooke admitted. "I know there was a plantation where Shellhaven now stands and that your ancestors were slaves who worked there."

"Typical," Felicia snapped.

They heard the toilet flush through the thin Sheetrock walls, and a moment later, Varina slowly emerged from the bathroom.

"All set?" she asked, smiling at her niece.

"Yes, ma'am," Felicia said, taking her arm. She looked over at Brooke. "Do you have a business card or something? I'll make some phone calls after I get her home, and then I'll email you the names and addresses of the Oyster Bluff folks."

"Any idea how many people we're talking about? Like, maybe a ballpark figure?"

"My guess? Nine or ten families," Felicia said.

Brooke fetched a card from her desk and offered it to her visitor, and at the same time, Varina Shaddix reached up and planted a kiss on Brooke's cheek. "You tell Josephine I'm coming to see her real soon," she whispered in Brooke's ear. "You tell her I'll be praying that demon cancer lets loose of her. Will you do that?"

"Yes, ma'am," Brooke said. "I'll let her know."

16

Felicia Shaddix had hit on a matter that had been worrying Brooke ever since she'd changed her mind and decided to work for Josephine Warrick. The State of Georgia was, as her client said, circling like buzzards, trying to force Josephine to sell Shellhaven and the land surrounding it to add to the existing park on the other end of the island.

Brooke knew little to nothing about statutes pertaining to condemnation law. The good news was that she knew somebody who would be able to school her on the issues. The bad news was that he was a senior partner in her old Savannah law firm. And she hadn't spoken to Gabe Wynant since the day she'd turned in her resignation letter four years ago.

He had actually been the one who'd hired her, been a mentor and a friend to her, and Brooke could still see the look of disappointment on his face the day she'd shown up, unannounced and dripping wet in his office doorway, to tell him she was quitting and leaving town.

The morning she'd quit, Brooke had to make three circles of the block around Calhoun Square, where the Farrell, Wynant offices were located, before finding a curbside parking space a block away. And of course, she'd left her umbrella at home. By the time she stepped into the office's marble-floored reception area, she looked like a drowned rat.

"Gabe?"

He was sitting at his desk, his suit jacket draped over the back of his chair, his face still ruddy from having just showered and shaved in the bathroom adjoining his office.

"Brooke! My God, what happened to you?"

She gestured toward the bow window that looked out on the live oaks of the square. "Poor planning," she said. Rain streamed down her face and her legs, leaving a puddle on the jewel-toned Oriental rug.

He stood, went into his bathroom, and came back with a thick, white monogrammed bath towel. "Here, see if this will help."

She toweled off her hair, made a halfhearted attempt to mop up the worst of the water, then draped the towel over her shoulders.

"Sit," he said, gesturing toward one of the leather wingback chairs facing his desk. "Unless you want to go home and change first. I'm sure whatever it is can wait."

"No," she'd said quietly. "I'm afraid if I leave now, I'll lose my nerve."

"You? Never," Gabe said. "But I don't like the look on your face right now. As a matter of fact, aren't you supposed to be on your honeymoon?"

Gabe Wynant was then in his late fifties, but he claimed his hair had turned white overnight after a particularly grueling lawsuit he'd filed against the City of Savannah. He was lean and tan, with a beaky oversized nose and dark eyes behind trendy tortoiseshell Warby Parker glasses.

Brooke took a deep breath. "I'm resigning."

"What? Why? Aren't you happy here?"

"I have been. I was." She felt her upper lip quivering and swallowed. "I thought you would have heard by now. Harris and I . . . anyway, the wedding's off."

"I just got back from vacation, so no, I hadn't heard," Gabe said. "I'm sorry, Brooke. We all really liked Harris. He's a nice guy."

"The best guy in the world," Brooke agreed. "And I'm the biggest idiot in the world. But I just can't . . ."

She was crying now, big, huge, crybaby tears. He sat and waited. Finally, he handed her a box of tissues.

"I'm not ready to be married," she said finally. "I thought I loved Harris enough to get past that, but I guess maybe I don't. Love him enough, I mean. In fact, I'm terrified of being married. And I was terrified to tell anybody, which is why I ran away."

"Okay," Gabe said slowly. "But just because you broke off your engagement, that doesn't mean you have to quit your job. Does it?"

"I can't stay here any longer," Brooke said. "I've lived in Savannah my whole life, except for when I was in school. I know this sounds like a horrible cliché, but sometimes clichés are true. For me anyway. I feel like I'm suffocating. I've made a huge mess of my life. I've let my family and friends down, hurt Harris and his family terribly. I'm a disaster. You don't want me working here, Gabe."

"You're the furthest thing from a disaster. You've got a fine legal mind. Your work here has been excellent, and all your clients adore you. The fact that you were savvy enough to walk away before getting entangled in a marriage you had doubts about means you've got a good head on your shoulders."

"I didn't walk away. I ran. All the way to Cumberland Island. I was a coward. I'm still a coward. I snuck into town last night. My parents don't even know I'm here. Harris is still at his parents' house in South Carolina. I've packed up the rest of my stuff, and as soon as you and I are done talking, I'm headed back down there. I can't face anybody, Gabe. It was all I could do to make myself come in here this morning, to hand in my resignation in person. I thought it was the least I owed you."

Gabe nodded. "I appreciate that, Brooke. And you're not a coward, so please stop saying that. A coward would have gone through with the wedding, despite the misgivings. The way I did, twenty-five years ago."

It was an open secret around the office that Gabe Wynant's marriage was over. He and his wife, Sunny, still lived under the same roof, but Sunny was an alcoholic who'd been in and out of rehab three times just in the time Brooke had worked at Farrell, Wynant.

Brooke didn't know what to say to that. "I've gotta go," she said, standing. She stuck out her hand, and Gabe took it and clamped it in both of his.

"Good luck, then," he said.

She'd walked all the way back to her car before she realized she still had the firm's bath towel wrapped around her shoulders.

Brooke still had that towel. And she still had Gabe Wynant's direct number in her cell phone.

"Brooke? Is that really you?"

"Hi, Gabe," she said. "Yes, it's really me."

"My gosh, it's good to hear from you. How the hell are you? Are you still living down, where was it, Brunswick?"

"I'm fine, thanks. I'm living in St. Ann's. I even hung out my shingle here."

"Did you go with an established firm?"

"No, I'm solo," Brooke said. "My practice isn't anything like it was in Savannah. I do a little of this, a little of that, whatever the other guys in town don't want to take on."

"That's great. I'm so glad to hear you didn't quit law. You're not, by any chance, calling to tell me you want to come back to us at Farrell, Wynant, are you? Because my offer still stands. The firm would welcome you back with open arms."

Brooke's face flushed with pleasure. It was nice to be wanted.

"That's so kind of you, Gabe. I can't tell you what it means to have you say that. But no, I'm not calling about a job. What I could use is your advice. I've actually got a new client, and although I've tried to persuade her I don't have any expertise at what she needs, she's insistent that I'm the only lawyer she wants."

"Happy to help out if I can," Gabe said.

"Do you have a few minutes to chat? It's kind of a long story."

"I've got a meeting in ten minutes. Can you give me the condensed version?"

"I'll try," Brooke said. "Have you ever heard of Josephine Bettendorf Warrick?"

"Of course," Gabe said promptly. "The queen of Talisa. My dad was a friend of her late husband, Preiss. I met her a couple of times, years ago, when she and Preiss came up here for parties and such. Is she your new client?"

"Yes."

He whistled softly. "Did she dump her Atlanta law firm? Schaefer-Moody?"

"I wouldn't say she dumped them. But if you know Josephine, you know she's, um, fairly headstrong. And eccentric."

"What's she want from you?" Gabe asked.

"She wants me to keep the State of Georgia from condemning her house and the rest of the island. They want to annex her land into the existing state park on the other end of the island. They've made her an offer, and they're pressing hard."

"How much?"

"Six million."

"For the house and how much land?"

"Twelve thousand acres, give or take."

"I've never set foot on that island and I can tell you right now that's a bullshit offer," Gabe said.

"I agree. She's got the only deepwater dock on that end of the island, all the beachfront, and the only freshwater supply on the island. And get this — the state paid her cousins three million for their little bit of the island back in the seventies. That's where the existing state park is located now."

"So, obviously, you need to fight the condemnation," Gabe said. "Look, Brooke. I need to get to my appointment. Here's an idea. I'll be down at my place on Sea Island over the weekend. You're not that far from there, right? Why don't you come up and have dinner with me, and then you can give me more details and we can throw around some ideas."

"This weekend?"

"Yeah. I've got something Friday night, but I could do Saturday, or even Sunday night if I don't head home until Monday morning. What do you say?"

Brooke sighed. "I don't know, Gabe. That's so generous of you, but the thing is, it's tough getting a babysitter on weekends."

"You've got a kid?" He sounded shocked.

"Henry. He's almost three. That's another long story. Look. My mom is coming down to stay with us, and I guess maybe I could get away for a couple of hours. Is there any way I can let you know over the weekend?"

"Why not? I'm going to be on Sea Island anyway. You've got my number, so just call or text me. I won't make dinner reservations at the club until I hear from you."

Brooke grinned. "Thanks so much, Gabe. Really."

17

"Where's my little fella? Where's my sweet Henry?"

Marie Trappnell arrived at Brooke's house shortly after 6:00 P.M. on Thursday night with a rolling suitcase and a gigantic tote bag overflowing with groceries and wrapped gifts. She swept past her bemused daughter and into the house.

Hearing her voice, Henry sped across the living room and flung himself at her knees, repeating his name for his grandmother over and over again. "Ree! Ree!"

Marie plopped herself down on the floor and gently pulled him onto her lap.

"Oh, my sweet boy! My poor angel." Marie kissed his face and the top of his head. She looked over at Brooke. "He's breaking my heart. I'm not hurting him, am I?"

"He's not made of glass, Mom," Brooke said. "It's been six weeks and he's fine. Just don't fling him around the room."

Henry held his arm up awkwardly for his

grandmother's inspection. "Look, Ree. I got boo-boo."

"I see," Marie said. She kissed his arm. "Better?"

He beamed. "Better." But the colorfully wrapped gifts had already drawn his attention. He pointed. "What's that, Ree?"

Marie pulled the tote toward them and spilled the contents onto the floor. "Well, let's see."

Henry picked up a stuffed dog. "Puppy!" He waved it at Brooke. "I got puppy!"

After they'd eaten dinner and put Henry to bed on the mattress in Brooke's room, Marie took a good look around her daughter's living room.

"This is really nice," she said, taking another sip of her wine. "You've done a lot since the last time I was down."

"It's not Ardsley Park," Brooke said wryly.

She actually had taken pains to fix up her modest cottage. Marie had donated the furniture from her garage apartment in Savannah after the departure of her last tenant. The sofa and matching ottoman were comfortable but with ugly, eighties brown-plaid upholstery, which Brooke had covered with sets of washed and bleached canvas drop cloths.

She'd splurged on an indoor-outdoor rug from a big-box store at the mall in Brunswick and had assembled a gallery wall of inexpensive thrift store paintings along with Henry's framed crayon drawings.

Marie yawned and stretched her legs. Brooke thought she looked distinctly out of place in this room of castoffs. Her mother had an innate elegance and sense of style that Brooke had always envied.

After the divorce, Marie had stopped coloring her dark hair, and her now silver hair was cut in a sleek bob, just below her chin. Unlike Brooke, she never left the house without eyeliner, blush, and lipstick. Her clothes weren't showy, just classics, like the well-fitting jeans and oversized Eileen Fisher white linen blouse she wore tonight. Her hands were long and slender, with nails painted a neutral color. She wore no rings.

"I'm so glad Henry is okay," Marie said. "I was terrified when I heard about the surgery."

"If it makes you feel any better, even though Henry is fine and the arm has totally healed, I'm still a little freaked out about the whole thing."

"You don't show it," Marie said. "You never have. I think you're like your father that way."

Brooke held up her hand, traffic cop–style. "Don't. Please don't compare me to Dad."

"I didn't mean it as a dig, honey. Just a mother's observation."

Brooke took a gulp of wine. "I may look calm to you, but I'm really like those ducks at the Daffin Park pond back home. Gliding over the water on the surface, but underneath it all, I'm paddling like hell trying to keep afloat."

Marie cocked her head and studied her daughter. Brooke's dark hair was pinned up in a messy bun on the top of her head. She wore a loose-fitting T-shirt and denim shorts. She was barefoot and needed a pedicure. And there were dark circles under her eyes.

"I wish you'd called me sooner," Marie said. "I wish you'd let me pitch in and help. Not just with money, but with Henry. I know you prize your independence, but sometimes I feel like you're deliberately shutting me out. And it makes me sad. You and Henry are my world, Brooke."

"I know," Brooke said with a sigh. "I don't mean to shut you out. It's just . . . I guess I feel like I have something to prove. You know, that I can do this. Work. Raise a child. Just be a competent human being. But it's so damn frustrating. If I'm home with Henry, I'm anxious that I should be at work, doing lawyer stuff. And when I'm at work, with a client — not that I have that many — I feel guilty that I'm not home with my child. And, Mom, I suck. At everything. I suck at life. I really do!"

Marie got up and sat down beside her daughter on the sofa. She wrapped both arms around her and laughed. "You don't suck."

"No," Brooke insisted, "I do. What kind of mom lets her kid break an arm at the park? What kind of lawyer can't even make enough money to pay for decent health insurance for her family?"

"Don't you think you're being a little hard on yourself?" Marie asked. "Do yourself a favor and stop trying to be a superwoman."

"I'm not. I just want to be half as good a mom as you were when I was growing up."

"Is that what this is about?" Marie asked, raising an eyebrow. "You're comparing yourself to me? But that's crazy! You're a single working mom, raising a child in a town where you have no support system. I had the luxury of being able to quit my job when I had you, because your father was more than able to support us."

"And you did everything, and you did it perfectly," Brooke said. "Beautiful, spotless house, gourmet cook, on every committee in town . . . and I know Dad wasn't any help with any of that."

"It was a different time. None of the women in our social circle worked outside the home. Even the women who had MDs and PhDs and JDs after their names quit their jobs to stay home with their babies."

"You sound wistful about that," Brooke said. "Did you ever wish you hadn't quit?"

"Sometimes," Marie admitted. "Not at first. I mean, I waited until I was over forty to have you. So I'd had a great career, and when I finally did get pregnant, it was such a shock, I thought, well, I should just stay home and raise this miracle child of mine. And that ought to be enough."

"And then?" Brooke prompted.

"I couldn't get you to sleep or nurse. I was a miserable failure. And I wasn't used to failing at anything. I'd always been good at everything when I was working."

"So what did you do?"

Marie reached over and stroked Brooke's hair, tucking an errant strand behind her ear. "I did what you should have done. I finally called my mother and told her I needed help."

"That's when she moved down to Savannah to live with us?"

"Yes. She literally saved my life. Yours too."

"God. It must be an inherited trait. Remember? I had to quit nursing Henry after two months because he wasn't latching on. And he didn't sleep the whole night until he was almost two," Brooke said, shuddering at the memory.

"You should have told me," Marie scolded. "Why wouldn't you call me up and tell me what you were going through?"

"I don't know," Brooke said. "I guess I thought it would be like surrendering. Admitting that I couldn't take care of my own child."

"You can't do it all alone, honey," Marie

said softly. "Nobody can. Not even you."

"I see that now," Brooke said. She stretched out on the sofa and put her head in her mother's lap. "I don't know if it's the wine or just having you here, but all of a sudden, I sort of feel okay. I think maybe it's gonna be okay."

"I'm glad," Marie said. "You've changed, you know, since you moved down here."

"Is that a good thing or a bad thing?"

"I haven't made up my mind yet. One thing that I think is good is that you're not as driven as you used to be when you were working in Savannah. You used to scare me, you were so focused. Work, running, work. I used to wish you'd slow down and have some fun."

"And the bad?" Brooke was almost afraid to ask.

"Oh, Brooke." Marie sighed. "Your self-esteem is so low. What happened to my golden girl? The triumphant soccer player, the kid who went to summer camp by herself at the age of six and never looked back or acted homesick? It hurts me to see you being so hard on yourself."

Brooke felt a tear slide down her cheek. She swallowed hard and tried to find the words.

"I screwed up. Royally. Let you guys down. Left poor Harris standing at the altar. Left Dad holding the bag for that hideously expensive wedding. Quit my job, ran away from home, and if that's not enough, I got myself knocked up. Had a kid out of wedlock. I'm like some big, stupid sitcom. Only nobody's laughing."

Marie pushed Brooke off her lap and prodded her back into a sitting position. "Look at me, Brooke Marie. Tell me the truth. Do you regret not marrying Harris?"

"No," Brooke said quickly. "Just the way I handled everything."

"Do you regret having Henry?"

"Never! He's the best thing that's ever happened to me."

"That's what I thought," Marie said. "So you made some mistakes. Doesn't everybody?"

"Maybe," Brooke said, still unconvinced. "But you can't pretend you were thrilled that I got pregnant the way I did."

"The baby was definitely a surprise," Marie admitted. "I wasn't even aware you were seeing somebody. And you still haven't told me anything about Henry's father. All I know is that you say he's not in your life anymore. That's the part that's really hard for me. I know you, Brooke. I know you don't have casual relationships. So this man . . . this mystery man. He's still Henry's father. Our boy has his DNA. And I'm only human. I can't help but wonder about him. Why aren't you together? Did he hurt you that badly?

Are you still in love with him? Is he a good man?"

Brooke looked into her mother's dark blue eyes and saw only love and acceptance. She felt herself exhale slowly. Holding the secret of Pete, she realized, was exhausting. And senseless. And selfish.

"His name is Pete. Pete Haynes," she began. "Henry has his smile. And his big feet. And yes, he's a very good man. I think you'd like him. And I know he'd love you."

The words came tumbling out, like a dammed-up torrent of story and emotion.

She told her mother how she'd met Pete during her summer job in DC. Her harmless secret summer fling. How she'd run into him at the barbecue restaurant in Savannah, at a lunch meeting with her wedding florist, for God's sake!

"Seeing Pete, after all that time," Brooke said. "I can't even describe how I felt. It was terrifying. I was already having these nagging midnight doubts about me and Harris. If we were really right for each other. And then to run into Pete — two weeks before my wedding! It was like seeing a ghost, Mom. I hadn't thought about this guy in years. At the end of that summer, I came home and moved in with Harris and started law school. Mentally, I put Pete Haynes in a shoe box, taped it up, and shoved it in the back of my closet. But that day, at freaking Johnny Harris

Barbecue, the tape came off. And I couldn't stop it. I couldn't stop thinking about Pete."

"I wish you'd told me," Marie said quietly.

"I couldn't tell you, because I couldn't admit it to myself. I was having anxiety nightmares. Panic attacks. I got some Xanax from a girlfriend at work, but the Xanax just made me feel stoned. It didn't get Pete out of my head."

"So when you ran away, the night of your bachelorette party?" Marie asked.

"I got in the car and started driving. That day at Johnny Harris, Pete told me he was staying on Cumberland, working on some project for the National Park Service. I didn't have a plan. Not really. I told myself I was going to Loblolly just to hang out and give myself time to think. But that was a lie. I wasn't running away from Harris. I was running to Pete."

Brooke found her half-empty glass of wine and drained it.

"Of course, when I threw myself at him on Cumberland, he turned me down flat. Told me he didn't want to be my rebound boy."

At some point, Brooke got her phone and showed Marie the last photo she'd taken of Pete before he'd left for Alaska. It had been taken while they were kayaking on the river. He was bearded and bare-chested, laughing, the late-day sun making a halo around his shaggy, unkempt hair.

Marie peered down at the phone, enlarged the image, then tapped the photo with her index finger. "The freckles. That's where they came from. I've always wondered."

"It's uncanny," Brooke said. "Henry has the exact same number of freckles sprinkled over his nose and cheeks as his father. I know, because I counted them. While Pete was asleep. The morning after . . ." She blushed. "The morning after Henry was conceived."

Marie didn't seem shocked. "When did things change between you? I mean, you just told me he rejected you when you showed up on Cumberland Island after you called off the wedding."

"We mutually agreed that we should take things slowly. The old 'let's just be friends' kind of deal. I realized I wasn't in any kind of shape to start a new relationship, I was trying to get my law practice up and running, and Pete's a naturally cautious person. We were seeing each other casually, at least at first."

"And then?"

Brooke twisted a strand of hair around her finger, avoiding her mother's probing eyes.

"Pete had applied for this research grant to study elk migration patterns in the tundra. It meant living in this remote base camp in Alaska. That's where he is, by the way. Alaska. It's a three-year project. Out of nowhere, he told me he loved me and wanted to be with me. I guess that's when it hit me that things had changed between us. We'd gotten serious when neither of us expected to. So . . . one thing led to another. Spontaneous combustion, you might say. And by spontaneous, I mean, I wasn't on birth control."

"Oh, Brooke." Marie sighed.

"The next morning, Pete asked me to go with him."

"And you said?"

Brooke shrugged. "I wasn't very diplomatic. I mean, what was I going to do in the middle of the Alaskan tundra? Sue a moose? I drove him to the airport, and we talked about my flying out to see him at Christmas. Six weeks later, I figured out I was pregnant."

"And you never told him? Never let him know he was going to be a father?"

"I wanted to. We were Skyping every other day, and he was so excited about being in Alaska. Everything was new and fascinating, and his work was really intense. He'd be out in the field, four or five days at a time, camping and tracking these radio-collared elk. I thought, if I tell Pete I'm pregnant, he'll think he has to come back here to take care of me and the baby. It would mean giving up his grant."

"Shouldn't that have been his choice to make?"

"Maybe. But I was having doubts of my own. I loved Pete, but I didn't want to be trapped into having a relationship just because of a baby. What if he did come back? And it turned out we weren't actually good together?"

"That's just a risk you have to take in a relationship," Marie said. "In life. Nothing ventured, nothing gained."

"I'm not sure I agree with you," Brooke said, suppressing a yawn. "Henry and I, we're doing okay. It's not easy. In fact, most of the time, being a single mom is terrifying. But I don't regret it." She met her mother's steady gaze. "What about you, Mom? Any regrets?"

Marie stood slowly, then pulled Brooke to a standing position. "No. I don't regret giving up my career to have time to raise my brilliant, gorgeous daughter. I don't even regret marrying your dad. We had lots of good years, you know. I'd never give Patricia the power to take that away from me. The way I see it now, I got the better part of the deal. The man I married was young and fun, the adventurous and romantic Gordon. Look at him now. Yes, now he has more time and lots more money to spare, but Patricia's got the cranky, high blood pressure, potbellied Gordon. I saw them across the room at a wedding at the Oglethorpe Club a couple of weeks ago, and he looked miserable. Patricia couldn't even get him to go out on the dance floor."

"The two of you used to dance all the time, especially at weddings and Christmas parties," Brooke said. "When I was a teenager I thought it was sooooo gross. Parents dancing together!" She covered her eyes in mock horror.

Marie went into Henry's nursery, fetched a stack of bed linens, and proceeded to make up a bed on the sofa.

"See you in the morning," Brooke said, yawning and giving her mother a peck on the cheek. "I almost forgot. Were you planning on staying over Sunday night?"

"Yes. Why?"

"If you really don't mind staying and watching Henry, I'm supposed to go up to Sea Island Sunday afternoon to meet with Gabe Wynant."

"Really?" Marie arched an eyebrow.

"It's about Josephine Warrick. I'm going to take her case on, after all. But I don't know the first thing about condemnation law. So I called Gabe, and he's agreed to meet with me and try to walk me through it."

"That's awfully nice of him," Marie said. "It's just a shame about poor Sunny. You'd think it might be a kind of relief, after all he went through with her, but I hear he's really quite bereft."

"Bereft? Did something happen to Sunny Wynant?"

"You didn't know? She died."

"No! I had no idea. What happened?"

"Liver cancer. She drank herself to death. I

guess it's been over a year ago now. Maybe two? I used to know her from altar guild, before she started drinking. She used to be so much fun. She had a really wicked sense of humor." Marie shook her head. "Such a waste."

"That's terrible," Brooke said. "But I'm glad you told me before I see him."

"You say you decided to work for Josephine, after all?" Marie asked. "What changed your mind?"

"Josephine did. She just wouldn't take no for an answer. And maybe, just maybe, I'm ready for a challenge."

Brooke remembered the last conversation she'd had with the old lady.

"Mom? Did you know Granny was engaged to somebody else? Before Grandpop?"

"Hmm? Who told you that?"

"Josephine did. Her family threw an engagement party at Shellhaven for Granny and this man, but something awful happened, and the wedding got canceled."

"Really? This is the first I've heard of such a thing. It's hard for me to picture my mother with another man. She was so devoted to Pops. Did Josephine give you any more details than that?"

"No. She said the man, whoever he was, wasn't a good person."

"I'd definitely be interested in hearing more about this mystery man," Marie said.

"You can ask Josephine all about it when you and the other two women meet with her over on Talisa."

"You think she's really serious? About leaving the island to the three of us?"

"She's dead serious," Brooke assured her.

18

October 1941

Josephine tapped loudly on the guest room door. "Millie? Are you all right?"

The muffled reply came a minute later. "I'm all right." In another moment, the door opened slightly to reveal Millie, looking pale and exhausted, still wrapped in a bathrobe.

"It's nearly noon!" Josephine exclaimed. "Your mother and grandmother just left on the boat for St. Ann's." She peered at Millie's face. "You look terrible. Are you sick?"

"Maybe a little hungover. I don't think champagne agrees with me."

"Come down to lunch," Josephine said. "Mrs. Dorris will fix you something nice and light. Some soup or something."

"Ugh. Food. I'll come down, but I think I'll just stick to coffee. What about the others? Has everybody gone already?"

"A lot of people needed to get to Jacksonville to catch the train at two," Josephine said. "Ruth's still here, of course, and I think some of the men were planning an early-morning fishing trip."

"Have you seen Russell this morning?" Millie whispered.

"Not yet, but if I do see him, I might have to slap his face for the rude way he acted at the party last night. What a scene he made!"

"I'm so sorry," Millie said, tears pooling in her eyes.

"Don't you apologize for him," Josephine scolded. "You didn't do anything wrong."

"I shouldn't have danced with Gardiner," Millie said. "It didn't look right."

"Why shouldn't you dance with my brother? He was your host. And it wasn't as if your fiancé was dancing with you. Honestly, Millie, I don't understand why you have to marry him . . ."

"Don't!" Millie shook her head. "I'll be down in a few minutes."

She slipped into the dining room and chose the chair beside Ruth's.

"Good morning," Samuel Bettendorf boomed. "How's our bride today?"

"I'm fine, thank you," Millie said. "Please forgive me for oversleeping. I guess I'm not used to late hours and champagne. But it truly was a lovely party, Mr. B. Russell and I are so grateful for your hospitality."

Mrs. Dorris came into the room and offered a platter heaped high with golden fried chicken.

"No, thanks," Millie said quickly. "Is there any coffee?"

"Where is Russell?" Samuel asked.

Josephine rolled her eyes, and Ruth choked back a giggle.

"He talked about going fishing this morning," Millie said. "Or maybe hunting?"

"I know some of the fellows went out fishing on the big boat with Captain Morris because I saw them off," Samuel said. "Russell wasn't with them. If he did go out later, in the skiff, I hope he got Omar or one of the other boys to go out with him. These tidal creeks have so many twists and turns, it's easy to get lost if you're not familiar with the topography." He sipped his coffee and turned to his daughter. "And what are you young ladies up to this beautiful day?"

Josephine consulted her best friends. "Maybe some bridge, if we can scare up a fourth?"

"Good idea," Ruth said. "Maybe Gardiner can play."

Samuel set his coffee cup down with a clatter, got up, and abruptly left the room.

Josephine watched his departure with a sigh. "Gardiner's gone," she announced. "He took the early boat."

"Gone where?" Millie's blue eyes widened with surprise.

"Canada. He's joining the Royal Canadian

Air Force. He says he's not going to sit around and twiddle his thumbs while Hitler invades the rest of Europe. Papa's furious. He and Gardiner have been arguing about this for months. Papa says what happens in Czechoslovakia and Poland is none of our business, but Gardiner is dead set on doing this. You know he's had his pilot's license since he was eighteen."

"Gardiner's a gun jumper? Aren't you proud of him?" Ruth asked.

"He's really gone?" Millie repeated. "To Canada? You're sure?"

"I took him to the dock myself," Josephine said. "He was trying to leave without saying goodbye to anybody, but I caught him sneaking down the back stairs with his valise this morning, and I made him tell me what he was up to. He was afraid Papa would try to stop him from going."

"He never said a word," Millie mumbled.

"Gardiner's like Papa that way. He plays his cards close to his vest. I'm mad at him too, of course. To think he thought he could just disappear like that, without telling anybody. He said he planned to send a telegram once the train stopped in Atlanta, but honestly, that's so like a man."

"I think it's terribly exciting," Ruth said. "Think about it. He'll be going to Europe, fighting those awful Nazis. My father says Hitler won't stop at Czechoslovakia and

Poland. He won't stop until he's goose-stepped all the way across the continent."

"Don't let my papa hear you say that," Josephine warned. "He doesn't want our country dragged into another war. You know he fought in the last one."

"My father did too," Millie said. "Mother says he was never the same after he came home from France."

"Let's not talk about war anymore now," Ruth proclaimed. "It's too sad."

Josephine jumped up from her seat. "Agreed. Come on, girls. We'll take a ride in the roadster and stir up some kind of fun. And you know, there's a full moon tonight. I say it's time for the High Tide Club to meet. What do you say?"

Ruth clapped her hands. "Brilliant!"

"I'll get Mrs. Dorris to pack us a picnic dinner, and we'll send for Varina to come too." She looked over at Millie, who was gazing out the dining room's French doors at the garden outside.

"Did you hear, Millie? Tonight's the night!"

"I heard," Millie said.

Josephine drove the roadster to Oyster Bluff, and the others waited while she knocked on the door of the simple wood-frame house where the Shaddixes lived.

It was nearly dusk, and guinea hens roosted in the lower branches of the chinaberry tree that shaded the yard, which was swept sand neatly bordered with sun-bleached giant whelk shells.

"I can't come with y'all tonight," Varina said.

"Of course you can," Josephine said. "It's Saturday night, isn't it?" She lowered her voice. "We're going to Mermaid Beach. For the High Tide Club."

The girl shook her head. "No, I can't. My daddy won't let me."

A man's voice came from within the house. "Varina? Who's that you're talking to out there?"

"It's me, Josephine," the older girl called. "How are you tonight, Harley?"

Harley Shaddix's crutch thumped against the wooden floor with each step. He appeared in the doorway behind his daughter. "I'm fine, Miss Josephine. Hope you are too. I saw Mr. Gardiner over on the mainland this morning. He told me where he's going. Mighty proud of him."

"I'm proud too, but so sad to see him go. Harley, would it be all right if Varina took a ride with us in the car? We're going to take a picnic down to the beach."

Harley looked down at his daughter. Varina was dressed in a pair of her brother's outgrown, cast-off denim overalls and a long-sleeved blouse that had been her mother's. The pant legs and shirtsleeves were rolled up to size. She looked so tiny against her father's powerful mass. "You done your chores? Washed up in the kitchen? Memorized your scripture verses for tomorrow?"

"Yes, sir."

He smiled and patted her shoulder. "You been mopin' around this house all day. Time to get out and have a little fun. Go ahead on with Miss Josephine, then. And you mind your manners, you hear?"

He looked past Josephine at the car parked at the edge of the yard. "Just the ladies tonight? You know there's all kinds of critters skulking around this island at night. What happened to all the menfolk?"

"Most of them left this morning," Josephine said. "But don't worry about us." She patted the pocket of her skirt. "I've got Papa's .45, and I know how to use it."

"Maybe I oughta stay home," Varina said. "I got a headache."

Josephine took the girl's hand. "Come on, Varina. It'll be fun."

"Get out on the beach and get you a lungful of that good salt air, you'll be right as rain," Harley said firmly.

Josephine parked the roadster under a cluster of trees at the end of the crushed-shell path that ended at the point they'd dubbed Mermaid Beach.

A wide sand beach flattened out before

them, and the full moon's reflection shone on the surface of the water. Waves lapped gently at the shore.

"Isn't it beautiful, girls?" Josephine asked, turning to her friends, who were seated in the car's rumble seat. "Have you ever seen so many stars in your life?"

"The best," Ruth declared. "And the ocean's so much warmer down here! I swear, my lips were blue for a week after we skinny-dipped last year at Nantucket."

"Brrrr." Josephine laughed. She hopped out of the car, went around to the rear luggage rack, and unstrapped the wicker hamper.

"I'll bring the towels," Ruth said. She looked over her shoulder at Millie and Varina, who hadn't moved from the backseat. "Come on, you two."

Millie climbed out of the car, followed by the younger girl, and they trailed after Josephine to the spot on the beach where she unfolded a large woolen blanket.

Josephine sat down on the blanket, promptly removed her shoes, and dug her toes into the soft sand. "Ahhh."

The other girls followed suit, except for Varina, who was uncharacteristically quiet.

"Look here," Josephine announced, opening the picnic basket. "Champagne!" She produced the bottle and popped the cork, sending a plume of champagne into the warm night air.

"Not for me," Millie said. "I had more than enough last night."

"I've got whiskey too," Josephine said, displaying a pint bottle of Jim Beam. "Gardiner gave it to me this morning, as a goodbye gift."

"No, thanks," Millie repeated, shuddering.

"Don't be such a party pooper, Millie," Ruth said. She found a tin cup in the basket and held it out to Josephine. "Guess I'll just have to drink her share."

Josephine tipped the bottle and filled her friend's cup, then gestured toward the youngest member of the group.

"Varina? Have you ever had champagne?"

The girl shook her head vigorously. "No, ma'am. You know my daddy is a Church of God preacher. He doesn't hold with drinking spirits."

"But your brothers drink," Josephine said, taking a sip from the bottle. "Papa always gives them beer after they've been working at Shellhaven."

"It's different for girls," Varina replied. "Everything's different when you're a girl."

"Just take a sip," Josephine insisted. She poured some into a cup and held it out.

"Leave her be, Jo," Millie said sharply.

"Spoilsport," Josephine said. She crossed her eyes and stuck out her tongue at her best friend, then emptied the cup of champagne in one long swallow, with Ruth following suit.

"What else have you got in that basket?" Ruth asked. "Lunch was hours and hours ago, and I'm famished."

"Let's see what old Dorris gave us," Josephine said, inspecting items as she lifted them from the basket. "Fried chicken. Ham biscuits. Some kind of little sandwiches left over from the party. Oooh. Chocolate cake!"

"Yum." Ruth found tin plates in the basket and helped herself to a ham biscuit and a slice of cake.

"Come on, you two," Josephine said, handing plates to Millie and Varina. "This is a party, not a funeral."

When they'd eaten their fill, Josephine sprawled out on the blanket and stared up at the sky. "Just think," she said. "Pretty soon, Gardiner will be up there, maybe flying across the Atlantic, to drop a big bomb on those dirty Nazis."

Millie set aside the plate with her half-eaten sandwich. "Aren't you afraid for your brother? What if something happens to him?"

"Nothing's going to happen to Gardiner," Josephine declared. "He's too good a pilot for that. You wait, he'll be one of those flying aces in no time." She downed another cup of champagne. "Okay. Let's go swimming!"

She stood up and slipped out of her dress, kicking it aside, and stripped down to her satin-and-lace-embellished panties and bra. Ruth followed suit, leaving Millie and Varina huddled together on the blanket, still fully clothed.

"Well?" Josephine said impatiently.

"Somebody might see us," Varina said, turning and surveying the deserted beach. "If my daddy found out I was swimming naked, he'd skin me alive."

"Nobody's going to see us," Ruth retorted. "And your daddy doesn't have to find out. We'll never tell."

"You two go ahead," Millie said. "I'll stay here with Varina."

Josephine shrugged, then stripped off her undergarments. She stretched her arms overhead. She unpinned her long hair and shook it out so that it fell down her back and across her bare chest. A moment later, she ran toward the ocean and plunged into the waves.

"Wait for me," Ruth called. She gulped the rest of her champagne and peeled out of her panties and bra, then raced toward the waves, screaming at the top of her lungs.

For the next ten minutes the two women laughed and splashed, wading out of the water, then running back and diving into the waves, letting the current pull them out before paddling back toward the beach.

Finally, Josephine and Ruth headed back to their friends, who sat watching from the blanket.

"You've got to come in the water," Josephine insisted. "It's wonderful!" She shook her head like a dog, spraying salt water over Millie and Varina.

"I'll take your word for it," Millie said, drying her face with one of the towels. "I'm fine right where I am, thank you very much."

"Oh no you don't," Josephine said. She pulled Millie to her feet. "Why are you suddenly being so bashful? You didn't mind skinny-dipping at Nantucket, or Palm Beach, or here last year."

"That's right, Millie," Ruth chimed in. She tugged at the cuff of her friend's gauzy long-sleeved jacket. "Come on. You've got to be suffocating in this thing."

Josephine caught the end of the silk scarf wound around Millie's neck and began to unwind it, and in the meantime, Ruth had managed to strip away Millie's jacket and was pulling at the waistband of her skirt.

"Don't!" Millie said, swatting at her friends' hands, which made them more determined to help her disrobe. "I don't feel like swimming. Why can't you just leave me alone?"

"You know the rules. One swims, we all swim. Naked as the day we were born," Josephine said, giggling. "You too, Varina. It's your initiation into the High Tide Club."

The fourteen-year-old hugged her skinny legs tightly to her chest, her arms wound around them. "No, ma'am," she said firmly. "I changed my mind. I don't wanna be in your club."

Josephine managed to pull the scarf free but froze when the moonlight revealed the ring of ugly blue-black bruises encircling Millie's neck, and the corresponding bands of bruises on Millie's now-exposed upper arms and wrists.

"Oh my God," she whispered.

Millie's lightweight skirt fell away from her waist just at that moment. Ruth gasped and pointed. "Jo, look."

Fingerprints, in the form of bruises, marred the creamy skin of their friend's upper thighs.

Weeping softly, Millie sank down onto the blanket, clutching her clothes to her body.

"Russell! He did this, didn't he?" Josephine wrapped her arms around her friend. "Oh, Millie. Why didn't you tell us?"

Instead of answering, Millie reached for the whiskey bottle. She uncapped it and gulped down three fingers of the amber liquid, then handed it to Varina. The girl considered the bottle, shrugged, and took a swig.

"I'll kill the bastard," Ruth whispered. "I will. I swear it."

19

Brooke felt guilty. It was Sunday afternoon. She was making the forty-five-minute drive north to Sea Island, and she was almost delirious with the sense of freedom. She had the Volvo's radio cranked to the max, and she was singing along to Journey. Or maybe it was the Eagles. She didn't know and didn't care.

The weather had cooled a little overnight, but the sun was high, and the sky was a brilliant blue. She rolled the car window down and inhaled the scent of marsh mud and diesel fuel from passing trucks as she drove north on U.S. Route 17.

She couldn't really say why she felt so happy this morning.

Maybe Marie's extended visit was the source of her contentment. Her mother had visited before, but this was the first time she'd stayed more than twenty-four hours. And it was definitely the first time Brooke had revealed the truth about her son's father to anybody. It was a huge relief to finally share all her bottled-up emotions. Talking openly about Pete had dredged up emotions she hadn't allowed herself to feel since Henry's birth.

But for now, Brooke needed to figure out Josephine Warrick's dilemma. How could she hope to fight the state on this condemnation issue when much more experienced Atlanta lawyers who specialized in this issue hadn't been able to fend off the taking of Josephine's island?

Josephine didn't have much time left, and the state's lawyers were obviously aware of that. They could easily keep stonewalling until the old woman was dead. Brooke tapped her fingers on the steering wheel of the car, her mind ticking off all the nuances of this case. Josephine Warrick wasn't the least bit loveable, but you had to admire her determination and her dogged, if late-breaking, sense of loyalty to her oldest friends.

The issue of the High Tide Club girls whom Josephine wanted to leave the island to was another matter. If Marie was going to be a beneficiary of Josephine's estate, there was no way Brooke could have anything to do with it. Maybe Gabe Wynant would be willing to take on that piece of work.

Crossing the Torras Causeway to St. Simon's Island, Brooke glanced over at the cell phone on the passenger seat. Marie hadn't called. There were no emergencies. Life was okay.

Brooke easily navigated the road to Sea Island. She'd been coming here since childhood with her parents on mini-vacations to the Cloister, which was the island's five-star resort, and with friends whose families owned homes here.

Brooke knew rich. Her parents were wealthy, in a modest, understated kind of way. But they weren't Sea Island rich. Sea Island rich meant yachts and private jets. She'd been a little surprised that Gabe Wynant owned a home here.

She pulled the Volvo up to the guard shack and gave the uniformed officer her name. He smiled, handed her a large visitor's pass with the date and time, and gave her directions to Gabe's house, which was on Cottage Lane.

Sea Island was lush and green this time of year. The impeccably landscaped roadway was carpeted with thick fringes of ferns and colorful beds of blooming pink, white, and lavender impatiens. No weed would have dared poke its head here.

Four turns later, Brooke pulled into the driveway of the address Gabe had given her. The house was modest — by Sea Island standards — a U-shaped whitewashed stucco cottage with vaguely Mediterranean aspirations. A pair of wrought-iron gates led into a terra-cotta–tiled courtyard garden. A fountain in the center trickled water from an oversized cobalt pottery urn. The heavy-planked arched door was open, and Gabe Wynant was waving hello.

"Brooke!" His craggy face broke into a grin, and he gave her a bear hug. This was a Gabe Wynant she'd never seen before. He was barefoot, dressed in loud pink-and-turquoise madras Bermuda shorts and a pink collared golf shirt. She'd always seen her mentor and law partner dressed in either sweaty running gear or in a custom-tailored suit and tie.

"Hey, Gabe," she said, feeling suddenly shy. "Thanks for letting me impose on your Sunday off."

"Nonsense," he said, waving her inside. "I was happy as hell to hear from you."

She followed him into the living room. The whole back of the room was a wall of French doors that looked out over an overgrown yard shaded by live oak trees. With a whitewashed brick fireplace and shelves filled with thick coffee table books and pottery, the room looked comfortable and lived in. A life-size portrait hung over the mantel. The subject was a young girl of maybe seventeen or eighteen, dressed in a gauzy embroidered peasant-style blouse and faded jeans. The girl was posed in profile, with her shining mane of long blond hair falling nearly to her waist, like a sixties folk singer or maybe just an affluent hippie girl. Brooke didn't know a lot about art, but this painting, she knew, was the work of an accomplished, confident artist.

"Your home is lovely," Brooke said.

"Like it? It can be yours. I'm getting it ready to put on the market," Gabe said.

"What a shame," she said. "This place, it feels so homey. So charming."

"This was really Sunny's house more than mine. I'd come down occasionally to play golf or tennis or to entertain clients, but it was her getaway."

Brooke touched his arm lightly. "My mom just told me about Sunny. I'm so sorry, Gabe. That must have been very hard, losing her."

He closed his hand over hers briefly and then released it. "Truthfully? I didn't suddenly lose her eighteen months ago. It was more like an incremental loss over the years. She climbed into a bottle of Johnnie Walker Black, and over time, the Sunny I knew just . . . dissolved."

Brooke nodded at the painting. "I'm sorry we never met. Is that her?"

"Yeah," he said, gazing up at it. "That was the girl I married. Or so I thought."

"She was so beautiful. It's a wonderful painting."

"It's a self-portrait," Gabe said. "She was a really talented artist. That's one of the only portraits she ever did. She painted it as an anniversary gift for her parents. This was their house. After we inherited it, she wanted to take it down, but I wouldn't let her. I guess I hoped it would remind her of who and what she used to be, before things changed." He shook his head. "Anyway. That's enough of that. Come on in the kitchen. I hope you haven't eaten lunch yet because I'm starved."

"You cooked me lunch? I'm impressed."

"Don't be. I ordered barbecue from a joint on the island. You didn't turn vegan after you moved down here, did you?"

"Not a chance," Brooke said, following him into the kitchen. A grease-spattered brown paper bag and two jumbo Styrofoam cups sat on the kitchen table.

"Sit yourself down and eat," Gabe said. He opened the paper sacks and dished out the food; big sloppy sandwiches of pulled pork with tangy orange barbecue sauce on oversized buns, vinegary coleslaw, and baked beans.

Brooke heaped some coleslaw on her sandwich and added a couple of pickle slices. She took a greedy bite and rolled her eyes in ecstasy. "Best 'cue on the coast," she declared, washing it down with a sip of sweet tea.

Gabe followed suit. "Tell me about this case of yours," he said between bites.

Brooke quickly recapped Josephine Warrick's standoff with the State of Georgia.

"I had one of our law clerks pull all the

recent filings," Gabe told her, retrieving a file folder from the kitchen countertop.

"What do you think?" she asked eagerly.

He took a sip of iced tea. "You've got an uphill battle ahead of you. There are only two legal ways to challenge the state's right to condemn land. One way is to challenge the procedures by which the condemnation is initiated. The state has to make good-faith efforts to negotiate a fair price prior to the actual condemnation."

"Anyway," Brooke said, "the main issue is, she doesn't want to sell her land. Not at any price."

"Why not? She's what? Nearly a hundred years old? No heirs. Why not take the money, give it to her favorite charity, and get a life estate? She gets to live out her life there, and after that, it'll be a nice state park. Maybe they'd even name it after her."

"You don't know Josephine. She claims to have seen some secret long-range development plan that would have the state razing Shellhaven and putting in a big marina to allow for larger boats to ferry campers and visitors over from the mainland."

"Would that be such a bad thing? Just playing devil's advocate here."

"Her father, Samuel Bettendorf, whom she worshiped, hired Addison Mizner to design and build that mansion for her mother. So it's basically a shrine to her parents. Virtually nothing in the house has changed in decades. Bettendorf was an amateur naturalist, and Josephine and her late husband also made it their life's work, studying and preserving the land and the wildlife. As far as Josephine is concerned, Talisa and Shellhaven are her legacy, and she wants them preserved. And I can't say that I blame her."

"Very noble," Gabe said, nodding. "Talking about the wildlife over there. That could be another argument against developing Talisa. Say, if there were some kind of rare or endangered animal indigenous only to that specific island. The navy's development of the big sub base down at Kings Bay in that neck of the woods was delayed for years because of some obscure species of gopher turtles that nested down there. You might ask Josephine about that."

"I will," Brooke promised. "You said there are two ways to challenge the condemnation? What's the second?"

He chewed on some ice. "Well, theoretically, you *could* argue that the condemnation is not intended to serve the public trust. But realistically, how do you claim that a big new state park with acres and acres of pristine beaches and a new marina is a bad thing for citizens?"

Brooke's shoulders sagged, but she struggled valiantly to mount a defense against Gabe's reasoning.

"This state has dozens of parks already — which it doesn't have the funding to staff or maintain. Who's going to pay for not just the acquisition but the development of Talisa?"

"Nice try," Gabe allowed, doodling on a yellow legal pad. "But feasibility is not really something you can litigate." He grinned. "There is one place where that argument might work. The court of public opinion."

"You've lost me," Brooke said.

"I'm talking about politics," Gabe said. "Do an end run. Who are your state representatives down here? Call 'em up. Ask 'em to lunch and make your case to them. Or better yet, have Josephine Warrick call and raise hell with 'em."

"I can definitely call those guys," Brooke said, nodding. "And you're right about a phone call from Josephine. I just don't know if she's up to it. Health-wise."

"She's that sick?"

"End-stage lung cancer," Brooke said. "But she's still razor sharp and full of piss and vinegar. She might really enjoy unloading on some hapless state senator."

"Sounds like that could be your game plan," Gabe said.

He wadded up the empty paper sacks and put them in the trash, then took the lunch dishes and stacked them in the sink before returning to the table. He handed the file folder to Brooke. "This has got all my research and the relevant legal citations you'll need."

"Gabe. I can't thank you enough," Brooke said.

"This is going to be a fun one. I envy you, Brooke."

"That's your idea of a good time? Going up against the majesty of the state?"

"Sure. That's exactly what makes it fun. The law doesn't necessarily have to be dry and dusty. This is your chance to get creative. Think outside the box."

"If you say so." She opened the file and thumbed through the contents. "Hey, there's something else I wanted to talk to you about. Josephine says she wants to create a trust — with three beneficiaries."

"I know you didn't do a lot of estate work when you worked at our firm, but that should be pretty cut and dried," Gabe said.

"It might be, except for the fact that one of the beneficiaries is mom," Brooke said.

"You and Marie? Really?"

"Yeah. It's another long story. Josephine never had children, and she doesn't have any living family members, so she's decided she wants to leave Talisa to the heirs of her oldest, dearest friends, including a woman who worked for her family for many years. Coincidentally, my maternal grandmother, Mildred, who died years and years ago, was Josephine's best friend since kindergarten."

"So you've got a big conflict," Gabe said.

"Afraid so. She wanted me to track down the other friend's heir, which I've done. I contacted her last week to let her know Josephine wants to meet with her. Would you have any interest in handling the estate work?"

"Me?"

"Why not? If you're worried about the money, I don't think that should be a concern. She's apparently loaded."

"Money's not the issue," he said quietly. He looked around the room. "I'm fifty-nine, Brooke. I've been thinking maybe I should slow down my work schedule. Not retire, not yet, but maybe not take on any new clients."

"I guess that's understandable," Brooke said, trying not to show her disappointment. "Okay. I'm sure I can find somebody else locally."

"Oh, what the hell," Gabe said. "Who am I kidding? I'm selling this place because I never come down here. Work is what I do. Tell you what. Talk to your client, and if she agrees, I'll come down and talk to her and get the ball rolling on the trust."

"Really?" Brooke threw her arms around her old boss in an impulsive hug. "That would be awesome! We'll be working together again. It'll be just like old times."

"We'll see," Gabe said, patting her back awkwardly. "We'll see."

20

Josephine was standing in the front door at Shellhaven, leaning heavily on a cane. She was dressed in baggy khaki slacks cinched with a worn leather belt and a tucked-in long-sleeved pale pink blouse. A baseball cap with the Audubon Society logo shaded most of her face. With a shock, Brooke realized it was the first time she'd seen her client standing upright and outside the confines of the library-turned-bedroom. It was Monday afternoon.

Shug pulled the pickup truck in front of the door, and Brooke got out. She'd called the house on Sunday, during her drive back from Sea Island, to let Josephine know she wanted to come see her, and Louette had promised to give her the message.

Even before the old lady opened her mouth, Brooke sensed she was in a rare mood.

Shug leaned out the driver's-side window. "Hey, Miss Josephine," he said, also obviously startled by the boss lady's miraculous transformation. "Ain't you lookin' perky today."

"Hello, Shug," Josephine said. She nodded at Brooke. "So you changed your mind. Needed the money, is that it?"

"No. Well, sort of. My son had surgery recently, and my insurance is crappy."

"Surgery? What's wrong with the boy?"

"He fell off a jungle gym and broke his arm in two places."

It didn't miss Brooke's attention that the old lady hadn't offered any empathy or condolences for her son's injury. Not that she'd expected any.

"You must be feeling better," Brooke observed. "I'm glad."

Louette peeked out from the spot where she'd been standing at Josephine's elbow.

"She's got some new medicine making her feel way better."

"Steroids." Josephine grimaced. "They don't cure anything, but I'll admit my breathing is much improved. Although they make me feel like I'm about to jump out of my skin."

"She's eating way better," Louette confided. "Sleeps better too."

"Shug," Josephine called to her handyman. "Just leave the truck right there. I want to take Brooke around and show her the island while I have the energy."

His amiable face showed his alarm. "For

real? You don't need to bother about that, Miss Josephine. I can take her anyplace you want her to see."

"Not necessary," Josephine said firmly. She turned to Brooke. "I assume you can drive a stick shift? I know how, of course. But it might be better if I navigate and you drive."

"I know how to drive a stick," Brooke said.

"All right, then," Shug said reluctantly. He slid out from behind the steering wheel and held the door open, then ran around and helped Josephine onto the passenger seat.

"Ready?"

Josephine's face was pink with exertion, and she was breathing heavily as she adjusted the portable oxygen canister hanging from a strap on her shoulder.

She pointed toward the end of the driveway. "Down there, then take a sharp left where the road forks."

The old woman directed her driver on a road that took them toward the state park and nature center. The blacktop was crumbling in places and pitted with potholes. Wooden directional signs pointed toward a bathhouse, wilderness camping area, wildlife interpretive center, and conference center.

They drove under a thick canopy of live oaks, sweet gums, and pines. Clumps of palmettos crowded up against the shoulder of the road, and Brooke caught glimpses of some primitive-looking log cabin structures where the vegetation thinned out.

"Interpretive center," Josephine said, sniffing. "These fools don't know the first thing about the wildlife on this island." She pointed at a low concrete-block building with smoked-glass windows. "That's their conference center. Don't ask me what they confer about, though."

They rode in silence through the half-empty campground. Here and there, Brooke spotted tents and picnic pavilions, and occasionally they passed a family hiking or biking along the road. It looked innocuous — idyllic, even — but Brooke could feel the anger radiating from Josephine as she glared at what she saw as the state's intrusion on the environment.

"This is what they intend to do with my land if they succeed in taking it," Josephine said, scowling at two teenagers who sped by on all-terrain vehicles.

"That's what I wanted to talk to you about today," Brooke said, sensing an opening. "I conferred with a former colleague of mine, and he had some suggestions about how it might be possible to deal with the state's efforts to buy your land."

"Steal it, you mean. What sort of suggestions does this colleague of yours have?"

"First of all, we need to get an independent appraisal of your property. Do you know if your Atlanta lawyers have an updated appraisal?"

"Maybe," Josephine said. "I can't keep track of all the correspondence they've sent over the years."

"I can ask them to share their files, but you'll need to contact the law firm, by registered letter, to notify them that you've hired me to work on the matter. I drafted a letter, and if you approve, you can sign it, and I'll send it out today."

"All right."

"We can certainly continue challenging the state's offer as being unfair and inadequate," Brooke said. "But that doesn't halt the condemnation; it only slows it down."

"I want it stopped," Josephine said. Her bony fists clenched and unclenched. "That's what this is all about. I won't rest until I know the state will never be able to take my land."

"I understand," Brooke said soothingly. "But our options are fairly limited. One way we might approach it is through political means."

"How's that? I don't trust politicians. Never have."

"Do you have any connections in the state legislature?" Brooke asked. "Do you know your local state senators and representatives?"

Josephine wrinkled her nose. "I used to know Jimmy Carter's mama. She was nice, even if she was a Democrat. And Preiss played golf with Talbott Hicks, who was our U.S. senator from this district, but he's long dead. Back in my churchgoing days, I knew Maralai Graham, who was in the general assembly, but she's dead too. And Mike Stovall, he was our state senator, but I believe he got indicted for racketeering last year."

"How about anybody who's alive?" Brooke asked, stifling a laugh. "Or not currently incarcerated?"

"Jenks Cooper is still alive, and I don't believe he's gone to prison yet. He's the state representative from our district."

"Great. Do you know him?"

"I know his grandmother and his mother and his wife," Josephine said. "Lovely women. Jenks is a scalawag, but aren't they all? I believe he's some sort of vice president at my bank."

"Anybody else?"

"There's the governor," Josephine said.

"Ooh, good. You know Governor Traymore?"

"Of course. I've known Tubby since he was a child. I contributed to his election campaign, as a favor to his mother. Personally, I don't think Tubby is all that bright."

"Are you friendly with anybody in local politics? Like somebody on the county commission? Judges, anybody like that?"

"Certainly," Josephine said. "They all come here with their hats in their hands to ask for money. I never give them as much as they expect, but I don't send them away empty-handed."

"Do you feel up to making some phone calls and writing some letters?"

"I don't see why not. Do you really think it will do any good?"

"It might," Brooke said. "The state always seems to be strapped for money. They can't even maintain the parks we have. So how can the state justify spending millions and millions of dollars to acquire land for another park? Especially one you can't even get to by car?"

Josephine gave her an appraising look. "I believe I might have underestimated you."

"Let's not get ahead of ourselves," Brooke said. "When we get back to the house, if you're not too tired, I'll help you write letters to everybody you can think of at the state level, protesting the state's attempted land grab, pointing out what a giant misuse of taxpayers' money it would be, and so on. On the county level, we need to figure out what you pay in property taxes every year and remind the commissioners how much revenue will be lost if your land gets turned into a state park."

"All right," Josephine said. Behind the thick-lensed glasses, her eyes glittered with excitement. "Maybe I'll even call Virginia Traymore. After all, I did make a hundred-dollar contribution to her son's campaign."

Brooke rolled her eyes. Georgia's governor, Tubby Traymore, was a multimillionaire developer. He hardly needed Josephine Warrick's hundred dollars.

"My colleague has also offered to handle your estate work. As I said before, it's a conflict of interest for me to have anything to do with that, since my mother is a beneficiary."

"I'll want to meet him first," Josephine said. "When can he come see me?"

"As soon as you'd like," Brooke said.

They'd reached the exit sign for the state park, where the road veered sharply off to the left.

"Where now?" she asked.

"Take the beach road," Josephine said.

"Sure thing," Brooke said. "That's a part of the island I haven't seen yet."

After a quarter of a mile, the pavement transitioned to a bumpy crushed-shell road. Palmettos and cabbage palms closed in on either side, their fronds slapping against the side of the truck. Brooke slowed, downshifted into third gear, and steered the truck around the worst of the potholes, but some were unavoidable.

At one point she started to apologize for the rough ride, but a glance revealed Josephine with her head slumped against the passenger door, snoring softly. The interior of the truck was silent except for the soft shunting noise of the old woman's oxygen tank.

She drove for fifteen minutes, unsure about her exact location, but eventually, the terrain changed. Palmetto thickets gave way to dense stands of gnarled and stunted live oaks, whose dark gray trunks acted as a windbreak for the seashore just beyond the tree line.

Here and there on the other side of a towering hedgerow of sea grapes, Brooke glimpsed a stretch of beach and heard the waves crashing. The wind whipped her hair around her face, and she was thankful for the break in the oppressive heat in the truck's cab. Meanwhile, Josephine slept on.

Finally, she saw a pull-off point on her right, a hard-packed section of shell that gave way to a path down to the beach. Brooke pulled in and shut off the ignition. The beach stretched temptingly in front of her, totally empty of any sign of human activity. Blue-green waves lapped at the shore, and seabirds skittered along the sand. A mosquito buzzed against the windshield.

"Josephine?"

"Hmm?" The old woman blinked slowly, seemingly confused.

"Is this the spot you wanted me to drive to?" Brooke asked.

"Hmm?"

"The beach road," Brooke said. "You asked

me to take you to the beach road. Is this the spot you had in mind?"

Josephine nodded. She sat up straight, bracing her hands against the cracked vinyl dashboard, staring out at the seascape unrolled before her.

"It's beautiful," she said. "Just as I remembered it. Untouched. Unspoiled."

Brooke propped an elbow on the windowsill, and the two women sat, without speaking, for half an hour. It was mesmerizing, Brooke thought. She felt her pulse slow, heard her breaths begin to match the inexorable rhythm of the waves rolling into the shore. She watched the long-legged shorebirds and smiled at their graceful antics, rushing in and out of the foam, pausing to dip and sieve for food. A pod of dolphins cruised by, rolling in and out of the waves. It made her think of Henry, whose favorite beach pastime was looking for dolphins.

She glanced at her cell phone on the seat beside her, guiltily wondering how her mother was faring with her son, who'd woken up cranky and uncooperative that morning. She couldn't tell whether her mother had called, though, because again, she had no cell service.

"Was there something here you wanted me to see?" she asked her client.

Josephine waved her arm toward the horizon outside the truck's windshield. "This. It's the place I told you about. Mermaid Beach."

"Where the High Tide Club went skinny-dipping?"

Josephine nodded. "I haven't been up here since I got sick. Today, when I woke up, I thought, just for a minute, maybe I'm better."

"You certainly look better."

"Looks are deceiving," Josephine said. "I'm dying. The doctors did scans, and there are new tumors everywhere." She stared out at the water. "And please don't tell me you're sorry. I'm sick of hearing that."

"What should I say instead?" Brooke asked. Since Josephine felt so little empathy for others, it shouldn't have come as a surprise that she expected none for herself. Still, her client's matter-of-fact acceptance of her terminal diagnosis was unsettling.

Josephine turned dark, unblinking eyes toward the younger woman. "Tell me the real reason you decided to work for me. I know a little bit about people. You're broke, but you're not desperate, not by a long shot."

"Maybe it's the challenge. My colleague who's worked on these kinds of cases says that fighting a state on condemnation issues is mostly a lost cause. I like the puzzle-solving part of being a lawyer, and lately, there hasn't been a lot of that in my life."

Josephine's thin lips stretched into a ghostly smile. "You think I'm a lost cause?"

"You said it yourself."

"So you're a fighter, after all." Josephine coughed violently, holding a hand to her chest as though trying to soften the racking spasms.

"I found the women you wanted me to look for," Brooke said abruptly.

"Tell me."

"Your friend Ruth has a granddaughter who lives out in California. Her name is Lizzie. She's a freelance magazine writer."

"Lizzie. She must have been named after Ruth's daughter, who died when she was a teenager. Did you speak to this Lizzie person? When can she come?"

"I did speak to her, and she said she'll only come if you pay her way."

"Hmmph."

Brooke let it drop, knowing that if she pushed the matter her skinflint client would probably push back and refuse to underwrite Lizzie's travel expenses.

"Also, Varina and her great-niece Felicia came to see me."

"They came to you? How extraordinary."

"Not really. Louette told them how ill you are and mentioned that you'd hired me to help with fending off the state."

The old woman scowled. "Louette had no business saying anything to that girl about my private business."

"Felicia brought her great-aunt to town to

pick out a headstone for her great-uncle. Louette's a cousin. Saved me the trouble of tracking her down. If it means anything, Varina wants to come see you."

"Because of the money. That Felicia is all about the money."

"You're the one who wants to see her old friend. Who, by the way, is in her nineties and suffering from diabetes herself, but whose first concern is praying for your health."

"Preacher's kid," Josephine said dismissively.

Brooke threw up both hands in mock surrender. "I give up. Do you like anybody? Trust anybody? You asked me to find these women. I found them, and now you're looking for reasons to turn them away."

"Just being realistic," Josephine said. "Did you talk to your mother? Tell her I'm dying?"

"Yes. She's actually at my house right now, helping with Henry."

"And what did she say? When you told her about my intentions?"

"She doesn't understand why you feel so strongly about leaving the island to her and the others." Brooke paused. "You didn't even go to my grandmother's funeral. You didn't so much as send a card."

Josephine looked away. "Things changed. I've changed. Did she say she'd come?"

"She'll come."

21

Josephine dozed off on the way back to Shellhaven. Her face was pale again, and her breathing sounded a little labored, or maybe Brooke was just feeling particularly anxious about her client. After several fits and starts, now that she'd taken on this oddball case, she realized that she really wanted to see it through to its conclusion.

Brooke touched the old woman's shoulder lightly after she'd pulled the truck around to the front of the house. "Josephine?"

No reaction. Brooke touched the side of her face and was relieved to feel that it was warm and her client was still breathing.

"Josephine, we're home."

The old woman's eyes opened slowly. She sat up and looked around. "So we are."

"Do you feel okay?"

"Tired," Josephine said. "What time is it?"

"It's after three. I need to get home to my little boy. Shall I get Shug to carry you into the house?"

"No!" she said sharply. "I can walk. Just give me your arm and I'll be fine."

The front door opened, and Louette came out and opened the passenger-side door. She must have been watching and waiting for the truck's return.

Brooke took one arm and Louette took the other, and they easily lifted Josephine out of the seat and into the house. The two Chihuahuas met them at the door, eagerly barking and jumping at their mistress's leg.

"Silly girls," Josephine said, but she reached into the pocket of her slacks and tossed each of them a biscuit.

After they'd gotten the dogs calmed down and the old lady settled back in her recliner, Brooke sat down and rested her briefcase across her knees. "Do you feel like signing this letter to your Atlanta lawyers?"

"I'm fine," Josephine said. "Stop fussing over me."

Brooke produced the papers, which Josephine signed.

"What else?"

"We talked about your making phone calls and writing letters to the governor and any other politicians you think might help stop the condemnation effort."

"Not today," Josephine said. "What day is it anyway?"

"Monday."

"Come back Wednesday. We'll do it then.

Bring your lawyer colleague too. I've wasted enough time on this already. I want to get this done. And I want to see those women."

"Lizzie Quinlan won't come unless you pay for her expenses," Brooke reminded her. "And she lives all the way out in California. So this could take some time."

"Time is what I don't have. So yes, I'll pay her way."

"Shall I make the arrangements?"

"I certainly can't, so yes, you'll have to do it."

"And how will I pay for it?"

"Don't you have a credit card?"

"Don't you?"

"It's in my pocketbook, which is somewhere around here," Josephine said vaguely. She waved in the general direction of the room. "I'm not paying for first class," she warned. "You tell her that. I never took a first-class plane ride in my life, and she won't be taking one on my dime."

C. D. rode up to the dock on a small black motorbike just as Shug was dropping Brooke off. He leaned the bike against a tree, then motioned Brooke to follow him to the boat. He jumped easily onto the boat and started the motor before extending a hand to help her aboard.

"Thanks," she said, sinking down onto the fiberglass seat.

"You ready?" the boatman asked, and without waiting for her reply, he cast off the stern line and backed away from the Talisa dock.

Brooke clasped her briefcase to her chest and tried to steel herself for another jaw-rattling ride across the river to the mainland.

Instead, C. D. was content to putter across at a leisurely pace.

Brooke tilted her head back to look at the sky. She was running through the list of chores she needed to complete before her return to the island.

"How's your client doing today, Miss Lawyer?" C. D. blurted. "I saw y'all riding around the island in the truck earlier. That's good, right? I mean, last time I took her over to the mainland to see the docs down at Jacksonville, she looked like one good breeze might knock her down. She don't hardly go out of the house at all since she got sick."

"What?" Brooke was startled by his sudden concern for his employer. "Um, yes, she did seem better today. I think the new medicine is helping."

He nodded, chewing the plastic filter of his unlit cigarillo.

C. D. was an odd-looking creature, Brooke mused, with his sun-seared skin, bowlegs, and ever-present cigarillo, plus the braided gray ponytail that hung down almost to his waist.

"Hear tell she's fixing to give Oyster Bluff

back to Shug and Louette and the rest of them Geechees living up there," he said. His aviators shaded his eyes, so she couldn't tell from his expression whether or not he approved of Josephine's largesse.

"Where did you hear that?" Brooke asked, careful to neither confirm nor deny.

"Around," C. D. said. "Next thing you know, she'll be giving us all raises and insurance."

"Maybe so," Brooke said. She stared off into the distance.

"Wait 'til she hears I run off another set of assholes from the state." He chuckled. "She'll for sure give me a raise for doin' that."

"You saw some people from the state? On Talisa? When was that?"

"Early this morning, right after sunup. Caught a couple of 'em tied up at the dock with a mess of what looked like surveying instruments. One of 'em tried to show me some piece of paper claiming they had a right to be there. Something about an appraisal they needed to do on account of the state making the old lady sell up. I told 'em unless they had the sheriff with 'em, they needed to stay the hell off this island."

"I certainly hope you didn't threaten them," Brooke said.

He patted the holstered revolver on his bony hip and chuckled again. "Hell, I didn't even draw down on 'em. They saw I was carrying, and that was the end of that conversation."

"You took a risk, running those surveyors off. It might not have been the wisest thing to do, but I'm sure Josephine would appreciate your loyalty."

He shrugged. "Her island, her rules. Can I ask you something?"

"You can ask, but I can't guarantee I'll have an answer."

"What happens to all of us, when she dies? Can the state come in and run us all off?"

"When she dies," Brooke said carefully, "it's my understanding that the state will still have to negotiate to buy Josephine's land from her estate. They can't take the land without fair compensation. That's the law."

"And that's where you come in," C. D. said. "She wants you to make the state go away. So she can keep the island."

"Something like that."

"You say no matter what, the state has to buy the island from her estate. But who's that? She ain't got no family I ever heard of."

"I'm not at liberty to discuss that," Brooke said firmly.

"Oh."

"Are you worried about losing your home on the island, C. D.?"

"I got a little place," he said. "Comes with the job."

"So did you grow up on Talisa?"

"Here and there," he said, suddenly cagey. "Mostly Savannah."

"I thought I detected a Savannah accent. I'm from Savannah too."

"Oh yeah?"

"Born and raised. How about you? What high school did you go to?"

"I bet I know what high school you went to," he said. "Probably St. Vincent's. Or maybe Country Day School. That's where all the rich kids went when I was coming up."

She ignored the taunt about being rich. "Did you go to high school in Savannah?"

"Never finished. Dropped out, bummed around, got drafted, went over to Vietnam, and managed to come back alive. School of hard knocks, as they say."

Brooke didn't try to hide her surprise. "You're a Vietnam vet? Mind if I ask how old you are?"

He shrugged again. "Born in '42."

"I can't believe you're that old. Wow."

"I take care of myself," he said, preening a little, flexing a sinewy, tattooed bicep featuring an eagle atop a globe pierced with an anchor.

"You were a marine?"

"Semper fi, baby," he said. "How'd you know?"

"I used to know a marine," she said.

It was her turn to be cagey. Pete Haynes had gone to college on an ROTC scholarship, fulfilled his obligation with one tour in Iraq, gotten out of the service, and immediately enrolled in grad school on the GI bill. He'd been sheepish about his own tattoo, claiming he'd gotten it on an impulse, which he'd immediately regretted. Brooke had found it sexy, although she'd never told him so.

The tattoo was only one of a long list of things she'd never talked about with Pete, she realized. And now it was probably too late.

22

Farrah waltzed into the office an hour late on Tuesday. She wore an oversized off-the-shoulder black T-shirt and skin-tight white jeans so shredded Brooke could see more skin than jeans.

"You're late," Brooke said, looking up in annoyance.

"And you're not very nice," Farrah said, sticking out her tongue at her boss. "Especially since I got out of school an hour early just to get to the courthouse to work on this." With a flourish she produced a piece of lined loose-leaf notebook paper covered with her girlish handwriting.

"What is it?"

"Just that list of former landowners at Oyster Bluff on Talisa you assigned me."

"Good job." Brooke did a seated half bow. She scanned the list, which covered both sides of the paper. "Geez. This looks like a lot more names than Josephine told me there would be."

"For reals," Farrah said. "I counted twenty-three names. It wasn't easy. People owned a house, then left it to four or five kids, and then the kids sold off pieces of the land to somebody else . . . it's a mess. And so many people had the same last name. Like, there are Shaddixes and Hobarts and Langs and Franklins and Johnsons . . . it's hard to know who owns what if you look at the county's old deed books."

"Well, it's an island, and Louette says a lot of people intermarried," Brooke said.

"I researched as many names as I could online, and at least six of these people have died," Farrah said. She removed her backpack and dropped it on the receptionist's desk. She unzipped a pocket on the bag and produced another sheet of notebook paper.

"I managed to find six addresses that I think are current," Farrah said, handing her the list.

"Okay. Maybe Louette or Varina or her niece can help with some of the missing addresses," Brooke said. "At least it's a start."

The office phone rang, and Farrah grabbed for it. "Law offices of Brooke Trappnell and Associates," she said. "This is Farrah. How may I help you?"

Brooke picked up her own desk phone to start checking off items on her to-do list. She'd already called Gabe Wynant first thing that morning and arranged the meeting with

Josephine.

Next up was Lizzie Quinlan.

"Hi, Lizzie. It's Brooke Trappnell in Georgia."

"Who? Oh yeah. The lawyer, right? What's the word?"

Brooke took a deep breath. "Mrs. Warrick would very much like for you to fly out here this week. The sooner the better."

"Not happening," Lizzie said. "I've got to finish a piece I'm working on, and then I've got a bunch of interviews to do for another piece. I could maybe get out there late next week."

"Couldn't you do the phone interviews from here?"

"Maybe, but what's the big rush?"

"Mrs. Warrick's most recent scans show several new tumors," Brooke said. "You might have all the time in the world, but I assure you, she does not."

"Okay, I'll come. But she pays all my travel, right? Room and board, everything."

"That's correct. I'll book your flights today. Could you be here by Thursday?"

"This is already Tuesday. Are you crazy? I'll have to find a cat sitter, finish my magazine article . . ."

"Friday, then," Brooke relented. "I'm afraid there aren't a ton of hotel options here in town. Just chains."

"I'll leave it up to you. Just something clean

and near a liquor store," Lizzie said. "And I need to be home no later than Monday. Understood?"

"Perfectly," Brooke said. "I'll text you the flight details. See you then."

Felicia Shaddix wasn't as easily persuaded.

"Friday? I teach a class on Friday. And even if I didn't, my aunt has a standing hair appointment on Friday. I promise you, she won't go anywhere without that hair fixed just right. Not even if it was lunch with Barack Obama himself."

"Isn't your class an online one? Could it be taped? I've got one of the other beneficiaries flying in from LA on Friday morning, and it's going to be tricky to reschedule her."

"I don't know," Felicia grumbled. "The dean likes the classes to be live, with student interaction. She's pretty strict about that."

"Look," Brooke said, lowering her voice. "I don't want to upset your aunt, but Josephine really doesn't have a lot of time left. I was with her yesterday, and she said the latest scans showed that the cancer has metastasized. I'm sure you know the implications of that. I really need to get all of you together with her so we can move forward with the arrangements."

"Fine. I'll tell the dean it's an emergency, and I'll tell my aunt's hairdresser it's an emergency too, see if she'll fit her in on

Thursday afternoon instead."

"Thanks so much," Brooke said.

Her own mother was the last piece of the puzzle, and a surprisingly hard sell.

"Friday? Oh no. That's out of the question," Marie said. "I have a committee meeting on Friday morning. I was going to tell you tonight. I'll have to head home to Savannah on Thursday."

"Mom, I really, really need you to meet with Josephine and those other women Friday on the island. I've been through hell getting everybody's schedules lined up. I didn't expect it would be a problem with you."

"Sweetie, I'm sorry, but this is my Fresh Air Home board meeting. We're going through the applications for the children for summer camp. I really can't miss it."

"Mommmm." Brooke knew she sounded like a petulant teenager, but she couldn't help herself. "You're the chairman of the committee, so can't you just make an executive decision and reschedule? Those women don't have jobs or day care to figure out."

"Are you saying my friends and I are just idle, rich ladies who lunch?" Marie asked.

Damn it, Brooke thought. She'd bungled that one badly.

"No, not at all. I know how much good work you and your friends do and how hard you work at it," Brooke said hastily. "But couldn't you let your co-chair run the meeting? Please, Mom? For me?"

"Well, if it really means that much, I'll do it for you, but not for her. This seems like a lot of fuss," Marie complained. "I don't mean to second-guess you, Brooke, but how do you even know Josephine really and truly means to leave the island to a bunch of strangers? It's just so unbelievably odd. Are you sure this isn't some ploy, just to get attention or sympathy?"

"It had better not be," Brooke said.

23

Gabe Wynant was dressed for his Wednesday morning meeting with Josephine Warrick in what was apparently his idea of island casual — white button-down oxford cloth shirt (sans necktie), pressed khakis, and navy-blue blazer, accessorized by Topsiders (sans socks) and a briefcase. Brooke didn't have the heart to tell him that Shellhaven didn't have air-conditioning.

"Who's this?" C. D. asked Brooke as the two boarded the boat.

"Gabe Wynant," the visitor said, extending a hand in greeting.

C. D. reluctantly shook hands. "C. D. Anthony. You got a business card?"

Being the Southern gentleman he was, Gabe produced a thick velum card and handed it to the boatman.

"Another lawyer?" He raised one bushy eyebrow.

"How are you today, C. D.?" Brooke asked.

"Same as ever. Bursitis, arthritis, and

gastritis. Them VA doctors are all a bunch of quacks, if you ask me."

Gabe started to offer his condolences, but Brooke gave him a warning shake of her head to telegraph *Do not engage.*

"I haven't been over to Talisa probably since the eighties, when it was included on one of the Georgia Trust for Historic Preservation's rambles," Gabe said as they puttered slowly through the marina's no-wake zone. "At the time, the house wasn't open for tours. I've always been fascinated with the place."

"It's pretty much a living time capsule," Brooke said. "Josephine has tried to keep everything the same as it was at the time of her husband's death."

"When did he die?"

"Sometime in the sixties, I think." She glanced at C. D., whose back was turned to them. "The house and grounds are in pretty sad shape. Unfortunately, she doesn't have the manpower to keep up with all the needed maintenance. Even in its current condition, you can tell it was once pretty magnificent."

"I'm looking forward to seeing it. And, of course, to working with the lady of the house," Gabe said.

"You might change your mind about that once you actually meet her," C. D. said. He'd turned around and was facing them now, ready to insert himself into their conversation.

Brooke frowned and shot her colleague the *Do not engage* look again, which Gabe cheerfully ignored.

"Why's that?"

"Just sayin'. She's a tough old bird. Stingy as hell."

"Why do you stay?" Gabe asked. "I mean, if she's as bad as you say."

"I'm seventy-six years old. I got a bad leg and some might say a bad attitude. I ask you, who else is gonna hire me and give me a place to live, sorry as it is?"

"Exactly," Brooke said. She pointedly turned toward the bow of the boat, leaving her back to the boat's captain and effectively ending the conversation.

When C. D. pulled the boat alongside the dock at Shellhaven, the same little boy was stationed at the end of the dock, waiting. "Hey, C. D.," the boy called.

"Gimme a hand with the bowline, will ya, Lionel?" C. D. tossed him the bowline, and the kid knotted it around a cleat.

"You take me for a motorcycle ride?" Lionel asked eagerly.

"Maybe later," C. D. said, nodding at his departing passengers.

It was Louette, and not her husband, who was waiting for them at the dock this time.

She was driving a vehicle Brooke hadn't seen before, a gleaming aqua-and-white four-door Chrysler with the exaggerated tailfins of a fifties muscle car.

Brooke gamely climbed into the backseat of the car and introduced Gabe Wynant. "Where's Shug today?" she asked.

"He's up on the roof, trying to patch another hole," Louette said. "Silly me, I never did learn how to drive a stick shift, which is why I had to come fetch you in Nellybelle." She gave the turquoise vinyl dashboard a fond pat.

"My dad had a Chrysler like this, only his was brown and cream," Gabe said. "I can't believe this thing still runs."

"Shug likes to tinker with Miss Josephine's cars when he has the time," Louette explained. "This is one of his favorites."

"There are others?" Gabe asked.

"Oh, sure. The barn is full of 'em. She don't like to get rid of anything, especially if it had something to do with Mr. Preiss. Let's see, there's the Cadillac he bought her after they first got married. I guess it's from the fifties, like this. And there's her daddy's old Packard. I don't know how old that thing is. Shug can't find parts for it no more. The oldest car, the roadster, is one that belonged to her brother, Gardiner, the one who was killed in the war."

Gabe gestured at the cars parked nearby. "Is this some kind of junkyard?"

"Looks like it, don't it? No, this is where island folks leave their cars when they're going across to the mainland. We just leave the keys in 'em, in case somebody needs a ride somewhere," Louette said.

"And nobody worries about car theft?" Gabe asked.

"Who'd steal any of this mess?" Louette scoffed. "Anyway, it's an island. How far is somebody gonna get in a stolen car?"

"How's Josephine feeling today?" Brooke asked.

"She *says* she feels fine, but I know she didn't sleep much last night. I heard her get up two or three times in the night."

"You're sleeping in the house now?" Brooke was taken aback.

"Uh-huh. Miss Josephine fell and hurt herself Monday night. Said she tripped over one of the dogs. Somehow she managed to get up and get back in the bed. It's a miracle she didn't break a hip or crack her skull wide open. She fought me on it, but last night I fixed me a bed on the sofa in the living room, and that's where I'm gonna be staying until . . ." Louette's voice trailed off.

"Do you think Josephine needs round-the-clock nursing care?" Brooke asked.

"Maybe. But I know her, and she ain't gonna do that. No, ma'am. She ain't gonna want to spend the money on a nurse. It's funny. She's been telling me the doctor says this cancer will kill her, but she really ain't ready to admit yet just how sick she is."

Gabe turned around to Brooke. "Maybe that's something I could discuss with her, if we're redoing her will. She probably already has an advanced health care directive."

"It's worth a try," Brooke said.

"Y'all go on inside, please, while I park Nellybelle out back," Louette said when they'd reached the house. "She's in the living room. Got herself all fixed up today, on account of having herself a 'gentleman caller.' "

Gabe got out of the car and took a few steps backward to take in the house. The grass had been freshly cut, the formerly overgrown shrubbery nearest the house had been trimmed, and the flower beds weeded. He let out a low whistle under his breath. "So this is Shellhaven. Even with the decay, the photos don't do it justice. It's magnificent."

"Just wait," Brooke warned. "If you're into shabby gentility, this is the place for you."

She led the attorney through the foyer and down the hallway to the living room, where they found the lady of the house sitting in a high-backed chair angled in front of the fireplace, facing the sofa.

True to Louette's word, Josephine seemed to have transformed herself into an old-style grande dame for today's meeting. She was wearing a floor-length flowered silk caftan with a stunning double-strand pearl necklace and matching earrings, and a fluffy silver bouffant wig that sat slightly askew on her head. She wore bright pink lipstick and a thick application of face powder that failed to hide a bruise on the right side of her face, but she still managed to look formidably regal. A box fan had been propped in front of one of the windows, its blades barely managing to stir the blanketlike heat in the room.

"Josephine," Brooke said, "I want you to meet my former boss, Gabe Wynant."

"Forgive me for not standing to greet you," Josephine said, offering her hand to Gabe. "I took a tumble the other night and I haven't quite regained my equilibrium."

Gabe gently shook the old lady's hand. "It's a pleasure, Mrs. Warrick. Both to meet you and to see your beautiful home."

"Not as beautiful as it once was, but we do our best," their hostess said. She gestured toward the sofa, which had been liberated from its dust cover. "Please sit."

They exchanged pleasantries for a few minutes, the way Southerners do at a first meeting, while Gabe discreetly unbuttoned the top button of his dress shirt and slipped out of his blazer in deference to the heat.

"I believe I knew your father," Josephine said. "He was a lawyer too, isn't that right?"

"That's right. He was one of the founding partners of our law firm," Gabe said.

"And your mother's people?" she asked.

"Mama was a Poole. She grew up in Macon," Gabe said.

"Macon? I don't believe I know anybody from Macon." It was clear that to Josephine Bettendorf Warrick, Macon might as well have been Mars.

"Gabe's the senior partner at my old firm," Brooke said, hoping to move the conversation along to business. "I've filled him in a little on your legal situation."

"But I'd appreciate it if you'd tell me exactly what your wishes are in regard to this proposed trust and, of course, your estate planning," Gabe said, sliding a yellow legal pad from his briefcase and balancing it on his knees.

"We'll get to that," Josephine said airily. "Where did you grow up and go to school, Gabe, if you don't mind my asking."

"Don't mind at all," Gabe said. "I grew up in Ardsley Park, went to prep school at Benedictine, like most of the guys in my neighborhood. Went to University of Georgia, undergrad. Came home from school, messed around in Savannah for a year or so, and then my dad pointed out that it was pretty inevitable that I would go to law school. So I did."

"And what law school did you attend?" Josephine said. "UGA?"

"No, ma'am. That's where my dad went, but I was just ornery enough to want to go a different route, get a little farther away from home. I'm a proud Duke Blue Devil."

Josephine looked impressed. "You know, I believe Richard Nixon went to law school at Duke University."

"So I've heard," Gabe said, grinning. "It was a little before my time."

"Well, yes, you're obviously much, much younger," Josephine said. "More attractive too, I might add."

"You're too kind," Gabe said.

Brooke felt her jaw drop slightly. The old lady was actually flirting with Gabe Wynant. Ninety-nine years old and batting her eyelashes like a Chi O at a KA mixer.

"I suppose you've been married a long time?" Josephine asked.

Brooke held her breath for a second.

"I was, yes. Unfortunately, my wife passed away nearly two years ago," Gabe said.

"Oh, dear. I had no idea. I'm so sorry." Josephine looked flustered.

"You couldn't have known, so please don't apologize," Gabe said. "She, uh, had liver cancer, so I will say that it was mercifully quick."

"I have cancer myself," Josephine said. "The doctors tell me it's terminal. I just hope my illness will be as mercifully short as your late wife's."

"I hope so too, ma'am," Gabe said. He coughed politely. "Which is why, if you don't mind, we ought to get down to talking about the disposition of your estate."

"Yes, time is fleeting," Josephine agreed. She looked out the open living room window at the expanse of green lawn flowing down toward the ocean, and she touched the pearls at her neck. "As fleeting as summer."

"Josephine says she wants to leave the island and Shellhaven to three women," Brooke put in quickly, hoping to get the old lady to focus on the task at hand with Gabe.

"I've been thinking about that. Since Varina is in her nineties and Marie is in her midseventies now, I think I'll include Felicia and you, Brooke. Let's make it five beneficiaries."

Gabe's eyebrows rose slightly, and Brooke took a deep breath. "That's very generous of you, Josephine, but that makes it doubly important that I excuse myself so the two of you can talk."

"What do you mean?" Josephine demanded. "I want you here too."

"It's like I explained to you the first day we met," Brooke said patiently. "My participation in planning for your estate is a conflict of interest."

"Be that way, then," Josephine huffed. "I wanted to meet with Gabe privately anyway. Go on to the kitchen with you."

Brooke exchanged a look with Gabe. He would use his considerable tact to settle her down. “I think I’ll go see what Louette is up to.”

24

Brooke pushed the kitchen door open and found Louette stirring a boiling pot on the stovetop with a long wooden spoon. The housekeeper wore a faded blue bandanna over her hair and a white butcher's apron fastened around her waist.

"Can I get you something?" Louette asked, mopping her face with a dishtowel. Another box fan was propped in a large double window over the old-fashioned cast-iron sink, but it did little to cool the oven-like room.

"Sorry to intrude," Brooke said, stationing herself in front of the fan. "Josephine had to talk to Gabe in private. What are you cooking?"

"Chicken soup," Louette said. "Miss Josephine's gotten real finicky, but I can usually get her to eat some if I fix it special. White meat only. A tiny bit of onion and celery and carrots."

"Soup," Brooke grimaced. "How can you even stand to turn on the stove in this heat?"

"My mama used to say air-conditioning wasn't good for you. Gives folks head colds. She told us that to keep us from complaining, I know, but I guess I'm just used to it now. Wouldn't know how to act if I did have it."

Louette went to the refrigerator, a rust-spotted relic of a fifties-era Frigidaire, and brought out a heavy cut-glass pitcher of iced tea. She opened the icebox and brought out an aluminum tray. With one deft motion, she cracked the handle and dumped half the ice cubes into a tall glass. "Drink some iced tea, and that'll cool you down."

Brooke gratefully accepted the tea, resting the cold glass against a sweat-dampened temple. She placed her briefcase on the scarred red Formica countertop and produced the piece of notebook paper Farrah had prepared from her courthouse research.

"Hey, Louette. This is the list my assistant made of all the people who at one time owned property at Oyster Bluff. I'm wondering if you could take a look at the list and tell me who's still living and where I can contact them."

The housekeeper reached into the pocket of her apron, brought out a pair of reading glasses, and ran a finger down the list.

"Yeah, that's Angela. She's still living in the old home place. And that's Jerome. He moved off a few years ago after his wife died, but I know his son works at the Family Dollar store on the mainland. I can get Jerome's address from him."

She tapped the list. "This here's my sister Loreen, and she lives with my other sister Latrelle. They're both widows."

She kept reading names as Brooke made notes on each entry. "Did that help?" she asked when she'd reached the end. "How long do you think it'll take, 'til she gives us our houses back?"

"For people like you, who still live on the island, it's a fairly straightforward process," Brooke said. "I'll get the paperwork drawn up, and if Josephine signs off as she promised, it shouldn't take long at all. Tracking down the other families is a different matter."

"You don't think she'll change her mind?" Louette asked, putting her glasses back in her pocket. "About us getting our property back? Especially the church and the graveyard?"

"You know Josephine better than I do," Brooke said, wanting to be honest. "But she seems sincere in her desire to make things right."

"All I can do is pray," Louette said with a heavy sigh. "The rest is up to Jesus."

Brooke finished her iced tea and set it in the sink before bringing up another matter. "Something I've been meaning to ask you about. What's the story with C. D.?"

Louette laughed. "He's an odd one, isn't he?"

"How did he come to work for Josephine?"

"He just showed up one day, probably about a year ago. Knocked on the front door and asked if we had any work we needed doing. He claimed he knew about boats, so Miss Josephine hired him on."

"Where does he live?"

"He's got himself a little place fixed up in the old chauffeur's cottage by the barn. There's no real kitchen out there, just a hot plate, so he comes around and eats here sometimes."

"I hate to make more work for you, Louette, but Josephine is going to have company arriving on Friday."

"Friday? Miss Josephine didn't say nothing about company coming."

"I just firmed up the arrangements yesterday. It'll be four women."

"But that's the day after tomorrow," Louette said. "That means I got to get guest rooms ready and beds made up. Get some groceries in here . . . that's more company than we've had since, well, I don't rightly know when."

"They're not staying at Shellhaven. In fact, they're not even staying on the island. Except maybe Varina and Felicia, who I guess will stay with one of the nieces and nephews. The other woman, Lizzie, I'll get her a room on the mainland, and of course, my mother will be staying with me."

"Am I allowed to know why these folks are coming over here?" Louette asked, returning to the stove. "Something to do with Miss Josephine's will?"

"Something like that," Brooke said. "I'm sure Josephine will tell you what she wants as far as food."

"Lord Jesus," Louette muttered. "Now I got to get that dining room straightened out. Got to get me a grocery list together, probably need to bake some rolls and pies . . ."

The kitchen door swung open just then, and Gabe Wynant stuck his head inside. "Her Majesty has retreated to her bedchamber for a nap," he announced with a grin. "And we're dismissed."

When they got back to St. Ann's, Gabe followed Brooke to the restaurant where she'd promised him lunch, parking beside her in the nearly full lot outside Screen Door Seafood.

"Really?" Gabe nodded toward the restaurant behind him. "This is your idea of an awesome place to dine?"

In its past life, the building had been a wholesale seafood processing plant, and a pair of shrimp boats were still tied up to a wharf that ran along the riverfront. The low-slung rusting corrugated steel building was perched on wooden pilings, with large rollup doors on the side facing the street. These had once provided access to refrigerated tractor-trailer rigs. Now the doors were rolled up, with metal-cased windows revealing tables crowded with happy diners.

"Trust me," Brooke said. "You're gonna love it."

"Miss Brooke!" The young black man's face lit up with a wide smile, revealing a row of gleaming gold-capped front teeth. He flung muscular arms around her shoulders and hugged her tightly.

"Table for one like usual?" he asked, but before she could answer, he spotted Gabe and released her.

"Hey there! I bet you're Miss Brooke's daddy." He grabbed Gabe's hand and pumped it enthusiastically. "How you doin'? I'm Myles. I wanna tell you, this daughter of yours is a great lawyer. Really. She helped my mama so much. Took care of business. She's a great lawyer, sir, and I know you're real proud of her."

Gabe's face turned crimson.

"Uh, Myles, this is actually my friend and associate, Gabe. He's a lawyer too."

"Oh. Me and my big mouth." Myles slapped his forehead, then shook Gabe's hand again. "Wow, man, I'm sorry. I just . . . well, I know Miss Brooke don't have no husband, so I figured, you know, white-haired dude . . . hey, man, no offense."

"None taken," Gabe said quickly. "Although, for the record, her *actual* father is at least twenty years older than I am. And not nearly as good looking."

"Heh-heh." Myles grabbed two menus and flagged down a passing waitress. "Hey, Addie, take Miss Brooke to that two-top by the window and treat 'em real special, you hear?"

"That was awkward," Brooke said after they were seated at a prime table overlooking the river.

"Brutal," Gabe agreed.

Their waitress reappeared at their table with a frosty pitcher of frozen margaritas, two oversized goblets, and a complementary basket of hush puppies. "From Myles," she said. "On the house."

Brooke glanced at the host stand, and Myles waved and flashed her a thumbs-up, which she returned.

"Your buddy Myles is certainly a big fan," Gabe said. "How'd you meet him?"

She took a gulp of the margarita, then fanned her face. "Sorry. Brain freeze. Gimme a minute."

He waited.

"Myles's mom, Lillian, works in the county clerk's office, which is where I spend a lot of time. Anyway, Lillian hired some crooked contractor to put a new roof on her house. The guy ripped the old roof off, then demanded payment in full before he'd finish the job. She paid, and of course, he cashed the check and never came back. Even left his ladder, the dumbass. Lillian hired me, and I went after him in small claims court. She got her roof and even some damages. So now I'm a superhero in the eyes of the extended King family."

"Did you get paid?" Gabe asked.

"A little. Enough." She gestured at the pitcher of margaritas. "This happens every time I'm in here. You wait. We'll be getting dessert too, whether we want it or not. Also, Myles and his brother show up faithfully, every week, to take care of my yard. But best of all, there's Lillian. She knows all the judges and where all the bodies are buried in this county. She takes care of my filings. You can't buy that kind of loyalty. Right?"

They placed their orders — fried seafood platter for Gabe and for Brooke, broiled, stuffed flounder. And a craft brew for Gabe, who confessed he wasn't much of a margarita drinker.

"So," Gabe said after the waitress had gone, "you have a child. I had no idea. At all."

"Henry. He'll be three in July. Want to see?"

"Of course."

She took out her iPhone and scrolled

through the photo library, holding it out for Gabe to see. "This is his preschool photo. Here he is at the park, with my mom. That's us, eating ice cream in the backyard . . ."

"Good-looking little guy," Gabe said, picking up a hush puppy from the basket the waitress had left on their table. He chewed and processed the images and the information. "He really is a miniature version of you."

"I think he looks more like his father, especially when he's mad at me."

"And the father?" Gabe said, taking the opening. "If you don't mind my asking."

She downed a third of her margarita, then dabbed her lips with a napkin. "I don't mind your asking," Brooke said calmly. "But I would prefer that you keep this just between us. I know how people gossip in Savannah."

"You think I don't know gossip?" Gabe said bitterly. "All those years with Sunny? Arriving late or not at all to dinners with friends? Making excuses for when she was passed out cold in the middle of the day. I knew what people were saying."

"I'm sorry," Brooke said. "If it matters, I think you were a good and loyal husband all those years."

"Thanks." Gabe smiled. "It matters."

"His name is Pete." She blurted it out.

"Huh?"

"Henry's father. My baby daddy. His name is Pete. We first met the summer before I started law school. We had sort of a thing, I guess you'd call it."

"This guy Pete? He's why you left Harris?"

"No. I ran off because I wasn't ready to be married, to anybody. I'd been having doubts, but once that wedding freight train got rolling, I didn't have the balls to derail it."

"Probably for the best, then," Gabe said.

"Tell that to my dad," Brooke said.

"You mean your *actual* dad?"

They laughed in unison, and with perfect timing, their food arrived.

When he'd worked his way down to everything but the lemon-and-parsley garnish and the shrimp tails, Gabe groaned and pushed back from the table. "You were right about this place," he told Brooke. "Don't know when I've had seafood this fresh."

"Glad you liked it," Brooke said. She'd finished most of her salad and the flounder.

"You were telling me about Henry's father. Pete? When did he come back into the picture?"

"Pete's a wildlife biologist. He was working down here on the coast, over at Cumberland Island, doing some research. And when I left Savannah, I came down here, because I didn't have anyplace else to go."

"And that's when you got together with this Pete?"

"Not at first," Brooke said, blushing. "We

were just friends."

"Until you weren't."

"Something like that. I suppose it was probably inevitable. One night, he announced he'd gotten a grant to do research on elk migration patterns. In Alaska. And he wanted me to go with him."

Gabe cocked one eyebrow. "To Alaska?"

"Yeah. Big shock. At which point, things got, um, real serious real fast. I did give it some thought, but in the cold light of morning, the whole idea seemed impossible. So I took him to the airport and kissed him goodbye, and six weeks later, I realized I was pregnant."

"And what? He dumped you?"

"He doesn't know," Brooke said.

Gabe set his beer down carefully on the tabletop and gave her a quizzical look.

"I had my reasons for not telling him," Brooke said. "But according to my mom, he has a right to know that he has a son."

"And what do you think?"

"I'm . . . conflicted," she admitted. "Things are complicated between Pete and me. And the more time that goes by, the harder it is for me to reach out and tell him. I don't want anything from him. I don't expect anything."

"But maybe you're afraid Pete will want to have some part in raising your son? Maybe even attempt to take him from you?" Gabe asked.

"There's that. Henry's all I have."

"I think it suits you. Motherhood, I mean. Are you happy down here, Brooke?"

"Happy?" With her fingertip, she drew circles in the tabletop water rings.

"I guess that's relative. St. Ann's is a small town, and the lawyers here are a pretty clannish bunch. They didn't actually throw me a welcoming parade. So I take whatever cases I can get. As for the rest of it, I've been lucky. I've got good childcare, including Farrah, who helps out in the office and babysits when I need her. And my mom comes down as often as she can. She's here right now, watching Henry, and she'll stay until after this weird meet and greet with Josephine on Friday."

Now it was Brooke studying her old law partner and mentor. "Speaking of Josephine, are you going to tell me what that 'confidential meeting' was about?"

"Nope. Sorry, but she was insistent."

"I really can't figure her out. I mean, why hire me? I told her I have no experience with the legal work she needs done, but she's adamant that I'm the only girl for the job."

"She has her reasons," Gabe said. He looked down at his watch and then around the room. "I'd better get going if I'm going to make it back to Savannah."

As if on cue, Addie, their waitress, was back, with two towering slices of what looked like key lime pie. "From Myles," she said.

They turned to look, and Myles waved again.

25

Brooke and Marie Trappnell stood outside the baggage claim door at the Jacksonville airport. It had rained earlier, and now steam rose from the still-damp sidewalk and road. Brooke's cell phone dinged.

The automatic doors slid open, and a handful of passengers emerged: a young family with a baby in a stroller, a pair of suited businessmen, two college-aged girls dressed in tight white shorts and matching sorority jerseys, and the last, a tall, striking-looking woman with short, spiky, blue-streaked hair who had an animal crate tucked under one arm and was dragging a rolling suitcase.

"That's gotta be Lizzie," Brooke told her mother.

"And she brought a friend," Marie added.

Brooke stepped forward. "Lizzie?"

"That's me," the woman said. "You must be Brooke. Here," she said, thrusting the carrier at her. She gestured toward the Volvo parked at the curb. "I hope that's yours. We've got to get Dweezil into some air-conditioning. She's not used to this crazy humidity."

As if on cue, the animal inside the crate yowled loudly, reached a paw through the crate's metal bars, and raked Brooke's arm with her claws.

"Dweezil! That wasn't very nice," Lizzie said, taking the crate back. She looked up at Brooke. "Let's go. We've been up since midnight. I need a drink, and she needs a litter box."

Brooke looked down at the bleeding claw marks on her forearm. "Uh, sure."

Marie turned around from the front seat and extended her hand toward their passenger. "Hi. I'm Marie. Brooke's mom."

"I figured," Lizzie said, taking her hand and shaking it briefly. "Same nose and all."

She opened the carrier, and an enormous fluffy gray cat exploded onto her lap, yowling indignantly. "And this is Dweezil."

"My goodness," Marie said. "I've never seen a cat that large. She's beautiful. And so unusual looking. What kind of cat is she?"

"Maine coon cat," Lizzie said, burying her nose in the cat's fur. The cat purred happily and licked Lizzie's face. "Three-time, All-West best-in-breed." She looked out the window at the passing traffic. "About that drink?"

Brooke followed the airport signs toward

the interstate. "We're about an hour or so away from St. Ann's. Can you wait until we get to your hotel? I think there's a bar in the lobby."

"They don't have liquor stores in Florida?" Lizzie said pointedly.

"Riiiight," Brooke said. She flipped her turn signal and maneuvered the Volvo into the far-right lane. "I think there might be one at this next exit."

They waited in the car while Lizzie went into the liquor store. Dweezil was perched on the backseat, her face turned expectantly toward the window. A moment later, her owner was back, clutching a large brown sack under one arm and holding a smaller package with a straw poking out the top. Lizzie opened the back door and set the large sack on the floor, then clipped a leash to the cat's collar and tucked her under her arm.

"This could take a while," she warned. "Dweez doesn't like to poop in new territory."

"You walk your cat?" Brooke asked.

"Unless you want her to poop in your backseat, I do," Lizzie said. She slammed the door and walked around to the side of the liquor store, where she gently set the cat down on the concrete.

"Interesting woman," Marie said, raising one eyebrow.

■ ■ ■ ■

Lizzie settled herself into the backseat with her cat on her lap. She reached into the paper sack and brought out a six-pack with one can missing. "Anybody want a mojito?" she asked. She took a sip from her own can. "No clue what's in this, but it's not half-bad."

"I'm good," Brooke said.

"No, thank you," Marie added hastily.

"So," Lizzie said, after they were back on the road. "Tell me about this island we're about to inherit. Got any idea what it's worth?"

"Um, well, the State of Georgia previously offered her $6 million," Brooke said. "But Josephine doesn't want to sell her portion of Talisa. Not under any condition. She's going to fight the condemnation."

"But we could sell it after she's dead, right?" Lizzie asked. "That is, I could sell my portion, right? I mean, no offense to you girls, but I live in California. What do I need with an island in Georgia?"

"Actually, Josephine is adamant that the island shouldn't ever be sold," Brooke said. "That's why she hired me. She wants to establish a trust to ensure that it's left just as it is."

"In perpetuity," Marie added.

Lizzie took a long pull on her canned mojito. "Shit. But you're a lawyer, right?"

"Yes."

"If the state does force her to sell the island, who gets that money? When she's gone? I mean, you told me she's pushing the century mark and she doesn't have any family. That just leaves us, right?"

"Let's not get ahead of ourselves," Brooke cautioned. "At this point, Josephine wants to meet with you, Marie, and Varina. After that, I can't predict what will happen. She's, um, eccentric, to say the least."

"Are you trying to say that if she doesn't like me, she might write me out of her will?" Lizzie asked. She scratched the cat's ears. "That won't happen, will it, Dweez? Everybody loves your mommy. Right?"

Brooke and Marie exchanged amused glances.

"You'd asked about Talisa," Brooke said. "It's an amazing place. Mostly wild. There's a state park on the north end of the island, but otherwise, Shellhaven, the home Josephine's father built, and a small community called Oyster Bluff are the only houses on the island. The scenery is spectacular — and the beach, well, when you see it, I think you'll begin to understand Josephine's determination to keep things untouched. You really have to see the island before you can begin to appreciate its beauty."

"Doubtful," Lizzie said. "I'm a city girl.

Dweezil and I don't really *do* nature. Do we, Dweez?"

The cat yowled loudly as if in agreement.

"According to my research, there used to be a plantation on the island. Is anything left of it?" Lizzie asked.

"No. Union troops burned it during the Civil War," Brooke said. "I think there are some tabby ruins, but they're on a part of the midsection of the island that's largely gone wild."

"And the only way to get to the island is by boat? Is there, like, a ferry?"

"There's a small state-operated ferry that goes to the park on the north end, but Josephine keeps a boat at the dock on her end of the island, and that's how we'll get over there today," Brooke said. "It's only about a half-hour ride."

Lizzie glanced down at the cat stretched across her lap and frowned. "Dweez doesn't really like water. Or boats."

"Maybe you can leave her in your room at the hotel," Marie suggested.

"No way," Lizzie said flatly. "She goes where I go. But it's not that big a problem. I brought some chill pills. She can have some of mine."

Marie smiled weakly. "Lizzie, tell me about your grandmother Ruth. I think it's so interesting that she and Josephine and my mother were best friends."

Lizzie yawned. "Grandma was definitely a pistol. She dyed her hair flame red right up until her hairdresser died, and then I did it for her. She had great legs, and she loved to show them off every chance she got. And she was a real original thinker. My dad always said I was more like Grandma than him or my mom, which was true. Grandma was the one who turned me on to books and writing. My dad said Grandma was living her life through me. She never worked after she married my granddad, because, let's face it, he was rich as sin, and women in her circle didn't really have careers back then. If she'd been born in my mother's generation, she probably would have been in Congress or maybe even president. Instead, she marched and protested and raised funds and raised hell for the liberal causes she cared about."

"Brooke tells me Ruth was your paternal grandmother?" Marie asked.

Lizzie shrugged. "She pretty much raised me, off and on. My mom split when I was just a kid, and my dad, well, he wasn't really what you'd call *dad material.* They weren't even technically married, it turns out. Grandma said my dad was super smart in school, but then he got drafted and went to Vietnam, and he was pretty messed up when he got back. He drifts around, always has some crazy scheme he's working on. Grandma left him some money in her will, so

I guess that's what he lives on."

Brooke glanced at her guest in the rearview mirror. "It's none of my business, but when I contacted you, the first thing you told me was that you're broke. I guess I'm wondering why your grandmother didn't leave you any money."

"The broke part was just in case you were a scammer. Anyway, I didn't say she didn't leave me any money," Lizzie said, her smile tight. "Grandma didn't want me to end up like my dad — you know, just a stoner. Most of Grandpa's fortune she left to the American Civil Liberties Union, Planned Parenthood, and Greenpeace, which she told me she intended to do, so no surprise there."

Marie turned around in her seat to face Lizzie. "Didn't you resent that?"

"Not really. It was something she talked about a lot. She paid for me to go to a good college, said she was investing in me having a career so that I could make my own way without having to depend on some man to support me. She left me enough to buy a house — which, if you know anything about California real estate prices, was a pretty good chunk of change. I started out working at newspapers, but that's no longer sustainable. So I freelance, and I do okay."

"Why wasn't newspaper reporting 'sustainable'?" Marie asked.

"It was for a few years, right up until they

fired me," Lizzie said. "I might've survived the downsizing, but they wouldn't accept Dweezil as my emotional support animal."

"You mean you took your cat to work with you?" Brooke asked. She was beginning to wonder if maybe Lizzie had inherited some of her father's instability.

"Of course," Lizzie said. "But one day she ate my editor's desk plant and coughed it up on the linoleum floor of the break room. The publisher stepped on it, slid to the floor, and broke a hip. So they banished Dweez from the newsroom, which was entirely their loss, I assure you. Without her, my anxiety level soared. So when cuts were made, I was one of the first to go."

Brooke wasn't sure she wanted to hear how Lizzie's anxieties manifested themselves, so she decided to change the subject. "Your grandma sounds like somebody I would have loved to have known," Brooke said. "I guess it makes sense that she and Josephine were such good friends."

Now it was Lizzie's turn to ask the questions. "What was Millie like, Marie?"

"Mama was pure sweetness. Quietly religious, in her own way. She played the piano beautifully, and she was devoted to her home and her family. I know she and Josephine were in nursery school together, and later they met Ruth in boarding school, and they all went to the same college together, but I think she dropped out after her sophomore year. Her family had financial issues, the war had started, and she got married not long after that."

"I wish Granny had lived long enough for me to have really known her," Brooke said. "I just have these tiny fragments of memories — like, I remember her perfume. It smelled sort of like lilies. And I remember her hands. She had long, slender fingers, and I'd sit on her lap and she'd let me play with her rings."

"By the time you came along, she'd already started to show signs of early dementia," Marie said sadly. "She'd get frustrated and was so easily agitated. Holding you seemed to calm her down."

"It's funny to think about Granny and Ruth and Josephine being best friends," Brooke mused. "From what I can tell, listening to you two, they all had such different personalities."

"I have a couple of old pictures of the three of them together that I found in one of my grandmother's photo albums," Lizzie said.

Marie's face lit up. "You do? Oh, I'd love to see those."

"Me too," Brooke said.

"They're in my suitcase," Lizzie said. "I made copies for you."

"That's so thoughtful," Marie said. "I don't have many family photos at all. Mama was never much of a saver," she said wistfully. "I think she didn't see the point of it."

"Grandma was the opposite," Lizzie said. "She saved everything. Newspapers, old letters, play programs, diaries. And scrapbooks! I have an entire trunkful of her scrapbooks. I've always thought someday I'd get a book out of that stuff. Maybe even more than one."

"What kind of a book?" Brooke asked, intrigued.

"Well, there's that unsolved murder on the island, of course," Lizzie said.

Brooke stared at her passenger in the rearview mirror. "You don't mean Talisa."

"Of course I do," Lizzie said. "Hasn't Josephine mentioned Russell Strickland to you?"

"Noooo," Brooke said. She looked over at her mother. "Does that name mean anything to you?"

"Never heard it before," Marie said.

Lizzie sucked loudly on her mojito. "It was a huge mystery at the time. Let's see . . . 1941? Think that's right. I say it's a murder, but actually, nobody really knows what happened to the guy. One minute he was there, at a big fancy party at Shellhaven, and the next morning, he was gone. Poof! Never seen or heard from again."

"For real?" Brooke asked.

"Absolutely. It was in all the newspapers back in the day. There was even a piece in *The Saturday Evening Post.* I found all the clippings in Grandma's scrapbooks."

"Who was this Russell Strickland?" Brooke asked. "Why was he on Talisa? How did he know Josephine?"

Lizzie took the last sip of her mojito. "He was from a wealthy family in Boston. According to the newspapers, he came down to Talisa because Josephine's family was throwing an engagement party for him and his fiancée."

"Who was his fiancée?" Marie asked.

Lizzie stared at her intently. "Her name was Mildred Everhart."

26

October 1941

Ruth gingerly touched one of the angry bruises on Millie's exposed upper thigh. "Did he . . . ?"

Millie reached again for the whiskey bottle and gulped. "Not this time. He was about to, but Gardiner followed us out into the garden. He saw what was happening and made Russell stop." She blinked back more tears. "Gardiner said he'd kill Russell if he didn't get off the island. And then he took me back to the house."

"You said he didn't do it *this time,*" Josephine broke in. "Does that mean he'd . . ." She lowered her voice. "Has he forced himself on you before?"

Even in the moonlight, they could see Millie blush deeply. She looked away. "He only does it when he's drunk."

"When isn't he drunk?" Ruth demanded, her fists balled up as though she were about to launch a counterattack on her friend's fiancé. "You can't marry him, Millie. We won't let you, will we, girls?"

She looked to Josephine and Varina for an answer.

"No!" Josephine said.

Varina shook her head mutely, her eyes wide. She snuck another sip from the bottle of Jim Beam and this time immediately began coughing and wheezing.

"It burns!" she sputtered.

"Here, Varina," Millie said, handing the younger girl the cup of champagne. "This tastes much nicer."

Varina hesitated, then took the cup.

"Just a sip at first," Ruth suggested.

Varina took a cautious drink. "It tickles," she reported, giggling.

"Exactly," Ruth said. "That's the whole point of champagne. It's tickly and bubbly, and it makes you feel giddy."

"Even when you shouldn't," Millie added.

Varina smiled and took another sip, and then a few more. "Oooh," she said, looking up at the sky. "I'm dizzy!" She flopped backward onto the blanket. "Why you gotta marry that man?" she asked, poking Millie in the arm. "He hurt you bad, didn't he?"

Millie sighed. "You wouldn't understand, Varina. You have a father and three brothers to help take care of you. My father is dead, and Mother and I don't have any money. We have to depend on my grandmother to support us, and she's so mean about it."

Varina looked at Josephine and Ruth. "Your friends have money. Maybe they can share so you don't have to get married."

"She's right," Ruth said. "I bet if I told my father how awful Russell is, he'd help you."

"My papa would give you money too. Russell Strickland is not the only man in the world," Josephine declared.

"He's the only man in my world," Millie replied. She held out her left hand and waggled the finger upon which perched a perfect five-carat diamond solitaire. "My family is broke, girls, and that's no joke." She giggled at her rhyme.

"My mother says your granny is richer than God," Ruth scoffed.

"Ain't nobody richer than God," Varina said solemnly.

"We really are broke," Millie insisted. "Grandmama has been living on the interest of the money Granddad left her, but now that's gone, and she's dipping into capital to keep the house going. You girls know Mama sold our house last year and moved in with Grandmama. I just can't ask her to support me too."

"You could get a job," Josephine pointed out. "You're a smart girl, Millie. You always made the best grades in school."

"Doing what?" Millie scoffed. "I've never had a job in my life. I don't know how to type. I don't even have a college degree. Russell says there's no need for me to finish school, since we're getting married. And he'd never let me take a job, even if I could find one."

"You're not going to marry him," Ruth said fiercely. "We won't let you."

"Ruth is right. I don't care what we have to do, you are not going to marry Russell Strickland," Josephine said.

Millie picked up the champagne bottle and took another drink before handing the bottle to Ruth. "Let's not talk about it anymore. It's too depressing." She paused, then unfastened her bra and stepped out of her panties.

In the moonlight, the women could see the bruises on her thighs, hips, upper arms, and collarbone.

"Come on, girls. Eat, drink, and be merry, for next month I'll be married. This could be the last meeting of the High Tide Club!" She whooped loudly, then raced for the shore. Josephine shrugged and gestured at Varina.

"Come on, Varina. We can't let her swim all by herself."

Varina giggled and stood unsteadily. "Ooh. My daddy will tan my hide if he finds out I went swimming naked." She hesitated, then took off her shoes and unfastened the strap of her overalls.

"Come on in, girls," Millie called, splashing in the waves. "And bring the champagne!"

■ ■ ■ ■

Two hours later, dressed again, the four young women lolled on the blanket, gazing up at the stars.

Varina held up the empty champagne bottle and sighed heavily. "Too bad. I sure do like the taste of that stuff."

Ruth propped herself up on an elbow and yawned. "Wonder what time it is?"

"I don't know, but I'm hungry." Varina sat up and began rummaging through the picnic hamper. She held up a sandwich and greedily wolfed it down.

"Do you think we should be getting back?" Millie asked. "It has to be after midnight."

"I don't feel like going back yet," Josephine declared. "It's our last night together before everybody leaves the island. Let's make it special."

"Yes!" Ruth agreed. "Why should we go back to the house? Let's stay out all night."

"Whoopee!" Varina chortled. "I ain't ever had a spend-the-night before."

Josephine glanced over at her young friend. "Girls, I believe Varina is officially tiddled."

"Tiddled?" Varina frowned.

"Yep," Ruth nodded. "Sloshed. Rip-roaring."

"What's that?" Varina asked, grabbing another sandwich.

"Sweetie," Millie said, "I think you're . . ."

Before she could finish the sentence, Varina grimaced. "Uh-oh." She stood and dashed toward the nearest dune, before bending over and being violently sick.

"Drunk," Josephine agreed.

Varina made it back to the blanket, where she collapsed, holding her head between both her hands. "I don't feel so good. My head is spinning."

Millie found a napkin in the basket and dabbed Varina's face with it. "Sit up," she said gently. "You'll feel better."

"It's all my fault," Millie said after Varina made two more trips to the sand dune. "I never should have given her that champagne. She's too young to drink. I feel awful that she feels so awful."

Suddenly, they saw a flash of lightning on the water, followed by the low rumble of thunder in the distance. A moment later, fat, warm raindrops splashed onto the blanket.

They all looked up at the sky, where black-tinged clouds drifted across the full moon.

Josephine swatted at a mosquito feasting on her arm. "Storm coming, girls. I think we'd better go. And these darned skeeters are eating me alive." She pointed at Varina, who was sitting with her head buried in her hands. "But we can't take her home like this. Her father would never forgive me. He's a teetotaling Church of God preacher." She stood up and brushed the sand from her clothes.

"Should we take her back to Shellhaven?" Millie asked.

Josephine had a gleam in her eye. "I've got a better idea."

"I hope it's better than combining bourbon and champagne," Ruth said.

"We'll go to the old lighthouse. To the lighthouse keeper's cottage."

"What about the lighthouse keeper?" Millie asked. "Won't he object?"

"He's long gone. The government decommissioned the lighthouse a couple of years ago, and now the cottage is abandoned. Locked up tight."

"So how do we get in?"

Josephine grinned impishly. "I'm not supposed to know, but Gardiner keeps a key under the floor mat of the roadster. I think he used the cottage for his secret assignations."

"Assignations?" Ruth said with a hoot. "If it's such a secret, how do you happen to know about it?"

"That's easy. Like the good little girl detective I am, I followed him one night and peeped in the window."

"You didn't!" Millie said, shocked. But a moment later, she asked. "Who was he with?"

"Some silly little blond floozie that he met at a dance at the Cloister," Josephine said dismissively. "You should have heard her carrying on when Gardiner took off his shirt."

"Jo!" Millie said, shocked to her core. "You didn't actually watch!"

"Of course not," Josephine said. "There's no electricity, and Gardiner blew out the candle before things got really good." She rolled her eyes for comic effect. "But I sure could hear those old bedsprings squeaking."

"You're awful," Millie said, tossing the napkin at her best friend.

"Awfully resourceful, you mean." Josephine began gathering up the picnic hamper. Raindrops began to pelt them, and the wind picked up. "Ruth, Millie, I'll get the blanket, and you girls had better help Varina to the car."

"We're going for a car ride?" Varina asked, rousing herself. "Whoopee!"

"Hold the flashlight, Millie, so I can see." Josephine handed the flashlight to her friend while she fumbled with the old-fashioned skeleton key.

"Hurry up," Ruth whispered, trying to crowd closer to the door. "We're getting soaked!"

"Ta-da!" Josephine turned the rusted knob, and the heavy wooden door swung slowly inward. She stepped inside, gestured for the others to follow, and they all heard something scurry across the wooden floor.

"Rats!" Millie squealed. "I'm not staying here."

"Probably just a possum or a raccoon," Josephine said, putting on a brave face.

Varina made a show of holding her nose. "It stinks in here."

"Don't be so prissy." Josephine took the flashlight and swept it around the room.

The beam revealed a single large room. A makeshift kitchen with a sink, a propane stove, and an ancient icebox stood against the front wall. The room was sparsely furnished with a wooden table and two chairs, a davenport with cotton stuffing erupting from its cushions, and a large brass bed haphazardly covered with a faded cotton quilt. The wooden floor had a thick coating of cobwebs, leaves, and long-dead insects.

A small brick fireplace stood opposite the bed, and its hearth was littered with twigs, leaves, and bits of sofa stuffing, indicating that an animal had made a nest in the chimney.

Josephine hurried over to the window above the sink and, with effort, managed to raise the sash. She did the same with three other windows, and a tattered curtain remnant at the kitchen window fluttered faintly in the breeze coming off the ocean.

"See? Much better."

"Can you turn on the lights?" Millie asked, creeping closer.

“I could, but it won’t do any good. There isn’t any electricity anymore,” Josephine said.

“How about plumbing?” Ruth asked. “I really need to pee.”

“Me too,” Millie echoed.

Josephine turned on the kitchen faucet and after a moment, a thin stream of rusty water trickled into the sink. She pointed to an open doorway in the far corner of the room. “It should be okay. At least we have water. I think the bathroom’s over there.”

Ruth hurried over and gave the toilet a test flush. “Hooray!” she called. “Good thing I can’t see what this commode looks like.”

“I’m next,” Millie said.

Varina sank down onto the bed and wrapped thin arms around her abdomen. “I don’t like this place,” she whispered. “It’s spooky.”

“You don’t have to whisper,” Josephine pointed out. “It’s just us. And anyway, my papa owns this cottage, so it’s not like we’re really trespassing.” She sat down beside the younger girl and put a protective arm around her shoulder.

They heard the toilet flush again, and the rusty water pipes groaned when the faucet was turned on. Millie emerged from the bathroom carrying a damp cloth, which she placed on the back of Varina’s neck.

“Better?” she asked. She sat down beside Josephine and Varina, and the three of them laughed out loud when the bedsprings loudly protested.

"But where will we all sleep?" Ruth asked. "Is there another bed?"

"Nope. Just this one, although if you want the sofa, be my guest."

Ruth glanced at the ripped stuffing and shuddered. "No, thanks."

At Millie's insistence, they stripped the sagging mattress from the bed and turned it over. Then they all took turns sponging the salt spray off themselves in the bathroom's claw-foot bathtub.

When Josephine returned from her makeshift bath, she found that Millie had managed to find a broom, sweep the floor, and remake the bed using the coverlet as a bottom sheet and their blanket as a bedspread.

"Well, Millie, you really are going to make somebody a wonderful wife someday," Josephine said.

"Just not that bastard Russell Strickland," Ruth added.

The four of them crowded onto the bed, and Josephine switched off the flashlight.

"This isn't so bad," Millie said after a long yawn. "Remember, we used to do this all the time when we were at boarding school and I was so afraid of the thunderstorms."

"What I remember is that Jo snores worse than my grandpa," Ruth said drowsily.

"And you had terrible gas," Josephine retorted. "And Millie likes to talk in her sleep."

Varina giggled in the darkness.

"This'll probably be the last time we get to do something like this," Millie said, sounding wistful. "Once I'm married . . ."

"You are not marrying him," Jo said. "And we would never forget about you."

"I ain't ever getting married," Varina said.

"Sure you will," Millie answered. "Not right away, of course. But someday you'll find some nice boy and get married and have the sweetest babies ever."

"No, ma'am," Varina said forcefully. "I ain't ever gonna let some bad man beat up on me or drink too much or tell me what to do. Someday, I'm gonna get off this island, and I'm gonna get me a job and have me a house of my very own."

She expected an argument from the others, but after a moment, all she heard was a low rumbling snore emanating from Josephine on the far side of the bed. Varina closed her eyes tightly and turned on her side, toward the wall. She felt Millie's slight body, spooning into her back, heard her mutter something incoherent.

She heard the rain pelting the tin roof and saw flashes of lightning through the windows. The wind picked up and the curtains danced. She pulled the edge of the quilt over her eyes and burrowed deeper into the lumpy mattress.

The last thing Varina heard before drifting off to sleep herself was a faint *phhhhhht* coming from Ruth, who was stretched out between Josephine and Millie. She giggled softly.

27

Marie whipped her head around to stare at Lizzie. "What do you mean? Are you saying my mother was engaged to marry this man who just vanished?"

"According to the old newspaper accounts my grandmother saved, yes," Lizzie said calmly.

"That's impossible." Marie shook her head. "I've never even heard of this Russell . . . what did you say his name was?"

"Strickland. I can't believe this is news to you. It was a really big story back in the day."

Brooke reached over and touched her mother's hand. "That must be the man Josephine told me about. She said his name was Russell. Granny never said anything at all? About being engaged to somebody before she married Pops?"

"Never," Marie said. "In fact, after Pops died, I teased her once, saying she should find another husband. She was so young to be a widow, only in her forties, and so pretty too. She got really angry at me for even suggesting such a thing. I can still remember what she said. 'I had one true love — and he's gone. That's enough for one woman.' "

"So . . . is it possible she was talking about Russell Strickland and not Pops?" Brooke asked.

Marie didn't hesitate. "No. Mama was devoted to Pops. As he was to her."

"Maybe your mother just felt uncomfortable talking about this guy," Lizzie suggested. "That generation — your mother's and my grandmother's — could be pretty stoic. Or in denial. Or both. Take my dad. It was clear to anybody who met him that he had issues. I mean, he once set fire to my grandma's Cadillac when she wouldn't give him the keys — this after he showed up at her house, at nine in the morning, stoned out of his gourd. But she never once admitted that he might be an addict."

"Well, this certainly puts a whole intriguing new light on our trip to Talisa," Marie said.

The desk clerk at the Seafarer Motel looked at Lizzie Quinlan and then pointedly at the cat carrier she'd placed on the counter at the reception desk.

"Sorry, Miss, uh, Quinlan. But we don't allow cats."

Lizzie's eyes narrowed. "Dweezil is not just a cat. She's a certified emotional therapy support pet." She slapped an envelope on the counter. "Here's her registration from the California secretary of state's office."

The clerk ignored the envelope. "Ma'am? This is Georgia. And it's management policy. No cats, no dogs, no ferrets. No pets of any kind."

"Policy?" Lizzie shrieked. "Is your policy posted on your website? Is it posted on the property? I don't see any signs."

Brooke stepped up to the counter to intercede. "Can you recommend any of the other local hotels that do accept pets? It's just two nights."

He shook his head and pointed out the lobby's plate glass window, where knots of gaudily costumed adults dressed up in pirate garb strolled past on the sidewalk. "I guess you could try the Happy Wanderer. Myrtice, the owner, is a crazy cat lady. But you know, it's Buccaneer Ball weekend, and every hotel in town has been booked for months. We're all pretty slammed."

Dweezil yowled her annoyance.

"What the hell is a Buccaneer Ball?" Lizzie asked.

Brooke slapped her forehead. "I'd totally forgotten that was this weekend. It's a local festival. A big tourism draw. Grown men and women dress up as pirates and wenches and take turns invading each other. There's even a big parade."

Lizzie gave Brooke a winning smile. "Maybe I could stay with you. As you say, it's only two nights."

"I'm so sorry," Brooke said. "I have a tiny two-bedroom cottage, and I share it with my three-year-old son."

"A kid? Never mind. I don't do kids," Lizzie said quickly.

"And Mom is already sleeping on my sofa," Brooke added.

Lizzie's shoulders sagged as she gathered up the cat carrier and her rolling suitcase. "I guess it's Shellhaven and Talisa, then," she said, heading for the door.

"I'll call Louette and let her know to expect an overnight guest," Brooke said.

C. D. took Lizzie's suitcase and stowed it in the bow locker. "Y'all having some kind of a convention over on the island? This is the third boatload I've had today."

"Third?" Brooke asked. "I know Felicia and Varina were going over this morning, but who else have you taken to Talisa today?"

"That other lawyer fella," C. D. said, casting off the lines and easing the boat away from the pier. "Louette called me first thing this morning to tell me to pick him up. Wasn't even daylight."

"Lawyer? You mean Gabe Wynant?"

"Yup," C. D. said. He gestured toward Lizzie, who was clutching the pet carrier with both hands. Inside, despite having shared a tranquilizer with her owner, Dweezil yowled loudly and pitched herself against the carrier's sides. "A cat, huh?"

"Good guess," Lizzie said coldly.

C. D. stretched his neck to see inside the carrier. "Wow. That's one pretty kitty. Never seen one like that before."

"She's a Maine coon cat," Lizzie said, preening just a little. "She was actually cover kitten of the July 2015 issue of *Cat Fancier.*"

"Have to check that out," C. D. said as the boat puttered away from the city dock.

Lizzie looked over at Brooke. "Wynant. Is he the lawyer who's making Josephine's new will?"

"That's right," Brooke said. "He was my boss at the law firm I worked at in Savannah."

"Why don't you just draw up the will yourself?" Lizzie asked.

"I thought the same thing, but Brooke can't do it because of me being involved in the trust," Marie explained. "It's a conflict of interest."

"Who are the other two women he took over earlier?" Lizzie asked.

"Varina Shaddix is the only other surviving member of the High Tide Club, and Felicia is her great-niece," Brooke said. "Varina's Geechee, and as a young girl, she worked for the Bettendorf family."

"What's a Geechee?" Lizzie wanted to know.

"They're called that, for the Ogeechee River, which is one of the big tidal rivers in South Georgia," Marie said. "In South Carolina, they're called Gullah."

"The Geechees are the descendants of the slaves who were brought to Talisa from West Africa," Brooke added. "Varina's family, the Shaddixes, have lived at Oyster Bluff, in that settlement, for generations."

"So this Varina, she was black, and yet she was friends with Josephine and Millie and Ruth? Wasn't that kind of unusual? This being the South and all?" Lizzie asked.

Brooke shrugged. "Josephine's an unusual woman. Very conservative, politically, but on the other hand, she's deeply concerned about the environment and keeping Talisa from being developed. She said she and her friends regarded Varina as a sort of little sister, because she was five years younger."

"Even so, that puts her in her midnineties," Lizzie observed. "Does she still work for Josephine?"

"Not anymore. After she retired from her job in Jacksonville, she got homesick and moved back to Talisa and worked for Josephine in some capacity, but she currently lives with her great-niece Felicia, who's become her caregiver."

"What's Felicia like?" Marie asked, gazing

back toward the rapidly disappearing waterfront.

"Very smart and polished. She's a PhD, teaches African American studies. A little prickly, maybe. She's convinced Josephine has taken advantage of her Auntie Vee her entire life."

"And has she?" Lizzie asked.

"Not for me to say," Brooke said with a shrug. "I can tell you Josephine feels genuine affection for Varina. But there's something else, something she obviously feels guilty about in her relationship with all these women."

"Any idea what it is?" Marie asked.

"Wait until you meet her," Brooke said. "Josephine Warrick is not somebody who easily relinquishes her secrets."

Twenty minutes later, they were within sight of the island when the boat's motor sputtered, coughed, and quit.

"Sheeeuttt," C. D. muttered under his breath. The cigarillo fell from his lips onto the floor, but he didn't seem to notice.

"What's wrong?" Lizzie said. "Why'd we stop?"

"Mechanical difficulties," C. D. said. He switched the key in the ignition, and the engine turned over for a moment, then died again. His second and third attempts to start the motor achieved the same result.

"Damn it." He stood and yanked the cover from the outboard, fiddling and cursing for a full five minutes as the boat fell and rose gently with the tide.

"Don't tell me we're stuck out here," Lizzie said, sounding panicky. She wrapped her arms protectively around the cat carrier.

"Naw, it's probably just a fouled spark plug," C. D. said. He opened the door to the stern locker, reached in, and rummaged around but came up empty.

"Damn it." He stood with his hands on his narrow hips as the boat rocked up and down. The sun beat down on the three women who stared expectantly at their captain. The drug-addled cat mewed loudly, thrashing against the sides of the carrier.

"Now what?" Even Brooke felt a tiny prickle of anxiety. They could see the faint green outline of the island, just tantalizingly out of reach.

The old man sighed heavily and went back to the locker, finally extracting a long wooden oar.

"Now we paddle." He nodded at Lizzie, still seated on the bow. "You might wanna move, ma'am."

For the next thirty minutes, C. D., standing on the bow like a Viking boatman, poled the craft in the direction of the island. The tide and the current aided somewhat, but sweat drenched his shirt, and he finally took it off, using it to mop his gleaming face. His bare chest was sun-blackened, the skin as saggy and leathery as a saddlebag, with patches of kinky white chest hair. His damp pants hung limply on his hips, and he panted with exertion as the boat inched toward his target. Brooke worried that he might keel over at any minute, and from the worried look on her mother's face, she knew Marie was thinking the same thing.

A hundred yards from the dock, the wind died, and their progress slowed dramatically. "Tide's changed," C. D. said grimly. "Can't fight this current."

Without another word, he set the oar down, removed a timeworn billfold and a box of cigarillos from his hip pocket, and tucked it into the glove box.

Then he jumped into the water. Dogpaddling, he called to Brooke, "Throw me that bow line, would ya?"

"What are you doing?" Lizzie cried. "There are sharks in this river. I read all about it. Get back here immediately!"

"Gonna walk it in," C. D. said calmly, standing on the shallow river bottom. "Unless you know a better way."

"Call somebody," Lizzie ordered.

"Like who?"

"I don't know. The police. The Coast Guard. Get them to send a helicopter."

He chuckled. "My phone's dead. Anyway,

we ain't out in the open ocean, and this don't count as no life-threatening emergency. Ain't nobody gonna send a helicopter over here when we're just a hundred yards from the island. You ladies just sit tight."

As they watched, he tied the bow rope around his narrow waist and proceeded to do as he'd promised, walking the boat, at an agonizingly slow pace, toward the island. When they finally reached the dock, he tossed the line to Brooke. "See if you can tie us up to that piling," he instructed. "Then tip the outboard back into the water so I can climb up on the prop."

Five minutes later, the old man hauled himself up into the boat. He lay panting on the fiberglass floor, as dark and wet as an oversized otter.

Then, with effort, he heaved himself to his feet. "Goddamn, I need a drink."

"Me too," Marie said weakly.

Louette stood next to the red pickup truck, squinting into the sun. When she saw the boat arrive at the dock, she ran out to the end. "What happened?" she called. "I've been waiting here for an hour. I could see you out there, but there was nothing I could do."

"Engine conked out on me," C. D. replied. "Where's Shug?"

"He took the ferry into town to pick up Miss Josephine's medicine after I tried to call you but didn't get an answer."

"Phone's dead," C. D. said.

"Is Josephine okay?" Brooke asked, climbing out of the boat.

"Last night wasn't a good one," Louette said. "The doctor called in something stronger for the pain."

"Oh, my," Marie said quietly. "Will she feel well enough to see us?"

"Louette, this is my mom, Marie," Brooke said before climbing into the bed of the pickup. "And this is Lizzie. Her grandmother Ruth was one of Josephine's best friends."

"Nice to meet you ladies," Louette said. "Just slide up here on the front seat with me, if you don't mind being a little close for a few minutes. As for Miss Josephine, she's got herself set on seeing you no matter what. It's all she's talked about for days now."

She started the truck's engine, waved goodbye to C. D., who was tinkering with the outboard motor, and started off down the road toward Shellhaven.

28

Louette pulled the truck up to the front door at Shellhaven, and Marie, and then Lizzie, cat carrier in hand, hopped out.

"What a dump!" Lizzie exclaimed, looking up at the crumbling pink mansion. "The pictures made it look a lot nicer."

"I think it's beautiful," Marie said, looking over her shoulder at Brooke, who'd climbed out of the truck bed. "Didn't you say a famous architect designed it?"

"Addison Mizner," Brooke said. "Very famous, especially for the homes he designed in Palm Beach and Miami."

Louette stood motionless by the side of the truck, her usually cheerful, round face lined with worry.

Brooke walked over to her. "What's wrong, Louette?"

The older woman shook her head mutely.

"Where are the others?" Lizzie asked, pausing between taking photos of the house with her cell phone.

"Varina wanted to show Felicia her old house at Oyster Bluff, so Mr. Wynant drove them over there in my truck," Louette said. "They ought to be back pretty soon."

"I want to see that old slave settlement and the site of the plantation," Lizzie said. "But first, Dweezil needs to stretch her legs." She set the carrier down on the ground, and the cat bolted out, streaking across the lawn.

"Dweez!" Lizzie cried, taking off after her. Marie followed right behind.

Brooke pulled Louette aside. "Louette? What's wrong?"

"It's Josephine. She fired me and Shug."

"What? That can't be true."

"Yes, ma'am." Louette nodded for emphasis.

"But why? How? She can't mean it. She wouldn't fire you."

"But she did. I told you, she hasn't been sleeping; the pain's been so bad. So last night, I called up her doctor and told him he needed to give her something stronger. Which he agreed was the thing to do. What I didn't know was, somehow, Miss Josephine managed to get herself up out of bed and come looking for me in the kitchen. She heard me talking on the phone."

"Uh-oh," Brooke said.

"I've never seen her so mad. She said I had no cause to go messing in her private business and calling her doctor behind her back.

She yelled at me and carried on so bad, she had me crying. Called me names nobody ever called me. Then, Shug came in, and he heard the ruckus, and when he tried to stand up for me, she took after him too!" Louette bit her lip and blinked back tears. "Finally, Shug told her if she felt that way about us, we would just quit, and she could get somebody else to work for her."

"Oh no," Brooke moaned.

"That's when Josephine said we couldn't quit, because we were fired. And then she said, 'Oh yeah, I changed my mind too, and I'm not gonna give y'all back Oyster Bluff, after all.' " Louette burst into tears.

Brooke hesitated, then folded her arms around Louette's bulky shoulders. The older woman heaved with every sob. After a moment or two, she pulled away, obviously embarrassed by her outburst.

"I'm sorry," she said, taking a neatly pressed handkerchief from the pocket of her white uniform. "I didn't mean to be such a crybaby. I know Josephine's only acting this way 'cause she's old and sick and hurtin', but I just don't understand how she could be so ugly to me."

"I don't understand it either," Brooke said.

"I'm still sleeping in that room next to hers, and I hear her at night, she can't hardly breathe right, and she's not sleeping, and that's why I called the doctor. He told me there's no reason she needs to be in pain, so close to . . . you know. Her time."

"You absolutely did the right thing," Brooke said. "And I don't care how sick Josephine is. There is no excuse for this kind of behavior. You and Shug would certainly be justified in quitting, if that's what you want."

"Shug wants us to go. We've got money saved. We could go someplace like Brunswick and buy us a little house for our own. He can work anywhere, and he wants me to retire. But I don't know what I'd do if I wasn't working." Louette sniffed. "And then what happens to her?" She jerked her head in the direction of the house. "She can't take care of herself. She don't know how to cook, and she's weak as a kitten. Who'll stay here and look after her if we leave?"

"We caught her!" Lizzie emerged from a thicket of overgrown azaleas on the north side of the house, clutching the errant cat. "Jesus, I need a drink!"

Marie was close behind. She frowned when she saw Louette's distress. "Everything okay here?"

Brooke took a deep breath and tried to swallow the anger bubbling up from her gut. "It will be," she said. "Louette, I know Josephine thinks she fired you, but could you please take Lizzie and my mom to the kitchen and give them something cold to drink? It was pretty hot out there on the water today."

"Of course. I should have offered that as

soon as we got here," Louette said. She opened the front door. "Y'all come in and get out of this heat."

"And I'll go speak to Josephine and get this firing thing straightened out," Brooke said.

She found Josephine dozing in her recliner. Her face was paler than it had been, her lips cracked and bloodless. There were deep purplish circles under her eyes. Her mouth was ajar, and she snored softly, as did the two Chihuahuas who were cradled in her lap. As soon as Brooke approached, both dogs scrambled to their feet, instantly alert and on the defensive.

"Hi, girls," Brooke whispered. She reached out and touched each dog's head. Then she pulled a wooden chair closer to the recliner, sat down, and stared at her client.

Josephine's red-rimmed eyes opened slowly. She coughed violently, and when she could finally catch her breath, she spoke with difficulty.

"Teeny and Tiny must be used to you now," she said, wheezing. "They didn't even whimper when you came into the room."

Brooke was so angry she didn't trust herself to speak at first. "Why are you so hateful?" she blurted.

"Me?"

"You. Hateful, cruel, spiteful, ungrateful. How could you treat Shug and Louette the way you did?"

Josephine coughed again. "She had no right —"

"She had every right," Brooke interjected. "Unlike you, Louette is a good, kindhearted person. She has empathy for others, which is a quality you were seemingly born without. Louette saw that you were suffering, and she tried to do something about it. And for that you fired her and threatened to take away her home? I can't even deal with you, Josephine."

Josephine struggled to catch her breath between words. "Louette knows I didn't mean it."

"No, she doesn't. And here's the irony. It's not herself she's concerned about. She's worried about who'll take care of you when she and Shug are gone."

"No . . . no," Josephine protested. "I didn't mean it. I was upset. The doctor wants me to take more pain pills. I don't want them. They make everything fuzzy. Make me so groggy I can't think straight. And I need to be able to think."

She closed her eyes, and Brooke thought she'd drowsed off again.

But Josephine was only gathering strength. "Where is everybody? Did you bring them? I need to see them. Tell them to come here. Right now."

"No."

Josephine blinked. "What's that?"

"I said no. Something you're not used to hearing. I'm not going to enable your cruelty and bullying. Either you apologize to Louette and take back everything you said to her, including the part about you not giving back the land and homes at Oyster Bluff, or I quit."

Josephine coughed so violently the dogs jumped from her lap and began barking at Brooke, their mistress's tormentor.

"That's blackmail," she wheezed.

"Sue me," Brooke said, folding her arms across her chest.

"Louette," the old woman croaked. She raised her voice. "Louette, damn it! I need you."

Gabe Wynant sat at the table in the kitchen, squeezing lemon into a tall glass of iced tea, surrounded by the women who'd been called to gather on the island. They were all drinking tea and laughing and munching on pale iced cookies from a platter in the center of the table.

Lizzie's and Marie's faces were pink with sunburn, and Brooke realized she too had gotten burned during their breakdown on the trip to the island.

"What's so funny?" Brooke felt like a party crasher. "What'd I miss?"

"Varina was telling us about the first time she tried to bake these cookies," Gabe said, biting into one, ignoring the crumbs scattering across his shirtfront.

"In a wood-burning stove in their family's cabin — which didn't even have electricity until after the war," Lizzie added. "How is that even possible in the twentieth century?"

"Wouldn't have made a difference," Varina said with a chuckle. "This tea cake recipe — my mama had it written down on a piece of paper in her Bible, but I couldn't read her handwriting too good. Where it said to put in a quarter teaspoon of salt, I did four teaspoons! My daddy said those tea cakes weren't hardly fit to feed to the hogs."

Marie broke off a portion of one of the cookies and nibbled at the edge. "These are delicious. I wouldn't mind having this recipe myself."

"Louette got all the cooking talent in this family," Varina said. "I never did learn how."

"But I thought all Southern women were great cooks," Lizzie said.

"Not me," Varina said. "I wanted to be a career girl. My daddy used to fuss that I'd never catch a husband if I couldn't cook, but I didn't care."

"She's doing good to open a can of soup," Felicia said fondly.

Gabe cocked his head in the direction of the library. "Louette seems pretty upset. What's going on?"

"Josephine threw a conniption fit last night because Louette called her doctor without her permission. She threatened to fire both Louette and Shug. From what Louette told me, I wouldn't blame them if they both left her high and dry," Brooke said.

"Oh no," Varina said quickly. "Louette wouldn't do that to Josephine. Her being so sick. She would never."

"Oh noooo," Felicia said, her tone mocking. "Couldn't leave missy in the big house to take care of herself."

"Hush now," Varina said fiercely.

Lizzie looked around the homey kitchen with interest, taking in the outdated appliances, the worn linoleum, and the water-stained plaster ceiling. "As rich as Josephine is, I can't believe how shabby this place is." She pointed at the open kitchen window. "No air-conditioning? It's barbaric. How do people stand it?"

"That air-conditioning isn't healthy," Varina said. "Poisons your lungs. Good fresh air is what people need."

"Not me," Lizzie declared. "The air here is as thick as a swamp. Give me air-conditioning any day. That and a shot of tequila. Which reminds me. Wonder where the old lady keeps her liquor?"

Louette bustled back into the kitchen with a wan smile, dabbing at her eyes. "What kind of liquor do you want?" She opened a pantry door and sorted through cans and bottles with faded labels that looked like something out of a museum. "We got gin and vodka." She held up a bottle with a brown label. "Wild Turkey. Will this do?"

Lizzie took the bottle from her hand and studied the contents. "It's not tequila, but it'll do. You do have ice cubes, right?"

Brooke glanced at the kitchen clock. It was already after three. "As soon as everybody's finished their ice tea, I think we need to meet with Josephine. It's late, and I promised my babysitter I'd be back by six."

Louette looked startled. "Josephine said y'all are spending the night. I got all the guest rooms cleaned and ready."

"Can't," Brooke insisted. "I've got a three-year-old at home."

"I haven't heard from C. D. about the boat motor being fixed yet," Louette said.

"Can you call him?"

Louette turned to a black rotary phone mounted on the wall beside the pantry and started to dial. "I'll try calling him, but if I know C. D., it won't do no good."

"My God, it's like being in medieval times around here," Lizzie muttered.

"Right?" Felicia agreed. "Time-warp city."

"Went right to voice mail," Louette said, hanging up the receiver. She took a set of keys from a hook by the back door. "I'll be right back."

"What happens if the boat's not fixed?" Marie asked. "Can somebody else on the island give us a ride back to the mainland?"

"There's the ferry," Louette said. "Last trip of the night is six thirty."

29

Brooke felt odd being the one to usher the others through Shellhaven. Lizzie and Felicia gaped at the disused rooms as they made their way to the library.

"It's like Miss Havisham's dining room in *Great Expectations,*" Lizzie murmured.

"All it lacks is a moldy wedding cake," Felicia agreed.

Marie cast an appraising eye at the furnishings, tsk-tsking at the state of decay. "What a shame." She sighed, running a hand over the dining room table whose mahogany top was cloudy and freckled with grayish mildew. "This was once a gorgeous antique piece. It would probably sell for over ten thousand in an antique shop in Savannah. But the finish is ruined."

Brooke looked up and saw that the plaster ceiling around the chandelier had sustained water damage, leaving crumbling plaster and exposed lathe.

"Mmm-hmm." Varina clucked her tongue

in agreement. "Louette does her best, but this house is too big for one woman. Time she gets one room cleaned, the next one is about to fall in."

"Louette?" Josephine called from the library. "Where is everybody?"

The old woman's dark eyes gleamed with barely suppressed excitement as Brooke ushered them into the library. In just the few minutes since she'd last seen Josephine, a transformation had taken place. She'd removed the knit cap and was wearing the bouffant wig again. Bright lipstick made a vivid slash across her pale face, and she'd changed into a rumpled periwinkle-blue dress that had probably last seen the light of day during the Johnson administration.

"Hello," Josephine said as the women filed into the room with Gabe trailing behind. She pointed at the semicircle of straight-back chairs, which had been dragged in from the dining room. "Please, sit. Did Louette give you something to drink?"

"Sure did," Varina said, taking the chair next to her oldest friend. "Fixed us cookies too." She grasped Josephine's hands in hers. "I been praying for you," she said softly.

Josephine started to say something, but Brooke caught her eye and subtly shook her head. "Thank you," she said simply.

Brooke made the introductions, and Josephine silently studied the newcomers' faces.

"Thank you all for coming," she rasped.

"What do you want?" Felicia asked abruptly.

Varina gave her great-niece a disapproving look.

"What's that?" Josephine was clearly taken aback.

Felicia leaned in and raised her voice. "I said, what do you want from us?" She gestured at Varina, Lizzie, and Marie. "Why are we here?"

"Want? I don't want anything. I want to give you all the most precious thing I own. This house. This island."

"But why us?" Lizzie crossed and uncrossed her legs. "You never spoke to my grandmother again after the '72 election. You don't know anything about me or the rest of my family. Why give me anything?"

Josephine didn't seem put off by the younger woman's brashness. "You're Ruth, made over. Aren't you? Not in looks, of course. She was much prettier. All that glorious red hair. But personality-wise, you've definitely got her DNA. Her spunk. You're a fighter. I like that."

"And what about me?" Marie asked. "Brooke tells me you seem to think there's something you need to make amends for with us." She gestured at the women sitting in the semicircle, with Josephine at the center.

Josephine was studying Marie. "You're very like her, you know. Your mother had a quiet beauty. She radiated sweetness. I don't mean to say she was a pushover. But there was a gentleness that drew people to her. Ruth and I . . . I don't know how she put up with the two of us. We were bossy, brassy. Opinionated."

"Ha!" Varina chuckled. "Opinionated. You two sure were. But Millie? My goodness. She was an angel to me." Varina glanced over at Felicia. "You know, Millie gave me my first pair of high-heel shoes. Pink satin with rhinestone buckles and ankle straps. I was only fourteen, but I thought I was real grown up. They were the prettiest pair of shoes I ever owned. And Millie gave them to *me.*" She tapped her chest with pride.

"High heels with rhinestone buckles? On this island?" Felicia looked dubious. "You, Auntie Vee?"

Her great-aunt looked down at her feet, shod today in sensible beige crepe-soled walking shoes. "I didn't always wear ugly old-lady shoes, you know. I used to spend *all* my folding money on stylish shoes. Back when I was working for the railroad, if it was payday, I was going straight to the shoe store."

"Whatever happened to those shoes, Auntie? Do you still have them?"

Varina's face clouded. "No, child. I . . . lost 'em. Wore them that one time and never saw them again."

While Varina spoke, Josephine struggled to pull herself to an upright position in the recliner, ignoring the dogs on her lap, her eyes riveted on Varina, her face tense. Her breathing was raspy and irregular, and Brooke panicked for a moment. Should she call the doctor?

Teeny, or was it Tiny? Whichever one it was whined softly and delicately licked Josephine's chin, which seemed to relax her.

Brooke relaxed a little too, and sitting back, she spotted Gabe out of the corner of her eye. He'd seated himself in a distant corner of the room, and he was doing the same thing, his eyes darting back and forth between his client and Varina.

What did he know that she didn't? Had he drawn up the new will Josephine requested? Surely, that's why he was here. But she hadn't had time since they'd arrived on the island to pull him aside and inquire.

"You still haven't told us what you want from us," Marie reminded her hostess.

Josephine was still staring at Varina. "Forgiveness."

"What did you do that was so unforgiveable?" Lizzie asked.

Josephine folded her hands in her lap. "It was a long time ago. I've spent nearly seventy years trying to put it out of my mind. And now I'm dying, and it seems the chickens have come home to roost."

"Does it have anything to do with that man? The one who disappeared at the party here on Talisa — back in 1941?" Lizzie asked.

What little blood remained in Josephine's face seemed to drain away in the blink of an eye. "How do you know about that?"

She turned to Varina. "We all swore. We took an oath. Did Ruth say something?"

"Relax," Lizzie said. "Granny never mentioned it. But she kept a scrapbook. She clipped all the newspaper articles about the disappearance of . . . what was his name again?"

"Russell Strickland." As Josephine whispered the name, she reached over and briefly clutched Varina's hand.

"Right." Lizzie snapped her fingers. "Russell Strickland. Big mystery back in the day. There was even a story in *The Saturday Evening Post.* Granny pasted that in the scrapbook too. Along with some photos of three girls dressed up in fancy evening gowns. I'm guessing it was Granny, Millie, and you."

Josephine pressed her lips together and said nothing.

"Was this man actually engaged to my mother?" Marie asked. "Is it really true?"

Josephine's chest heaved and fell. She coughed, covered her mouth with her hand, and finally grabbed an inhaler from the table beside her chair and took two puffs.

"It was a mistake," she said when she'd regained her breath. "He was all wrong for Millie. A dreadful man. We tried to get her to break it off."

Brooke was intrigued. "What was so awful about him? And if all of you hated him, why would she agree to marry the guy?"

"She had no choice," Josephine said. "Millie's father . . ." She nodded at Marie. "Your maternal grandfather lost everything in the stock market crash in '29. He took his own life not long after that."

Marie looked shocked. "I didn't know."

"It was hushed up. I doubt Millie ever knew the truth. My papa told me, strictly in confidence. But Millie's mother was destitute. They had no money and were dependent on her grandmother."

Josephine continued with her story, meeting Marie's gaze as she spoke. "Your maternal grandmother's people, the Prestons, still had money and a certain position in Boston society." She smiled ruefully. "We all did. Our families — mine, Ruth's, Millie's — were what people called *robber barons.* We weren't Rockefeller or Vanderbilt wealthy, nothing as showy as that . . ."

"Oh, I don't know," Lizzie drawled. "I'd say owning your own private island is pretty damn showy."

"Touché," Josephine said. "Anyway, after her father died, Millie's mother and grandmother were determined that she would make a brilliant marriage. Russell Strickland's people — his grandfather, that is — owned banks, railroads, a seat on the New York Stock Exchange."

"In other words, he was mega-rich," Felicia said.

"I suppose." Josephine tugged the afghan on her lap, drawing it up to her shoulders. The room was suffocating, with only the box fan droning away in an open window, and everybody except the hostess dabbed at the perspiration on their faces.

"She met Russell at Ruth's coming-out party in Newport." Josephine's lips twisted into a bitter smile. "He cut quite the figure in white tie and tails. He was tall and rangy. Broad shoulders, dark hair, and the most arresting deep blue eyes. What we used to call *matinee idol looks.* He had buckets of money, and he threw it around like it was water. Anyway, he swept Millie off her feet — or rather, he swept Millie's mother and grandmother off *their* feet."

Marie's brow puckered. "He doesn't sound like Mama's type at all."

"No. Forgive me, dear Marie, but he was rich, which meant that he was your grandmother's type. By then, Millie had dropped out of college. Her mother didn't see the point of spending money on educating a girl, and anyway, Russell was in hot pursuit."

Felicia fanned herself with her hands and yawned. "Can we cut to the chase, please? Like, how did this Russell Strickland just up and disappear?"

Josephine fixed Varina's great-niece with an icy glare. "I was getting to that."

"Russell proposed, and Millie accepted," Josephine said. "At first, Ruth and I were happy for her. But then, the more we saw of him, the less we liked. He was loud and could be very intimidating. He was so possessive of Millie. Jealous, especially of her friendship with us, and he drank too much. And when he drank, he was mean. *Abusive,* we'd call it now.

"The wedding was set for November. Of 1941. Ruth and I were to be bridesmaids. Papa was so fond of Millie. He thought we should give an engagement party for her. Here on the island."

"Not back in Boston?" Lizzie asked.

"No. My mother had passed away the previous year, and Papa was devastated. He loved Talisa and spent as much time here as possible, especially after Mama was gone. So we planned the party. We brought in an orchestra from Jacksonville and the best caterer in Atlanta. It was the social event of the season. White orchids and gardenias flown in from Miami. The ballroom looked like a fairy tale."

"There's a ballroom?" Felicia asked incredulously. "Here?"

Josephine seemed not to have heard her. "Millie looked so beautiful that night. She had a couture gown, flowers in her hair. We all had new dresses." She looked over at Varina and smiled. "Even Varina."

"Oh yes," Varina said dreamily. "Josephine gave me a dress, pink, the nicest thing I'd ever owned. And Millie gave me those pretty shoes to match."

"You were invited to the party?" Felicia looked dubious. "In the Jim Crow South? In 1941?"

"Not exactly," Varina said.

"We wanted her to come, but my father thought it wasn't the right thing," Josephine said. "Remember, she was only fourteen at the time."

"And black," Felicia said.

"I was getting paid to work in the kitchen that night," Varina said. "But the girls, they knew what a special night it was for all of us, and they wanted me to be all dressed up, to be a part of it."

"Before Cinderella's coach turned into a pumpkin," Felicia said caustically.

Brooke glanced down at her watch. It was getting late, and Josephine's narrative about the party was close to being derailed. She needed to nudge things along.

"What happened at the party?" she asked.

"Russell had been drinking all night with his fraternity brothers who'd come down for the party. And not just champagne. They were out on the veranda, passing a flask around. Poor Millie, he never even danced with her. She was a wallflower at her own engagement party. So Papa asked Gardiner, my brother, to dance with her. It was totally harmless. Gardiner had known Millie for years. She was like a kid sister to him. Unfortunately, Russell came into the ballroom, saw them dancing together, and there was an incident."

"You mean, like a fight?" Lizzie was clearly intrigued.

"Not there in the ballroom. Even Russell Strickland wasn't that gauche. He said something to Gardiner — I couldn't hear what — then he grabbed Millie by the arm and dragged her out of the ballroom."

"Poor Mama," Marie said. "She must have been terrified."

30

There was a soft knock at the library door, then Louette poked her head inside. "Miss Josephine, sorry to interrupt, but I need to let these ladies know that I finally tracked down C. D. He says the water pump on the boat motor is broke."

"What does that mean?" Brooke asked. From the expression on Louette's face, Brooke had a feeling that this was not good news.

"Too late to do anything about it today. He'll have to go on up to Brunswick tomorrow to try to get a new one," Louette said.

Brooke glanced again at her watch. It was nearly five o'clock. "If he can't take us back to the mainland, can we take the ferry?"

"Afraid not. I called the office, and they said the whole boat is booked with some folks who've been up at the conference center for a two-day corporate retreat. Not even a single seat is available."

"Is there another boat on the island — one

we could charter to take us back?" Gabe asked, half standing.

"Not one you'd want to get on," Louette said. "A few folks at Oyster Bluff have boats, but they're just little bitty wooden bateaux for fishing in the creek. I'm sorry, but it looks like you'll have to stay over tonight."

Gabe sank back down onto the chair and pulled out his phone. "I'm supposed to take a deposition in the morning. I need to call the office."

Brooke took her phone from her pocketbook and glanced down at the screen. As she'd feared, it read, NO SERVICE.

"Don't bother," she told Gabe. "Cell phone reception is almost nonexistent over here."

"So what do we do?" he asked, annoyed. "I really have a busy day tomorrow. Not to mention a dog at home who needs to be let out and fed."

"And I've got to call my babysitter and let her know I'm stuck over here," Brooke added. "I just pray she'll agree to spend the night with Henry."

"Come on out to the kitchen. You can use the landline there," the housekeeper offered.

As they followed Louette down the hall, Gabe checked his phone one more time. "You'd better believe I'm billing Josephine if I have to spend the night."

Which made Brooke laugh despite her worry over childcare arrangements. "Good idea. I'll bill her for the cost of my babysitter, assuming Farrah will stay."

"Is everything okay?" Marie asked when Brooke and Gabe returned to the library.

"As good as can be expected," Brooke said, sitting down again. "Thank God, Farrah broke up with her loser boyfriend, Jaxson, today. She's usually not available to sit on Friday nights. She volunteered to take Henry out for pizza, and then they have a date with some LEGOs."

"I got a neighbor to feed and walk my dog," Gabe reported. "And I arranged for my paralegal to handle the deposition."

"Did Louette tell you she has rooms ready for you?" Josephine asked. "I thought I'd made it clear that I expected everybody to stay over."

Brooke bit back her retort. Josephine Warrick at ninety-nine was still very much used to getting her way.

Instead, Brooke shrugged off her irritation. "Louette gave me a tour of the upstairs and showed me our rooms and asked us to let you know dinner will be ready at seven, if that's all right."

"That'll be fine," Josephine said regally.

Brooke held out a white paper bag. "And in the meantime, Shug got back from the mainland with your new medicine. You're supposed to take it at dinnertime."

"Pills. Always more pills," Josephine fretted.

"She also suggested you probably need to rest before then, since you didn't sleep at all last night," Brooke said. "And I have to agree." She looked at the others. "Since we're apparently all staying for dinner, I guess the rest of this story can wait until then."

"And people say *I'm* bossy," Josephine said, making a face. She waved her hand. "All right. For once, she's right. I suppose I could close my eyes for a few minutes."

Brooke led the group up the broad staircase to the second floor. The silk damask wallpaper in the stair hall was peeling off in sheets, the Persian stair runner was faded and threadbare, and the curved mahogany handrail wobbled beneath their hands.

"I can't even imagine what it cost to build this place over a hundred years ago," Marie said, pointing up at the once glittering, multitiered chandelier above them. "If I'm not mistaken, that's Waterford crystal."

"I can't imagine what it would cost to make it livable again," Lizzie said. She glanced back at Gabe, who was bringing up the rear of the caravan, behind Felicia, who was slowly guiding her great-aunt up the stairs. "Is she leaving money for the upkeep of this white elephant?"

He smiled and said nothing.

At the top of the landing, Brooke pointed to the right. "Lizzie, your bedroom is the second doorway from the end. There's a bathroom right next door, although it's not attached. Mom, you and I are doubling up in what used to be the master bedroom, which is at the very end." She pointed to the left. "That's Gabe's bedroom down there. Louette said it was Gardiner's before the war, and it does have a bathroom, although there's a tub and no shower." She pointed to a double doorway halfway down the left wing. "Felicia, this room is yours and Varina's. There are two double beds, but the best thing is there's an attached bathroom."

"I need that bathroom right now," Varina said, a note of urgency in her voice. She took her walker from Gabe, who'd carried it upstairs, and scuttled in the direction of the bedroom.

"God," Lizzie said, wiping her glistening face with the back of her hand. "Tell me there's air-conditioning in my room."

"It's only a window unit, but Louette turned it on and she swears the room will cool down nicely," Brooke said.

Dweezil yowled and batted against the side of the cat carrier, echoing Lizzie's annoyance.

Brooke sat gingerly on one side of the narrow bed and patted the lumpy mattress, which was covered with a quilted satin throw.

"Isn't it funny to think of married couples sleeping on something this small?"

The master bed had a towering carved mahogany headboard that reached halfway to the ceiling and a footboard so high that being in the bed felt like being in a boat.

Marie sat down on the other side of the bed, the one nearest the window, and bounced up and down. "Your father and I slept on double beds for years when we first got married. We didn't think anything of it at the time. Now I get claustrophobic sleeping alone in a queen."

"Sorry about having to share a bed with me," Brooke said.

"It'll be fine," Marie said lightly. "Taking family closeness to a whole new level. Although I do wish I had a toothbrush and nightie with me."

"Louette put new toothbrushes in the bathroom for both of us," Brooke said, "and she said we should just help ourselves to whatever we find in the closet for clothes."

Marie flopped backward onto the bed. "Later," she said wearily. "Right now, I feel like I'm the nonagenarian. There has been a *lot* of drama already today." She turned onto her side and yawned. "Wake me up ten minutes before dinner so I can at least wash my face. Okay?"

Brooke curled up beside her mother and

stared at the wall. The wallpaper was a scenic toile featuring flowers and trees and birds and animals that she guessed were native to Talisa, all done in shades of pea green. She managed to pick out a sea turtle, a running deer, some kind of long-necked seabird, pine trees, oaks, palms . . . and the next thing she knew, her mother was gently poking her in the side.

"Come on, Brooke," Marie said, laughing. "It's dinnertime. And did you know you snore?"

"Do not," Brooke yawned, sitting up.

"Do too," Marie said. "Let's go. I'm starved."

The others were already seated in the dining room, which had also undergone a transformation. A snowy white damask tablecloth covered the table, which was set with gold-rimmed porcelain dishes, heavy sterling flatware, and crystal stemware. A pair of tall silver candelabras adorned the center of the table with lit tapers.

Josephine sat at the head of the table, sipping from a glass of wine. She was dressed in the silk caftan again, and diamonds twinkled from her earrings, necklace, and a solitaire cocktail ring on her right hand. When Louette bustled into the room, delicious scents wafted from the direction of the kitchen.

"What are we having tonight?" Josephine asked.

"Paper-bag baked redfish," Louette said. "C. D. was fishing off the dock when he oughta have been fixing that boat motor, but at least we got dinner out of it. There's red rice to go with the fish, salad from the garden, and some lady peas out of the freezer. I didn't have time to bake yeast rolls, but I managed to throw some biscuits together."

Gabe moaned out loud. "Redfish. My favorite. And lady peas. My mother used to fix them with fatback."

"Mmm-hmm, that's how I do 'em too," Louette said, setting the dishes on the sideboard. She held up a bottle of white wine that had been sitting in a silver cooler. "Can I pour anybody some more wine? The man at the wine store says this is real nice with fish."

Josephine held up her nearly empty glass. "You can top me off."

Louette shook her head vigorously. "Noooo. You know your pain pills have it written right on the bottle — *Do not consume with alcohol.*" She moved around the table, filling the other extended glasses.

"Louette, I said you can top me off." Josephine's voice held a warning note. "What does it matter if I drink with my medicine? I'm not operating heavy machinery. And I already have stage-four lung cancer, so what's the worst that can happen?"

The housekeeper muttered something under her breath but did as she'd been ordered.

Dinner proceeded, with the guests around the table complimenting the fish, which was the best Brooke had ever tasted, and the wine, which was also a surprisingly good quality. Their hostess, Brooke noticed, barely picked at her plate, merely moving food from one side of her plate to the other and occasionally tossing morsels to Teeny and Tiny, who sat on the floor by her chair.

At last, Marie folded her napkin and placed it beside her plate. "Josephine, that was absolutely a divine dinner." She toyed with her dinner fork. "Do you want to know something funny? I think I have this same silver pattern. Francis First, right?"

Josephine sipped her wine. "Yes, I believe that's the name of this pattern." She waved her hand at the table with its elegant trappings. "I don't really care for this kind of thing, but Louette insisted. This was my mother's wedding silver."

"Mine was my grandmother's," Marie said. "The war was going on when Mama got married, so she said she didn't really get a lot of wedding gifts."

Lizzie picked up her fork and looked at it. "Granny had boxes and boxes of this kind of family stuff. I think it's all still in storage. At some point, I guess I'll get it all out and deal with it, but what do I need with pickle tongs and monogrammed pillowcases? I live alone and mostly eat carryout Chinese."

Brooke tried not to think about all the wedding gifts she'd had to return after she'd canceled her own wedding to Harris Strayhorn.

She turned to their hostess. "Josephine, you didn't go to Millie's wedding, did you? Or Ruth's either, for that matter. Isn't that what you told me?"

Color flooded the old woman's parchment-like skin. "As Marie pointed out, it was during the war. Gas was rationed, and travel was difficult. And, well, as I've admitted, we were estranged."

"Did you have a fight?" Felicia asked eagerly. "What did you fight about?"

"No fight," Josephine said. "We just . . . drifted apart."

"Because of the thing with Russell Strickland?" Lizzie asked. "Don't forget, you promised to tell us the rest of the story."

Josephine's fingers toyed with something on the collar of her dress. Brooke leaned closer and saw that it was the brooch she'd shown her previously. The High Tide Club pin.

"Yes. What happened after that man dragged my mother out of the ballroom?" Marie asked.

The door to the kitchen swung open, and

as Louette walked in, Brooke glimpsed C. D. sitting at the kitchen table, mopping up sauce with half of a huge biscuit.

"I made coffee," Louette announced, brandishing a pot. Josephine glared at Louette. "But you're not having any, and I don't care how much you fuss at me. It's too late for you to be drinking coffee."

"Fine. Open a bottle of port and bring me that," Josephine said. She looked around the table. "At one time, Papa had the finest wine cellar on the coast. We might as well have some of his port, don't you think?"

When the coffee had been drunk and the port poured, Josephine resumed her story.

"Russell was absolutely livid after he saw Millie dancing with Gardiner," Josephine said. "I wasn't out in the garden where he attacked her, so I only know what we managed to coax out of her the next night."

"I seen it all," Varina said quietly.

Every head in the room swiveled to look at her. She was such a tiny figure, almost child-sized, against the bulk of the enormous chair she sat in.

"You did?" Josephine seemed taken aback. "You never said so, all those years ago."

"Nobody asked," Varina said, shrugging. "Anyway, I was just a girl. I was so shocked at first, I couldn't believe what I was seeing and hearing."

"Auntie, how did you happen to see it?" Felicia asked. She reached over and gently removed a crumb of biscuit from her great-aunt's blouse, which was when Brooke noticed, for the first time, that Varina was also wearing a High Tide Club pin.

"I'd finished up working in the kitchen, and Mrs. Dorris — she was the housekeeper back then — she told me to go ahead on home. I was supposed to wait for my brother to come fetch me and walk me home, but I knew he wasn't coming for another hour, and anyway, I wanted to peek at all the fancy dresses in the ballroom. So I changed back into my pink party dress and heels, and I sorta snuck around to the back of the house so I could look in the doors from the veranda. About the time I got there, I saw that man hauling Millie out of there." Varina looked over at Marie. "I'm sorry you have to hear this."

"It's all right," Marie said. "It was a long time ago."

"Millie was crying, telling him he was hurting her, but he didn't care, and he didn't slow down," Varina said. "He drug her into the garden, way back where the camellia bushes were head-high. And that's right near where I'd jumped into the bushes to hide."

Varina closed her eyes as though she were reliving the scene from memory. "It was a full moon that night, so I could see things I wished I hadn't. That man, he shoved her up against a tree, and he had his hands all up and down in her dress."

She glanced over at Gabe, blushed, and looked away. "Millie was begging him to stop. She was afraid somebody would see them, like her mama or her grandmama, but he said he could do what he wanted because they were getting married. I saw him push her dress up, and then he unfastened his trousers . . ."

"Oh my God." Lizzie breathed. "He raped her. The bastard raped her."

Marie was clutching her napkin in both hands, twisting it into a rope, her face ashen. Brooke reached over and touched her shoulder, but her mother didn't seem to notice.

"He didn't get the chance," Varina said. "Right about that time, Mr. Gardiner came busting in on them. I think he must have followed her out of the ballroom, because just before that, I saw him standing on the veranda, like he was looking for somebody. I guess he caught sight of Millie's dress, because he ran right over to them. He yelled at that man to stop it, and the bad man told him to mind his own business because he could do what he wanted, and the next thing I knew, Mr. Gardiner yanked him clean away from Millie. They had a fight, and even though the other man was way bigger, Mr. Gardiner punched him in the face and the gut and knocked him clean off his feet."

"Good for him," Lizzie said. "What happened after that?"

"Mr. Gardiner had already told Millie to go on back to the house. So then he told that bad man he'd better leave this island. He told him if he was still there in the morning, he'd kill him. And then he left."

"Gardiner really was a hero," Josephine said, sighing. "Not just a war hero, although he was that too. He was all our heroes. The best brother a girl could ask for."

Her face sagged, and her speech was slightly slurred. The pain meds, Brooke thought, must be kicking in.

"Did he . . . make it through the war?" Lizzie asked.

"No. He didn't," Josephine said. "His plane was shot down at Midway. Gardiner was a gun jumper, you know."

"What's that?" Felicia asked.

"He got tired of waiting for the United States to get into the war. He'd gotten his pilot's license just about the same time he got his driver's license. Gardiner hated what was happening in Europe. After Hitler marched into Poland and then Holland and Belgium, his mind was made up. He and Papa had terrible fights about it because my father was still an isolationist at that point. Anyway, Gardiner decided to join the Royal Canadian Air Force. The morning after the engagement party, he took the early ferry to the mainland, and from there he took the train to Canada."

"You must have been so proud of him," Marie said.

"At the time, I thought it was terribly romantic," Josephine said. "And heroic. Of course, that was October, and in early December, Pearl Harbor happened, and the United States did get into the war."

"Did you ever see Gardiner again?" Marie asked.

"Just once, and only for a few hours. He came home briefly, after training and before he was shipped out. By then, Papa had closed up this house. Most of the men on the island, including all the Shaddix boys, went off to fight the war, plus German U-boats were prowling the coast, and he didn't think it was safe for us to stay."

Gabe looked up from his glass of port. "I never heard that before."

"Oh yes. In 1941, at least five Allied merchant ships were torpedoed by the Germans between here and Savannah, and I believe four or five U-boats were sunk, right off the coast here." Josephine drained most of her port and, setting the glass down, tipped the rest onto the tablecloth, watching idly while the deep purple stain pooled on the white damask.

"I should really be getting to bed," she said. Her eyelids drooped, and she slumped back in her chair.

"Oh no," Lizzie objected. "You still haven't told us how Russell Strickland disappeared."

31

Louette hovered in the doorway, anxiously observing her employer's body language. "Y'all need to let her go to bed now," she warned as she mopped up the spilled port. "She's flat wore out."

Josephine's eyelids fluttered, and she seemed to struggle to stay awake. "No," she protested, raising a bony hand. "No, it's all right." She coughed, then recovered. "I owe them this much. Go back out in the kitchen, Louette, and leave me be."

"You were saying?" Lizzie prompted.

"We all slept late the morning after the party, but at breakfast, Millie seemed different. She was edgy and agitated. Of course, at the time, we had no way of knowing what had gone on the night before. As Varina said, it was a full moon. We had this silly custom — a ritual, I suppose you'd call it — of skinny-dipping on a full moon at high tide if we were near a beach. We called ourselves the High Tide Club."

Josephine's fingers found the brooch on her collar, and with trembling fingers, she managed to unfasten it and hold it out in the flat of her palm for the others to see. "Millie had these made for Ruth and me, as bridesmaid's gifts."

"She gave me one too," Varina said proudly, pointing to the pin fastened to her chest.

"Mom? Did Granny have a pin like this too?"

"May I see it?"

Josephine handed the pin to Marie.

"No, at least I never saw her wear one like this, but then she never wore much jewelry. Just her wedding band and engagement ring. Is that a diamond . . . on her nipple?" she asked, raising an eyebrow. "I never knew Mama had a naughty side to her."

"Yes," Josephine said. "She could be as silly as the rest of us. We were just girls. Anyway, we'd skinny-dipped at Millie's grandmother's beach house and at Ruth's family house at Palm Beach and at Cape Cod, all during the full moon, and that weekend seemed like the perfect time. The moon was full and high tide was around nine that night. Millie claimed she had a headache and didn't want to go, but Ruth and I pestered her until she finally gave in and agreed to come with us."

Felicia gave her great-aunt a sideways look. "Auntie Vee — did you skinny-dip too? I'm shocked!"

Varina ducked her head and then looked away.

"It was peer pressure," Josephine said. "We took Gardiner's roadster, picked Varina up at Oyster Bluff, and sweet-talked her daddy into letting her go with us. We said we were having a beach picnic, which was true, but we left out the part about skinny-dipping."

"My daddy was a Church of God preacher," Varina told the others. "He never would have let me go if he'd known what those fool girls were up to."

"There's a place on the island — not far from the lighthouse, a little secluded spot that we named Mermaid Beach. That's where we were headed," Josephine said. "I'd gotten the cook to fix us a picnic basket, and I snuck in a bottle of champagne and a bottle of Gardiner's bourbon. We had a fine supper, but when it came time to go swimming, Millie flat refused."

"Mama was always so modest," Marie said. "I don't think I ever saw her undressed the whole time I was growing up."

"It wasn't just that," Josephine said sadly. "Ruth and I had both been drinking, and we were sort of teasing Millie, telling her she had to swim, and I guess I pulled at the jacket she was wearing — long-sleeved, even in the heat — and that's when we saw the bruises."

Brooke felt herself recoil at the thought of Millie, just a girl of nineteen, and a victim of sexual abuse.

"She had bruises up and down her arms and on her shoulders and thighs," Josephine said. Her eyes filled with tears. "Our dear, sweet Millie. That's when she broke down and told us what that bastard Russell had done to her. She as much as told us Russell violated her whenever he was drinking — and he drank a lot. He was a violent, abusive drunk."

"Dear God," Marie said. She was clutching the edge of the table like a life preserver.

"Ruth told her she couldn't marry Russell. So did I. We both tried to talk her into breaking the engagement, but she said it was too late. She said it was the only way out of her mother's money problems."

"I'd never heard of rich people with money problems before," Varina said. "I thought rich folks didn't have problems like the rest of us."

"Millie insisted there was no way out of her predicament. She drank some more, and then we all went skinny-dipping and finished off the champagne and the whiskey," Josephine said. She looked over at her old friend, sitting at the opposite end of the table.

"You too, Auntie?" Felicia said, her eyes widening in disbelief.

"I'd never had a drop of alcohol before," Varina said. "That whiskey tasted nasty and burned my throat, but the champagne, that was a different story."

"It was very good champagne," Josephine added. "Moët & Chandon."

"I did like that champagne," Varina admitted. "It had bubbles like a Coca-Cola, only it tasted different. I didn't have but maybe a whole cupful."

"But you were so small, it didn't take much to get you drunk," Josephine said.

"My first and last time drinking alcohol," Varina said. "I guess I was cutting up pretty bad."

"It had gotten late, after midnight. And we didn't dare take her home drunk," Josephine said. "And anyway, none of us wanted to go home. We had this crazy idea about staying out all night — under the stars. Millie wanted to do it. She thought it would be her last night with all of us before she got married."

"But the bugs . . . oooh, the bugs were bad back then," Varina said.

"And it started to rain. Then I remembered the old lighthouse keeper's cottage. The government had decommissioned it several years earlier, but I knew Gardiner had a key to the cottage hidden under the roadster's doormat. So I drove us over there, the key worked, and we all piled onto the only bed in the place."

"Four girls in one bed?" Lizzie wrinkled her nose at the idea.

"Four very drunk girls," Josephine said. "I

was the tallest, and Ruth wasn't exactly tiny, but Millie and Varina were so petite, they didn't take up any room at all." She yawned, not bothering to cover her mouth. "Oh my. Maybe I overdid it tonight. Or maybe it's just these damn pills." The old woman shook herself slightly as though she were shaking off her weariness. "I can't remember who woke up first, but I know it was early, because that bed was facing east, so the sun was shining right in our eyes."

"Y'all didn't hear me creeping out of that bed, getting sick in the middle of the night, I guess," Varina said. She held her head between her hands at the memory of it. "Ooh, I had a headache, and I'd never been so sick in my life."

Felicia laughed. "I'm sorry, Auntie. I just can't picture you hungover."

"Girls do lots of crazy things when they're young," Varina said. "I seem to remember your mama and daddy putting up with all kinds of foolishness from you."

"That's true," Felicia agreed. "I was a real handful."

"We were all a little worried, because it was Sunday morning, and we didn't want Varina to get in trouble for missing church, so we got dressed and hurried back to Oyster Bluff. We hadn't gotten very far when I spotted something up ahead, in the middle of the road. As I got closer, I could see it was buzzards. Three of the biggest, boldest buzzards I'd ever seen. There was another, pecking at something off in the tall grass. And they didn't fly off, even when the car was almost on top of them. At first I assumed it was a dead animal, like a deer or a feral hog or something. But as we got closer, I realized it was . . . a person."

"I'll bet it was Russell Strickland," Lizzie said.

"Was he . . . ?" Marie's hand reached for her wineglass, but it was empty.

"Yes. He was dead." Josephine looked back at the sideboard, where another bottle of port rested on a silver trivet. She pointed at Gabe. "Be a dear and fetch that, will you? We're all going to need another drink."

When everyone but Varina had a refilled glass, Josephine went on talking.

"He must have weighed nearly 250 pounds, and of course, all of it was deadweight. I still don't know how we managed to lift him. I suppose it was adrenaline or something. Somehow, we got him into the rumble seat, and then, of course, we had to figure out what to do with the body."

"Wait! Hold the phone," Felicia said, her voice rising. "How did he die? Who killed him? Are you saying you just hid the body?"

"Mmm-hmm." Varina nodded calmly. "That's right."

"But how did he die?" Lizzie persisted. "It was Russell Strickland, right? So who killed him?"

"Yes, it was him. He'd been shot. He didn't tell us who did it, and we didn't ask," Josephine said.

Gabe had been silent throughout most of the dinner, but now he was shaking his head. "You didn't notify law enforcement?"

"We did not," Josephine said.

"Why not? He'd been murdered. A crime had been committed."

"Russell Strickland was a monster," Josephine said, her voice cold, detached even. "We've already established that. Varina saw him assault Millie. He was twice her size! He would have kept on assaulting her, and nobody could have stopped him. Whoever killed him did the world a favor."

"So you got rid of the body. Just like that?" Gabe reached for the port bottle. "You didn't wonder who the murderer was?"

"It didn't matter. The four of us — Millie, Ruth, Varina, and me — we all agreed not to ask any questions. And never to tell what had happened. And we didn't."

"Until tonight," Brooke said.

"Do I dare ask what you did with the body?" Gabe asked.

Josephine regarded him with cool dispassion. "Why do you want to know? Are you going to report me to the authorities?"

"I am an officer of the court," Gabe said. He nodded toward Brooke. "And so is she. Did you kill him?"

"If I had, I wouldn't tell you," Josephine said.

"Do you know who killed him, Auntie?" Felicia peered at her great-aunt.

"Maybe I do, maybe I don't. We swore that night, and I won't go back on my word," Varina said.

"It couldn't have been you," Felicia said forcefully. "You're the most God-fearing woman I've ever known. You wouldn't hurt a fly."

Varina gave her an indulgent smile. "Child, we are all sinners in this world. I have tried to live the Lord's word the best way I know how, but the Bible tells us we are all born sinners, craving the Lord's forgiveness."

"It couldn't have been Granny, no matter what he did to her," Brooke said. "I bet she didn't even know how to fire a gun."

"We *all* knew how to shoot," Josephine corrected her. "We learned to shoot sporting clays at summer camp. And of course, Gardiner taught me how to hunt." She pointed at a pair of impressive deer mounts on the wall above the sideboard. "That eight-point buck is one I shot when I was twelve. That one" — she pointed to the mount on the right — "Gardiner shot just a week before the party."

She nodded at Varina. "You know how to shoot, don't you?"

"Oh yes," Varina said. "On an island like this — with rattlesnakes and gators and wild hogs, every family has a gun and every child learns how to shoot it, even little bitty girls like me. My daddy had a big ol' pistol, and he made me learn how to use it."

"This is just unbelievable," Lizzie said, slapping the tabletop for emphasis. "But it doesn't really solve the big mysteries of the night. What happened to Russell Strickland's body? Was it ever discovered? Granny's scrapbooks just covered the year he disappeared. And it was a huge story at the time."

"To my knowledge, the body was never found," Josephine said.

32

October 1941

Harley Shaddix's shoulders sagged as he parked the rusted pickup in front of Shell-haven. Samuel Bettendorf had been waiting for him, nervously pacing back and forth in front of the house, wearing a path in the lush green grass.

Dusk was approaching. Most of their house-guests had departed on the four o'clock ferry, including Millie Everhart's mother and grandmother, but it had been hours since anyone had seen or heard from Russell Strickland. The knot of worry burned in his gut.

The hound tethered to a cleat in the bed of the pickup truck hung his head over the side, panting heavily.

"Anything?" Bettendorf asked.

"No, sir," Harley said. He pointed at his dog. "Butch, he picked up a scent out in that dove field and followed it right close to the deer stand. Then, coming back down the road, he acted like he picked it up again, but I couldn't find no sign of Mr. Strickland."

"His kit and all his clothes and suitcases are still in his room," Bettendorf said. "I can't tell what's missing, other than his shotgun. Poor Millie is so upset, I hate to ask her to look through his things. Josephine and Ruth are with her now, trying to keep her calm."

"I talked to my boys," Harley said. "Homer said he showed Mr. Russell the spot where we seen that big ol' buck Mr. Gardiner's been tracking. And Friday, he talked about he was gonna bag him a trophy while he was on the island." Harley winced as he tried to take the weight off his bad leg. "I got Omar and Otis out in the bateau, looking in the creek in case he decided to go fishing."

"Good idea," Bettendorf said. "I wish to God Gardiner were here right now. He'd know where to look."

"Varina tells me your boy's gone off to fight in the war," Harley said.

Bettendorf's posture stiffened. "He's a goddamn fool. What happens in Europe is not this country's concern. But I couldn't talk him out of it. Couldn't stop him from going."

"He's a grown man," Harley said. "My boys, they say they're gonna sign up first chance they get." He sighed. "I can't talk no sense into them neither."

The two men, one black, one white, leaned

against the bed of the truck, gazing up at the sky, where the last orange streaks of sunlight were visible through the tree line.

"Getting dark," Harley said, scratching at the stubble of beard on his chin. "City boy like that, how's he gonna do alone at night in a place like this?"

Ruth peered out the window at the scene below. "Your father's back with the truck," she told Varina, who crouched uneasily on the chair at the dressing table. "He's got a huge dog with him. I've never seen a dog like that."

Varina craned her neck to see. "That's Butch. My brothers take him coon hunting. He can scent anything. Daddy must have been out looking for that bad man." She wouldn't say his name out loud. She would never say his name.

Millie sat on the bed, her knees drawn up tightly against her chest. "What if they find where we put Russell? What if the dog finds that place and they dig him up?"

Josephine stood by the window now, looking down at the two men. "They won't go near that oyster mound. It's a special Indian place for the Geechees. Right, Varina?"

"Mmm-hmm." Varina nodded agreement. "Supposed to be evil haints there."

"But you're Geechee, aren't you?" Ruth asked. "And you were right there with us."

"Dead Indians don't scare me," Varina said. "And I don't believe in haints. Anyway, I'm not gonna be afraid anymore."

"I'm not going to be afraid either," Millie said, lifting her chin. "I'm going to be like you girls."

"The High Tide Club," Josephine said. "We're like the Three Musketeers, plus one."

"All for one, and one for all," Ruth said.

Millie clapped a hand to her mouth and jumped up from the bed. She scrabbled in her suitcase, spilling slips and stockings and dresses onto the carpet. "Oh my gosh! I almost forgot."

She brought out a small package. "Here!" She opened the wrapping and brought out three small black velvet boxes, which she passed around to each of the girls. "These were to have been your bridesmaids' gifts," she said.

Josephine was the first to open the box. She held up the tiny brooch, squinting at it and then laughing delightedly. "Millie, you scamp! She's naked!"

Ruth clapped her hands. "Mildred Everhart, this is the most perfect gift anybody has ever given me. And I will treasure it always."

Varina stared down at the pin nested in its white satin wrapping. "But I'm not a bridesmaid."

"Neither are we. Now," Ruth drawled.

"You're better than a bridesmaid," Millie

said, hugging the younger girl. "You went skinny-dipping with us last night, didn't you?"

"And helped us bury you-know-who this morning," Josephine pointed out. "I'd say you've paid your initiation fees in full."

Varina lifted the pin from the box and held it up to the light. "That ain't a real diamond, is it?"

"They're just chips, but they're real. Granny gave me a pair of her earrings, and I had the jeweler use them for the pins."

From outside, they heard an engine starting, then backfiring. Ruth parted the curtains again. "Your father is leaving, Varina. And, Josephine, your father is in the truck with him."

"Maybe they're going for the sheriff," Millie fretted. "Maybe they'll bring more dogs and men who aren't afraid of dead Indians and haints. And they'll figure it out and we'll all be arrested."

"It won't matter. They won't find Russell. As long as we stick together, nobody will ever know what happened to him," Josephine said.

33

"No, the body was never found," Josephine said.

"And the family never did anything about that?" Lizzie persisted. "They didn't, I don't know, hire a private detective or try to call in the FBI?"

"Russell Strickland's parents were both killed in a car wreck when he was a boy. He was raised by his grandparents, who were old and ill at the time. They did send somebody down to conduct an investigation, but you have to understand, the sheriff in this county at that time was part of a political dynasty who'd run things here for generations. He didn't appreciate having a Boston lawyer question his methods and practices."

"And I'd venture a guess that your father, being the wealthiest taxpayer in these parts, probably had some political sway with the sheriff and his cronies," Gabe said.

"Papa believed in being generous to this community. Among other things, he paid for two new squad cars, and he built the high school football field. The sheriff was . . . grateful," Josephine said.

"So the investigation never went anywhere," Felicia said.

"The war started, and people had bigger things to worry about," Josephine said. She pushed her chair back and stood with great effort. "And now, if you'll excuse me, I think I really must go to bed." She snapped her fingers at the dogs, asleep on the carpet. "Come along, girls."

The old woman took one faltering, wobbly step.

Gabe jumped up and offered her his arm. "May I assist you?"

She shrugged. "If you must."

34

"Miss Brooke, Miss Brooke." Someone was knocking on the bedroom door. She sat up in bed, awakened from a deep, dreamless sleep. She looked around the room, disoriented. Her mother was in bed beside her. Where was she? And then the knock again. She saw the wallpaper, the blurry green tangled vines and creatures, and it came to her. She was in a bedroom at Shellhaven. She reached for her phone on the nightstand and glanced at the digital time readout. 7:15 A.M.

She jumped out of bed and opened the door. Louette stood in the hallway, barefoot and wild-eyed, with a cotton bathrobe cinched loosely around her waist. Brooke stepped into the hallway and gently closed the door to keep from waking her mother.

"What's wrong, Louette?"

"It's Josephine. I think she's dead. I need you to come downstairs and see about her."

Brooke felt as though she'd just touched a live wire. "What happened?" She was already moving down the hallway toward the stairs with Louette in tow.

"I don't know. I found her on the bathroom floor. She must have fallen. There's blood. And she's not moving, and she's not breathing."

They'd reached the door to the library-turned-bedroom, which was closed, but Brooke could already hear the dogs inside, whining and scratching at the door.

"That's what woke me up," Louette said as they slipped into the library, quickly closing the door behind them. "Since I been sleeping in the house, I usually get up at six, because she's up by then, needing her medicine and such, but today when she wasn't up, I thought that was a good sign. Maybe she was sleeping late. I went back to sleep, but then I heard Teeny and Tiny barking and carrying on, so I went to check, and that's when I found her."

The dogs were in a state of frenzy, barking, jumping at their heels. Brooke saw puddles of urine on the carpet. "Better grab them, Louette, before they wake up the whole house. I'll see about Josephine."

Louette nodded, scooping up a dog with each hand.

Brooke walked toward the bathroom door, but as she got nearer, she saw a ghostly white foot, turned at an odd angle, and then the pale, blue-veined leg belonging to the foot and then the other foot, and then, finally, Josephine Bettendorf Warrick.

There could be no doubt she was dead. The body was sprawled on the tiled floor. She was dressed in a moth-eaten gray sweater over a pale yellow cotton nightgown, her body awkwardly twisted, faceup on the tile floor, in a pool of blood.

Brooke swallowed hard, once, twice, and clenched her jaws, fighting the wave of nausea that swept over her. She knelt beside the old woman and tentatively touched the side of her neck. It was cool to the touch, and there was no sign of a pulse.

She heard the library door open and looked over her shoulder. Louette stood motionless in the doorway, a dog tucked under each arm. "I was right. She's dead, isn't she?"

"I'm afraid so," Brooke said, standing and backing out of the bathroom.

"That poor old thing," Louette said. "It's all my fault. I never should have given her that wine last night. Not when she was taking that medicine. She hadn't had no wine since she got sick, so she wasn't used to it. Mixing it with those pills, that's what killed her."

Louette began to cry, and to her surprise, Brooke felt tears streaming down her own face. Louette set the Chihuahuas gently onto the floor, reached out, folded Brooke into her arms, and they stood like that, quietly crying. Teeny and Tiny sat on their haunches, their ears pricked up, small bodies trembling, attuned to the emotions unfolding before them.

Brooke finally pulled away and wiped her eyes with the sleeve of the man's cotton pajama top she'd found neatly folded in the master bedroom upstairs.

"What should we do?" Louette asked, wringing her hands. "Should I go get Shug?"

"Let me think," Brooke said, taking a deep breath. But her mind was a whirl of emotions. Panic, dread, grief, confusion. Josephine was dead. What happens next?

"Look here," Louette said, pointing down at the top of one of the dog's heads. "Is that blood?"

Brooke scooped up the dog and examined her head. Sure enough, there were several droplets of dried blood on the dog's face and muzzle, but as she searched the dog's body, she could find no obvious wounds.

"I bet I know what happened," Louette said. "Josephine probably got up in the middle of the night to go to the bathroom, and it woke up these dogs. They followed her wherever she went. She wasn't right last night, doped up on those pills and all that wine. Probably she tripped over Teeny, or maybe Tiny. And that's how she fell and hit her head."

"You're probably right," Brooke said. "I guess you'd better go get Shug. In the meantime, I'll use the house phone to call the sheriff."

"Sheriff?" Louette stiffened at the word.

"I think that's the correct procedure," Brooke said. "But before you fetch Shug, I think we're going to need a big pot of coffee ready before I wake the others."

35

"Carter County Sheriff's Office. Is this a life-threatening emergency?" The dispatcher's voice was calm and detached, the exact opposite of how Brooke was feeling at that moment.

"Er, no — that is, the person is already dead," Brooke replied.

She could hear the tapping of computer keys on the other end of the line.

"Ma'am, can you tell me the manner of death?"

"She's, uh, ninety-nine years old, and I believe she fell and hit her head."

"Accidental, then. I see you're calling from over there on Talisa Island?"

"That's right."

"Name of deceased?" More tapping.

"Josephine Bettendorf Warrick," Brooke said.

"Ohhhhh," the dispatcher said. "That's so sad, and I'm very sorry to hear it. Miss Josephine did a lot of good things for this community."

"Yes, it is a shame."

"All right, hon. I'm gonna call Sheriff Goolsby, because he was a personal friend of Miss Josephine's, and I'll ask him to call you right back. Is this a good number?"

"It's the only number," Brooke said. "My cell doesn't have good reception here."

"Okay, well, you sit tight while I get ahold of the sheriff. What's your name, hon?"

Brooke told her.

"I know you!" The dispatcher's voice warmed. "My niece Farrah works for you. This is her aunt Jodee. Now, you being a lawyer and all, you probably already know this, but y'all just leave Miss Josephine right where she's at. Don't try moving her or nothing like that."

"I promise you, nobody is going to move her body."

After she'd hung up, Brooke took a few more sips of coffee and waited. She really wanted to call Farrah and check on Henry, but she also didn't want to miss the sheriff's call.

She paced around the kitchen, looking out the window for the return of Louette and Shug, trying not to think of Josephine's lifeless body stretched out on the bathroom floor. Ten minutes later the phone rang, and she grabbed it.

"Sheriff Goolsby here. Is this Brooke Trappnell?"

"This is she."

"Jodee tells me Miss Josephine has taken a fall and died?"

"Yes. We think she got up in the middle of the night to go to the bathroom and perhaps tripped over one of her dogs and hit her head when she fell. There's quite a bit of blood."

"Don't touch a thing," the sheriff said sternly. "At all. Are you able to close off that bathroom?"

"Yes."

"Do that. I'll call the funeral home and try to raise the coroner, and we'll be over there ASAP. Don't touch anything. Understand?"

Brooke rolled her eyes. "Yes, I've got the message. If you'll call this number when you're close to the Shellhaven dock, somebody will come down and bring you up to the house."

She glanced over at the kitchen clock. Just past eight. Henry would have been up for at least two hours by now. She dialed her babysitter's number, crossing her fingers that all would be well. One crisis per morning was all she was equipped to handle.

"Farrah? How's it going?"

"Oh, Brooke, hey. Everything's cool. Henry's being a really good boy. Aren't you, Henry?"

She could hear the tinny theme song of her

son's favorite cartoon show. Then her son's voice. "Yes! I'm good boy."

"He really has been pretty good," Farrah said. "I got him to sleep almost the whole night in his new bed. He's had breakfast, and now we're just chilling with some *Caillou.*"

Brooke smiled despite herself. "Ugh. I hate that show."

"For real. Whatever happened to Barney the purple dinosaur like I used to watch?"

"Dunno. Listen, Farrah. Would it be possible for you to stay 'til later in the day?"

"I guess. I mean, it's not like I've got anything else to do since me and Jaxson are broken up. How late are we talking about?"

"Not sure yet."

"Is everything okay? You sound kind of stressed."

"Yeah, well, stressed is putting it mildly. The thing is, Josephine is dead."

"What! For real? What happened?"

Brooke described the scene she'd found in the bathroom.

"Oh, man. That really sucks. What happens now, with the island and everything?"

"It's way too soon to tell. I've called the sheriff's office, and he'll be over pretty soon. In the meantime, I've got to deal with things here, which could get complicated. Which is why I'd really, really appreciate it if you could keep watching Henry. I'll pay extra, of course."

"No problem. It'll be fun. Maybe we'll head over to the park in a little while."

"Good idea," Brooke said. "I can't thank you enough, Farrah. Can you put Henry on the phone?"

"Sure thing," she said. "Henry!" the babysitter called. "Hey, Henry, come here. Your mama's on the phone. She wants to talk to you."

"No!"

"Come on, buddy," Farrah coaxed. "Don't you want to tell Mama about the awesome thing you did last night?"

"No!"

"Never mind," Brooke said, sighing. "I'll get home as soon as I can. Give him a kiss for me, okay?"

"All day long," Farrah promised.

"Just out of curiosity, what did he do last night?"

"Oh. Big news. Huge news. He pooped in the potty."

"Major breakthrough," Brooke said, laughing. "I'll call you later."

Gabe Wynant was just emerging from his bedroom, dressed, with his briefcase tucked under his arm. "Oh, good," he said, seeing Brooke approach. "You're up. I was going to see if somebody could give us a ride to the ferry . . ." He left the sentence unfinished, noticing her pained expression. "What's wrong?" He clutched her arm.

"Josephine's dead," she said.

"Oh no." He shook his head. "Heart attack?"

"Maybe, but maybe not. Louette found her lying on the bathroom floor. It looks like she fell and hit her head on the tile."

He glanced up and down the corridor at the closed doors. "Have you told the others?"

"No, I just got off the phone with the sheriff's office. He'll be over with the coroner as soon as he can. I was just about to start the process of letting the others know. My mom's still sleeping. But I'm glad you're the first. I guess we need to talk about what comes next, right?"

"Yeah," he said with a long sigh. "But first, coffee. And maybe some aspirin."

When they'd reached the first floor, Gabe turned away from the kitchen and toward the library. Brooke intercepted him before he opened the door.

"Gabe, the sheriff said not to let anybody near the body, or to touch anything."

He pulled his cell phone from his pocket and nodded. "I promise not to touch anything, but as her attorney, I think I need to see her body."

Brooke used the hem of her shirt to turn the doorknob. Inside, the room was already hot, despite the early hour and the fan whirring in the open window. "She's in there," she said, pointing to the open bathroom door. Unwilling to see her client's body again, she posted herself beside Josephine's recliner. The knitted afghan was carefully folded across the back of the chair, but the covers of the nearby bed were rumpled. Josephine's favorite sneakers, with the laces removed, were neatly lined up at the foot of the bed, and the wig was on the nightstand.

She looked up when she heard Gabe's cell phone shutter clicking off multiple frames. When he emerged from the bathroom, his face was pale under his ruddy tan. "Coffee," he said.

Gabe helped himself to a mug of coffee, then poured more for his associate. "This has been a hell of a twenty-four hours," he said, draining half the cup.

"What comes next?" Brooke asked.

"Assuming the authorities don't think foul play is involved, I suppose the body will be removed to the funeral home at St. Ann's."

"Will there be an autopsy?" Brooke cringed as soon as she'd said the word.

"Up to the sheriff and the coroner. I mean, she was old and terminally ill. And as far as we know, nobody would have a motive to want her dead, right?"

"Not that I know of," Brooke said.

"If that's the case, they'll start the work to

issue a death certificate. After that is when the fun begins."

"What's that mean?" Brooke asked. "You drew up a new will and executed it yesterday before I got here. Right?"

He set the coffee mug on the table and massaged his temples with both hands. "Not quite. I did draw up the will. Josephine read and approved it, but we needed two witnesses. Louette was supposed to fetch a couple of folks from Oyster Bluff, but then there was the trouble with the boat, and Josephine was excited about seeing your mother and Lizzie, and the will got pushed onto the back burner."

"Oh no," Brooke moaned. "I thought everything was signed and sealed."

"Christ!" He stared down at the table. "This is going to be a hell of a mess, and it's totally my fault. I knew I should have pressed her to get those witnesses over here yesterday, but Josephine was adamant about greeting her guests first."

"Not blaming you at all, but couldn't you have gotten Louette and maybe C. D. as witnesses?"

"No. She'd left them small bequests, so they had the same conflict as you."

"Which means that Josephine died intestate."

"As far as I know, yes."

Brooke gestured upward with her chin. "So

this means we tell everybody — Varina and Felicia, Lizzie, Mom, and of course, Louette and Shug — that they don't inherit?" She stood and began rifling cupboards, banging the warped wooden doors as she searched.

"What are you looking for?" Gabe asked.

"Aspirin. Let's hope there's an industrial-sized bottle somewhere in here."

36

"Good morning, ladies," Louette murmured, head down, eyes averted. She set a tray of fruit, coffee, and tea down on the sideboard. "Breakfast will be just a few minutes."

Brooke looked around the table, wondering how she would break the news to the women that their hostess was dead. As a delaying tactic, she got up and began filling coffee cups.

"I'll get your tea, Auntie Vee," Felicia volunteered.

"I reckon Josephine is sleeping late this morning," Varina said, chuckling. "We sure did have a late night." She reached over and patted Lizzie's hand. "How did you sleep last night, honey, after that long plane ride all the way from California?"

Lizzie yawned. "Not that great. The sun was shining right in my eyes. Plus, that mattress in my room felt like it was stuffed with corncobs or something."

"Sorry about that," Brooke said. She

cleared her throat nervously, looking down the table at Gabe, who'd just joined the group in the dining room.

"Is something wrong?" Marie asked, studying her daughter's face.

Brooke hesitated. Marie knew her all too well. She'd never been able to hide anything from her mother's all-seeing gaze.

"I'm afraid so."

Every pair of eyes in the room turned toward her, coffee cups suspended in midair.

"There's no easy way to tell you this, so I'm just going to say it. Josephine is gone."

"You mean she's dead?" Felicia looked from Brooke to Gabe and then back at Brooke again.

"Yes."

"Lord Jesus!" Varina exclaimed.

"How?" Lizzie frowned. "I know she was old and sick, but she seemed fine last night."

"The Lord took her," Varina said, tears streaming down her face. She clasped her hands over her chest.

"Exactly how did Josephine die? And when?" Felicia asked.

"That's what I'd like to know," Lizzie echoed.

Marie said nothing, watching her daughter over the rim of her bone china coffee cup. The swinging door from the kitchen opened again, and Louette placed their breakfast on the table, a platter of scrambled eggs, bacon and sausages, a bowl of steaming grits, and a basket of biscuits, covered with a checked napkin. Through the open door, Brooke spied C. D. hunched over a plate of food at the kitchen table. He gave her a solemn nod, then kept eating.

But all eyes in the dining room were riveted on Brooke.

"We can't be sure, but from the looks of it, Josephine got up sometime in the night to go to the bathroom, and she tripped, maybe over one of the dogs, and fell and hit her head," Brooke said. "Louette found her there this morning, and that's when she came and woke me up."

"I thought she was just tired from being up so late last night," Louette said, wiping the palms of her hands on the skirt of her polyester uniform. "But then I heard the dogs scratching at the door wanting to get out. So I went in to take them outside, and that's when I found her . . ." She bit her lip and looked away, tears welling up in her eyes.

"Oh, Louette," Marie said. "That must have been so upsetting for you."

"Yes, ma'am," Louette said. "I ain't gonna forget that sight. Not ever." She turned and quickly left the room.

Lizzie shrugged and reached for the food, sliding bacon and eggs onto her plate. She looked askance at the steaming bowl of grits with a melting pat of butter in the middle.

"What's this? Mashed potatoes? For breakfast?"

"It's grits," Felicia said, rolling her eyes. "Your first time in the South?" She took a biscuit from the basket, sliced it, paused, then reached for the butter dish. "So that's it? Josephine is gone?" She glanced at her great-aunt. "I'm sorry, Auntie Vee."

"She was my oldest friend in the world," Varina said, dabbing at her eyes with a tissue plucked from the sleeve of her blouse. She looked out the open dining room window, past the thick green screen of overgrown azalea branches. "Josephine, she was the last of the line. All the Bettendorfs, all of them, Miss Elsie, Mr. Samuel, Mr. Gardiner, and now, Josephine. All gone. I can't believe it. And what's going to happen to this house now? To Talisa?"

"That's what I'd like to know," Lizzie said, gesturing with her fork at Gabe. "Mr. Wynant? Can you enlighten us?"

"Surely that can wait," Marie demurred. "This is hardly the time."

"Why not?" Felicia said. "Josephine invited all of us here to discuss leaving her estate to us. She told us last night, told all of us, that she wanted to make amends. And it's my understanding she intended for us to be her beneficiaries. Isn't that right, Brooke?"

"That was her intent," Brooke admitted.

"Then let's get down to brass tacks," Lizzie

said. "No disrespect or anything, but I just met the old girl for the first time last night. So it would be totally insincere of me to pretend I'm grief-stricken. She was ninety-nine years old, and she was dying. But the rest of us are alive, and I think I can speak for all of us when I say, what's next? When do we inherit?"

"Leave it to a Yankee," Felicia muttered, shaking her head.

"I'm not a Yankee. I'm a Californian, although technically, Ruth, Josephine, and Millie were all Yankees." Lizzie grabbed a biscuit from the basket and dipped it into the bowl of grits. She took a bite, chewed, and nodded. "Hmm. Not bad." She added, "Are you saying you don't care what happens to Josephine's estate, Felicia?"

"Nooo," Felicia said cautiously. "I mean, yes, I do care, but for God's sake, have some tact. The woman's body is barely even cold."

Varina sniffed loudly.

"What about funeral plans, Brooke?" Marie asked. "Do we know anything about arrangements yet?"

"No. I've notified the sheriff's office, and he and the coroner should be on the way over by now," Brooke began.

"Coroner!" Lizzie and Felicia said in unison.

"It's strictly procedural," Gabe said. "Especially in a case like this, when the, uh, deceased has met with an accident."

"So after that?" Lizzie crossed her arms over her chest.

"Assuming everything is, uh, as it should be, Mrs. Warrick will be taken to the funeral home in St. Ann's, and a death certificate will be issued."

"And then we start probate, or however you do things in Georgia, correct?" Lizzie asked. She jerked her head in Felicia's direction. "I only ask because at some point, Dweezil and I need to get back to California. I've got stories to write and deadlines to meet. It would be good if we could get all the paperwork wrapped up ASAP."

Gabe frowned and nodded meaningfully at Brooke.

"We have a problem," Brooke said.

"What kind of problem?" Felicia demanded.

"It's about the will," Brooke said slowly.

"Oh, shit. Here we go," Felicia said. "What? She changed her mind?"

"This is all my fault, so I think I'd better be the one to tell you," Gabe said. "Mrs. Warrick had every intention of leaving her estate to be put into a trust and divided among you five women — Brooke, Marie, Lizzie, Varina, and Felicia. I drafted the will as she dictated it last week, and as you know, I brought it back here yesterday for her to review and approve. Which she did."

"Thank God for that," Felicia said.

"Unfortunately . . ."

"Oh, shit," Lizzie said.

"Unfortunately, for the will to be legally binding, it had to be signed by Mrs. Warrick in the presence of two witnesses. And that, I regret to tell you, did not happen. I had every intention of sending for two witnesses first thing this morning, but as you now know, it would have been too late."

"Run that by me again?" Lizzie said. "Are you saying we don't inherit? Like, anything?"

"Yes," Gabe said, looking defeated. "That is correct. For all intents and purposes, Mrs. Warrick died intestate."

Felicia pounded the tabletop with the flat of her hand, sending coffee cups and plates bouncing and clattering. "I knew it! I knew this was just some bullshit white guilt trip."

"All because of a frigging piece of paper you didn't get signed?" Lizzie demanded. "We can fix that. Send for the witnesses now. Get Louette and that weird guy who drives the boat. Have them sign the will, backdate it, then slip them a couple of hundred bucks to keep their mouths shut, and it's all good. The will is in effect, and everybody's happy."

Gabe shook his head. "It's not that simple. For one thing, Mrs. Warrick left both Louette and C. D. bequests, which means they are ineligible to be witnesses. But more importantly, even if they hadn't been named as beneficiaries, such an action would constitute fraud, and as an officer of the court, I cannot and will not be a party to that."

"The sheriff just called. He and the coroner should be docking in a few minutes," Louette announced, returning to the dining room. "I said I'd send Shug to fetch them." She circled the table with the coffeepot, hovering quietly in the background as the unhappy news sank in.

It was Lizzie who asked the question that had already occurred to everybody.

"If none of us inherits everything, who does? Josephine didn't have any family, right?"

"Actually, she did," Brooke said. "There are a couple of distant relatives. Second or third cousins, I believe?" She looked to Varina for verification.

"Those Underwood girls." Varina frowned. "Josephine never did take to them."

"She couldn't stand those women," Louette agreed. "She always blamed them for ruining that end of the island by selling their land to the state to make a park out of it."

"Did either of you ever meet these cousins?" Gabe asked.

"Just the one time," Varina said. "Those two . . . I forget their first names . . ."

"Dorcas and Delphine," Louette put in. "But I don't know their married names."

"Ooh, yes," Varina said. "Long time ago. Josephine wouldn't even let 'em in the house. She stood right in that front doorway out there and told them they could get off her property and never come back. Then one of them started to say something about burying the hatchet and acting like family again, considering they were all cousins, and that's when she told them they'd better not hold their breath waiting on her to leave them anything, because she'd leave it all to her dogs before she gave them a single red cent," Varina said.

"But guess who'll be having the last laugh now?" Lizzie said gloomily.

"Is that right, Mr. Wynant?" Varina asked, turning to Gabe. "Will everything really go to those Double D girls? Isn't there anything you can do to stop that from happening?"

"That's for a judge to decide, but yes, barring any other claims on the estate, and if these cousins truly are her only other living relatives, that's a possibility."

"Excuse me, Mr. Wynant, but what happens in the meantime?" Louette asked. "To the house and the island and to me and Shug and C. D.? And all the folks living at Oyster Bluff? She was going to give that land back to all of us, wasn't she, Brooke?"

"Yes, that was her intent. I had all the paperwork drawn up, but again, it was never signed and witnessed."

"So we're all out of a job, and now we're fixing to get kicked out of our houses and off this island," Louette said sadly. She turned and hurried back to the kitchen.

"Isn't there anything we can do?" Brooke appealed to Gabe. "I know the law's the law, but you and I also know how Josephine wanted her estate disposed of. This all seems so heartless."

"I can petition the county to be named administrator of the estate," Gabe conceded. "If approved, I would be able to keep the staff on here, to maintain the house and grounds. That might buy us some time."

"Time to do what?" Lizzie asked, draining her coffee cup.

"I don't know," Brooke admitted. "Do some research. See if Josephine left an earlier will, anything that would keep her cousins — or ultimately the state — from taking over the island. It's a long shot, but I can tell you this — Josephine Bettendorf Warrick had been living in this house full-time since the war was over. That's nearly seventy years. And judging just from the papers she had me look through in the library, when I was trying to track you and Varina down, she was a world-class pack rat."

"Can we do that? Legally?" Felicia asked.

"Maybe." But Gabe sounded dubious.

37

"Sheriff's here," Louette said, gesturing to the man and the woman who stood in the front hallway at Shellhaven.

The man stepped forward and held out a hand to Gabe and then to Brooke. He was trim, probably midforties, with steel-framed glasses and dressed in a khaki uniform. When he removed his cap, his closely shaved head gleamed in the dim light.

"Good morning," he said. "Howard Goolsby, Carter County. And this here," he said, referring to his companion, a sturdily built middle-aged brunette dressed in civilian clothes, "is Kendra Younts, our county coroner."

After the introductions were made, Goolsby wasted no time.

"Who found the body?"

"I did," Louette said.

"And you are?"

"Louette Aycock. That was my husband, Shug, who just picked you up at the dock.

We both work for Miss Josephine."

"Can you show us?"

"Yes, sir," Louette said. "Right down this hallway."

"Will you need us?" Brooke asked, not anxious to revisit the death scene.

"Stick around, if you would. I'll need to talk to you after this," Goolsby said.

Brooke and Gabe sat on the stiff upholstered furniture in the living room.

"I feel like I'm living in the middle of an Agatha Christie novel," Brooke said, clasping and unclasping her hands.

"If Agatha Christie had ever written a book set on the Georgia coast," Gabe said.

"You don't think they'll think something . . . bad happened, right?"

"I don't see why they would," Gabe said. "This is all strictly procedural."

"This is all just so . . . bizarre," Brooke said. "I'm sorry I dragged you into this mess."

"Don't be. I'm glad I got to meet Josephine Warrick and see all of this," he said, indicating the house. "The whole story she told us last night was unbelievably fascinating. And of course, I'm glad to be working with you again, Brooke. I just wish we'd gotten that damn will executed."

She heard herself say her father's favorite phrase. One she'd always hated. "It is what it is." Brooke nodded in the direction of the closed library door. "Yeah. About that. Should we mention Russell Strickland to the sheriff?"

"God, no," Gabe said quickly. "It's just a story, right? No need to muddy the water, especially since we have no firsthand knowledge of what happened back then."

"That's what I hoped you'd say," Brooke said. "I also don't want to drag Varina into any kind of trouble since, as far as we know, she's the only living witness to . . . that night."

The library door opened, and Louette emerged. "They want to talk to y'all," she said.

Brooke was relieved to see that a blanket had been placed over Josephine's body. Kendra Younts was busily dumping Josephine's medications into a plastic bag, and Sheriff Goolsby was sitting on the chintz wing chair, scribbling in a small notebook.

"Y'all can come in," he said without looking up from his notes. "Just finishing up here."

"Okay, Howard," Kendra said. "I'm gonna bring in the stretcher if you're all set here."

"All set," the sheriff said.

He looked up at Brooke and seemed puzzled. "You look awful familiar. Have we met before?"

"Probably. I'm a lawyer, and I think our paths have crossed at the courthouse."

He snapped his fingers. "Now I got it. You're Brittni Miles's lawyer, right?"

"Afraid so," Brooke said, laughing. "But please don't judge me by my clients."

"I'll try not to," Goolsby said. "That is one crazy little gal, though. You know she went on a hunger strike because my deputies wouldn't bring her a Diet Dr. Pepper?"

"She's still in your jail? I thought her stepfather was going to bail her out."

"Not yet. If he doesn't come get her pretty soon, though, we're fixing to take up a collection and bail her out ourselves." He closed his notebook and rested it on one knee. "What's your connection to Mrs. Warrick?"

"She hired me a couple of weeks ago, in a legal capacity, to help her find the heirs of her oldest friends. And she also wanted me to draw up a new will."

"And did you do that?"

"We ran into some complications. It turns out that one of the people she wanted to leave a bequest to, the daughter of her late best friend, is my mother, Marie Trappnell. Which is why she hired me in the first place. Once I realized we had a conflict, I suggested she hire Gabe, who I used to work for in Savannah."

Goolsby nodded at Gabe Wynant. "Savannah, huh? You know Wayne duBose?"

"I know Sheriff duBose quite well," Gabe said. "We're in Rotary Club together."

"Wayne's a good man," Goolsby said. "Comes down here fishing with me when he can get away from the big city." He tapped his notebook with a pen. "I think we're about set here. I'd heard Mrs. Warrick was terminally ill, and the housekeeper confirmed that. She was on some pretty strong new pain meds, is that right?"

"Yes."

"And she consumed some alcohol at dinner last night, even though the housekeeper warned her against mixing the pills with alcohol?"

"That's correct," Gabe said. "We finished dinner around ten o'clock, and I helped her from the dining room because she was somewhat unsteady on her feet."

"Did she seem okay, otherwise?"

"She was groggy," Brooke said.

"And there were some dogs in here? The housekeeper mentioned she might have tripped over them?"

"Two Chihuahuas," Brooke said. "Teeny and Tiny. You rarely saw Josephine without those dogs at her feet. I guess Louette must have put them in another room now. But they were here this morning when I came down."

"Okay, then," Goolsby said. "Kendra and I agree, this is a textbook accidental death, likely alcohol-and-drug-related. Hell of a way for the old lady to go, though. She was pretty much a legend around here. Her family did a lot of good in this county."

"She told me her father was always very community-minded, even though he wasn't originally from here," Brooke said.

"That was way before my time, of course, but my granddaddy used to talk about what a fine person Mr. Bettendorf was. What happens to all of this now?" Goolsby asked. "She never had any kids, did she?"

"No children, no close surviving family," Gabe said. "And unfortunately, as far as we can tell, she died intestate."

Goolsby blinked. "I thought you said you did her will."

"I did, but she died before it could be witnessed."

The door opened, and Kendra Younts wheeled in a gleaming chrome collapsible stretcher.

"Son of a bitch," the sheriff said.

Gabe pointed at the stretcher. "That might not be necessary. Mrs. Warrick specified that she wanted to be buried in the family plot here on the island. According to Louette, she even has a handmade casket out in the barn. So why transport the body over to the mainland when it's just going to end up back here?"

"That's a pretty unusual request," Kendra said.

Brooke imagined the coroner mentally calculating the amount of money her family's funeral home would not be billing to Josephine's estate. No transport. No embalming or cremation. No bronze coffin, no visitation in the Younts Mortuary's Palmetto Parlor, no hearse . . .

"Josephine Warrick was a pretty unusual woman," the sheriff said. He nodded at Kendra. "We're agreed it's an accidental death, but I think we might want to touch base with her doctors to confirm their diagnosis of her illness and all. So we'll go ahead and take her over to the morgue at the hospital just in case. Afterward, we can release the body to be brought back over here."

"That sounds reasonable," Brooke agreed.

"First thing Monday, I'll petition with the court to be named administrator of the estate," Gabe said. He stood and handed business cards to the sheriff and the coroner. "Please let me know if you have any questions, and of course, I'd appreciate it if you could notify me when the death certificate is ready."

Brooke quickly left the room before they began transferring Josephine to the stretcher. The dining room was empty and had been cleared of all traces of breakfast. When she went looking for more coffee, she found Louette and Shug standing in the kitchen. Shug had his arm around his wife's waist, and Louette's head rested on his shoulder. Their backs were to her, but she could hear Louette's racking sobs from where she stood.

She backed out of the room to leave them alone with their grief.

She was walking back toward the living room when she heard scratching and whining from behind another door.

Brooke opened the door slightly, and Teeny and Tiny came scrambling out, barking indignantly and flinging themselves at her ankles.

On an impulse, she scooped them both up and cradled one under each arm. "Hey, girls," she crooned. "Poor little girls. I guess we sort of forgot about you in all this excitement."

One of the dogs raised her head up and began licking Brooke's neck. She read the tag on the collar. "So you're Tiny." She held the dog at arm's length. "How am I gonna tell you apart from your sister? Oh, okay. Your ears are way longer than Teeny's. And no offense, but you've kind of got an overbite. How did I miss that?"

The back door opened, and C. D. poked his head inside the hallway and cleared his throat.

"Hey, uh, Brooke. Can I talk to you for a minute?"

"Of course. Did you already take the sheriff back to the dock?"

"Yeah. Them and Josephine."

"I probably need to let the girls outside for

a potty break," Brooke said. "Can we talk outside?"

"Yeah. That'd be okay."

It took her eyes a moment to adjust to the dazzling sunlight after the dim half-light of the house. The moment she set the dogs down, they ran straight for a clump of oleander bushes at the edge of the veranda.

Brooke pointed at a rusting wrought iron table and two chairs. It was the only furniture left on what must have once been a beautiful spot overlooking the ocean. The slate tiles were crumbling, with weeds poking up through the cracks. Still, a fine breeze ruffled the palms at the edge of the low wall, bringing the scent of gardenias blooming in what was left of the garden just beyond.

She studied C. D., who sat stiffly, staring out at the ocean. He still wore his ever-present oversized aviator sunglasses, but today he was dressed in a loose-fitting short-sleeved shirt, tucked neatly into a pair of baggy jeans whose hems just brushed the top of his bare brown feet. This, she realized, was as dressed up as she'd ever seen him.

"What's on your mind?" she asked finally.

He looked at her now. "This morning, I was out in the kitchen, and I heard y'all talking about Josephine and how she didn't have no close kin or nuthin'."

"That's right," Brooke said. "If you're worried about your job, though —"

"The thing is, she does have kin."

"Yes, we know about the cousins, and they'll be notified —"

"I'm not talking about the cousins. I'm talking about me." He thumped his bony chest and raised his glasses to look her straight in the eye. "Me. I'm Josephine's son. I reckon that's about as close a kin as you can get."

38

May 1942

"You're the doctor? Thank God!" The woman who'd met him at the door was wrapped in a thin cotton bathrobe and didn't wait for his answer. "She's having an awful time. Please hurry."

Thomas Carlyle was getting accustomed to receiving urgent phone calls in the middle of the night. All the younger physicians in Savannah, even the middle-aged ones, had enlisted in the war effort in the immediate aftermath of Pearl Harbor. But he was in his seventies, and his fondness for gin was well known among a certain clientele in the city.

Still, he was surprised to be summoned to this particular address. It was a handsome, pale pink double town house on one of the most fashionable blocks of West Jones Street, so he'd dressed for the occasion; his only black suit, too large for him now and full of moth holes, and a heavily starched white dress shirt, although no necktie. He was poised to ring the bell when the door opened.

He heard the moans and shrieks as soon as he began to climb the narrow stairs, which did nothing to quicken his steps. He'd heard it all hundreds of times before, and in his experience, babies took their own time.

He found the patient stretched out on a bed with an elaborate mahogany carved headboard. She'd thrown off most of the bed-covers and was thrashing around on the mattress, wild-eyed and clearly terrified. Her face, neck, and narrow arms were slick with sweat. Blood pooled on the white sheets.

"How long has this been going on?" Carlyle asked. He removed his suit coat, tossed it onto a chair, rolled up his shirtsleeves, and opened the satchel he kept packed by his front door.

"The labor pains started around two this afternoon," the woman said, leaning down to stroke the younger woman's hair. She crooned something inaudible, which seemed to calm the patient a little.

"And how far along is she?"

"Maybe seven months? It's too early, I know. The bleeding won't stop. I didn't know there would be so much blood."

"She should have been taken to a hospital hours ago," Carlyle said, frowning down at the patient.

"I told you, that's not possible."

"No!" the patient cried. "No hospitals. My

mother died in the hospital." Her eyes widened again, and she cried out as another wave of contractions racked her body.

He sighed and reached into the satchel, bringing out a small clear vial and a hypodermic needle, which he set on the table beside the bed. He rummaged around again and brought out a brown paper packet of cotton balls. "Damn it," he muttered. He reached for his jacket and extracted a half-empty pint of gin from the inside pocket.

Carlyle uncapped the gin and dribbled some on the cotton ball. He stuck the hypodermic in the vial of liquid, drew back the plunger and flicked the tube once, twice with a forefinger, to dispel any air bubbles.

He nodded at the woman. "I'll need you to hold her down for a moment."

"I'll try," she whispered, standing to lean across the bed.

"Noooo!" the patient cried.

"Just a small prick," he said pleasantly. "Then you'll have a nice sleep, and when you wake up, this will all be over."

Her body tensed as another contraction began, and she writhed in pain.

"Hold her down!" he barked, and he jabbed the needle into her arm.

When he emerged from the bedroom, he carried a tiny, squalling infant wrapped in a pillowcase.

"It's a boy," Dr. Carlyle said, thrusting the baby into the woman's arms.

"Healthy?" She looked down at the beet-red infant. "He's so tiny."

"Because he's too early," Carlyle said. His shirt was sweat-soaked and clung to his chest, his forearms were flecked with blood, and his white hair was plastered to his skull.

"Where's the bathroom? I need to wash up."

"Just there." She pointed to the next door. "And how is she?" The woman gazed anxiously through the open doorway where the patient lay unconscious atop a mound of blood-soaked sheets and towels.

"She'll live. But there won't be any more surprise pregnancies, I'll tell you that."

"Just as well," she murmured.

She heard water running. She looked down at the baby, no bigger than an undersized roasting hen. She didn't particularly like babies, but she felt a strange pang of sympathy for this one. She touched a tentative finger to his fist, and he stopped crying, grabbed hold, and clung on with a surprising ferocity.

Carlyle was wiping his hands on a clean towel. "You'll want to wash her properly when she wakes up, keep the incision clean, watch that she doesn't run a fever, which is a sign of infection. If she does seem feverish, call me immediately before she becomes septic."

"And what about the baby?"

"What about it?"

The woman looked down at the now sleeping infant and then pointed with her chin toward the bedroom. "She's not married, you know. If anybody found out . . ."

He yawned, impatient to get home to his bed. "What are you trying to say?"

She bit her lip. "It would be better if she thought . . . well, if she thought the baby died."

Carlyle bristled and feigned shock, though in his line of work this was a very old story.

"What if we could find somebody to take care of it?" the woman went on.

"What are you suggesting?"

"Surely there are orphanages?"

"This baby is not an orphan," he said. "In any case, orphanages require paperwork. Questions would be asked."

"Oh."

He looked at her, waiting, expectant.

She sighed and went for her pocketbook. He took the money without comment.

The woman slumped with exhaustion. He considered her, considered his surroundings. He knew the owner of this house, had even socialized with him, in long-ago, happier times. Money would not be an issue for this family. If he could provide the answers to nosy questions, perhaps everybody's problems would be solved.

"I know a couple," he said slowly.

When he left, he took the sleeping infant with him, bundled in a wicker shopping basket. She went into the bedroom and began gathering up the soiled linens. Carlyle's gin bottle stood on the nightstand, empty now.

39

Gabe Wynant was getting accustomed to the unexpected that day at Shellhaven. But nothing could have readied him for the story he was about to hear in the library-turned-bedroom so recently vacated by Josephine Bettendorf Warrick.

Brooke caught him as he took the last stair. He was dressed and ready to leave, his briefcase again tucked under his arm.

"What now?" he said, noting the grim expression on her face.

She glanced upward, toward the second floor. "Where are the others?"

"I heard lots of cursing coming from Lizzie's bedroom. And the cat was yowling, so it's a good guess they're getting ready to leave. I think Felicia and Varina went out somewhere with Louette."

"I think you'd better come with me," she said.

C. D. had seated himself in the recliner and

was idly leafing through a leather-bound book he'd picked at random from one of the bookcases.

"You remember C. D.," she told Gabe.

"Yes?" Gabe said, leaning against the doorjamb.

"C. D., could you please tell my colleague what you just told me?"

"You mean the part where I tell him I'm Josephine's son?" C. D. seemed pleased to have a story worth telling and retelling.

Gabe blinked and looked at Brooke for her reaction. She nodded. "Yes. And start from the beginning, please."

"Which beginning? You mean how she dropped me off at the orphanage in Savannah when I was just a baby? Not even a month old? And bribed them nuns to keep me and not tell anybody she'd had a bastard? Or do you want me to begin when I got too old to stay with the little kiddies, so they packed me off to Good Shepherd Home for Boys?"

"Whoa. Whoa!" Gabe exclaimed. "She? You are referring to Josephine Warrick?"

"Who else?" C. D. asked.

"You're telling me you are Josephine Warrick's son?"

"And only living heir," C. D. said. He picked up a pen and extended it toward the lawyer. "Write it all down if you want, 'cause it's all true and I can prove it."

40

C. D. folded his sunglasses and placed them in his breast pocket. His pale blue eyes flickered around the library, taking inventory, finally resting on the side-by-side oil portraits of Josephine and Preiss Warrick.

Preiss was posed casually in a tweed jacket, sitting on a tree stump, with a shotgun propped in the crook of his elbow. His left hand rested on the head of a black-and-white English setter who had a dead bird clenched between its jaws. Preiss had been a handsome man, with a narrow, bony face, deep-set eyes, and full lips. The painting's backdrop was a romanticized version of Talisa with moss-draped oaks, blue sky, and puffy cotton-candy clouds.

Josephine appeared to have been costumed for a fancy dress party in her portrait, in a floor-length emerald-green satin dress, triple strands of pearls, and a full-length mink tossed artfully around her shoulders. The backdrop matched the portrait of her husband, right down to the tree stump and the trailing Spanish moss. But in Josephine's portrait the setter was curled up, asleep at her feet.

C. D. drummed his fingertips on the leather-bound book cover.

"We're waiting," Gabe said, tiring of the dramatics.

"You were raised at Good Shepherd? In Savannah?" Brooke asked. Like most in Savannah, she knew that the former children's home, founded in pre–Revolutionary War times, was considered the oldest child-caring institution in the country.

"Back in my day, it was called Good Shepherd Home for Boys," C. D. said. "They changed the name along the way. But I didn't get sent over to Good Shepherd until the nuns closed up the orphanage I'd been in. St. Joseph's Foundling Home, it was called."

"Never heard of it," Gabe said flatly. "And I'm Catholic, and I was raised in Savannah."

C. D. shrugged. "You probably never heard of it, 'cause like I said, the nuns closed it up a long time ago. It was on Habersham Street, right where there's a grocery store today. They shut St. Joe's down sometime in the fifties, but they kept on running the girls' orphanage. I reckon they decided boys were too much trouble."

"How does Josephine Warrick figure into all of this?" Gabe asked.

"How do you think? She got herself knocked up. And she wasn't married, either, so she did what rich girls did back then. She paid somebody to take the kid — that's me — off her hands. The nuns took me in, then when I was five, they shipped me out to Good Shepherd."

C. D.'s mouth smiled, but his eyes were wary. "And that's where I stayed, working on that damn cattle farm of theirs, until I got into trouble, and then I ran away before they could bounce me out."

"How old were you when you left Good Shepherd?" Brooke asked.

"Sixteen."

"And where did you finish high school?"

That smile again. "Who says I did? I was on my own, had to get a job, which I did. After a while, I was sick of Savannah, so I hitchhiked clear out to California and then back east. I ran into a recruiter in Baton Rouge, after an all-night bender, who promised me that I'd see the world if I signed up for the marines. Next thing I know, I'm at Parris Island, then right after that, I started seeing the world with the Third Marine Division in Vietnam."

C. D. rolled up his shirtsleeve to display the tattoo on his bicep. "Semper fi, motherfucker." He nodded at Gabe Wynant. "How 'bout you? Did you ever serve?"

"Nope. I turned eighteen in '72, but I had

a student deferment," Gabe said.

"College boy," C. D. said. "Figures."

"I suppose you have some proof that Josephine Warrick was your birth mother?" Gabe asked. "Adoption records, birth certificate, something like that?"

C. D.'s smile dimmed a bit. "That ain't how it worked back then. Everything was hush-hush."

"Okay, what proof do you have?" Brooke asked. She couldn't decide whether she was intrigued or horrified by C. D.'s unfolding story. A little of both, probably. "It's not up to us, but a judge is going to want proof of the validity of your claim."

C. D. leaned forward and brought out a worn leather billfold that was attached by a chain to his belt. He slid a packet of papers from the billfold and smoothed them out across his knees.

He held out a photocopy of a black-and-white newspaper photo of a small child of no more than two or three, dressed in cotton print pajamas and holding a toy truck, balanced on the knee of a woman who was looking away from the camera. "That's me," he said, tapping the image of the child. "And that's Josephine."

"Can I see that?"

C. D. passed the clipping to Gabe Wynant, who examined it closely and then handed it to Brooke.

The newspaper photo was date-stamped SAVANNAH MORNING NEWS, June 18, 1945. The woman in the photo was dressed in a dark dress, with a frivolous feathered hat perched on her dark hair. She held the child stiffly at arm's length from her chest.

LOCAL BENEFACTRESS VISITS CHILDREN'S HOME, the caption read. Underneath, the copy said:

> Miss Josephine Bettendorf distributed smiles and Christmas gifts to orphaned boys this week at the St. Joseph's Foundling Home. Three-year-old Charles Anthony delighted in receiving a new toy truck.

Brooke studied C. D.'s face.

"Charles Anthony is me," he said. "And I still got that truck."

"That's an amazing coincidence," Gabe said. "But Josephine was probably just doing what wealthy socialites did back then. It was a charity visit, not a mother-son reunion."

"No way," C. D. said. "She came to that home every year while I was there, at Christmas. She handed out candy and toothbrushes and pajamas to them other kids. But I was the only one who got a real toy." He leaned forward, showing off a narrow white scar that ran through his left eyebrow. "Some other kid tried to take my truck the last year I was at the orphanage. I slugged him, and he hit me with the truck, which is how I got this scar and how he lost his two front teeth."

"Sorry, but that's not really proof that you were her child," Gabe said. "Maybe she just thought you were cute, or she felt sorry for you."

"I figured you'd say something like that," C. D. said. He leafed through the packet of papers on his lap and held up another document. It was a photocopy of a typed page.

"Now this here is what's called the intake report from St. Joseph's. The sister in charge filled it out when they took in a kid. This is a copy of my intake page. Take a look at that, why don't you?"

Brooke scooted her chair next to Gabe's, peering over his shoulder. There were spaces on the page for the date, name, and address of parent or parents, child's name and date of birth, weight, height, eye and hair color, and race. At the bottom, a space was reserved for comments.

According to the report, on May 5, 1942, a male child named Charles D. Anthony arrived at the orphanage. Weight was eleven pounds, six ounces. The child's hair color was listed as brown. Eye color: blue. Race: W. In the spaces for the child's mother and father, someone had typed *Unknown.* Also unknown were the child's exact date of birth, although someone had typed *Approx. six months of age.*

The comments block had been filled out in

Spenserian black script.

> Father Ryan brought male child to home last Sunday, stated he was found asleep, under pew, in church today, after 8:00 A.M. mass. No parishioners have any knowledge of child. Father stated hopes parent will return to claim child, but fears child has been abandoned. The boy is docile, in good health. Father Ryan believes that boy was born out of wedlock. Mother Superior advises we will accept child pending further investigation.

"Somebody left a child? A six-month-old baby in a church?" Brooke said, aghast.

"Yeah. That was me," C. D. said. "Turns out since they didn't know my real name, they named me after that priest. Charles David. For a last name, they gave me the name of one of the nun's favorite saints, which was St. Anthony." He chuckled. "Can you imagine that? Me named after a saint?"

Brooke found herself speechless, pondering the reality of C. D.'s childhood. She'd always known who she was, who her people were, and who *their* people were. Family and a sense of family identity were ingrained in every Southerner she knew, especially Savannahians, who were obsessed with family connections. What would it be like to wonder your entire life who you really were?

"How did you find out about all of this?" Brooke asked. "Or did you always know about the orphanage?"

C. D. rubbed the gray stubble on his chin. "I always remembered bits and pieces from the time I was in the orphanage. Like how us little kids all slept in one big room, with rows and rows of these iron cribs that had high sides so you couldn't climb out. Even when we got older and were big enough to sleep in a real bed, they kept us in those cribs, almost like a cage, you know?"

Brooke thought guiltily about the crib her own Henry had been sleeping in until recently. Would he too remember, someday, and wonder if he had been kept a prisoner there?

"How were you able to track down these records?" Gabe asked.

"That's kind of a funny coincidence," C. D. said. "After I came home from Vietnam, I'd been living in Savannah off and on for about twenty years. Retired there, after working as a longshoreman out at the Port Authority, and I knew a couple of guys, like me, who were Good Shepherd alumni. One of 'em told me about a reunion they were having a couple of years ago. It was the home's 275th anniversary. So I went along out there, 'cause I was curious to see how the place had changed."

"I imagine there's been quite a bit of change since you lived there," Gabe offered.

"Yeah, the 'cottage' I lived in, it's some kind of classroom now," C. D. said. "The whole place is a boys' prep school now, 'cause you really don't have a lot of honest-to-God orphans these days."

"My mom has a friend whose father and two brothers grew up at Good Shepherd, back in the Depression years," Brooke said. "Their father had died, and their mother had to work and couldn't care for three boys. So she kept his sisters and the boys were raised at the Children's home."

"That happened a lot," C. D. said. "Anyway, at the reunion party, I ran into a guy who lived in my cottage. He was a couple of years older than me, but like me, he'd been at St. Joseph's before Good Shepherd. And he was telling me that he'd been able to look up his records. In the church office. I forget what they call it."

"The archdiocesan office," Gabe said. "All the diocesan records were moved there after the girls' orphanage was closed and remodeled."

C. D. snapped his fingers. "Yeah, that's what it's called. Anyway, they won't let you look at the records unless you can prove you were what they call a former 'resident.' I told the woman there, 'Hell, I wasn't a resident, I was an orphan.' " He rattled the papers on his lap. "That's where I found all this stuff." He smoothed the newspaper clipping. "They let me look in my file. How about that? I found this clipping. And when I saw the picture of *her* holding me on her lap, something clicked. And I remembered her. How she come to see me, every year, at Christmas, and on my birthday, or what they told me was my birthday. I remembered she smelled like some kind of flowery perfume. And she had a pearl necklace, and I tried to play with it, but she'd slap my hand away."

C. D. paused in his story. "Now you tell me, why would she come see some little kid in an orphanage, bring him presents and all like that, unless she had a connection to him?"

"Good question," Gabe conceded.

"When you came to work here, did you tell Josephine you thought she was your mother?" Brooke asked.

He shook his head emphatically. "No. Because I wasn't sure yet. I kinda wanted to get the lay of the land, check things out. I came over on the ferry, talked to Shug and asked about a job, and he's the one brought me up to the house and told Josephine maybe I could run the boat and help with some other stuff around here."

"And she never recognized you? Didn't recognize your name?" Gabe sounded skeptical. "Come on, C. D. This is an entertaining story, but none of it proves that you are her son or her heir."

"How about this?" C. D. asked. He handed over a faded color snapshot of a brick cottage surrounded by towering oaks similar to the ones on Talisa. Brooke squinted to read a plaque.

"That's the Samuel Bettendorf Cottage at Good Shepherd," C. D. said. "I looked it up in the records. Josephine donated the money for it to be built in 1946 — the year I got put over there once they closed the orphanage."

"And what do you think that signifies?" Gabe asked.

"It means she felt guilty about walking away and giving me up," C. D. said, throwing up his hands in exasperation. "Hell, I can't explain why she did the stuff she did. I just know I am her son, and after all these years, it's about damn time she did right by me."

He looked from Brooke to Gabe, then back at Brooke again, and then donned his sunglasses. "Kinda upsets your apple cart, don't it? You and your mom and those women upstairs? Looks like none of y'all are gonna be heiresses after all."

Brooke shrugged. She didn't know what to say or how to feel. Just the night before, the mistress of Shellhaven had shocked them all by telling them about a murder that had happened nearly eighty years ago, right here on this island. This morning, Josephine was dead, her estate left in limbo. Horror, grief, shock, disbelief. And now this. She was numb.

She stood up and held out a hand to C. D. "Good luck to you, C. D. I hope you're able to prove your claim. And I truly mean that. If Josephine really did walk away and leave you in an orphanage all those years ago, you deserve to inherit. But in the meantime, I need to get back to the mainland. To my own son."

41

They found Marie and Lizzie in the kitchen, having lunch. Louette looked up from the sandwich she was eating.

"Did C. D. tell y'all that crazy story of his? 'Bout how he's Josephine's son?"

"What's that?" Marie asked, startled. "You mean C. D., the man who pilots the boat? He's Josephine's son?"

"That's what *he* thinks." Louette's voice dripped scorn. She stood up and motioned for Brooke to take her chair. "Sit here. You want some lunch? I got chicken salad and crab salad."

Gabe dragged a chair up to the table. "I'd love a crab salad sandwich."

"I'm not really hungry," Brooke said. "But if it's all right, I'd like to call the ferry to book a ride back to the mainland."

"Oh, I already took care of that," Louette said. "You're on the two o'clock, if that's all right."

Brooke gestured to Lizzie. "Will that give

us enough time to get you to the airport for your flight back to California?"

Lizzie reached for a potato chip from the bowl in the center of the table. "I'm not going home. Not just yet. I canceled my flight."

"But . . . I thought you were in such a rush to get back. For your deadline and everything," Brooke said.

"I was, until last night, when Josephine started spinning that amazing story of hers, and then, after what happened this morning, it dawned on me, there's a story right here. Like, a once-in-a-lifetime story. And I'm a part of it. So instead of packing this morning, I pounded out a query letter and emailed it to a couple of magazine editors I know in New York, and I heard back from one right away, and she loves the idea. So I'm staying."

"Here?" Gabe asked. "At Shellhaven?"

"Why not? Louette doesn't have a problem with that, do you, Louette?"

"Be nice to have company, especially with Josephine gone," Louette said.

"Do you have a problem with me staying here?" Lizzie asked Gabe pointedly.

"No. I mean, as I said, I'll petition the court to be named administrator of the estate, but in the meantime, I guess there's no reason you couldn't stay on."

"Then it's settled," Lizzie said. "Now what's all this about C. D.? He really claims he's Josephine's long-lost son?"

While Gabe polished off two crab salad sandwiches, a homemade pickle, and a couple of tea cakes, Brooke recited what the lawyers had just heard from C. D.

"This story just keeps getting better and better," Lizzie said, rubbing her hands together gleefully. "Josephine, an unwed mother! Now it's not just a magazine article or a book. We're talking potential movie deal."

"I wouldn't go that far," Gabe said, brushing cookie crumbs from the front of his golf shirt. "I hated to burst the guy's bubble, but an old newspaper clipping of her holding a little orphaned tyke at Christmas probably isn't going to hold water in court."

"That man is crazy," Louette said, shaking her head. "I never heard a story so crazy. Even if it were true, don't you think Josephine would have recognized her own flesh and blood?"

"It does strain the imagination," Marie said. "Abandoning a baby in a church? And then going to the orphanage every year at Christmas to visit him? How could anybody be that cruel? Even Josephine?"

Varina pushed her walker slowly into the kitchen, with Felicia following behind. "Is Josephine . . . gone? Did the funeral home man come?"

"Yes, but actually, the coroner is a woman. Her family owns the funeral home too. They took her body back over to the mainland, just until the funeral arrangements can be made," Gabe said, scrambling to his feet to offer his chair to the old woman.

"But they'll bring her back, won't they?" Varina asked anxiously.

"Yes, I understand those were her wishes," Gabe said.

"Auntie Vee, you need to eat some lunch before we get on the ferry so your blood sugar doesn't get too low," Felicia said.

"I got her a nice sandwich right here," Louette said, sliding a plate of food in front of Varina.

"She's all the time fussing over me," Varina told Marie. "Does Brooke fuss at you like that?"

"Usually not," Marie said. "More likely I'm fussing at her."

"What time does that ferry leave?" Varina asked, nibbling on her sandwich.

"Not 'til two, so you've got plenty of time to eat," Louette said.

"Then maybe Shug will take us by the old place at Oyster Bluff first." Varina looked across the table at Brooke. "Have you been over to Oyster Bluff yet?"

"No, ma'am," Brooke said. "I've heard a lot about it, though."

"I'd love to see it," Lizzie said. "Research for my magazine article. What is this Oyster Bluff place?"

"It's my home. Where my people have always lived," Varina said, her voice quivering slightly. "Where I'm going to stay, 'til the good Lord decides to take me."

"Maybe someday," Felicia said with a vague smile.

"Not someday. This day," Varina said, her face serene. "I was reading my Bible just now, and the scripture spoke to me, clear as a bell. Isaiah. This island here is my home, where I am fixing to stay until such time as my Father takes me to his home."

"Now, Auntie, we have talked about this," Felicia said. "You're living with me now, because the doctors say you've got to have somebody to make sure you eat and take your medicine."

Varina nodded and ignored her great-niece. "Louette, could you please ask Shug to ride us over to Oyster Bluff in that fancy new truck of his before these ladies need to take the ferry back?"

Louette reached for the phone. "I'll call him right now."

Shug turned off the paved main road onto a wide shell road. Varina was propped up next to him, and Brooke sat by the window. Lizzie, Marie, and a grumbling Felicia sat in the second row of cab seats.

Varina pointed to a wide, weedy pasture area surrounded by cypress and oak trees. A pair of rusted-out trucks were parked at the edge of the field along with a tractor that leaned crazily on rotted tires. "That there is part of the old plantation, where they grew cotton and sugarcane. It was way before my time, of course, but my grandmama used to talk about working in that field."

"What was the plantation called?" Lizzie asked from the backseat. "Did the Bettendorfs own it?"

"Oh no. Mr. Samuel didn't buy the island until long after plantation times." Varina turned to her great-niece. "What did they call that place, honey?"

"Friendship," Felicia said. "Great name for a business that bought and sold slaves, don't you think?"

Shug turned the truck in a wide arc around the pasture, and in half a mile the small community came into view. A hand-painted sign tacked to a tree proclaimed, "Historic Oyster Bluff. Pop. 45."

"More like twenty. Or twenty-five on a good day," he observed. He slowed the truck over the rutted dirt road as two chickens raced across it. Varina pointed to a long, low, wood-frame building with a rusted tin roof. Six or seven junked cars were parked haphazardly in the crushed-shell parking lot, their hoods up, weeds growing out from broken windshields.

"What's up with all the abandoned cars?"

Lizzie asked.

"Costs fifty dollars to barge a vehicle back over to the mainland," Shug said. "If it can't be fixed, that car dies right here."

"That's the old commissary," Varina said, pointing to the building. "Back when I was a child, Mr. Samuel paid all his people in script we called 'Bettendorf Bucks.' You could use it like money to buy whatever you needed. We didn't need much back then. Everybody had a garden, and we fished in the creek, raked oysters. My daddy knew how to knit a cast net, so we had as much shrimp as we wanted. There's wild cows on the island, and every year, my daddy and brothers would catch one, fatten him up, and then butcher it. They hunted too; deer and hogs and turkey and dove. But it was a big treat when I used to take my little bit of money to the commissary and buy candy and Coca-Colas."

"One of Louette's cousins runs it now, we just call it the Store," Shug said. "It ain't open except Thursday through Sunday, and that's only if he's sober and out of jail."

He turned down another lane and pointed proudly to a snug cottage with a wide front porch that looked out onto the marsh. Baskets of ferns and geraniums hung from the ceiling beams, and a carport housed another car and a golf cart.

"That's our place. I built that front porch so we can sit out there and watch the sunset.

Got me a deck on the back where I do my grilling. Louette wants me to put in a new kitchen, but we were waiting to see if Miss Josephine was gonna let us buy the place back before we put any more money in it." His shoulders sagged, and he passed a hand over his jaw. "Don't know what will happen now."

The truck rolled slowly down the road, passing half a dozen small homes in various states of disrepair, while Varina provided a running commentary of residents past and present. "That's the Johnsons, but I think they all moved off. That there was where the preacher used to live. This house right here is where my best little friend Marjean lived. Her mama was real sweet to me, because I didn't have a mama of my own. Miss Stokes had the best garden on this whole island. Grew the sweetest corn and the prettiest flowers you ever saw."

"How'd she keep the deer and hogs from eating everything up?" Shug asked.

"Ooh, she had her a stout wooden fence all around that garden plot, and she had a big mean dog, Mitzi, would scare anything away that came near," Varina said, laughing.

Shug pulled the truck in front of a small wooden tin-roofed cottage. Faded green paint peeked from behind thickly festooned vines that threatened to swallow the house whole. The front porch columns were whitewashed tree trunks, and the windows on either side of the front door were boarded up with plywood.

"This is my house," Varina said, her eyes glowing with pride. "My daddy built it with his own two hands. He cut the trees down and milled the planks right here on this island. Mr. Samuel counted on my daddy. He sold him the land for our house, and I been keeping up with the taxes all this time."

"It must be a really special place for you," Marie said from the backseat.

"It's adorable," Lizzie said, peering out the window at the cottage. "It's like one of those tiny houses they show on HGTV. I wish I could move in here myself."

Felicia glared at Lizzie and silently mouthed the word, *"Nooooo."*

"Yes, ma'am," Varina said. "And now I'm fixing to move right back home."

"Here?" Felicia's voice was panicky. "I know it's special, but look at this place, Auntie. It's falling down."

"Then I'll fix it back up." Varina patted Shug's arm. "This man here can do anything. You'll help me, won't you, baby?"

"Why not?" He opened the door and planted one boot onto the weedy yard and appraised the house with a thoughtful eye. "This house has been standing all this time, so it must be sound. Gonna need a new roof, though."

"You can't stay here," Felicia insisted. "Does it even have plumbing? Or electricity? Tell her, Shug."

"It actually does have plumbing. And electricity, although we probably need to update the panel. Homer was living here until he got too sick and moved over to hospice. It hasn't been empty but a couple of years."

"Okay, but it's gonna need a lot of work before it's even remotely habitable. It'll probably take months and months. And where will you stay in the meantime? You can't get up and down the stairs at Josephine's house."

"Plenty of room at our place," Shug said. "The kids and grandkids hardly come over at all anymore 'cause they've got sports and all that. Louette's gonna be getting lonesome without having Josephine to look after and cook for."

"Oh no, we couldn't put you out," Felicia started.

"We got two guest rooms. Plenty of room for both of y'all," Shug said.

"Thank you, baby," Varina said, beaming at her benefactor.

"Auntie, that's just not possible," Felicia said. "It's sweet of Shug to offer, but I'm your caregiver, and I have to work."

Varina's jaw set stubbornly. "Didn't you tell me you do all your teaching on a computer now? And don't they have computers and all that here on Talisa?"

"Yes, ma'am, we got Wi-Fi here," Shug said. "Me and Louette FaceTime the grandkids all the time on our computer."

"See that?" Varina nodded enthusiastically. "So it's all set, then. We can go on back to Jacksonville today and pack up our stuff and then be back for the morning ferry. Isn't that a blessing?"

Lizzie grinned and poked Felicia in the ribs. "Sounds like a blessing to me."

42

The ferry was waiting at the dock, along with a crowd of three dozen passengers — campers, day-trippers, and a group of middle-aged birdwatchers bristling with cameras, binoculars, and backpacks. Brooke was surprised to see just how large the ferry was, a gleaming white affair with two observation decks, with the name painted in large letters across the stern: *The Miss Elsie Bettendorf.*

"I wonder if that was Josephine's mother," Marie said as the group approached the boarding dock.

"That's right. Miss Elsie was Josephine's mama," Varina said, coming slowly up beside them. "Those state people thought they were buttering Josephine up, naming the ferry after Miss Elsie, but that made her madder than a mule with a mouthful of bumblebees. She wrote all kind of letters trying to make them change the name, but it was too late. She wouldn't even get near this new ferry, no matter what."

"I guess it's a good thing Josephine's not still alive to know that her final trip across the river was on *The Miss Elsie,*" Felicia said.

"Ooh, child," Varina said, chuckling despite herself. "She'd come back and haunt us all."

They found an empty row of shaded wooden seats on the first deck.

"Remind me why you're going back across to the mainland, since you're staying on at Shellhaven?" Felicia asked Lizzie.

"Supplies," Lizzie said, ticking off her list. "Cat food for Dweezil, a few more clothes, including a bathing suit, since I only packed enough stuff for the weekend, white wine, tequila, Xanax . . . just the basics."

Felicia cocked her head and regarded Lizzie with real interest. "So you're going to write a magazine article about Josephine and Talisa? Seriously? Who'd want to read about some backwater island in the middle of nowhere?"

"Who wouldn't? This story has more turns and twists than a daytime soap opera, but the best part is, it's all true. Just look at the latest development: this C. D. character coming to Brooke and Gabe this morning to say that he's Josephine's long-lost son and only living heir. How surreal is that?"

"Oh, please," Felicia said with a snort. "If he's kin to Josephine, I'm Diana Ross."

"What did you just say?" Varina leaned forward from her seat next to Felicia to face

Lizzie. "Who's kin to who?"

Lizzie raised her voice and enunciated slowly. "I said C. D. is now claiming to be Josephine's son."

Varina's eyes behind her thick-lensed glasses widened. "Oh no. That can't be right. That boy is crazy. What's he saying that for?"

"Easy. For the money," Felicia said, frowning. "He wants to inherit the house, the island, Josephine's money, all of it." She glared in Gabe's direction. "Just because *somebody* didn't get her will signed and witnessed before she died."

Gabe flushed slightly but said nothing.

"Brooke, Mr. Gabe, did that man really say Josephine was his mama?" Varina asked.

"That's his story," Brooke said. "It's kind of complicated, but in a nutshell, C. D. says he believes that Josephine abandoned him as an infant — left him in a church in Savannah. The church turned him over to a Catholic orphanage there, and they, in turn, placed him in Good Shepherd Home for Boys, where he lived until he ran away at sixteen."

"No, no, no," Varina insisted. She clenched the wooden bench slats with both hands. "That's not true. It can't be true. I would have known." She continued, shaking her head, "How old is that man?"

"He told me this weekend that he's seventy-six. Born in '42, I think he said."

Varina's forehead puckered in distress. "See, that's a lie. No, ma'am. Josephine never had no baby, never. I would have known if she'd had a child. She didn't even meet Mr. Preiss until the war was over."

"His story is pretty far-fetched," Marie said gently, "but isn't it just possible that since Josephine was unmarried, she would have kept her pregnancy a secret because of the scandal? She could have told you and everybody else that she was going away to 'visit family.' That's what young girls did back then. At one time, there was even a home for unwed mothers, The Florence Crittenton home, just a few blocks from my house in Ardsley Park, where girls went to have their babies. Afterward, the babies were adopted and the girls went back home and nobody was any wiser."

"I don't care. It's a lie. That man is telling a lie," Varina said angrily.

Lizzie leaned back and stretched and yawned. "I think I'll see about renting a car. That way I can shoot up to Savannah this week to try to verify C. D.'s story."

Gabe reached into his pocket and brought out a plastic bag containing two smaller plastic bags.

"You can double-check his story if you like. I think it's a good idea. But in the meantime, I took the liberty of getting Louette to collect some of Josephine's hair from her hairbrush. And I paid a visit to C. D., who, after some persuading, donated a bit of that ponytail of his."

"Hair?" Varina wrinkled her nose. "What are you gonna do with that?"

"It's for DNA testing, Auntie," Felicia said.

"I'll send it off to a testing laboratory, and they should be able to tell us whether or not C. D. is related to Josephine," Gabe explained.

"I don't need a bag of hair to tell you that," Varina said. "Because that man is definitely no kin to Josephine Warrick." Her hands shook slightly as she gesticulated.

Felicia placed a hand on her aunt's arm. "Auntie, I think we need to test your blood sugar and see if it's time for your meds. Let's go to the ladies' room. Okay?"

The old woman was still muttering under her breath as her great-niece helped her to her feet and they began making their laborious way to the ferry's restroom.

After the ferry landed and their group had disembarked, Brooke motioned for Lizzie to follow them to her car. "I don't think you'll be able to rent a car in St. Ann's. We might need to take you to Brunswick to the airport for that."

"I'm headed back to St. Simon's, so Brunswick is on my way, and I'm happy to give you a ride," Gabe said.

"Fine with me," Lizzie said. She turned and

watched as Felicia tried to juggle two overnight bags and Varina. "Let me go see if I can give those two a hand."

"You're not going back to Savannah?" Brooke asked Gabe.

"No, I want to get to the courthouse here first thing tomorrow to petition the court to become administrator of Josephine's estate."

"I need to figure out what my next move is too. Josephine paid me a retainer, and I need to make a good-faith effort to follow through and stop the state from taking her land."

"Your client is dead," Gabe said. "Your obligation to her has expired. I suppose you can raise the matter with her heirs, when and if we track them down, or learn the truth about C. D.'s claim." He leaned in closer to her, his voice low in her ear. "Have dinner with me tonight, Brooke. Please?"

"Tonight? I can't, Gabe. I haven't seen Henry in two days. I'm already feeling guilty about leaving him with Farrah for this long. Maybe we can catch up tomorrow, after you make your filing? We can compare notes."

He sighed. "Okay, if lunch is all you can do. But, Brooke, I didn't mean for this to be a business meeting." He searched her face for a reaction.

Her face grew hot, and she could feel herself blushing.

"Never mind," he said quickly. "Call me tomorrow if you want, and we can meet.

Strictly professional if that's how you want it."

He turned and walked hurriedly toward his car.

43

Marie waited until they were in the car. "What was that all about?"

"What?" Brooke felt heat creeping up from her collarbone.

"That whispered conference back there with Gabe."

"Oh, you know, just legal stuff. He's going to stay over at Sea Island tonight so he can be at the courthouse here first thing in the morning to petition to become administrator of Josephine's estate."

"This is your mother, Brooke. I know something else was going on back there."

Brooke sighed. "I think maybe Gabe just asked me out on a date."

"Maybe? You're not sure?"

"Okay, so yes, he asked me to dinner. But I totally blew it and embarrassed both of us."

"What did you say?"

"The first thing that occurred to me. Which was that I'd been away from Henry for two days, and I couldn't possibly go out to dinner. Then he asked me to have lunch with him, and at that point he made it very clear that he wasn't talking about a business meeting when he asked me out for dinner."

"Ohhhh. So how do you feel about that? About seeing Gabe socially?"

"I don't know," Brooke wailed. "God, I suck at this boy-girl stuff. I never was good at it. Maybe that's why after I started dating Harris in college, I decided he was the one. It was such a relief, you know, to not have to go through this whole bizarre dating ritual."

Marie laughed. "How did I raise such an odd duck as you? Brooke, honey, this is not all that tricky. Take it slow. Break it down to the basics. A nice man asked you out to dinner. He's single; you're single. Now. How do you feel about Gabe? On a personal basis?"

"Don't you think he's way too old for me? I mean, the last time we went out to dinner, somebody mistook him for my dad! It was super embarrassing."

"Gabe Wynant is much younger than Gordon and, just between us girls, much better looking. Anyway, why do you care what I think or what some stupid waiter thinks? What do you think? That's the only thing that matters."

Brooke took a deep breath. "He's a nice guy. When we worked together, he never talked down to me, never hit on me like some of the other, older partners in the law firm.

We used to run together, you know? He really listened to me and respected my opinions."

"What else?"

Brooke shrugged. "I guess I like how he treats women. He never said anything negative about his wife, ever, even though she must have put him through hell. He's old-school like that, but not an old fogey, like Dad."

"And?"

"Okay, I guess he is kind of hot, in a silver-haired-fox kind of way. He's fit, but not obsessed with himself. Does that make sense?"

"Yes. And I'd agree with everything you said."

"Then maybe *you* should go out to dinner with him."

"He didn't ask me," Marie said. "Or I would. Now, what are the negatives?"

"Like I said, he's way too old for me. What do we even have in common?"

"Hmm. You both like to run. You're both interested in the law. I don't know. That's the reason you go to dinner with somebody. To figure that stuff out. It's part of that whole 'bizarre dating ritual thing' that you seem to think you suck at."

"I do suck at it," Brooke insisted. "Anyway, the big thing is, it's creepy. It's like that whole Woody Allen obsession with younger chicks thing."

"It's nothing like that," Marie said sharply. "You're not an impressionable teenager. If you're not interested, just say, 'No, thanks.' Gabe's no dummy. He won't pursue it if you decline."

"But I don't want to hurt his feelings! I like him. I like him a lot!"

"Then go to dinner. Or lunch. Or meet him for a drink. Or coffee. But if you think you have even a little interest, say yes. That's the one thing I've learned, getting older, going through a divorce, reinventing myself. Say yes to the possibility."

Brooke pulled the Volvo into the driveway of her house. "You sound like you have some personal experience in this whole game. Are you saying you've been dating?"

Marie's smile was sphinxlike.

"Mom! You have been dating. Why didn't you say so?"

The front door to the cottage opened, and seconds later, Farrah stood in the doorway, waving at them as Henry hurtled through the yard and into his mother's arms.

44

"Hey," Farrah said as soon as Brooke walked into the office on Monday afternoon. "We need to get over to the jail. There's a situation with Brittni."

"We?" Brooke asked. "Did you graduate from law school and pass the bar exam over the weekend?"

"No, but Brittni's mom called me a little while ago. Britt got locked up again yesterday and she's in deep shit."

"Her stepfather still owes me for Brittni's last scrape with the law," Brooke pointed out.

"I told Aunt Charla that, and she's gonna meet us at the jail with the money she owes you, plus another check for $5,000 as a retainer. Happy?"

"What exactly did Brittni do?" Brooke asked as they were getting into the Volvo.

"Aunt Charla was kinda hysterical when she called, but she kept using words like *kidnapping* and *aggravated assault.* Also *crimi-*

nal trespass," Farrah said.

Brittni Miles had bleached-blond hair, two black eyes, and an orange jumpsuit. She glared at her visitors from the other side of a plexiglass divider in the visiting room at the Carter County Jail.

"I told Mama not to call y'all," Brittni said sullenly.

"Too bad," Farrah said. "Since your mama is the one who's payin', she gets to do the sayin'."

Brooke looked down at the copy of the arrest report she'd been given, but the police officer's handwritten narrative was nearly unreadable. "Brittni, if I'm going to represent you, I need you to tell me what happened. This says the victim's name is Kelsy Cotterell. Is she the cashier from the SwiftyMart? The one you threw the ice at?"

"She doesn't work there anymore," Brittni said smugly. "Got fired for gettin' arrested for what she done to me."

"Which was what?" Farrah asked.

"Put a big ol' bag of flaming dog poop on my mama's doorstep Friday night," Brittni said. "Only she didn't know Mama put one of those motion-activated video cameras on our front porch. The dumb ho looked right at the camera while she was doing it. The bag caught the whole porch on fire, and Mama called Aunt Jodee, and the cops looked at the video and arrested her, right there at the SwiftyMart."

"Oh-kayyyy," Brooke said slowly. "But that doesn't explain the criminal trespass, kidnapping, and aggravated assault charges against you. Do you want to walk us through that?"

"Kelsy posted bail the same night she was arrested!" Brittni exclaimed. "Then she called my cell and left a message saying next time she'd burn down our whole house. So I decided to, like, keep an eye on her. Saturday night, I followed her Camaro, and you know where she went? Right to Wayne's place! That ho."

Farrah glanced over at Brooke. "Wayne is Brittni's boyfriend."

"Ex-boyfriend."

"Whatever," Farrah said. "Does Wayne still live in those apartments by the school?"

"Uh-uh. He bought an RV, which he parks at his sister's place. Wayne told me he had to work a late shift Saturday night, but his truck was parked right there in his sister's driveway. The lying sack of crap. I watched her go in, and five minutes later, I saw the lights in the RV go out, and the next thing you know, that thing was rockin' back and forth to beat the band."

"Uh-oh," Farrah said.

"Right then, I think I might have had, like, an outer body experience," Brittni said. "I, like, lost control. Next thing you know, I was running over to the cab of the RV. I was just gonna bang on the side to scare them, but the keys were in the ignition, so I fired it up and floored it. Who knew a twelve-year-old Winnebago could do sixty on a dirt road? I could hear Wayne and Kelsy bouncing around back there and hollering at me to stop, but it was like the devil took hold of me. You know how that is, right?"

"Uh, no," Brooke said.

"Wayne came up front, buck naked, and he was trying to yank the wheel away from me, and then Kelsy was right on top of me too, pulling my hair and screaming at me to stop, and while I was trying to fight her off and defend myself, the RV went off the road and slammed into a pecan tree. The airbags deployed, and I was knocked unconscious. And when I came to, all I saw was blue lights and gold badges."

"Okay," Brooke said. "Do you still have Kelsy's message on your phone?"

"Yeah."

"Good. Forward that to me. That's called making terroristic threats. Serious stuff. If she came onto your property without permission, that's trespassing. How much damage did the flaming dog poop do?"

"A lot!" Brittni said. "The fire spread from the porch to the carport, and the whole thing collapsed on top of my stepdad's 1968 El Camino, which he's been restoring."

"All good stuff," Brooke said. "I've got to get back to the office now, but I'm going to call the district attorney and offer to show him the video of Kelsy trying to burn down your house, and I'll let him know about the threats too, and hopefully he'll see that this was just a love triangle gone wrong. In the meantime, if they do drop the charges, I'd urge you to stay away from Kelsy."

"She'd better stay the hell away from me too," Brittni said, glowering.

Charla Miles was waiting outside when Farrah and Brooke emerged from the jail.

"How'd it go?" she asked, handing an envelope to Farrah.

"As well as can be expected," Brooke reported. "I'll speak to the district attorney and see if we can't work out something that doesn't involve jail time. Best-case scenario, Brittni pays for the damage to the RV, does some community service hours, and takes some anger management classes."

Charla threw her arms around Farrah and hugged her tight. "Thank God!"

"No, Aunt Charla," Farrah said, "thank Brooke. And don't forget, if she gets Brittni off without doing any more jail time, you agreed to let her represent you on your next divorce." She handed the envelope of money to Brooke.

"I won't forget," Charla said. "Martin's so

mad about Brittni getting his El Camino burned up, I could be callin' y'all any day now."

When they returned to the office, Brooke spotted an envelope lying on the middle of her desktop. The envelope had the official seal of the University of Georgia.

"What's this?" she asked, turning to Farrah.

"Oh my God, I almost forgot with all of Brittni's drama!" Farrah exclaimed. "I did it, Brooke. I got in! I got into UGA!"

She grabbed both of Brooke's hands and the two of them hopped up and down in an impromptu happy dance. "We did it!" Farrah shouted.

"You did it," Brooke corrected. "Yaaaay!"

They were both out of breath and laughing and crying at the end of the dance.

"I told you so. I knew you'd get in, but I thought you said you weren't going to apply," Brooke said with a mock-accusing tone.

"I just told everybody that, so that way, when I got rejected, nobody but me would know," Farrah said. "I didn't even tell my mom. Or Jaxson, which I felt kind of guilty about."

"Jaxson's not an issue anymore, right?"

"Maybe. I'm not sure. He wants us to get back together. He's been texting me, and I've seen him drive by the house a bunch of times at night. I think he's checking up on me."

Brooke knew better than to give unsolicited

advice, but she couldn't help herself. "Farrah, please listen to me. You've got such an incredible, bright future ahead of you. I hate to see you tether yourself to your hometown honey."

"I didn't say I was getting back with him."

"But you're thinking about it. And if he's texting you, he's going to come around begging you to take him back. And he'll make you feel guilty about going off to school in Athens and leaving him behind. And the next thing you know, you'll think about what *he* wants, instead of what *you* need."

Farrah's phone dinged. She took it out of the pocket of her jeans, read the text, typed something rapidly, and pushed Send.

"Okay, I'm ready to get to work," she announced, sitting at her desk and powering up her computer.

"Was that Jaxson?"

Farrah nodded but didn't look up from the document she'd just opened.

"Did you tell him you didn't want to get back together with him?" Brooke asked.

The girl still didn't look up. "Brooke?"

"Yes?"

"Not another word."

Brooke's own cell phone rang. She checked the caller ID screen. It was Gabe Wynant.

She glanced at Farrah, picked up the phone, and headed for the powder room, which was, for her, the equivalent of a conference room. She closed the bathroom door, took a deep breath, and answered. "Hi, Gabe!"

"I know it's last minute, but is there any way you could sit for Henry tonight?" she asked Farrah, trying desperately to sound casual.

"Sure. I could use the extra money. UGA ain't cheap, ya know." She flashed a big grin.

"Great. Why don't you come over around 6:30? I'll fix something for dinner for you and Henry, and you can give him a bath and get him ready for bed before I leave around 7:00."

"That's fine. But you're going out on a weeknight?"

"Yes."

"Business meeting?"

"Not exactly. More like an, uh, date."

"Oh. My. God!" Farrah spun around on her chair so that she was facing Brooke. "Finally. Who's the guy?"

"Just a lawyer I used to work with in Savannah. An old friend, that's all."

"Suuuuure."

"Farrah?"

"Yeah?"

"Not another word."

45

Farrah peeked out the small window in the front door. "I think he's here."

"Get away from that window," Brooke said. "Aren't you supposed to be putting my son to bed?"

"Oh my God. He's totally driving a Porsche 911. Who is this guy?"

"Farrah!"

"Just let me get a good look at him. You know, to make sure he's not an ax murderer or something. I wish I could see his license plate."

"Farrah!"

"Okay, he's getting out of the car. Wait. He's got white hair. Seriously, how old is this dude?" She whipped her cell phone out, held it against the window, and clicked off three frames in rapid succession.

"Farrah!" Brooke's teeth were clenched. She wiped her sweaty palms on the side of her white jeans. Her stomach was doing flip-flops, and she could already feel the familiar heat creeping up from her collarbone. She'd felt like this for the past hour. It was as though she were reliving junior high again. Why in God's name had she agreed to go out with Gabe Wynant?

"Okay, he's standing by the car, but he's not moving. He's looking at his watch. He actually dresses kind of cool for an old guy. He's not even wearing dad jeans." She snapped off a few more photos.

"What do you think you're doing?"

"I'm taking his picture, so if you don't come back tonight, I'll have something to take to the cops."

"Farrah!"

"I'm going."

The doorbell rang. Brooke took a last gulp of her white wine and pasted a smile on her face.

"Hey, you," she said.

"Hey, you too," Gabe said. He was dressed casually, in dark wash — but not dad-style — jeans and a crisp, pale yellow dress shirt with rolled cuffs. He wore Gucci loafers, but no socks. "Ready to go?"

"Come on in for a minute. I just need to look in on Henry and kiss him good —"

"Noooooooo!" The three-year-old ran into the living room, dressed in his pajama top, but naked from the waist down. He threw himself against Brooke's legs, wrapping his arms around her knees. "Nooooo. I don't want you to gooooo!"

Farrah darted into the room after him. "Sorry," she said breathlessly. "I turned to grab his pull-ups and he made a run for the door."

"Come on, Henry," she said, gently trying to coax the boy away from his mother. "It's story time. *Good Night, Good Night, Construction Site.* Your favorite."

Henry tried to slap away the babysitter's hands. "No. I go with Mama."

Brooke leaned down and hoisted the boy into her arms. "Hey, little man. It's time for bed. You go with Farrah and help her read, and I'll be home before you know it."

He shook his head, then stared at Gabe. "Who that?"

Gabe smiled nervously. "Hi, Henry. I'm Gabe."

"This is Mama's friend," Brooke added. "Can you say, 'Hi, Gabe'?"

"Gimme five!" Gabe said, holding his hand out, palm up.

Henry buried his face in Brooke's shoulder. "Noooo!" he wailed.

Farrah reached out and managed to peel the boy off his mother. "Let's go, Henry McBenry," she said, heading back to the bedroom. "Have a good time, Brooke," she called over her shoulder. "Nice to meet you, Gabe."

■ ■ ■ ■

He'd chosen a new restaurant she'd been meaning to check out. It was Italian, located in a restored craftsman cottage a block away from the waterfront. There were flowers and candles on the table, which actually had a white tablecloth.

Gabe smiled at her as the waiter brought their wine. "Are you as nervous as I am?"

She sipped her wine. "That depends. Is your pulse racing? Do you feel like you might vomit at any moment?"

"Check and check. Plus I had to change my shirt twice before I left the house tonight, because of all the flop sweat."

She laughed. "Okay, I didn't require a wardrobe change, which makes me feel marginally better, so thanks for that."

"It's just dinner. That's what I've been telling myself all night. Right? Dinner with an old friend and colleague."

"Absolutely." She nodded and sipped her wine.

He took a gulp of his own wine. "I'm sixty-three, by the way."

"Okay . . ."

"I just thought I'd get that out of the way. In case you were wondering and trying to figure out if I really am too old for you, which I hope I'm not."

"I've got a confession to make," Brooke said, emboldened by the wine. "I already knew that. I checked on Martindale-Hubbell."

"I Googled and checked you on LinkedIn," he countered. "Very impressive. I'd forgotten you graduated near the top of your class."

"So we're two smarty-pants lawyers. We should be able to get through a simple no-risk dinner together, right?"

"Not a problem," he said. "And since you mentioned the lawyer thing, I've got good news. The court appointed me administrator of Josephine's estate today."

"Wow. That was fast."

"One of the circuit judges was a law school classmate of mine," Gabe said.

"Ah yes, the good-old-boy network," Brooke said, hoping she didn't sound bitter.

"In this case, it was helpful. We can speed things up and start wrapping up Josephine's estate."

"It's hard for me to believe she's gone," Brooke said wistfully. "Even though I only knew her for a short time, and of course, her illness diminished her on an hourly basis, she was such a strong life force with such an amazing story to tell."

"I agree. It's sad."

"I'm really pissed she died without telling us who killed Russell Strickland or where the body is buried," Brooke admitted. "My one hope is that Lizzie really will be able to unravel all of Josephine's secrets while she's staying at Shellhaven."

Gabe frowned. "I'm not sure it's such a good idea for Lizzie to be living there. I mean, I personally don't really have a problem with it, but as administrator, once I track down those cousins of hers — the heirs apparent, as it were — they might not like it at all."

"It's not like she's moving in for the rest of her life," Brooke protested. "And it's a good thing that Shellhaven isn't empty, with Josephine gone now. What's it going to hurt?"

"Maybe you're right," Gabe said hastily. "Anyway, for the short term, I suppose it's okay."

Their appetizers arrived then, and the discussion segued into favorite restaurants, gossip about Savannah, old clients, and mutual friends.

It wasn't until their desserts arrived — chocolate sea salt gelato with biscotti for her, a glass of port for him — that Brooke realized two hours had flown by.

She dug out the last bite of gelato with the tip of a biscotti, tasted, and rolled her eyes. "So good."

"Like this evening," Gabe said, watching her over the rim of his glass. "I love seeing you like this, Brooke."

He reached over with his napkin and

dabbed at a bit of gelato on the corner of her mouth. His hand lingered there for only a moment, but she felt herself blushing.

"You mean with food all over my face? That's an everyday occurrence. I'm an even messier eater than my three-year-old."

"He's a pretty cute kid, by the way. No, I meant seeing you relaxed, enjoying yourself, just being yourself."

"Are you saying I've changed? Since we worked together in Savannah?"

"Definitely. You were always so driven and focused when you were working for the firm in Savannah. I don't think I was ever with you when you completely let your hair down, the way you have tonight. It's a nice change. It suits you."

"Well . . . thanks. I've had kind of a rough three years, raising a child by myself in a new town. There were weeks and months I didn't think I'd make it. Henry was not an easy baby, and I didn't get a lot of sleep. But somehow, I guess we weathered the storm. Henry sleeps through the night now, mostly. My practice is finally starting to grow, slowly. I've got good childcare — Farrah, who you met tonight, is a godsend. She's my right-hand girl in the office too. She adores Henry, and the feeling is mutual, and she's smart as a whip. I don't know what I'll do in the fall when she goes off to school in Athens."

Gabe swirled the port in his glass. "And

what about your personal life?"

She raised an eyebrow. "Personal life? Who has time for that?"

"Now you sound like the old Brooke," he chided. "Don't you have any desire to see what life is like outside the office? Or Henry's nursery?"

"You mean date?"

"Yeah. That."

She sat back in her chair and took a long look at him. His silver hair glinted in the candlelight, and his eyes were frank and appraising.

"I haven't given it a lot of thought," she said finally. "For one thing, there's not exactly a deep dating pool of eligible men in these parts. I mean, sure, I get hit on by your garden-variety rednecks and the occasional horny, inappropriate married guy. And I've had some very tempting offers to provide oral gratification to some of the inmates at the county lockup . . ."

Gabe laughed.

"But otherwise, I haven't met anybody down here that I'd want to date. And I haven't felt the need to go looking, despite Farrah's pleas to set me up with a Tinder account. Now. Turnabout is fair play, Gabe Wynant. What about you? Are you a Match.com guy, or are you more of an eHarmony type? Or maybe Christian Mingle?"

"None of the above. I swear. You know how

it is in Savannah, though. For a while after Sunny died, I was fresh meat in the dating supermarket. Her old friends — hell, *my* old friends — all wanted to set me up, either with themselves or somebody they knew. And I'll admit, it was lonely. I went out a few times, saw a couple of women for third or fourth dates, but there was never any real connection, so I just kind of gave up."

"It's much less stressful to stay home in my yoga pants, read a book, have a glass of wine, and enjoy my own company," Brooke said.

"Bingo," Gabe said. "The easy way out. But that gets old too, you know?"

She smiled noncommittally.

The waiter brought the check, Gabe presented his credit card, and he and Brooke drifted out of the restaurant. A breeze was blowing off the river, and as they walked to his car, which he'd had to park a block away, Gabe caught his hand in hers in an easy, natural movement.

"Nice night out," he said. "Not even that humid."

"For Georgia. In May," she agreed.

"Want to take a walk?"

She hesitated, trying to estimate the time.

"Aw, come on. It's not that late," he said, reading her thoughts. "It's not even ten."

"Okay. But just down to the docks and then back. It's a school night for me, and Henry's up at six every morning."

They swung their hands companionably as they walked along the waterfront. The air smelled of marsh mud and salt water and faintly of fish. The sky was pricked with stars. She thought if she squinted she could see the lights of shrimp boats headed out to sea.

"You look beautiful tonight, by the way," Gabe said as they reached the municipal docks.

"Um, thanks," she said. She'd deliberately dressed down for the occasion; white jeans, a simple V-necked navy cotton sweater, and a necklace she'd splurged on at a local boutique, white coral beads with an oyster-shell medallion in the middle.

"Nice to see you not swathed in your typical lady lawyer battle armor of a business suit and heels," Gabe said.

"Not much call for business suits and heels down here," Brooke said. "I'll wear one if I'm in court, in front of a judge, but this is as dressy as it gets for me these days."

"If you did feel the urge to dress up, I'd love to take you to dinner up at the Cloister," Gabe said. "They've got a great new chef, and there's an orchestra and dancing on Saturday nights."

"Oh my gosh. They still have those? My parents used to take me to those when I was a teenager. Mom would make Dad dance with me, and it was total agony."

"Oh." He looked disappointed. "You don't

like to dance?"

"I love to dance. And so did he, but it was so damn embarrassing, dancing with your father, who was trying to be all hip and happening. I'll never forget the night he tried to do the Macarena. The memory is permanently seared onto my brainpan."

Gabe winced. "If I promise not to try to break out any new dance moves, would you consider coming to dinner with me Saturday night?"

"At the Cloister? But that's like an hour away."

"You could stay over," Gabe said. "Not at my place. I mean, you could stay at my place. There's room, and I swear I wouldn't hit on you. But what I meant was I'd book you a room at the hotel. And I'd bring you home first thing in the morning."

"I don't know," she said slowly. "I'd have to see if Farrah is available to stay over. It's a lot. And you saw how clingy Henry can be. Don't get me wrong, it sounds like fun, but . . ."

"Just think about it, okay?"

"I will. Now I'd better get home, or Farrah will have the state patrol out looking for me."

The ride home took only five minutes. When Gabe pulled into the driveway, they saw a quick flick of the front window curtains.

"Told ya," Brooke said. "She's very protective of me."

"Hmm," Gabe said.

"But she totally approved of this car. Whatever happened to the Mercedes?"

"I still have it. The Porsche was a complete surprise. Turns out, Sunny bought it without ever saying a word to me. I found it covered by a tarp in the garage at the house at Sea Island the first time I came down after she died."

"A Porsche 911? She just bought it on a whim?"

He shrugged. "More like on a toot. I'll sell it eventually, when I sell the house, but for tonight, I thought maybe I'd impress a girl with it."

"You totally did," Brooke said.

And before she could say anything else, he leaned over and kissed her softly on the lips. "Don't tell the babysitter," he whispered.

46

"Brooke?" There was more than a note of panic in Louette's voice.

It was Wednesday morning. She'd just walked into her office and hadn't even had time to fire up the coffee maker or laptop before her cell phone rang.

"What's wrong?" Brooke asked.

"Those cousins of Josephine's, Dorcas and Delphine, they're here! They just come riding up here in a Jeep with some man from the state park. I let 'em in, 'cause I didn't know what else to do, but now they're walking around, talking like they own the place. I think you'd better come quick."

"How the hell did they even find out Josephine is dead?"

"They said there was a big piece in the newspapers yesterday. They already called a lawyer, and he told them they're fixin' to inherit this whole island, including the house."

"What newspaper?" Brooke walked around

the office, looking for her copy of the local paper, a weekly that was published on Wednesdays.

"I don't know. Maybe the Savannah paper? Or Atlanta? We don't get a paper over here. Shug reads the sports page online."

"I'll head over there right now. Can you have C. D. pick me up at the city dock?"

"We ain't seen C. D. in a couple of days. I'll send Shug over. He's off work today."

"Okay, see you soon. And try not to worry, Louette."

Brooke flipped her laptop open and did a quick Google search on Josephine's name. The first citation was an article from the previous day's edition of *The Atlanta Journal-Constitution.*

Talisa Island, GA. Josephine Bettendorf Warrick, the legendary heiress owner of this wildest of Georgia's untamed barrier islands, died last week at the age of 99. Her death signals what is almost certainly the last chapter of private ownership of the 12,000-acre Talisa.

Mrs. Warrick's father, Samuel G. Bettendorf, was a Boston shipping magnate who purchased the Carter County island more than a century ago with two cousins. He commissioned famed Gilded-Age architect Addison Mizner to design and build a pink stucco Beaux-Arts-inspired twenty-room mansion he dubbed Shellhaven.

Carter County sheriff Howard Goolsby confirmed Mrs. Warrick's death, saying that the nonagenarian, who'd recently been diagnosed with terminal lung cancer, died of a head injury last Saturday after a fall. There are no known survivors.

Bettendorf's only son, Samuel Gardiner Bettendorf Jr., who was known as Gardiner, enlisted in the Royal Canadian Air Force at the age of 23 and was killed when the Spitfire he piloted was shot down over Nazi-occupied France in early 1942. The senior Bettendorf died one year later, leaving his daughter as sole owner of much of the island, with the exception of a smaller tract of land on the northern tip of Talisa, which was retained by distant relatives who sold their land to the state for a park in 1978.

In 1949, Josephine Bettendorf married Preiss H. Warrick, a naval captain she met at a bridge party on Sea Island, Georgia. The couple, both amateur naturalists, made the protection of Talisa and its wildlife their life's work. Preiss Warrick died in 1966 of renal disease.

The couple never had children, and Mrs. Warrick spent the remainder of her life as a fierce guardian of the island, mounting a thirty-year fight to fend off the state's efforts to buy it.

Brooke closed the laptop and called Gabe Wynant. The phone rang three times, and she got his voice mail.

"Hi, Gabe. Sorry to bother you, but Louette just called to say that Josephine's long-lost cousins turned up at Shellhaven this morning and are already acting pretty possessive. I'm going over there right now, and I just wanted to give you a heads-up. Talk soon."

Shug eased the boat away from the slip at the municipal dock. The water was calm, and seagulls wheeled and soared overhead as they crossed the river.

"How are Varina and Felicia doing?" Brooke asked, as they rode through the no-wake zone.

"Varina's happy as a clam, but that Felicia, I don't think she really takes to island life," Shug said with a chuckle. "She spends most of her time on that computer, teaching her online classes and reading. And she doesn't leave the house unless she sprays all over with bug spray. Still, she's got a good heart, taking care of her auntie the way she does."

"Have you started working on Varina's house?"

"Oh yeah. We got all the vines and brush tore off outside, and cleared out a whole nest of raccoons that had been living in the chimney. The roofing shingles and insulation and windows and such I ordered should be here by Friday. And you ought to see that little old lady Varina, leaning on her walker and sweeping and mopping the inside of that house."

"You're a saint to house them and help them out this way, Shug."

"Just doin' what's right," he said. "Family's family."

"And what about Louette? How's she holding up with all this stress?"

"Not so good," he admitted. "Her blood pressure's up, and she's worried somebody's gonna make us move off the island. I told her, 'Honey, we got money, and we got a place to go,' but we both know she's true Geechee. Only place she's ever gonna be happy is right there in that little house at Oyster Bluff."

Louette met her at the front door at Shellhaven. She pointed down the hall toward the library. "They're back there, and I'm afraid Lizzie is about to snatch 'em bald."

"I'll see if I can referee," Brooke promised.

She heard raised voices as she approached the library's open door.

"You can't just ransack our family's belongings this way," a woman was saying.

"Hi!" Brooke said, stepping inside.

Two women whirled around to confront the newcomer.

The cousins looked enough alike that they could have been twins. They were skinny, probably in their mid- to late seventies, with dyed strawberry-blond hair so thinned that large patches of pink scalp showed beneath their matching golf visors. They wore T-shirts tucked into their elastic-waisted khaki slacks and sturdy, blindingly white tennis shoes, and they were both glaring at Lizzie, who'd constructed a makeshift office on a card table in the middle of the room.

"Hi, Brooke!" Lizzie looked profoundly grateful for her arrival. She gestured at the women. "These are Josephine's long-lost cousins, Dorcas and Delphine. Or is it Delphine and Dorcas?"

"I'm Dorcas Fentress, and this is my cousin Delphine McElwain," said the taller of the two, whose T-shirt was hot pink with a design of sequined kittens. "And you're the lawyer our cousin supposedly hired to handle her affairs, despite the fact that she had a perfectly capable law firm in Atlanta?"

"That's me," Brooke said, extending her hand. "Brooke Trappnell. My grandmother Millie was one of Josephine's best friends growing up."

"And my grandmother Ruth Mattingly Quinlan was one of her other best friends," Lizzie said. "They all went to boarding school together."

"I never heard Josephine mention either of

those names," Delphine said. Her blue T-shirt had a motif of dancing dolphins, and her wire-rimmed glasses had blue-tinted lenses.

"When was the last time you ladies saw Josephine?" Brooke asked.

The two women exchanged glances. "It's been some years now," Dorcas admitted. "Josephine had become such a shut-in late in life, you know, but Delphine and I made several attempts to contact her."

"It was my understanding that she refused to see you," Brooke said. "She was still furious at you for selling your land to the state."

"That's all water under the bridge now," Dorcas said, pressing her narrow lips together. "I must say, it was very upsetting for both Delphine and me to learn about Josephine's death through a newspaper article."

"Horrifying," Delphine said. "We had no idea Josie had even been sick. It breaks my heart to think of our cousin spending her last months so ill and then dying here, all alone, with none of her family around. If only somebody had had the decency to notify us . . ."

"Oh, she wasn't alone that night," Lizzie said cheerfully. "I was here, Brooke and her mother, Marie, were here, Varina and Felicia were here, and of course, Louette, the housekeeper, was here too. And her other lawyer. We had dinner together."

Dorcas favored Lizzie with a withering

stare. "I find it hard to believe that a dying woman would have hosted a dinner party."

"More like a house party," Lizzie said. "We all spent the night."

"And why would she have invited a bunch of strangers to a house party?" Dorcas asked.

Lizzie gestured around the library. "She was going to leave —"

"She was feeling nostalgic," Brooke said, deliberately cutting Lizzie off. At this point, there was no need to let the cousins know of Josephine's intent to create a trust to protect Talisa. She would let Gabe Wynant deal with all that. Maybe there was still hope that he would find some loophole to prevent the dreaded Ds from inheriting.

"We should have been notified that she was sick," Dorcas said. "We would have come immediately. We were her only living family, you know."

Brooke shrugged. "No offense, but I think Josephine would have contacted you herself if she'd wanted to see you. She was by no means a shut-in. She was making regular visits to her doctors in Jacksonville, and she knew the cancer diagnosis was terminal. That's why she reached out and asked me to gather these women together. She wanted to meet them and make amends."

"So you say," Delphine said.

"Amends for what?" Dorcas asked. She glanced down at Lizzie's work space, with the scattered file folders, yellowing newspaper clippings, and stacks of old correspondence. Brooke realized that Lizzie, the journalist, had begun digging into Josephine's past, delving into the secrets she'd been so reluctant to share.

"Old slights. Fractured friendships. It was Josephine's story to tell, not mine," Brooke said.

"Very touching," Dorcas said. "But none of that explains what this woman" — she pointed at Lizzie — "is doing here, trespassing in our family's home, meddling with our cousin's private papers."

"Just some genealogy work," Lizzie said with an impish grin. "I'm harmless, really."

"By whose authority?" Delphine asked.

"Mine, actually," a man's voice said.

Gabe was standing in the doorway, with Louette and Felicia right behind him.

Gabe was dressed in a somber gray business suit. "Gabe Wynant," he said, extending a business card to each of the cousins. "I'm the court-appointed administrator of Josephine Warrick's estate. Mrs. Warrick had mentioned that she had some distant cousins, but we had no names or addresses, since it seems you were estranged. I asked Lizzie here to search Mrs. Warrick's papers for your contact information."

"We certainly were not estranged," Dorcas said, bristling.

"Never mind," Delphine said, reading the business card. "Mr. Wynant, is it?"

"That's right," Gabe said.

"My cousin and I have hired a lawyer to see that our rights as Josephine's closest heirs are protected. He'll be in contact with you."

"I look forward to speaking to him," Gabe said. "Anything else I can do for you ladies today? No? Shug is outside with his truck, and he'll be happy to take you back to the ferry if you'd like."

Lizzie waited until the women were out of earshot before offering Gabe a high five.

"Well done, sir." She laughed. "Here's your hat, what's your hurry? And not even offering to have Shug take them back to the mainland instead of waiting on the ferry? I call that cold!"

"Shug has other work to attend to," Gabe said. "I've asked him to stay on here and take over the outside maintenance again."

"Thank you, Jesus," Louette said fervently. "That grass was getting so high I was afraid what might be hiding in it."

Gabe reached into the inner pocket of his jacket and brought out an envelope. "I've brought both your paychecks too," he said. "And I hope the past few days haven't been too stressful for you."

Louette tucked the envelope in the pocket of her slacks. For the first time, Brooke realized that with the death of her former employer, Louette had stopped wearing the white uniform and switched to more casual clothing.

"Thanks for coming over so quickly," Brooke said to Gabe. "Things were getting pretty sticky with those two."

"Yeah, they look like they're gonna be major pains in the ass," Lizzie said. "I think they thought I was going to put a match to Josephine's papers."

Gabe frowned. "I hate to say it, Lizzie, and I didn't want to mention it in front of the cousins, but it is somewhat problematic for you to be riffling through Josephine's personal effects."

"Why?" Lizzie asked. "I'm just doing research for my magazine article, that's all. And I'm actually doing you a favor, organizing and indexing everything I find." She gestured at the cardboard file boxes surrounding the card table. "Besides, maybe I'll find a clue to who actually killed Russell Strickland and where he's buried."

"If they do get a lawyer involved, he may raise an objection with the court," Gabe said.

"You're now the administrator of the estate, right? You could counter that by pointing out that Lizzie's research is necessary to make sure Josephine's papers are in order," Brooke said. She pointed to the secretary. "Josephine was a total pack rat. That thing is full to overflowing with old letters, cards, correspondence, and who knows what? Josephine had me going through it on one of my first visits here, to try to track down Ruth's and Varina's families, and I barely scratched the surface of what's in there. Maybe there actually are other living heirs that need to be notified of her death. Maybe she'll find something that will either prove or disprove C. D.'s claim that he's Josephine's son."

"Doubtful," Gabe said, shaking his head. "I'm sorry, but this is just not a good idea."

Lizzie rolled her eyes but said nothing.

"Look, Gabe. Just let her finish cataloging the contents of the secretary and whatever else is in the room. Okay? If some judge asks questions, you can say you hired her to provide archival services."

"Except that Lizzie, as astute a journalist as she is, is not a forensic archivist," Gabe said.

"Give me a week. One week, that's all I ask," Lizzie chimed in. "I'll put everything in order and notify you of anything and everything I find."

"Please, Gabe?" Brooke asked.

He glanced at his watch. "All right. I've got court up in Glynn County this afternoon. You've got a week, Lizzie, then I really have to insist that you decamp. Let me know what you find."

47

"Who died and left him boss?" Lizzie asked.

"Josephine did, remember?" Felicia said. She picked up an envelope from the card table. "Find anything interesting yet in all this mess?"

"Lots. Josephine really led a fascinating life. She was a prodigious letter writer." Lizzie picked up a file folder. "She was mad as hell at her 'dear cousins' for selling their land to the state. There are carbon copies here of all the letters she sent — to them, to her state representative, the governor. She even wrote letters to Jimmy Carter. Turns out she contributed a hundred bucks to his campaign when he ran for governor of Georgia, so naturally she thought he should intervene on her behalf."

"Did he write back?"

"Nope. And when she didn't hear from him, she fired off a scathing follow-up letter telling him she was glad she'd voted for Ronald Reagan against him," Lizzie said.

Brooke sighed. "Well, you heard the man. You've only got a week before Gabe kicks you out of here and cuts off your access to these papers."

"What exactly are you looking for?" Felicia asked, sitting in Josephine's recliner, a seat Brooke had consciously avoided.

"Answers. Why did Josephine cut off contact with Millie and Ruth — and Varina, to some extent? I mean, she went to all that trouble having Brooke invite us over here, but she never really gave us any answers. And of course, I'm hoping to figure out this thing with the unsolved disappearance of Russell Strickland," said Lizzie.

"Wasting your time," Felicia said. "Why don't you find some way to prove that C. D. wasn't Josephine's son?"

"I've been trying, but like Brooke said, there are a ton of papers just in that secretary. I did find these, though." She picked up a shoe box and held it out.

Felicia and Brooke peered into the box, which held a jumble of small, thin leather-bound books. Brooke picked one up at random. The cover was stamped in gold with *1965*.

"Datebooks?"

"Yup. They start in 1938 and run all the way through the mideighties. And before you ask, I've looked at the relevant years. No mention of killing anybody or birthing any illegitimate babies."

Brooke riffled the pages of the book in her hand and read aloud from the first entry. " 'Dentist appointment, Brunswick, January 12.' And then there's this, in February: 'Lunch with Emma.' "

Lizzie nodded. "From what I can tell from skimming her calendars, she had a lot of lunch dates, played bridge with some ladies at the Cloister every other week, went to fund-raisers for various good causes, and she was diligent about getting her teeth cleaned and her cars and boat serviced. She also noted the tide charts, how many deer and feral hogs were shot on the island, and how many sea turtle nests she observed on the beach every summer."

"Do we know what year C. D. was born?" Felicia asked.

"He claims he was born in '42," Brooke said.

Lizzie sifted through the shoe box contents. "Here's the datebook from 1942. Help yourself, but I'm telling you there's nothing about having a baby."

Felicia pulled a pair of glasses from her pocket and began skimming, turning pages, occasionally reading aloud. "Josephine was living in Savannah then, right?"

"Yes," Brooke said. "Once the war started, her father closed up Shellhaven. I believe he went back to Boston, but Josephine lived in a town house in Savannah that her family owned."

Felicia ran her finger down the calendar pages. "War bond drives. Bridge parties. Luncheons. Dinners. Josephine was quite the social butterfly. Wait. Here's a notation about a doctor's appointment. In February," Felicia said.

Brooke looked over Felicia's shoulder. "But it doesn't say the doctor's name."

"No." Felicia turned over a few more pages. "Another one in April. Still no doctor's name."

Brooke looked down at the penciled notation. "That doesn't necessarily mean anything. I mean, maybe she had heartburn. Or migraines. Or bunions."

"Or God forbid, a bun in the oven," Felicia said dryly.

"Hey!" Lizzie said, lightly punching Felicia's arm. "That was funny! You actually *do* have a sense of humor."

Felicia looked from Lizzie to Brooke. "Did you think otherwise?"

"You seem pretty serious most of the time," Brooke said.

"I think that's Southern for 'You go around acting like you have a stick up your butt,' " Lizzie said. "Maybe you could lighten up just a little?"

Felicia blinked, then pushed her glasses farther up the bridge of her nose. "You sound like some of my students. I mean, I teach African American studies. It's serious stuff. And as an African American woman, I've spent my whole career trying to take my work seriously."

"We're not your students," Lizzie pointed out. "We're your friends. Or we're trying to be."

"Okay. Point taken. Lighten up. Loosen up. Anything else?"

"Yeah. Turn the page on that datebook. Any other interesting entries?" Lizzie asked.

"Hmm. Red Cross committee meeting. Junior League committee meeting." Felicia flipped pages. "Bond drive." She looked up, startled. "March 20. Maternity clothes."

Lizzie reached for the datebook. "Let me see that."

Felicia stabbed the notation with her index finger. "Right here. See?"

"It actually says, 'Mtnty clothes,' but yeah, you're right. Shit. Maybe C. D. is for real," Lizzie said. "Why else would she be shopping for maternity clothes?"

"Okay, I think we shouldn't start jumping to conclusions," Brooke said, trying to be the voice of caution. "Lizzie, maybe you and Felicia can team up to finish going through all Josephine's papers."

"Or maybe —" Lizzie started.

"We go to Savannah and start doing some primary research," Felicia finished. "Talk to that Catholic whatever-it-is. Visit the orphanage where C. D. says he was raised."

"Brilliant!" Lizzie beamed at her newfound colleague. "Let's do it." She turned to Brooke. "I say we head up to Savannah first thing in the morning. And since you're a native daughter, you can be our Savannah tour guide."

"I can't just drop everything. I've got a job, you know. And a child," Brooke said.

"Have your calls forwarded to your cell phone and get the babysitter to take care of the kid," Lizzie said. "Come on, Brooke. You know people in Savannah, and we don't. This is important. To all of us."

"It's just one day," Felicia said.

Brooke sighed. "Okay. This is crazy, but I'll do it."

"High fives!" Lizzie declared, and the three slapped palms and bumped fists. "Now group hugs!" she added.

"Let's not get carried away," Felicia drawled.

48

Brooke was standing beside the Volvo, waiting, as Felicia and Lizzie walked toward the marina parking lot.

"Shotgun," Felicia said, climbing into the front seat.

Lizzie rolled her eyes and opened the rear door. "Um, Brooke?"

Henry was belted into his car seat, quietly munching on a toaster waffle. His face and hair and hands were smeared with peanut butter.

"Ladies, this is my son, Henry. Henry, that's Lizzie. And this is Felicia, up front with me."

"Hi, Henry," Felicia said, turning around to wave.

"Heyya, Henry," Lizzie added.

"He was running a little temperature this morning, which meant I couldn't take him to day care, and Farrah, my babysitter, has graduation practice today and she couldn't keep him," Brooke explained. "So we're going to drop him off at my mom's house in Savannah before we go do our thing. And Henry's going to be a really good boy today. Aren't you, Henry?"

"No," Henry said, throwing his sippy cup onto the floor.

"He'll fall asleep any minute now, I promise," Brooke said.

"He'd better," Lizzie muttered. "So what's our game plan?"

"I thought we'd start where C. D. says he got his initial information, at the archdiocesan office in Savannah. It's just a few blocks from my mom's house in Ardsley Park. Depending on what we find out, we'll hopefully also make it out to Good Shepherd too."

"Remind me exactly what that place is?" Felicia said.

"It *was* the oldest continuously operating home for boys in the country. But their mission has changed over the years, and now it's morphed into a privately operated all-boys prep school," Brooke said. "C. D. says he lived there from the time this Catholic orphanage placed him there at six until he ran away at sixteen."

"Louette says she almost hopes we can prove C. D. is Josephine's son," Felicia said. "He's definitely a strange one, but she says he's way better than those awful cousins."

"I think we have to try to go into this with an open mind," Lizzie said. "Ask the right questions and just follow the bread crumbs until we reach the truth."

"Agreed," Brooke said. "But realistically, I don't have high hopes that the archdiocese will share much information with us, especially where it relates to those old adoption records. I'm sure they'll cite privacy concerns."

Lizzie leaned forward in her seat. "Listen, I dig up dirt for a living. It's my job to outrun or outsmart every version of the answer *no.* When we get there, how about I ask the questions?"

"Works for me," Felicia said.

"So whatever kind of pretext I come up with, you guys just go with it. Okay?"

Brooke felt uneasy. "You're not going to tell any outright lies or try to make me do anything unethical, right?"

"We'll see," Lizzie said.

Marie met them at the front door of the Ardsley Park home where Brooke had grown up. She transferred the limp, dozing toddler to her mother's outstretched arms.

"He feels a little warm," Marie whispered, touching the child's pink cheek.

"There's some children's Tylenol in here," Brooke said, handing her mother the diaper bag. "Give him that with some juice."

"We'll be fine," Marie said. "Call me and let me know how it's going."

"I will. Thanks again for pinch-hitting, Mom. Love you."

Brooke made the turn from Victory Drive onto the impressive-looking grounds of the Catholic diocese campus. "This used to be a children's home too," she told her passengers. "When I was growing up, it was St. Elizabeth's. But the grounds were so overgrown with trees and moss, it looked really spooky."

They parked and started walking toward the entry. "Rule number one for seeking information you probably don't have any right to is always make friends with clerks and secretaries," Lizzie said as they mounted the marble steps.

"You mean suck up to the man?" Felicia asked.

"No. Not the man. The man's secretary or assistant or clerk, who is almost always a woman. The gatekeeper, if you will. Now watch and learn," Lizzie said.

She swung open the door and approached a middle-aged woman at a reception desk.

"Hi," she said brightly. "I'm Lizzie Quinlan."

"Hello." The woman looked quizzical. "How can I help you ladies?"

"I'd like to see some records from a now-defunct Catholic children's home here in town, and I understand you have those on microfilm? The years I'm interested in are roughly 1942 through 1948 or '49. And I'd be happy to pay whatever photocopying costs are incurred."

"I'm sorry. We have strict privacy rules. Those records are only open to the actual children who were placed in the home and their biological mothers."

"Oh." Lizzie's shoulders slumped dramatically. She stared down at the clerk's nameplate, which said *Debbie Winters.*

"Well, I guess I did see something about that on the archdiocesan website, but I just thought maybe, because of the special circumstances, you all might make an exception, just this one time. And we've come such a long way too."

"That's a shame," Debbie said. "Where are you ladies from?"

"I'm actually from California, and she's from Florida," Lizzie said, pointing to Felicia. "You see, Debbie," she continued, "our dad is very, very ill. He's in his seventies and we really don't know how much longer we'll have him with us."

"Is it . . . ?"

"Cancer? Yes. Very advanced. And very, very aggressive."

"My sympathy to you girls," Debbie said.

"He only recently shared with us the story of how his mother left him — abandoned him, actually — in a church here in Savannah. It was the first time he's completely opened up to any of us about this. Naturally, my sisters and I wanted to follow up and get to the truth."

"Naturally." Debbie nodded.

"He told us that the priest in one of the churches in town found him under a pew when he was an infant after mass one Sunday morning."

Debbie's face registered her disbelief. "But that's horrifying."

"Shocking," Felicia put in. "We had no idea."

Debbie looked from Felicia to Lizzie, obviously puzzled. "Who is this?"

"Oh, uh, that's my sister, Felicia. From Florida."

"Half sister," Felicia corrected. "Same dad. Different mamas."

"Same for me," Brooke said.

"Three daughters by three different women? How unusual," Debbie said.

"Anyway, the three of us, we're at that time in our lives, we really need some answers. For our peace of mind, and of course, to find out about our family medical history," Lizzie went on. "You can empathize with that, can't you?"

"Yes, but —"

"Before Dad dies," Lizzie said. "Ticking clock," Felicia added.

"Dad told us the parish priest who found him took him to a Catholic orphanage here."

"From the sound of it, that would be St.

Joseph's. It closed in the mid-1950s, and the children were moved over here to St. Elizabeth's," Debbie said.

"You still have all the records though, right?" Felicia said eagerly.

"As I said, those records are sealed to the general public."

"But we're not the general public," Lizzie said.

"If you bring your father in here, with some proof of identity, we'd be happy to share the records with him," Debbie offered.

"Not possible," Felicia said.

"Or his authorized representative. If you could bring in a notarized letter, signed by your father, I could speak to my supervisor and I think we could possibly work something out," Debbie said.

"But we want it to be a surprise," Lizzie said.

Brooke had an idea. "Daddy said he'd heard that the priest's name was Father Ryan? Maybe Charles Ryan? He's the one who turned him over to the nuns at St. Joseph's. We know it's a slim chance, but maybe if Father Ryan were still alive . . ."

"What year did you say this was?" Debbie asked.

"Nineteen forty-two. We think," Felicia said.

"I'm sure Father Ryan is long gone," Debbie said.

Lizzie sighed heavily. "Is there, like, a roster

or something in your computer that you could check?"

Debbie's fingers danced over the keyboard of her desktop computer. "Well, just as I suspected. Father Ryan, God rest his soul, passed away in 1982. According to our records, he was pastor at Church of the Apostles until his retirement in 1976. Unfortunately, that church was closed in 1987, and its parish was absorbed into another church."

The three women looked at each other, waiting for an idea to occur to their self-appointed leader.

"I just wish, for Dad's sake," Lizzie said dramatically. "I wish there were some way to find out if the story is true, about him being found under a pew. I mean, it's so bizarre, you'd think somebody who was around back then would remember."

"It was a very long time ago," Debbie said.

Lizzie snapped her fingers. "All right. Let's try this from another angle. After a good bit of prodding from us, Dad said he's always believed his biological mother was a woman named Josephine Bettendorf Warrick. Would it be possible to see if she was a parishioner?"

"I can check, but not all the parishes in the diocese kept good records. And in some cases, when churches closed, their records were simply destroyed, which I think is a shame, don't you?" Debbie began typing. "Spell that name, please?"

Lizzie spelled it out, then repeated it.

"No. Not in our database."

"Dad has an old newspaper clipping from that time," Brooke said. "He showed it to us. It shows Mrs. Warrick at the orphanage at Christmastime with a child identified as Charlie Anthony on her lap. Dad says he remembers she came every year to donate toys and gifts, and every year, he got special gifts the other children didn't."

"That's right," Lizzie said. "Why would Josephine do that, if she didn't have a connection to our dad or to the orphanage or to the church where Dad was left?"

"Right." Debbie's brow was wrinkled as she considered the question. She chewed on the end of a pencil. "Maybe . . . ," she said slowly. "I think you should go speak to Sister Theresa. She's the oldest nun still living in Savannah from that time. She's ninety-nine and almost blind, but she's still sharp as a tack. If anybody would remember this story, it would be Sister Theresa."

"Perfect," Felicia said eagerly. "How do we find her?"

"She lives at the Rose of Sharon Apartments, in midtown." Debbie spun the wheel of a Rolodex and plucked a yellowing card. "One of the younger nuns from her order does all Sister's shopping and acts as a sort of de facto caregiver. Let me call Joan and see if she thinks Sister is up for visitors today."

A moment later, Debbie scrawled an address on a scrap of paper. "Joan says Sister loves company, and you're welcome to go see her right away, if that's convenient."

"Oh!" Lizzie exclaimed. "God bless you, Debbie! We'll all keep you in our prayers."

"My pleasure," Debbie said, blushing.

"Laying it on a little thick back there, weren't you?" Felicia asked as they climbed back into the Volvo.

"The Lord moved me," Lizzie said with a broad wink.

49

Sister Theresa Monahan's grip was firm as she greeted each of her visitors. "I'm so pleased to meet you," she said in a quavery voice that still bore traces of a Boston accent, despite having lived in the South for more than seventy years. "Now, Joanie says you girls have some questions for me?"

She was a short, plump woman, and she wore a navy-blue St. Vincent's Academy sweatshirt and navy sweatpants. Her bright blue eyes were clouded, but her round face was miraculously unlined. She sat in an overstuffed armchair in a neat but sparsely furnished studio apartment. The television was turned to a Braves baseball game but she pointed the remote at the set and turned down the volume.

"Now. I'm all set. Ask away."

Lizzie repeated the pertinent parts of their pretext story.

Sister Theresa nodded sympathetically. "I'll put your father in my devotionals," she said.

"Charles Anthony, you said his name is?"

"He goes by C. D. now," Lizzie said. "He has some memory of the nuns at St. Joseph's telling him he was named after the priest who found him, Charles Ryan."

"Of course. I knew Father Ryan."

"The sisters gave him the last name of Anthony, after their favorite saint," Brooke added.

"Goodness. I haven't thought of this in years and years!" Sister exclaimed. "Now, I don't remember the baby's name, I'm afraid, but at the time, back in the war years, I went to St. Joseph's once or twice a week to teach music to the little ones, and I do remember the story about Father Ryan finding an infant in that church. He was a scrawny little thing."

"Yes?" Lizzie said anxiously.

Sister hesitated and picked up a string of well-worn rosary beads. "Now, I would never want to speak ill of the dead or call dear Father Ryan a liar, but I will say that we always wondered if that story was completely truthful."

"Why is that?"

Sister Theresa smiled. "Of course, we take vows of poverty when we accept our vocations, you know. I think Father Ryan came from a very, very impoverished part of Ireland. But when he came to the States, and Savannah, he discovered he had a taste for the nicer things in life. Things that don't come easily when you're the pastor of one of the poorest inner-city churches in Savannah."

"He had a black parish?" Felicia asked.

"Yes. That's right. Many of his parishioners worked for some of the wealthiest families in Savannah as maids or gardeners or handymen. Wonderful people, but of modest means. So it did raise some eyebrows when Father started driving a shiny new Packard. Coincidentally, right around the time the sisters took in that poor little baby you mentioned."

"Did Father Ryan say how he was able to buy such a nice car?" Felicia asked.

"A generous gift from an anonymous benefactor," Sister said with a mischievous glint in her sightless eyes.

Wow! Felicia mouthed.

"And you and the rest of the sisters, you didn't really believe that story?" Lizzie said.

"We might have been nuns, dear, but we weren't dummies," Sister said tartly. "We did wonder what Father Ryan did to deserve such a splendid gift."

"What do you think he did?" Brooke asked.

"It was just speculation, you know. We all assumed one of his parishioners, who worked for one of those very wealthy families, was asked to be the go-between between the baby's mother and Father Ryan — and that Father Ryan was handsomely rewarded in return for his discretion," Sister said.

It was Brooke's turn now. "Wow," she whispered.

"Sister? Did you ever know a woman named Josephine Bettendorf Warrick?" Lizzie asked.

The nun smiled. "I never did have the pleasure of meeting that great lady, but of course, we were all very gratified when she donated the money for the new nursery wing at the children's home. Such a lovely gesture, especially considering she wasn't even of our faith."

"She paid for a wing at the children's home, yet she didn't have children and she wasn't Catholic?" Lizzie asked.

"Oh no. I believe her family attended St. John's Episcopal. As for the children part, I don't believe she was married at that point. The new wing was named the Bettendorf Nursery."

Brooke spoke up, choosing her words carefully. "Was there, well . . . was there any speculation, at the time, about the baby Father Ryan claimed he 'found' in his church? Were there any rumors that the baby could have been Josephine Bettendorf's own baby? Maybe a child she had out of wedlock? Could Josephine have been the anonymous donor of the Packard? And could that be the reason she donated the money for the nursery at the home?"

"You think baby Charlie was Josephine Bettendorf's?" The idea seemed to intrigue the elderly nun.

"We've heard a story to that effect, but we don't have any real proof," Lizzie said. "That's why we came to you."

"I don't think any of us, at the time, thought anything like that," Sister Theresa said. "We all just assumed Josephine was a wealthy young lady from a good family who'd been raised to perform good works. Although, now that I think about it, I remember one of the sisters was always puzzled about why Miss Bettendorf made such a point of visiting the home and spending time with the children, especially at Christmas, when she was so very clearly uncomfortable around little ones."

"Good question," Felicia said.

Sister nodded. "Is there anything else I can help you with? I've really enjoyed our visit, but I'll confess, I'm anxious to get back to my ball game. I try never to miss a Braves game. Can one of you tell me the score?"

Brooke stepped closer to the television. "Looks like it's the top of the ninth, and it's all tied up, and the Braves are at bat."

Sister clapped her hands gleefully. "Who's on deck?"

"Um, I can't pronounce that name," Brooke said. "Lots of consonants."

"Never mind. That must be Vlad. He's my favorite." She put down the rosary beads and picked up the remote, turning the volume on high.

"Goodbye, Sister Theresa," Lizzie said, leaning down to give the old woman a peck on the cheek. "We've enjoyed talking to you, and really appreciate the information."

"Entirely my pleasure, I assure you. Come again, anytime. I always enjoy talking about the old days."

"We'll do that," Brooke said, heading for the door.

"One more thing, girls!" Sister called out. "Something I just thought of. You said the nuns named Charlie after St. Anthony because he was their favorite saint. I'm afraid that's wrong. I'm quite sure he was named that because Anthony of Padua is the patron saint of the lost. And that poor baby was definitely lost."

"Excuse me?" Felicia said.

"Obviously you're not Catholic." Sister chuckled. "My late mother, God rest her soul, whenever she misplaced her pocketbook or house key, she would always make us children get down on our knees and pray to St. Anthony for assistance. I can still remember the prayer. 'Tony, Tony, turn around. Something's lost and must be found.' Probably highly sacrilegious, but I still pray to St. Anthony when I can't find my doggone remote."

50

The women sat in the parked Volvo in the parking lot at the rebranded Good Shepherd Academy.

Felicia gestured toward the manicured grounds dotted with moss-hung towering oaks, head-high azaleas, and redbrick buildings. "This place doesn't look at all like a children's home. I've been on college campuses that don't look this impressive. Hell, I've worked at campuses that weren't this nice."

The bronze plaque over the door told them they were looking at the administration building and visitor's center.

"Remind me what we're doing here?" Felicia asked.

"We're trying to dig up the truth about C. D.'s origin story," Brooke said. "That orphanage he was taken to as an infant is long gone, and this was his next stop. He says he lived here from the time he was six until he was sixteen. To tell you the truth, I'm not really sure what we're looking for."

"After what Sister Theresa said, I think we might be on the right track," Felicia said. "That sweet old lady wouldn't lie, would she?"

"I believed her. And now I'm thinking maybe there really is something to C. D.'s story. It's just weird enough to be true," Lizzie agreed.

"I don't know," Brooke said. "Josephine was so intent on making amends with her oldest friends, and by extension, us. Right up until the night she died. But if she wanted to make things right, why wouldn't she mention the fact that she'd given a child up for adoption? Why wouldn't she try to find him?"

"Not just given him up. Abandoned him," Felicia said. "And bought off a priest in the process to keep her secret."

"Of course, we don't have any proof of that," Lizzie reminded them. "Just an elderly blind nun's suspicions."

"You know what I've been wondering?" Felicia said. "What's C. D. been using to prove his identity all these years? Does he have a birth certificate? Social security card? How'd he get those things if he was supposedly the equivalent of a Catholic Cabbage Patch Kid?"

"Good question," Lizzie said. "Maybe I can look it up online."

"Except you can't," Brooke said. "Privacy issues again. Only the holder of the birth certificate, or a first-degree relative, or a duly authorized representative of the party in question, like a guardian or attorney, has access to those records in Georgia."

"So what's our approach when we get in there?" Felicia asked. "Is Lizzie still our liar in chief?"

"Same general pretext," Lizzie said. "I'm probably just going to wing it. So nod and agree with whatever I say. I think the aim is to see if we can get a gander at C. D.'s records."

Brooke had been staring at the administration building, trying to recall some obscure detail that had been nagging at her since she'd driven through the Good Shepherd entrance arch. Something C. D. had said.

She got out of the car and walked toward a nearby building, a brick one-story affair. A brass plaque proclaimed it the Halberg Cottage. She turned and got back in the car.

"What was that all about?" Lizzie asked.

"Just remembering something C. D. said. It was the morning Josephine died when he came to tell us he was Josephine's son. He said he'd come to a reunion here at Good Shepherd and bumped into a man he'd known all those years ago. Somebody who'd been at St. Joseph's and then transferred here to Good Shepherd, the same way C. D. had, when he turned six. He was the one who told C. D. he could look up the old records at the archdiocesan offices."

"Did he mention a name?" Felicia asked.

"I don't think so," Brooke said. "If he did, I don't remember it. Maybe this man could corroborate C. D.'s story." She pulled out her cell phone and found Louette's number in her contact list.

Louette answered on the third ring. "Hey, Brooke. How you doing? Finding out anything up there in Savannah?"

"We've made some progress, but I'd like to ask C. D. a couple of questions. Do you have his phone number, Louette?"

"I got a number for him, but he don't ever use a phone," Louette said. "Half the time it's turned off or he's left it behind somewhere."

"Can you tell me the number anyway? It's worth a shot. And if you see C. D., will you ask him to call me?"

"I will, but I don't know where that man's got to. Haven't hardly seen him at all this week."

After she disconnected from Louette, Brooke tried C. D.'s number. Her call went directly to voice mail. She left a message. "C. D., it's Brooke. I'm in Savannah, trying to track down any records that might prove you're related to Josephine. Call me, please, as soon as you get this."

A small sign in the lobby of the administration building directed visitors to the upstairs offices. It was late afternoon, nearly four, and the open space with office cubicles lining the outside walls was mostly deserted.

"Hello?" A trim, middle-aged man with a salt-and-pepper goatee walked out of his office with a smile. The placard on the wall said DON SMALLS, DIRECTOR OF DEVELOPMENT.

"Anything I can do for you ladies?"

"Hi," Lizzie said smoothly. She went into her pretext again, this time adding more drama and substance.

"Dad is at the end of his life," she said sadly. "And this place has meant so much to him. He's sort of searching for his identity, I guess, so that he can pass it along to his daughters."

Smalls adjusted his wire-rimmed glasses. "Are all three of you sisters?"

"Half sisters," Felicia said, picking up her cue. "We had three different mothers. They're all gone now, and Dad's all we have left."

"I totally understand," Smalls said. "Was your father looking to make some sort of bequest to Good Shepherd? As a memoriam?"

"Not at this time, although that could change," Lizzie said. "His birthday is coming up and we thought we'd put together a memory book as a surprise. He suffers from dementia now, you know. The problem is, we don't have anything substantive to put in there from his childhood."

"We were hoping maybe the home had some old photos or documents in their archives that we could make copies of," Felicia said.

"We'd be happy to pay any copying charges," Brooke added.

"Well . . ." Smalls crossed his arms over his chest. "I don't know what documents you're looking for. Most of that stuff would be considered confidential."

"Really?" Felicia wrinkled her nose in disbelief. "After all these years? I mean, he's nearly eighty. Why all the secrecy?"

"You have to remember, at the time this institution was a children's home, there was somewhat of a social stigma attached to having been placed here. After all, living here meant either that you had no parents or that your parents were too poor or unfit to raise you themselves. Most of our alumni are quite proud of what they achieved, coming from such humble beginnings, but others would just as soon hide their connection with Good Shepherd."

"So there's nothing?" Lizzie asked, shoulders drooping dramatically to signal her disappointment.

"You're welcome to look through the exhibits in the museum and the scrapbooks," Smalls said. "They're all downstairs in our museum, and they're organized by year.

Maybe you'll find some photos or clippings from his time here. And although it's not usually done, I don't see any harm in letting you make photocopies here in the development office."

"Awesome!" Lizzie said.

"We do ask for a minimal donation for entry to the museum," Smalls said, reaching for his key ring. "Seven dollars."

After the women had paid, he walked them downstairs and unlocked the doors. "I'll be upstairs finishing a report. Look around all you want, and if you do see something you want to copy, feel free. And, ladies? We close at five. I have a board meeting tonight, so I really won't be able to keep the museum open any longer than that."

They spent ten minutes or so browsing the exhibits and then made their way to a small anteroom where they found metal shelves loaded with rows of black leather-bound scrapbooks.

Brooke ran her fingers over the spines of the books, searching for the right years.

"C. D. would have come here in 1948, by my reckoning," she said, pulling a book with the appropriate year stamped in gold on the spine.

The three women crowded around a table as Brooke opened the scrapbook. The pages were of brittle black construction paper with newspaper clippings, black-and-white snapshots, and the miscellanea of a bygone era glued to the paper.

"Look at this," Brooke said, tapping a faded mimeographed sheet of paper. "It's a play program. *Oliver Twist.* Appropriate, huh? Orphans putting on a play about an orphan boy." She ran her finger down the names of the cast and was surprised to see a name she recognized.

"Oh my gosh. Here's George Trautwein. He used to own the biggest Cadillac dealership in Savannah. I went to Savannah Country Day with his granddaughter Ginger."

"Fascinating," Felicia said. "Let's keep going. We don't have much time."

"Right," Lizzie agreed. "Eyes on the prize."

She flipped more pages, and some of the old paper seemed to crumble under her fingertips. "What's with all the pictures of cows?" Lizzie asked.

"They've always had a cattle operation here, and a working farm," Brooke said. "I think it was part of the whole vocational, self-sustaining model."

A few pages later, they found a typed report of the minutes of the Good Shepherd Alumni Association annual meeting.

Lizzie read aloud. "Okay. Discussion about raising funds for a new roof for the hay barn. Announcements about new cottage parents. Announcements about fellow alumni, births, deaths, marriages . . . oh, hello!" She tapped a line item with her fingertip. " 'Construction has begun on a new cottage, to be named in memory of local benefactor Samuel G. Bettendorf.' "

"Looking better and better for our buddy C. D.," Felicia muttered. "First Josephine bought a new wing at St. Joseph's, and then a new cottage here. Some guilt trip, huh?"

"Keep flipping those pages," Lizzie said.

Two-thirds of the way through the book, they found a section devoted to black-and-white group photos of boys, organized by cottages.

"Here!" Felicia stabbed a slightly out-of-focus photo of eight young boys posed in front of a small brick house. "These kids look to be the right age."

The boys stared into the camera, squinting in the sunlight. They were dressed in dungarees mostly, with two of the smallest ones wearing knickers and high socks. Their clothes were rumpled, and some wore baseball caps. A small balding man who wore pince-nez glasses stood behind the children, his hand on the shoulder of a dour-looking woman in a dark print dress.

The handwritten caption on the page read: "Cole Cottage, 6–8 yrs."

"Do any of these kids look like C. D. to you?" Lizzie asked, peering down at the photo.

"I've only laid eyes on him a couple of times, so I can't imagine what he looked like over seventy years ago," Felicia said. "One thing catches my eye. They're all white kids, right? What happened to black children who had nobody to look after them?"

"There used to be a home for black children in Savannah, according to my mom, but I don't know too much about it. As for recognizing C. D., I've seen him and talked to him several times, but I've got no clue either," Brooke admitted. "But look. You can see some writing on the back." With a fingernail, she worked at the glued-down corners at the bottom of the photo. A moment later, she carefully turned the photo over to find a handwritten list of the children.

"Dicky Abbott, Buck Anthony, Frank Armour, Sid Babcock, Bobby Bass, Mickey Beaman, Chick Garber, Timmy Potts."

"Buck Anthony," she repeated. "That's gotta be our guy. Bingo."

"Which one?" Lizzie asked, leaning down to get a closer look.

Brooke shook her head. "I don't know. It looks like they listed the kids' names alphabetically, but there's no telling if they're lined up that way."

Lizzie reached for her cell phone and snapped a photo of the list, then flipped the photo over and shot one of the picture itself.

They leafed rapidly through the rest of the

scrapbook but found nothing else that showed a boy who could be C. D. "Buck" Anthony.

"Now what?" Brooke asked, looking at her watch. "We've only got ten more minutes before closing. That's not really enough time to go through any more scrapbooks."

"We've got a list of the boys who lived with him in that cottage," Lizzie said.

"And we know at least one of them is still living, or he was as of a few months ago, when C. D. ran into him at that reunion," Brooke said. "But which one? And how do we contact him?"

"Through the alumni association," Felicia said. "That's how my alma mater always reaches out to put the squeeze to me for donations."

They heard the door open, and Don Smalls popped his head inside. "All set, ladies? I need to set the alarm and lock the place up now."

"But it's not five yet," Lizzie protested.

"Sorry. I can't be late for that board meeting," Smalls said.

"Can you do us a huge favor?" Lizzie asked, walking rapidly toward him. "We found a picture of my dad, along with the rest of the boys who lived in his cottage in 1948, the year he came here. And we found a list of the names of the boys on the back. I took a photo with my phone. Maybe you could take a look and see if you recognize any names? Dad said he ran into one of his pals at the last reunion, but he couldn't remember the name because of the dementia. But it's likely this man belongs to the alumni association if he came to a reunion, right?"

"Maybe," Smalls said.

Lizzie scrolled through her camera roll until she found the photo, and then she enlarged it.

Smalls read the list aloud. "Hmm. No, never heard of Dicky Abbott or Sid Babcock. Dowling, Garber, Potts, I've seen their names in old alumni newsletters, but I believe they're all deceased. But Mickey Beaman, yeah. Mickey's still active in the association. His son drives him to all the meetings and functions."

Brooke's heart leaped. "Do you by chance have contact information for Mickey Beaman?"

"No, but this time of day you can usually catch him at his son's business. He likes to hang out there and chat with any old-timers who wander in. Mickey's pretty loquacious. He'll talk your ear off if you give him half a chance."

"What's the business?" Lizzie asked eagerly.

"Mr. B's Quality Beverages," Smalls said. He jangled his key chain to signal that their time was up.

51

Mr. B's was a liquor store on West Broad Street, on the fringes of the Savannah College of Art and Design campus.

"We used to try to use fake IDs to buy booze here when I was in high school," Brooke remarked after she'd parked.

An electronic doorbell rang as they entered the store, which was dark and cramped with narrow aisles built of liquor cartons, the walls lined with shelves of cut-rate wine. A glass partition separated the cashier stand from the rest of the shop, and behind it, an Asian woman with white-streaked dark hair was counting back change to a college kid with a case of beer tucked under his arm.

"I don't think this place has been cleaned since the last time I was in here," Brooke muttered to Lizzie. "And that's definitely the same lady who called the cops on us."

She waited until the store's sole customer had departed and stepped up to the counter and gave a friendly smile to the cashier, who remained stone-faced.

"Hi. I'm looking for Mr. Beaman?"

"My husband's out," the woman said. "What do you want? Not another charity donation, I hope. You people are bleeding us broke with all these silent auctions and wine dinners."

"I'm actually looking for Mickey Beaman," Brooke said.

"Why?" The cashier looked over Brooke's shoulder, regarding Lizzie and Felicia, who were loitering near the door, with growing suspicion.

"Well, uh . . . ," Brooke stammered, caught off guard by the woman's hostility.

"We're trying to find somebody who lived at Good Shepherd at the same time as a relative," said Lizzie, stepping into the fray. "We just came from there, and a man in the development office suggested we talk to Mr. Beaman."

The woman rolled her eyes and turned toward a partially open door behind her. "Dad!" she hollered. "Dad! Some people wanna talk to you out here."

She waited a moment. "I'm warning you, once you get him talking about that place, he'll never shut up."

The door opened, and an old man shuffled out of the back room. His thinning gray hair was combed across his balding head. He wore a Budweiser-logoed golf shirt stretched tightly over a massive stomach.

"These ladies want to ask you some stuff about one of your Good Shepherd cronies," the woman said.

Mickey Beaman's eyes lit up at the mention of his alma mater. "What do you want to know?" he asked, leaning against the counter.

"Not here," his daughter-in-law said. She pushed a button and they heard a buzz, and then a door opened between the store and the cash stand. "Take them back to the stockroom."

A small card table and four folding chairs were shoved up against an ancient refrigerator in the stockroom, delineating what passed as Mr. B's break room.

"You ladies have a seat," Beaman said with a gallant gesture toward the table.

"Mr. Beaman," Lizzie started.

"It's Mickey. Nobody calls me Mr. Beaman anymore," he insisted. "Now, what can I tell you about Good Shepherd? Have you been out to see the new museum? Did you see the video? That's me at the three-minute mark, talking about the values that were instilled in boys like me."

"That museum is very impressive," Lizzie said. "We only got to spend a few minutes there today, so we missed out on the video. I guess we'll check it out the next time."

"You do that," Mickey urged. "Jimmy Yaz—

that's Jimmy Yazbek, he was three years younger than me — lived in the Blatner Cottage. His son is a big-deal cameraman on one of those TV shows, I forget the name of the show, but Jimmy Junior made that video. For free."

"Speaking of your classmates, we're trying to help a relative of ours, C. D. Anthony, put together some information about his early life, both at St. Joseph's and at Good Shepherd," Brooke said.

Mickey's brow furrowed. "Say the name again?"

"C. D. Anthony. The nuns called him Charlie, but when we were at Good Shepherd just now, we saw a photo showing all the boys who lived in your cottage. He was listed as Buck Anthony," Lizzie said. "Does that name ring a bell?"

"Buck? Oh yeah. I knew Buck Anthony. Like you say, we were both at St. Joseph's, and then when we turned six, we were sent to Good Shepherd. I think I was maybe older than him. I'm seventy-nine, you know. Still drive, although Yvonne out there, she's trying to get my son to make me stop. What can I tell you about old Buck? He was a hell-raiser as a kid, that's for sure. He was always small for his age, but you didn't want to cross him. The guy had a temper and a wicked undercut. We used to box, you know. I don't think they teach boxing to boys these days, which is a shame. Boxing is a great life lesson."

"It sure is," Lizzie said, trying to steer Mickey back toward the topic at hand. "Do you remember ever hearing about how Buck came to live at St. Joseph's?"

"Somebody left him in a church was what I always heard," Mickey said promptly. "Not like me. My mom passed when I was two, and my dad was a traveling salesman. My grandma did what she could, but she was too old to raise a kid like me. And then my dad got killed in the war, Iwo Jima, so then I was a real orphan. But my grandma would come see me, when she could, take me out for my birthday, stuff like that. I don't think hardly anybody ever came to see Buck, which maybe explains why he sort of had a chip on his shoulder, excuse the expression."

"By any chance, do you remember a woman named Josephine Bettendorf, who might have visited him while he was living at St. Joseph's?" Brooke asked.

"Bettendorf? The family the cottage is named after? At Good Shepherd?"

"Yes," Brooke said. "C. D. — I mean, Buck — says he remembers her coming every Christmas while he lived at St. Joseph's. He says she brought all the kids gifts, but he got special ones. Like a toy truck."

"You want a drink?" Mickey asked suddenly. He stood and opened the refrigerator door. "We get all kinds of samples, for free.

The sales reps are always trying to get us to order whatever's new in their lines." He held up a can. "Red Bull? The SCAD kids all love Red Bull. Or lemme see, how about a Peach Sunset Tea? Or maybe some Chocolate Mint wine? What will you have? It's on the house. Just don't tell Yvonne."

"No, thanks," Brooke said. "We were talking about the Christmas visits? From Josephine Bettendorf?"

"I wouldn't mind trying that wine," Lizzie spoke up. "Strictly for research."

"Great! Take the whole bottle," Mickey handed her the bottle and a plastic wineglass. "Now what were we talking about?"

Lizzie twisted the metal cap from the bottle and poured an inch of milky brown liquid into the glass. She sipped, shuddered, shrugged, then sipped again.

"Christmas visits? At the children's home?" Lizzie reminded him.

"There were several ladies who used to come around the holidays. They'd bring us kids candy canes and oranges. One year a Jewish lady whose husband owned a shoe store downtown brought us each a pair of new shoes. I tell ya, I was so proud of those shoes, I wore 'em 'til those nuns made me turn 'em over to one of the younger kids because they were way too small for me. I can't think of the name of that store. But it's right there on Broughton, near Levy's Jewelers. Or used to be."

"How about Josephine Bettendorf?" Lizzie prompted. "Can you remember her coming to the home? She was tall, with dark hair. Very striking. And C. D. says she gave him a toy truck one year."

"The truck!" Mickey said, roaring with laughter. "I don't remember that dark-haired lady, but I do remember a red truck. A beauty. The other kids were real jealous of Buck and his truck. This one boy — I can see his face, but I can't remember his name . . . a big red-headed kid with freckles — grabbed that truck and bashed Buck in the eye with it. Buck yanked it back and busted the boy in the mouth. Kid bled all over the place. After that, nobody tried to take nothing offa Buck."

"That's what he told me too," Brooke marveled. "Do you have any other memories of Buck? From his time at Good Shepherd? Did the dark-haired woman ever visit him there?"

Mickey popped the top on a can of Budweiser and sipped. "Not saying it didn't happen, just saying I don't recall it. But I remember him staying in trouble. Wouldn't do his chores. Wouldn't listen to the house parents. Fighting, like that. I heard he ran away after he got caught stealing cigarettes from a candy store nearby."

"That sounds about right," Brooke agreed.

"I was surprised he showed up at the reunion, to tell you the truth," Mickey said. "I've never missed one since I left — been president of the alumni association. But that's the only time he ever came to one. I don't judge, but it looked to me like he'd had a hard kind of life."

Brooke glanced at Lizzie to see if she'd thought of any more questions for Mickey Beaman.

Lizzie cleared her throat. "Mickey, there's something I'm curious about. The nuns named him Charles, after the priest who found him, and they called him Charlie. So why did everybody at Good Shepherd call him Buck?"

"It was just a nickname. Everybody had a nickname back then. My name was Mickey, but the guys called me Mouse. You know, for Mickey Mouse? We had a guy called Jughead because he had big ears."

"Where did the name *Buck* come from?" Brooke asked.

Mickey glanced at Felicia, then looked away. "It was different times back then, you know? We weren't what you'd call politically correct. If you really want to know, *Buck* was short for *Buckwheat.* You know? Buckwheat, the little colored kid from the *Our Gang* shows?"

"I remember Buckwheat," Felicia said, her voice icy.

"How did he get the nickname *Buckwheat*?" Lizzie asked.

The stockroom door swung open, and Yvonne stuck her head inside. "Dad, I've gotta go home and get supper started. I need you to come run the register until Michael comes back."

"Sure thing," Mickey said, lumbering to his feet, eager to escape the prying eyes of these three women. "Sorry, ladies, I gotta go to work now."

"The nickname," Lizzie repeated. "How did Buck get that nickname?"

Mickey squirmed and gulped his beer. "I didn't name him that, you understand. It was one of the older guys who started it, and after that, it just stuck. Charlie, or C. D., whatever you wanna call him, he had this wild, kinky hair. You know, like that colored kid from *Our Gang.*"

Lizzie thought about that for a moment. She pulled out her cell phone and pulled up the photo she'd copied from the Good Shepherd yearbook.

"This is a photo of the boys from your cottage, isn't it?"

The old man's face softened. "Son of a gun. It sure is. Look at that. We look like the Dead End kids, don't we? There I am, right there in the middle."

"Which of the boys is Buck?" Lizzie asked, handing him the phone.

He stared down at the photo and finally tapped one face. "I can't be sure, but I think maybe this is him. He was for sure the smallest kid in our cottage, and he's wearing a ball cap, like Buck always used to do. Maybe because he was trying to hide the kinky hair."

Felicia's eyes were blazing, but her voice was calm. "Are you saying Charlie looked black? Like he was African American?"

"His skin wasn't all that dark, not as dark as yours," Mickey said. "Like maybe just real tan. You know how kids are. They say stupid stuff. The guy who gave him that nickname, he said he bet Buck was part colored. And that's why his mama left him in a church. Because she didn't want anybody to know she had a colored baby."

"Dad! Are you coming?" Yvonne screeched.

Mickey downed the rest of his beer and scurried out of the stockroom.

52

"What planet was that old dude from?" Lizzie asked as they drove away from the liquor store. " 'Buckwheat'? 'Colored kid'? What a dinosaur."

"Nothing new to me," Felicia said, turning around from her perch in the front seat of the Volvo. "You've been living in your little bubble out in California all this time. Wake up, girl. This is the Deep South. We got more crackers here than a box of saltines."

"Could it be true?" Brooke asked. "Could C. D. be Josephine's son? And biracial?"

"You think just because I'm black I can spot that one drop of chocolate in the glass of milk?" Felicia demanded.

"That's not how I meant it, and you know it," Brooke said, the blood rushing to her face.

"Relax," Felicia said, laughing. "I was just yanking your chain. 'Cause I've lightened up." She held out her hand to Lizzie. "Let me see that picture again."

Lizzie pulled up the photo and handed over the phone.

With two fingers, Felicia enlarged the image until the blurry face of a runty six-year-old filled the iPhone screen. Shadow cast from the bill of his cap obscured most of the upper half of his face, but the slight smile was visible.

"It's possible," she said, studying the photo. "His lips are sort of full, and maybe his nose is a bit flatter and broader. His skin tone? No darker than some of my Italian friends. Of course, I can't see his hair because of that cap. But yeah, he could be passing."

"I don't think I've ever seen C. D. without a hat. And a cigarillo," Brooke said. "And he's spent a lifetime out in the sun. The question is, what do we do with this gem of information?"

"Let's go see Sister Theresa, show her this photo, and ask if there was ever any discussion that Charlie, or Buck, or whatever you want to call him could have been biracial," Lizzie said.

"Can't. I've gotta pick up Henry from Mom's by five, and I'm already late," Brooke said.

"And I've got to make sure Auntie Vee has eaten and taken her meds," Felicia said. "Louette's been great about letting us stay there, but I'm the one responsible for Vee's health."

"Maybe you could tactfully broach the subject of C. D. with Varina again, given what we learned today," Lizzie said.

Felicia laughed. "She was absolutely adamant that Josephine never had a child. I don't know what her reaction would be if I ask her if Josephine had a child with a black man. Her head might just spin all the way off her neck at the very idea."

"If C. D. would ever return my call, I'd ask him about it," Brooke said, glancing at her own phone, which hadn't rung. "I guess I'll let Gabe know what we learned today. After all, he's the administrator of Josephine's estate. Let him sort it all out."

53

By the time she'd fed and bathed Henry and yawned her way through story time and bedtime, it was after nine o'clock, which was an hour past his normal bedtime and what felt like an eternity past her own.

Brooke peeled out of her clothes and crawled into her unmade bed wearing an old T-shirt. Her laptop rested on her nightstand, but she didn't have the energy to even lift the top. She had emails to return, legal issues to research, documents to draft. The corner of her bedroom was piled high with this week's dirty laundry and last week's laundry that she'd never gotten around to folding. She wouldn't get to any of it tonight, and based on what she knew of her upcoming schedule, tomorrow wasn't looking good either.

Which left only Saturday. In her past life, Saturdays were for long runs followed by endless Bloody Mary–soaked brunches, followed by a trip to the nail salon and maybe shopping with a girlfriend, and then date night with Harris.

But that life was ancient history. It would be a miracle if she managed to muck out her house, get to the grocery store, and maybe do some laundry this Saturday.

Saturday! She flopped backward onto the mattress. This Saturday was supposed to be date night with Gabe Wynant. She'd allowed herself to be sweet-talked into going to a dinner dance with him at the Cloister, but she'd forgotten to line up a babysitter.

She reached for her phone, keeping her fingers crossed that Farrah would be available.

There was a missed call on her phone from an unfamiliar number and an area code she'd never seen before. The caller had left a message. She touched the Play button, and as soon as she heard the voice her pulse rocketed.

"Hey, Brooke. It's Pete. Look, I know it's short notice, but I'm back on the East Coast, headed to a conference in Miami. I've got a stopover in Savannah, where one of my former colleagues from the Park Service is picking me up, then we're driving down to the conference together. I'm wondering — no, I'm hoping, you might agree to meet me at the Savannah airport. I bought a cheap plane ticket, which means I'm about to board my first of three legs of the flight, which is supposed to get me in around ten tomorrow morning. Maybe we could do an early lunch and catch up before my colleague picks me up? Okay, anyway, I really hope to see you tomorrow. I've missed you, you know?"

Pete Haynes missed her. He wanted to see her. Have lunch. Catch up. After three plus years. She could already picture the conversation.

Her: How was Alaska? How are the caribou? Is it really cold there?

Him: Alaska's great. The caribou are awesome, and it's cold as shit. How about you? What have you been up to?

Her: Oh, you know, the usual. Practicing law and raising your son. Wanna split dessert?

She ran her fingers through her hair and groaned. This could not be happening. The call had come in while she was bathing Henry. It was too late to call Pete and try to beg off.

Instead, she texted Farrah.

> Hey. Can you keep Henry for me tomorrow morning? Gotta run up to Savannah. Also need sitter for Saturday night. Heavy date. I'll pay double your usual rate.

Farrah's reply came back in less than a minute.

> So sorry! Can't tomorrow. It's graduation.

I'm a maybe for Saturday night. Can I tell you tomorrow?

No! she wanted to shout. *Commit already.* But she couldn't really blame Farrah. This was a big weekend for a graduating senior. Who wanted to be saddled with babysitting? And maybe it was for the best. Maybe this was the universe telling her she needed to stay home and take care of her kid and concentrate on building some kind of a career.

Or maybe it was the universe telling her to call her mother.

Good thing Marie was a bit of a night owl, Brooke thought.

"Hi!" Marie said. "Shouldn't you be in bed by now?"

"I was, and then I had a missed call. From Pete."

"Oooh. Tell."

"He's got a layover at the Savannah airport tomorrow on his way to a conference in Miami, and he wants me to meet him for lunch and to catch up."

"You're going, right?"

"Not sure. He gets in at ten. But Henry gets out of day care at noon tomorrow because of teacher conferences. And Farrah's graduation is tomorrow, so she can't pick him up and keep him. I hate to ask, especially after you had him all day today . . ."

"Bring him to me," Marie said quickly. "How was he tonight? I didn't want to jinx anything, but he was a little crabby. And he hardly ate anything."

"He seemed fine," Brooke assured her. "We were both wiped out after the long drive home. In fact, he fell asleep in the bathtub after dinner."

"How are you feeling about seeing Pete tomorrow? Are you excited? Nervous?"

"I haven't had time to process it yet. A little of both. Oh, shit!" Brooke wailed. "I have to figure out what to wear. I haven't even done laundry since I got home from Talisa."

"I looked in your closet when I was putting away clothes last time I was there," Marie said. "You have half a dozen pairs of white jeans. Put on a cute top that shows some cleavage. Wear those sexy black sandals I gave you for your birthday. Pull your hair back with those tortoise clips, and wear some dangly earrings."

"Mom! Pete gets in at ten. I'll look like a hooker on the stroll for a john if I show up at the airport in cleavage and spike heels at that hour of the morning."

"You wish. And don't forget to wear makeup, for heaven's sake. You do still know how to apply makeup, right?"

"Very funny. I wear makeup all the time."

"Like when?"

"Like if I have a court date or something."

"You're going to tell Pete about Henry tomorrow, aren't you?"

"I haven't decided," Brooke said. "I thought I'd see how it goes."

"No matter how it goes, you have to tell him," Marie insisted. "Henry is his son. He has a right to know, and you have a responsibility to your son to allow him to have a father in his life. Even if you decide that your relationship with Pete is over, you need to do this, Brooke."

"We'll see," Brooke said. "I gotta hang up now. See you in the morning."

"Makeup. Heels. Cleavage. Earrings," Marie said. "And courage."

She rang the doorbell at her mother's Ardsley Park house and then fumbled in her purse for the house key. The door swung open.

Marie stood in the hallway dressed in her bathrobe and slippers, which was unheard of. This was a woman who never left her bedroom unless she was dressed and perfectly groomed.

But there she stood with lank, unwashed hair. Her eyes were red-rimmed with dark circles beneath. She held a tissue to her nose.

"Mom!" Brooke shifted Henry from one hip to the other. "You look like death. What's wrong?"

"Fever. Chills. Started an hour ago. You look nice," her mother said, giving an approving nod to Brooke's deep V-neck top and eyeliner. "I, on the other hand, feel like I've been run over by a dump truck." Marie's voice was a hoarse rasp.

"You should have called before I left home. I would have just canceled," Brooke said. She stepped into the hallway and took Marie by the elbow. "Come on. I'll fix you some tea with lemon and honey, then you need to get back to bed."

"No," Marie croaked. "Go. Just go. I'm going back to bed. But you need to go to the airport and see Pete. Go. Shoo." She made shooing motions with her hands.

"And take Henry? Are you nuts? What'll I say? What will he say?"

"You two will figure it out," Marie said, turning her head aside to cough. "No matter what else happens, he'll fall in love with Henry. Who wouldn't? Promise me you'll go. Promise me you won't back out and run away again."

Run away. Again. Like she had the weekend of her wedding. The words stung. Because they were true.

"All right," Brooke said. "We're going."

Pete had neglected to tell her where he was flying in from, so she had no idea of his flight number or where they should meet. She'd been so keyed up about the meeting that she'd arrived at the airport thirty minutes early and had spent the past ten minutes pacing up and down the airport's carpeted retail concourse. Her back ached from carrying the heavy toddler, so she finally put him down.

"Toy!" Henry cried, pointing to a gift shop where a giant stuffed Snoopy was perched in the front window. He set off at a run for the shop.

"Whoa there," she said, following after, scooping him up just before the boy made it to his quarry. The back of his pants were damp. She held him aloft, sniffed, and gagged.

"Oh, Henry, nooooo. Not now."

"I poop," he said proudly.

"We poop in the potty, remember?"

"No potty," Henry said.

She'd almost left his diaper bag in the car but at the last minute had shoved her purse inside and looped the bag over her shoulder. It was navy blue, quilted cotton with a pattern of elephants and tigers. Not nearly as cute as the black designer clutch she'd planned to carry. She hurried to the ladies' room, breathing through her mouth while she stripped off the boy's shorts on a drop-down changing table. "What we have here is a shituation," she muttered, stuffing his soiled shorts, shirt, even his socks into a plastic sack she kept in the diaper bag for just such emergencies. She used half a bag of baby wipes cleaning him up, then dressed him in a fresh outfit.

Finally, she went to the sink to wash her hands and check her makeup. "Oh God," she moaned, looking at the mirror. Her cute low-cut top had somehow come into contact with Henry's soiled backside. Gagging, she scrubbed at the top with a wet paper towel. The quarter-sized damp spot grew to the size of a half-dollar, directly over her left nipple.

Brooke grabbed Henry's hand and dragged him in the direction of the gift shop. Surely they sold a few items of women's clothing, right?

She was in the process of paying for the only top she could find, a hideous bile-green tank top with SAVANNAH spelled out in sequins when Henry spied his heart's desire. It was a board book featuring his favorite thing in the whole world, the hairless Canadian cartoon character, propped on a display next to the cash register.

"Caillou!" Henry crowed, grabbing for the book at the same moment Brooke was in the process of handing her credit card to the cashier.

Without thinking, Brooke snatched his chubby hand away from the book, which shared shelf space with dozens of tiny cheesy breakable souvenir trinkets. "Henry, no," she said sharply. "You already have that book."

Her son's face crumpled into agony. "I want it!" he cried. "I want Caillou!"

"Anything else?" the cashier asked, her hands poised over the register. "Chips, gum, soft drinks, magazine?"

"Just the shirt, thanks," Brooke said tersely, keeping an eye on the concourse. It was ten after ten, and a sudden wave of passengers had disembarked their flights and were passing by, laughing and talking.

"Please, Mommy," Henry whined. "I want Caillou."

"Can I have your email for your receipt?" the cashier asked.

"No!" Brooke said. "Stop it right this minute."

"Excuse me?" the clerk said.

"Sorry, I was talking to my son. Just print out the receipt and put it in the bag, please," Brooke said through clenched teeth. She released Henry's hand to retrieve her card.

Henry saw an opening and seized it. He grabbed the book with both hands. "Mine!"

Without thinking, she snatched the book back. She knelt down so that she was at eye level with her son. "Absolutely not. You have this exact same book at home, and I am not buying you another one."

She stood up and tried to compose herself. Another wave of passengers was passing. She saw a familiar face in the crowd. It was Pete, striding down the concourse, one arm flung casually across the shoulder of a young blond woman. She was in her midtwenties, slender and petite with a long Nordic-looking braid cascading down her back. She wore form-fitting green hiking shorts and had a backpack over one shoulder. Pete leaned in, laughing and talking with her.

Brooke felt herself shrink away from the gift shop entrance. She wanted to flee, to melt into the woodwork. As soon as Pete and his friend had passed, she tugged gently at her son's hand. "Come on, buddy. Let's go home."

"Nooooooo!" Henry wailed, throwing himself onto the floor. He grabbed the book and hugged it to his chest. "I want Caillou! I want it, I want it!" His face was scarlet with rage. She bent over and tried to pry the book away. *"Noooooo!"* he screamed, kicking his tiny feet at her ankles.

Brooke saw Pete pause. He turned, said something to his female companion, and frowned, looking to see where the commotion was coming from. His eyes met hers. People surged around him, but Pete Haynes stopped dead in his tracks.

54

He strode toward the gift shop. Stopped, then wrapped Brooke in an awkward embrace. "I'm so glad you showed up," he murmured in her ear. "I wasn't sure you would."

"I wasn't sure either," Brooke said, her voice shaky. "It's been so long. But I'm really glad you called." She saw the woman who'd been walking with Pete, standing discreetly nearby, watching their reunion with undisguised interest.

Sensing he'd lost his audience, Henry abandoned his tantrum, stood and raised his arms. "Mama. I pick you up."

Brooke took a step backward and scooped her son into her arms.

"Who's this?" Pete asked warily.

"Pete, this is my son, Henry. Henry, can you say hello to Pete?"

Henry turned away, burying his face in her shoulder.

"Hi, Henry," Pete said, lightly tapping the boy's back. "How old are you?"

Henry lifted his head and observed the stranger, his expression grave. He held out three chubby fingers. "I'm fwee."

"Obviously, we've got some catching up to do," Pete said.

"Who's your friend?" Brooke asked, gesturing toward the girl who was now slouching against a nearby wall.

"That's Hope, a grad student I've been working with. Hey, Hope," he called. "C'mere. There's somebody I want you to meet."

"Hello," the young woman said, offering a wide smile showing perfectly straight, blindingly white teeth. "You've got to be Brooke. Pete's told me so much about you."

"Great to meet you, Hope," Brooke said. "This is my son, Henry, who was doing his best howler monkey impression a minute ago."

"Oooh, Henry, is that Curious George on your shirt? I used to love him, and the man with the yellow hat."

Henry peeped shyly at the girl, nodded, then turned his head and hid again. Hope's face registered a flicker of recognition as she looked from Henry to Pete.

"Okay, well, uh, Pete, I'm going to hit the ladies' room and then maybe find a magazine for the ride to Miami. I'll let you two have some private time together," Hope said.

"Thanks. How about we meet outside at noon?"

"I'll see you there. Bye, Brooke. Bye, Henry."

They found a corner booth at the bar. When the waitress arrived to take their order, Brooke gave her what she hoped was a winning smile. "Is it okay for me to have my little boy in here?"

The waitress looked around at the lounge, which was half-empty at that hour. "Okay by me, but if one of my other customers complains, you'll have to leave."

Pete ordered a beer, and although Brooke longed for something to quell her bad case of jitters, she ordered coffee for herself and orange juice for Henry.

"You don't want any food?" Pete asked, scanning the menu. "I've gotta eat something. I've been on planes for twenty-four hours, and all I've had was some mini-pretzels and a stale bagel." He ordered crab cakes and french fries, and Brooke ordered a grilled cheese to split with Henry, who was already curled up on the booth with his head in her lap.

They made polite, inane conversation about the weather in Alaska, southern Atlantic hurricanes, blue crabs versus snow crabs, and politics while waiting what seemed like an interminable amount of time for the food.

She tried not to stare at Pete. His hair was longer than she'd ever seen it before, brushing his shoulders and falling across his eyes. He'd grown a thick beard too and had lost weight so that the planes and angles of his face stood in sharp relief. But his biceps bulged beneath the short sleeves of his dark gray T-shirt, and his belly was noticeably flat.

Brooke was vaguely aware that Pete was talking about the GPS devices they'd implanted in the caribou to allow them to track migration patterns, but she was only half listening. Instead, she was mentally mapping the contours of his shoulders, the scar on his lower back where he'd impaled a fishhook in his own flesh as a kid, his chest and the way it had felt to lay her cheek against it that one fateful night more than three years ago.

She longed to reach out, touch a finger to his lips. *Shh,* she wanted to say. *No more talk of caribou or grizzly bears or how they collected blood samples to measure hormone levels in the female caribou. Later. All that can come later. Tell me about you,* she wanted to say. *Tell me it was lonely without me. Tell me you love me.*

He stopped talking once or twice. Sat back, sipped his beer, and seemed to be taking measure of her, puzzling something over in his mind. Had he guessed? Did he know?

After the waitress brought their order, Pete

dove into his crab cakes, and Brooke picked at her sandwich, tearing off bites and offering them to her drowsy son like a mama bird feeding her chick. She had no appetite, although she would have loved a glass of wine.

Finally, Pete stopped eating. His face was unreadable. "So. Got any news you want to share with me? Your child is three, and that's about how long it's been since we last talked."

"Pete, I'm sorry," Brooke started.

"He's the real reason you wouldn't come to Alaska that Christmas? The reason you quit Skyping and then just quit answering my phone calls and emails altogether?"

The lump in her throat felt like concrete. She nodded, miserable.

"And his father? Anybody I know?"

Brooke felt herself tense. How could Pete look at Henry and not recognize his own DNA? How could he gaze into the boy's eyes and not see in them a mirror image of his own smoky blue eyes, fringed with lashes so thick and lush they seemed to weigh down his eyelids?

"Are you married?" Pete asked incredulously. "When did that happen? Were you seeing this guy the whole time we were together? Damn it, Brooke, don't just sit there, staring at me like that."

"I'm not married," she managed. "He . . . Henry's father isn't in our lives. He hasn't been in a long time."

Pete frowned. "The guy just left you? Pregnant with his kid? What kind of swine does something like that?"

"It's not his fault. I'm the one who let myself get pregnant. You know how I am. I decided I could do it all by myself. And I have. Mostly. I found a place to rent at St. Ann's, hung up my shingle. I'm practicing law again."

He pushed his plate away. It was dotted with the breading from the crab cakes, and the streaks of ketchup from the french fries reminded her of blood, and the stabbing pains she felt in her chest as she so artlessly avoided telling Pete the truth about his son. Not lying. Just not being entirely honest.

His voice was hoarse. "Any chance you and this guy will get back together? For Henry's sake?"

She saw Hope approaching. She'd applied fresh makeup and her braid was brushed out, with blond hair flowing loose over her shoulders. She wore black jeans and a spotless white T-shirt and looked as fresh and lovely as a wildflower. Brooke was painfully aware of her own appearance, the large damp spot over her left breast, her shirt and lap covered with bits of Henry's sandwich. She was a hot, unwed mother of a mess.

"It's not looking good for me and Henry's dad. Not right now anyway. What about you and her?" She jerked her head in the girl's direction. Pete turned and flashed her a smile as she neared the table, then backed away, aware that she was interrupting something intense.

"She's a colleague," he said firmly. "She's been collecting data on caribou from another location on the tundra, and we've collaborated on this paper we're presenting at the conference in Miami."

"And there's nothing between you?" Brooke raised an eyebrow, hoping she sounded as though she didn't care.

"We're colleagues. And friends. I thought, I mean, I hoped, maybe, there was still some chance of us, you know, you and me, reconnecting. I successfully defended my dissertation three months ago. When I get down to Miami, I'm meeting with the head of a nonprofit foundation that has funding to study the deer population on all the barrier islands — Talisa, Sapelo, Ossabaw, Cumberland. They've got deep pockets, and it's a great opportunity for me."

"Pete! That's wonderful," Brooke impulsively reached out to grasp his hands in hers.

"Hey, Pete," Hope said, edging toward their table. "I hate to break this up, but Ralph just texted me. He's parked in a no-parking zone at the curb, and he says if we don't get our butts out there right now, we can find our own way to the conference."

"Coming." He stood and threw money on

the table. "This should cover the check."

Brooke made a move to stand, but she was trapped in the booth with Henry, sound asleep with his head in her lap.

"Don't wake him up," Pete said. He leaned over and touched the top of Henry's messy curls. "Cute kid." Then he straightened. "This was probably a bad idea, huh?"

"Not at all," Brooke said. "It was great to see you. I just wish we'd had more time to talk. My mom was going to take Henry, but this morning she woke up with some kind of bug." Her mouth was dry, and she didn't know what to say.

He hesitated. "I'm flying out of here next week. This time, the ball's in your court, Brooke. If you call me, we'll meet. If not, I'll know it wasn't meant to be." He brushed his lips against her cheek, turned, and hurried out of the lounge, with Hope following.

"You didn't tell him, did you?" Marie's tone was more resigned than accusatory. They sat at the kitchen table. It was a dark Irish Georgian oak with carved ball and claw feet, and the chairs were of the same wood, but in a Chinese Chippendale style.

Her mother squeezed lemon into a glass of iced tea and handed the glass to Brooke.

"How are you feeling? You look a little better than you did this morning. Have you taken your temperature?" Brooke asked.

"I'm okay. Now, did you or did you not tell Pete that he has a son?"

"I wanted to," Brooke said, sipping her drink. "But when he didn't even notice how much Henry looks like him, I don't know. Something inside me just shut down."

"Your backbone?"

"How could he not recognize his own child?" Brooke cried. "Even that alleged colleague who was with him, the enchantingly lovely Hope, I know she saw the resemblance the minute she laid eyes on Henry."

Marie sipped her own tea. "Oh, Brooke, you know how clueless men are about stuff like that. When you were born, your father stood outside the nursery window at Candler Hospital proudly telling everybody within listening distance that a total stranger's newborn was his beautiful new daughter. And get this — the child was a boy, and he weighed twelve pounds, eight ounces, which was exactly twice what you weighed."

"I've never heard that story before," Brooke said. "Are you sure you didn't just make it up?"

Her mother slid her phone across the table. "Call and ask him if you don't believe me." She glanced fondly at her grandson, who at that moment was happily coloring at a child-sized table Marie had brought down from the attic for him. "Did Pete even get a really good look at him?"

Brooke shrugged. "You know how shy Henry gets around strangers. He sort of buried his head against my shirt when Pete was talking to him. But he did tell Pete he was three, which, if the man had any brains in his head, should have told him that Henry was the fruit of his loom. He even had the nerve to ask me if I'd been seeing Henry's father while we were together!"

"What did you tell him?"

"I told him the father hadn't been in our lives in a long time, which was the truth."

"I just don't understand why you didn't simply tell him the truth: that you got pregnant the last night you were together and then couldn't quite get up the nerve to tell him about his child."

Brooke jiggled the ice cubes in her glass. "I wanted to. Truly, I did. But the food took so long to get there, and it was so weird and awkward between us, and then after the food did arrive and we finally got around to talking about us, that damn girl showed up to say that their ride was there and they needed to leave. I swear, she did it on purpose."

"Didn't he tell you they were just colleagues? Nothing romantic?"

"I guess. Maybe I'm just paranoid. Pete did tell me he's coming back through town to fly back to Alaska after the conference ends next week. He said I should call him if I want to see him — and that this time the ball's in my court."

"Fair enough," Marie declared. "Next week, you call him. You get a sitter for Henry, and you arrange to meet Pete somewhere other than the airport, at a nice restaurant, and without his little friend Hope. And you sit down and put all your cards on the table."

"He'll hate me," Brooke said. "Or worse. What if he decides he doesn't want to be with me but he wants me to share custody of Henry? What if he tries to take him away from me?"

Marie rolled her eyes. "He has a right to be angry, but he's not going to try to take your son. You're being ridiculous, and you know it. Stop being so paranoid. I know you, Brooke. If you cared enough about this man to sleep with him, you know his character. Right?"

"Maybe. But it's been three years. Maybe he's changed. He grew a big, awful Grizzly Adams beard that hides his beautiful face. And he's been pumping iron too. He's, like, beefcake now. Who knows what else is going on with him?"

"You're giving me a headache," Marie said wearily. "I can't talk any sense into you. Are you going to see Pete again or not?"

"Truthfully, I don't know. My life is complicated enough right now. And part of that's your fault."

"Mine? What did I do?"

"You're the one who told me it was okay to date Gabe Wynant. So I'm doing it. He's taking me to the dinner dance at the Cloister tomorrow night, and he wants me to spend the night at his place after."

"Oh, he does, does he?"

"He swears he'll be a gentleman," Brooke said.

"They always do," Marie said primly. "Are you on any kind of birth control?"

"That's none of your business," Brooke said. But she wasn't. There hadn't been any need in a long time. As far as she was concerned, the combination of a rambunctious three-year-old and an exhausted single mother was the most effective birth control on the market.

Marie cocked her head and studied her daughter.

"What? What's that look?" Brooke demanded.

"Nothing. Just thinking."

"I hate it when you do that. It's like you're psychoanalyzing me."

"Has it occurred to you that you're at a fork in the road? The father of your child apparently wants to be in your life again. And in the meanwhile, Gabe Wynant has come a-courting. I know I encouraged you to see Gabe, but that was before all this business with Pete."

"Yes, Mom, it has occurred to me. Trust me, I know what I'm doing."

"I certainly hope so. Anyway, you never told me what you and the girls found out on your fact-finding mission yesterday. Do you really think there's a chance C. D. is Josephine's son?" Marie asked.

Brooke shared the results of the previous day's investigation, and Marie listened carefully. "Have you spoken to C. D. yet? If it's true that his father might have been black, that's going to come as a huge shock to someone of his generation."

"I've left him messages, but nobody's seen or talked to him. I'm starting to get a little worried about him, to tell you the truth," Brooke said. "Lizzie was going to try to track him down today. I'll call her on my way home to see what she knows."

"Keep me posted," Marie said. "And be careful driving home. Call me Sunday and fill me in on all the gory details of your night with Gabe."

"A lady never kisses and tells," Brooke said, grinning impishly.

"Except to her mother," Marie said.

55

When Shug dropped her off at the dock at Talisa, Felicia and Lizzie were waiting, with Lizzie behind the wheel of the pickup truck. Shug waved goodbye as he backed the boat away from the dock, headed back to the mainland to run errands for Louette.

"I was kind of surprised to hear from you this morning," Lizzie said as the two other women scooted in close to her in the front seat of the truck.

"After you told me yesterday that C. D. seems to be missing in action, it made me a little nervous. I mean, right now, he's Josephine's heir apparent," Brooke said.

"Or at least, he's *our* preferred heir apparent," Felicia said. "Not that we have any say in the matter."

"Did you talk to Varina? Ask her about the possibility that a black man could have fathered Josephine's child?"

Felicia shook her head. "I can't. She's still pretty frail. And she's so protective of Josephine's reputation. Her main concern right now is when Josephine will be buried. She hates the idea of her body locked up in a freezer drawer at the morgue. Have you heard anything?"

"We're waiting on the sheriff to release the body," Brooke said. "I'll ask Gabe when I see him tonight. Maybe, now that he's been named administrator, he can speed things up."

"You're seeing Gabe tonight?" Lizzie asked, nudging Felicia.

"You two are so juvenile," Brooke said.

"I told you so," Felicia said, addressing Lizzie. "I definitely sensed some kind of a spark between those two."

Lizzie wrinkled her nose. "It's none of my business, but . . ."

"It really isn't, so let's change the subject," Brooke said good-naturedly. "Talk to me about C. D. When was the last time anybody actually saw him?"

"Shug rode him over to the mainland last Monday," Felicia said.

"Did C. D. say where he was going? And how does he get around when he's over there? Does he have a car in St. Ann's?"

"According to Shug, C. D. has an old Vega. A real rust bucket he keeps parked at the city marina," Felicia said. "And Louette thinks he might have a girlfriend there too."

"How does he get around on the island?

Does he always use Josephine's truck?"

"I've seen him a couple of times on a motor scooter," Lizzie said. "Don't know if it's actually his or if it belonged to Josephine."

"I find it hard to picture Josephine on a motor scooter," Brooke said. "Does anybody know where C. D. was headed when he went to the mainland?"

"He told Shug he was going shopping for a new boat so he'd be ready to buy it when his inheritance from Josephine comes through," Felicia said. "Which gave everybody a good laugh."

The trunk bounced down the long drive to Shellhaven.

"Looks like Shug's been busy," Brooke said. The huge expanse of grass had been mowed. All the fallen palm fronds and tree branches had been picked up, and the flower beds had been weeded.

"Finally getting a paycheck was a real morale booster," Lizzie said. "But Shug can't keep these grounds up all by himself. He's got to have help, from C. D. or somebody."

"Louette says C. D. wasn't that much help with the lawn maintenance anyway," Felicia said. "He mainly wanted to take care of the boat and run errands on the mainland. She says he's forever wandering off and disappearing for a day or two."

"Does she have any guess where he goes?"

"Maybe shacked up with the girlfriend?"

■ ■ ■ ■

They walked over to the barn, a creaky wooden structure that seemed to lean at a near forty-five-degree angle. It was painted a weathered white, and sunlight shone through cracks in the old boards.

"Shug says the barn roof is in worse shape than the house," Lizzie remarked. "He'd finally talked Josephine into shelling out the money to hire roofers to do it, but then, after she got so sick, the roof sort of got put on the back burner."

"She wanted her husband's cars preserved, Louette says," Felicia added. "I walked over here and looked at them this week. If you're into cars, it's a pretty amazing collection."

Lizzie grasped one of the barn doors, and the rusted hinges squealed a protest. Inside, it was dim and relatively cool and smelled of mildew and mouse droppings. Four shadowy hulks were shrouded in dusty tarps.

She walked over to the car on the end and yanked off the cover to reveal a gleaming vintage roadster.

"This was the last car Gardiner owned, and we know Josephine worshiped him. And this car," Brooke said, running a hand over the hood of the roadster.

Felicia walked slowly around the roadster and peered in the back. "Is this the same car she told us they dumped Russell Strickland's body in when they went to bury him?"

"It must be," Brooke said.

Felicia jumped away from the car, eliciting a belly laugh from Lizzie.

"What's the matter, Felicia? You getting spooked by an old car?"

"Must be 'cause I'm spending all my time with these Geechees," Felicia admitted. "I had no idea how superstitious my people are. Even Auntie Vee. You can't leave a broom in a corner because she says that means somebody's fixing to die. And don't you let her catch you leaving a pocketbook on a bed, either. I've started writing it all down. It's really pretty fascinating."

Brooke carefully returned the dustcover to the roadster. "How far is C. D.'s place from here?"

"Just a little ways away," Lizzie said. "It used to be the chauffeur's house."

The house stood in the shadow of an enormous oak tree. It was a step up from the humble slave cottages they'd seen at Oyster Bluff — wood frame, with a small front porch ornamented with simple Victorian-inspired gingerbread trim. Once, the house had been white, but only traces of the paint remained now. A front door with a small window was flanked on either side with tall windows.

Lizzie stepped onto the porch and boldly jiggled the doorknob.

"Lizzie!" Felicia scolded.

"He could be in there, hurt and unable to call out to anybody," Lizzie said. She stepped to the right and pressed her face against the wavy window glass, which was smeared with ancient layers of grime and cobwebs. "Can't see a thing through all this dirt," she complained.

Brooke peered through the other window but saw only a shadowy interior.

"Let's look around back," Lizzie said, leading them around the east side of the house. A lean-to roof jutted off the back of the house. The wooden floorboards groaned under her footsteps. A weathered broom, rag mop, and dustpan hung from nails, and a fishing pole and plastic bait bucket stood beside the door.

Lizzie rattled the door handle. "Locked." She took a step backward and lifted the edge of the doormat. Grinning, she extracted a large brass skeleton key, which she fit into the lock.

"Stop. You can't just break into the man's house," Brooke said.

"Technically, it's not his house. Louette says he doesn't even pay rent. Josephine just let him stay here as part of the job. So technically, it belongs to the estate. Also, he could actually be in here, hurt or passed out or something, so really, this is a welfare check." Undeterred, Lizzie opened the door and stepped inside.

"Nobody home." She popped her head outside the door. "Come on in. Don't be so prissy. If he comes back and catches us, you can say I was the evildoer."

Felicia looked at Brooke and shrugged. "Might as well."

They were standing in a compact galley kitchen. There were exactly four wooden cabinets, their doors warped from humidity. An opened plastic Sunbeam bread bag on the Formica countertop held a moldy heel of bread, swarming with black ants, and a jar of store-brand mustard was open, with a butter knife stuck into it. A greasy plastic ziplocked container held only the red stringy rinds of a half pound of bologna. The small stainless steel sink held a used coffee mug, a teaspoon, and a plate. An ashtray on the counter was full of cigarillo butts.

Lizzie sniffed the air. "Yeah, this is C. D.'s place, all right."

"It looks like wherever he was going, he decided to pack a picnic," Felicia said.

They followed her into the small front room, which looked like it had been furnished with cast-offs from the big house. The sofa, a 1940s relic, had worn maroon tufted upholstery and another overflowing ashtray was perched on the arm. The glass-topped coffee table was part of an old wrought iron patio set. It was littered with file folders and photocopied news clippings.

Lizzie ducked into the adjacent room. "Here's his bedroom. No sign of C. D., though."

"We should get out of here," Brooke said uneasily. "This doesn't feel right."

Felicia perched on the edge of the sofa and began sifting through the papers. "Hey. Looks like he's been reading up on Josephine and the Bettendorfs. Look at all this stuff."

"Let me see." Lizzie sat beside her. She picked up a paper. "He's been spending time in the library, going through the old microfiche issues of the Savannah and Atlanta newspapers, dating all the way back to the mid-1930s. I'm kind of surprised he knew to do that."

"Yeah, he doesn't strike me as the researching type," Felicia agreed. She looked up at Brooke. "He's gotten copies of the old property tax records from the Carter County courthouse too."

"It's a matter of public record," Brooke said. Against her better judgment, she stepped into the bedroom. Like the rest of the house, it was tiny, with worn wooden floorboards. The cracked plaster walls were bare except for a calendar from a marine supply store, the page turned to the current month. The old brass bed was unmade, covered with a cheap white cotton bedspread and a pair of lumpy feather pillows. A nightstand held an ugly, oversized lamp, an empty beer can, and the usual ashtray full of cigarillo butts. A pair of worn jeans hung from the doorknob of a narrow closet.

The drawers of a cheap wooden dresser facing the bed were pulled out.

"I feel like a Peeping Tom," Brooke muttered.

But she looked inside the top drawer, which held balled-up crew socks and a folded stack of worn-looking white cotton briefs that had been pushed aside. An empty leather binocular case lay atop the briefs, and beside them was a half-empty cardboard box of bullets.

She felt queasy. "Hey, y'all," she called.

Lizzie and Felicia approached and stared down at the cardboard box. "Nine-millimeter bullets," Lizzie said. "I guess they're for that holstered pistol he carries."

"So wherever C. D. went, he left in a hurry, and he took binoculars and extra ammo," Felicia said. "And a picnic."

"And he probably lied when he told Shug he was going boat shopping," Lizzie added. "But why? And where was he really going?"

"I think we should leave," Brooke said, slamming the dresser drawer closed. "As soon as I get back to St. Ann's, I'm calling Gabe. Something weird is going on here."

56

Henry reached across the kitchen table and touched Brooke's sparkly diamond-and-pearl-drop earrings. "Pretty!" His face and hands were smeared with spaghetti sauce, but at that moment something in his expression so closely resembled Pete Haynes it took her breath away. She caught her son's chubby hand in hers, kissed it, then pretended to munch on his fingers.

He giggled, then presented his other hand for similar treatment, but the doorbell rang.

"Farrah's here," she told him.

Her heels clicked across the wooden floor, and she caught a glimpse of herself reflected in the living room window. She couldn't even remember the last time she'd gotten really dressed up for a date. But fortunately, the strapless black cocktail dress she'd bought to wear to a long-forgotten party in Savannah still fit, and the earrings her parents had gifted her as a law school graduation gift were timeless.

Brooke opened the door and frowned. Not at Farrah but at her companion, Jaxson, who stood beside her on the doorstep.

"Wow!" Farrah said, following her into the house. "You look amazing." She nudged Jaxson. "Doesn't she look great?"

"Uh, yeah, awesome," Jaxson said. He'd changed since the last time Brooke had seen him. The greasy blond mullet and scraggly Fu Manchu mustache were gone. His head was newly buzzed, and he was clean-shaven. He carried a large cardboard pizza box in both hands and was setting it down on the coffee table.

"New haircut?" she asked as he settled himself on the sofa.

"Yeah," he said, opening the box and shoving a gooey slice of pizza into his mouth.

"Jaxson's going into the army!" Farrah announced. "He leaves Monday for basic training."

"Congratulations, Jaxson. Farrah, why don't you come into the kitchen and say hi to Henry. He's just finishing his supper."

"Fawwah!" Henry called, reaching out his arms to his favorite babysitter.

The teenager lifted him out of his booster chair and swung him up in the air. "Henry McBenry!" She sat him on the kitchen counter, wet a paper towel, and began cleaning him up. "I already know what you're going to say about Jaxson," she said, her voice low. "So save it. We are not getting back together. He's just a good friend, okay?"

"That's fine, but it would have been nice if you'd asked me if he could come with you tonight," Brooke said. "I'm not really comfortable leaving you and Jaxson here alone with Henry while I'm away overnight."

"For God's sake, we're not going to have sex on your sofa or anything," Farrah retorted. "We'll eat some pizza, watch some television, and then he'll go home. Okay? Don't be such a buzzkill. Like my mom."

Brooke glanced at the kitchen clock. "I don't have time to argue with you about this now. I should have left fifteen minutes ago. Jaxson can stay, but I want him out of here by no later than eleven o'clock. Understood?"

"Whatever." Farrah set Henry on the floor and began cleaning up the kitchen table.

"There's breakfast stuff in the fridge," Brooke said. "I think there are some Cokes somewhere around here too. Don't forget to lock the front and back doors before you go to bed, okay? I put clean sheets by the sofa bed. And let's see. Remember to —"

"Quit stalling." Farrah handed Brooke the overnight bag she'd packed earlier in the evening. "Henry and I will be fine. I'll see you tomorrow."

"Call me if anything comes up. Okay? No matter what time. In fact, I want you to check in with me at eleven. The pediatrician's number is on the fridge. I'll text you Gabe's cell number too. And you've got my mom's phone number, right? Just in case?"

"Yes, yes, and yes. And remember," Farrah said, giving her an exaggerated wink, "don't do anything I wouldn't do."

She called Gabe on the drive to Sea Island to tell him she was running late.

"Damn. Well, I guess that means we won't have cocktails at the house before we head over to the Cloister," he said, sounding annoyed. "Dinner starts at seven."

"Sorry. Babysitter complications. I'll fill you in when I get there."

"I've left you a guest pass at the gate. Park at the Cloister and meet me inside."

As soon as she'd driven through the gatehouse at Sea Island, Brooke felt herself slipping into her privileged past. Everything about the grounds and buildings at the resort and second-home community whispered power and money and taste. There was even a row of moss-draped oaks, each of which had been planted by successive presidents, starting with Calvin Coolidge right up to the most recent occupant of the White House. She pulled up to the entrance to the Cloister, and a uniformed doorman stepped out to whisk her car away.

The lobby was crowded with people dressed in elegant evening wear, and when she saw Gabe beaming as he walked rapidly toward her, a martini in one hand and a glass of champagne in the other, she realized that her date might be the most attractive man in the room.

Black tie suited Gabe Wynant. His jacket was custom-tailored to his slender frame, and his silver hair was just long enough to be hip, but short enough to be considered not trying too hard. Her pulse blipped at the sight of him, and she couldn't have said if she was nervous or giddy at the prospect of the evening ahead.

He handed her the champagne and kissed her lightly on the cheek. "You look beautiful," he said before tucking her arm in his. "And I am the luckiest man on this island tonight. Maybe in this state."

They were seated at a round table with three other couples, all of whom were Gabe's old friends or business associates. Despite her misgivings that she'd be seated with a bunch of strangers, theirs was a congenial group: the Johnsons, who'd recently retired and moved from Minneapolis to Sea Island, Dave and Susie (he was a business consultant, she did something in marketing), and Jack and Sharon, both closer in age to Brooke, and from the looks of it, still celebrating their recent marriage, because they held hands every moment they weren't eating or drinking.

The new chef Gabe had touted lived up to his reputation, producing a French-accented five-course dinner that had them all oohing and aahing — and groaning at the thought of the calorie count.

Even the orchestra was a nice surprise — a versatile sextet that played everything from Big Band standards to sixties soul to eighties rock.

"Hope you're not too bored," Gabe said as he led her out to the dance floor. The band was playing a respectable version of "Unchained Melody," and it felt good to be in a man's arms again. He held her closely, his hand resting lightly on the small of her back, and he was easy to follow.

"You smell nice," he said, his lips close to her ear. "I know this perfume. You've worn it for years, right? Even when you were at the law firm?"

"Since high school," Brooke said. "It's Joy. Mom gives me a bottle every year for Christmas. I can't believe you remembered my perfume from when we worked together."

"I notice a lot people don't give me credit for," Gabe said. "What does Marie have to say about your seeing me?"

"She was all for it," Brooke said. "She says age shouldn't matter."

"Smart lady. And your dad?"

"He'd probably call you a dirty old man. He doesn't approve of much that I do anymore, but then, I can't say I approve of all his choices either."

Gabe chuckled and let his hand slide farther down her back. "If I'm gonna get called a dirty old man, I might as well act like one."

"I like your friends," Brooke said. "I was afraid I'd get stuck listening to a bunch of grumpy old men talking about tax reform and prostate surgery tonight."

"Not a chance. They like you too. Especially Byron. Which is good, because he just sold his share of a startup tech company, and he wants to start doing some estate planning. It'll be a nice piece of business. He's got two sets of kids: one set from his first wife, all of whom are in their early thirties, and his kids with Micki, who are eight and six."

"Really?" Brooke looked over his shoulder at the Johnsons, who were dancing together at the far side of the ballroom. "He's got grade-school kids? How old is he?"

"Only a couple of years older than I am. Do you think that's too old to have young kids?"

"I guess I'm just surprised he'd want to start over raising a family."

Gabe looked down at her. "Personally, I wouldn't rule it out. Why not? I'm healthy, I can afford it, and I've always wanted kids."

"But Sunny didn't?"

"No," he said succinctly. He tilted his head. "How about you? Has being a single mom turned you off to having more kids?"

"Not necessarily," Brooke said. "I was an only child of an only child. It can be lonely, you know?"

"I was never an only child. I have two brothers. But I do know about loneliness. People treat you differently when you're not half of a couple. They might bring casseroles and potted plants when you're first widowed, but after that, it's a whole lot of single-serve microwave dinners and Netflix binge-watching."

"You should try being single in a town like St. Ann's," Brooke said.

"Maybe you should move back to Savannah and find a nice guy to settle down with," Gabe said, nuzzling her neck. "Somebody who'd bring you coffee in bed in the morning and rub your feet at night."

"Mmm," she said, sighing and sinking into him. "That does sound tempting. Where do I sign up?"

"Right here," Gabe said.

She looked up at him. He'd had two or three martinis before dinner, and they'd both had a little wine with dinner, but what she'd thought had been casual flirting had suddenly taken an unexpected turn.

He was still holding her hand when they returned to their table. Coffee and after-dinner drinks were being served, and jokes were being told. Gabe scooted his chair next to hers, so close her bare shoulder brushed his dinner jacket. Brooke glanced surreptitiously at his gold wristwatch. It was nearly eleven. She excused herself and headed for the ladies' lounge.

Checking her phone, she saw that she had no missed calls and no text messages. She combed her hair, reapplied lipstick, then sat in one of the lounge chairs and stared at her phone, waiting for the babysitter's call. At five after eleven, she called Farrah's cell. No answer.

"Damn it, Farrah," she muttered.

She went back to the table and waved away Gabe's offer of more champagne. "I was about to send out a search party for you," he said, his voice low. "Everything okay?"

She shook her head. "Farrah promised to check in with me at eleven. I waited a few minutes and then I called, but there's no answer."

"She's eighteen, right? Just graduated from high school?"

"That's right."

"And she's usually very responsible? I mean, she works in your office too, right?"

"Yes, but this is different. When she showed up tonight, she had her boyfriend with her.

Or ex-boyfriend. I'm not sure which. I let her know I wasn't happy about the situation, but what could I do? That's why I was late leaving the house."

"She probably forgot and fell asleep," Gabe said.

The band was breaking into another slow song, "When a Man Loves a Woman." It was one her parents had danced to back during the rosy-hued years when they'd dragged her along to parties at the Cloister. She could remember being deeply embarrassed at the way they'd clung to each other on the dance floor.

"Come on," Gabe said, taking her hand. "The band will be packing it in pretty soon. Let's dance, and then you can try calling the babysitter later."

He held her even closer than before as they danced. "I was dead serious about that offer I made you earlier," Gabe said, taking her hand and kissing the back, and then the palm. "I can tell you're struggling with the solo practice, single parenting, finances, all of it. I've thought a lot about this, Brooke. Come back to Savannah. You can practice law with me again, or not. Let me take care of you and Henry."

She was so taken aback by the proposal, she stumbled briefly, but he helped her regain her footing. "I . . . don't know what to say," she said, feeling herself blush.

Gabe smiled. "I'm rushing you, right? Damn it! My timing is usually better than this. Look, we can talk about this later. Just chalk it up to the music and the wine." He nuzzled her neck again. "And that perfume of yours, which is driving me out of my mind."

The party was breaking up. Goodbyes were said, hugs and contact information exchanged. The moon was three-quarters full as they stood outside, with a salt-scented breeze gently ruffling the palm fronds near the entrance, waiting for the valet to bring their cars around.

"Gorgeous night tonight," Gabe said, his arm around her shoulders. "What do you say we take a walk on the beach when we get back to my place?"

"That sounds nice," Brooke said, trying not to sound distracted. It was after midnight, and she still hadn't heard from Farrah.

The Porsche sped around the corner from the parking deck and stopped abruptly inches from where they stood. The booming thump of head-banging rock music assaulted them when the valet driver hopped out of the car.

Gabe snatched the parking stub from the driver's hand. "Where the hell do you think you are, you dumb fuck? This isn't the Indie 500. That's a $175,000 car you just mishandled."

"Sorry, sir," the driver said. "I'm not used to all that horsepower."

Gabe whipped his cell phone from the inner pocket of his dinner jacket and quickly snapped a photo of the driver, who wore a brass nameplate pinned to his uniform shirt.

"Lopez, right?" Gabe said. "I'll email this to your supervisor in the morning."

Before the kid could reply, another valet pulled up, at a more sedate speed, in Brooke's Volvo.

Gabe held the door while she slid behind the driver's seat, his rage seemingly forgotten. "You remember the way to my house, right? Turn left at the first roundabout, then a quick right and two more lefts."

She waited until she was out of sight of the clubhouse before calling Farrah again. She called two more times, each time waiting until the girl's voice recording played.

Hey, this is Farrah. Leave me a message, and I'll hit you back later.

Brooke pounded the steering wheel in frustration. This wasn't like Farrah. Something had to be wrong. Instead of taking a left at the first roundabout, she made a right. When she'd reached the causeway that would take her back south to St. Ann's, she winced and tapped Gabe's number on her cell phone. He'd be pissed, she knew, but if he was sincere in his concern for her as a mother, he'd have to understand. Henry came first.

He answered on the first ring. "Are you lost? I knew I should have had you follow me home."

"Actually, I'm not coming to your place. I'm so sorry, Gabe, but Farrah hasn't answered any of my calls, and I'm already sick with worry. I'm heading back to St. Ann's. I'm hoping you'll give me a rain check."

There was a deafening silence from the other end of the call. "You're kidding, right?"

"Not at all. This isn't like Farrah. I'm terrified something could have happened. You understand, don't you?"

"Not really." His voice was cold. "You said yourself the girl is very responsible. It seems to me that this is you looking for an excuse to pull another disappearing act."

His words felt like a slap in the face.

"I see. Well, thanks for a lovely evening." She disconnected the phone, her cheeks burning with anger and indignation.

57

Brooke kept the Volvo's speedometer at seventy-nine miles per hour on the drive back to St. Ann's. Any faster than that, the car's whole chassis would have vibrated, plus she would have been ticket bait for the cops, who ran a notorious speed trap on that section of highway. She was grateful she'd limited her alcohol intake to two drinks over the course of the long evening. And she didn't really slow down until she reached the turnoff for St. Ann's.

Jaxson's black Ford F-150 truck was still parked at the curb in front of her house. She could see the lights in the kitchen window, but the front of the house was dark. She'd been rehearsing the lecture she'd give Farrah when she got home — assuming she still had a home when she got there — but seeing the boy's vehicle further fueled her anger.

She opened the front door, which she noted was unlocked, and stepped inside. The television was on, and two bodies were slumped sideways on the sofa. Brooke gasped. And then she saw the coffee table. The pizza box was still there, along with an empty liter bottle of Coke and a mostly empty liquor bottle.

Brooke stomped over to the sofa and picked up the bottle. Captain Morgan rum. An inch of brown liquid sloshed in the bottom, and from the looks of it, the rest had been consumed by Farrah and Jaxson. His head lolled against the back of the sofa cushions, mouth open, snoring. Farrah's head rested on his chest, and a thin trickle of drool dampened his T-shirt. She slammed the bottle back down onto the table, but neither of them stirred. They were both alive, but dead drunk.

Henry was asleep in his bed, tucked between his green stuffed Ninja Turtle and a large Clifford the Big Red Dog stuffed animal. She bent down and kissed his cheek, then went to her own room, where she quickly stripped out of her party dress and diamond-and-pearl earrings and into a pair of lightweight summer pajamas.

She took a cotton bedspread from the closet and draped it loosely over the sleeping couple. It was nearly two o'clock. In the morning, she promised herself, she would raise hell with those two. But for now, she needed to sleep more than she needed to vent.

■ ■ ■ ■

Bleeeeechhhhh. Bleeechhhhh. Brooke sat up in bed, momentarily confused. Where was she? It was still dark outside — 6:15 A.M. according to the digital clock on her nightstand. The horrific noise was coming from the hall bathroom. She got out of bed to investigate.

Farrah was hunched over the commode, her head nearly invisible.

"Hey." Brooke sat down on the edge of the bathtub.

The girl raised her head and gazed at Brooke from bloodshot eyes. She looked like hell.

"Hey," she said weakly.

"You look like hell," Brooke said. "I'd say Captain Morgan is no friend of yours."

Farrah retched for another five minutes. Brooke found an elastic band and fastened the girl's hair. She ran cold water over a washcloth and placed it on the back of her neck.

Brooke tiptoed out to the living room in time to see the black pickup zoom away from the curb. Picking up the pizza crusts, Solo cups, and rum bottle, she noted with grim satisfaction that Jaxson had been in such a rush to depart that he'd left behind a pair of nearly new, expensive-looking basketball shoes. She picked them up and deposited everything in the trash.

Back in the bathroom, she found Farrah sprawled, facedown, on the tile floor. "Your super-classy boyfriend had to leave," she said.

"Uuuuggghhhh. He is *so* not my boyfriend." Farrah managed to pull herself up to a sitting position. "And I want to die."

"Okay," Brooke said pleasantly. She turned on the shower. "But we need to clean up your corpse before we bury you. A hot shower is your first step to salvation."

By the time Farrah stumbled into the kitchen, Henry had finished his frozen waffle and was happily knocking back a sippy cup of milk. She sank down onto a chair and gratefully accepted the mug of coffee Brooke offered.

"Fawwah!" Henry yelled. He held out his cup. "You want some milk?"

The girl's face turned a new shade of green. "You drink it, Henry."

"How're you feeling?" Brooke asked. "Any better?"

"Not really. I mean, I stopped barfing, so I guess that's something." The girl looked balefully at her employer. "I'm really, really, really sorry I let you down, Brooke."

"Yeah. Me too. I expected better of you."

Farrah hung her head. "I know. I was so stupid. I should never have let Jaxson come over here with me last night. You were right. He's nothing but bad news."

"Whose idea was the rum?"

"His. But I went along with it, you know? He didn't pour it down my throat or anything."

Brooke took a sip of her own coffee. "Was Henry awake when you started drinking?"

"No! He was asleep. I swear. But I wouldn't blame you if you wanted to fire me."

"I don't *want* to fire you. My son adores you. I adore you, or I did until I drove back here like a maniac last night after you didn't call, only to find you and Jaxson passed out on my sofa."

"I really fucked up your big night, didn't I?" Farrah pressed her fingers to her temples. "I bet Gabe is really mad."

Brooke mentally replayed Gabe's cutting remark about her pulling "another disappearing act." It hurt as much now as it had when he'd said it last night.

"He wasn't thrilled. He had big plans for the rest of the evening, and then I pulled the plug. I think it's safe to say our fine little romance is kaput."

"Oh God. I'm such a screwup."

"Just as well it happened now. Gabe never had kids, so he doesn't understand where my priorities are. And if he can't understand that, there's really no future for the two of us."

Brooke went to the pantry and got a packet of crackers. She placed them on the table in front of Farrah. "Eat those."

"Food? No. Gross."

"They'll help settle your stomach. I'll get you some ginger ale too. Then, if you keep that down, you can take some aspirin for that headache I'm sure you have."

Farrah took fifteen minutes to nibble half of one cracker, washed down with four sips of ginger ale. Brooke handed her two aspirin, which she swallowed. She held her head in both hands, a pathetic, miserable sight.

"Are you going to tell my mom?" Farrah asked.

"What would she do if I did tell her?"

"Probably ground me for the rest of the summer. Maybe take away my car. For sure she wouldn't let me see Jaxson again."

"If she grounds you and takes away your car, that hurts me as much as it hurts you. If I hadn't been so tired last night, I would have throttled you both with my bare hands."

"I deserve it. And so does he."

"True. But I need an assistant at the office, and Henry needs a babysitter who loves him so very much, so I'm going to give you a second chance, and I'm not going to tell your mom. This time."

Farrah let out a long sigh of relief. "Thanks. I'll make it up to you. I swear. And hey, no charge for last night."

"Oh, don't worry," Brooke said. "I wasn't going to pay you anyway. Go on home and get some sleep now, okay? And if Jaxson calls, you can tell him I threw his shoes in the trash."

Brooke puttered around the house most of the morning, doing multiple loads of laundry, cleaning and disinfecting the bathroom, dumping the clothes Farrah had left on the floor into a grocery bag, and helping Henry put together one of his puzzles. He'd begged to go to the park, but by mid-morning it was broiling out, the temperature already hovering around ninety with sauna-level humidity, so she'd compromised by letting him watch an hour of cartoons on her laptop. Did that make her a terrible mother? Maybe, but she didn't care.

At eleven, she put her son down for a nap and decided to color her hair. Like Marie's, Brooke's hair had begun going gray when she was in her midtwenties. In the past, Genevieve, the stylist at her trendy Savannah salon, had colored her hair, but these days, rather than spend $175 a pop every six weeks, she colored her own hair with the stuff that came in a box from the drugstore.

It took thirty minutes to apply the grape gravy–colored goop to her wet hair. She was still barefoot in a ratty terry cloth bathrobe when the doorbell rang. *Probably Farrah returning to reclaim her clothes,* she thought as she went to open the door.

Gabe Wynant stood on the doorstep with a

huge bouquet of pink peonies in one hand and a large Harris Teeter paper sack in the other. "Hi," he said, eyeing her uneasily. "Um, maybe I should have called first?"

Brooke's hands flew to her hair. "Oh, shit." She must have looked like something from a bad seventies sitcom.

"I just wanted to apologize for last night," he said, thrusting the flowers at her. "I was a jerk and an unforgiveable ass."

"You really were," Brooke agreed, sniffing the flowers.

He held the paper sack in both hands now, looking like a penitent first grader. "I brought you a peace offering. Coffee, fresh-squeezed orange juice, croissants . . ."

"Come on in, then," Brooke said, opening the door wider. She gestured toward the small, shabby living room, grateful that she'd picked up all the toys and preschooler detritus that usually littered the room. "Sit there and pour yourself some coffee. I have to deal with this." She pointed toward her head.

Thirty minutes later, she emerged from her bedroom dressed in shorts and a T-shirt, her hair freshly blown dry and styled. She'd even applied a little lipstick.

"Hi," Gabe said, standing when she walked into the living room. He'd found a vase for the peonies and arranged a buffet on the coffee table; a bowl of raspberries, blueberries, and strawberries, a carafe of orange juice, a plate of croissants, plates, napkins, silverware, even a miniature jar of marmalade, and two steaming mugs of coffee.

Brooke nodded and sat down on the sofa. "I'm sort of amazed you didn't head for the hills just now, after you saw me in my natural habitat."

"It takes a lot more than that to scare me off," Gabe said, smiling. "And I'm the one who's amazed — that you didn't tell me to take a hike when I showed up here uninvited."

She fixed herself a plate of fruit and buttered a croissant. "The least I can do is listen to your apology. Anyway, I didn't have any breakfast this morning."

Gabe looked around the room. "I see the house is still standing. So, I guess everything was okay when you got home last night?"

"Farrah and her boyfriend were drunk, passed out on the sofa," Brooke said, biting into the croissant.

"Christ! Where was your kid? Was he all right?"

"Henry was sound asleep in his bed," Brooke said, taking another bite of the croissant, ignoring the shards of pastry showering onto her shirt. "Crisis averted, narrowly."

"I hope you fired the girl," he said.

"Nope. Farrah's a good kid. She made a really dumb decision. I'm giving her a second chance."

He gave her a winning smile. "So . . . how about me? Do I get a second chance? I don't know what came over me last night. I could blame the martinis. I should have stopped after two."

"You really should have," Brooke said. "Nobody likes a mean drunk. And that's what you were last night, Gabe. You were mean. First when you went off on that poor valet kid, threatening to get him fired, and then to me. You were mean and rude."

"I know." He shook his head. "So no excuses. I want you to know I went back over to the Cloister this morning. I left the kid a note of apology and a big tip."

She sipped her coffee and waited for what would come next. Did she even want to hear it?

He ran his fingers through his hair, which was uncharacteristically messy. Come to think of it, Gabe was uncharacteristically messy this morning. Gray stubble, dark bags under his eyes, and he wore beltless khaki slacks that needed ironing, a faded gray T-shirt, and scuffed up Topsiders.

"Look," he said, his dark eyes pleading. "I'm not a kid anymore. I haven't courted a woman in . . . well, a long time, and I'm not sure I was good at it back in my twenties. I'm in foreign waters here, you know?"

He took Brooke's hand and pressed it between his. "I wish you could forget the ugly turn the evening took last night. Because I want to. I'll never forget how it felt, holding you in my arms, watching every other man in the room watching you and envying me, because I was the lucky guy you were with."

He brushed a tendril of hair behind her ear. "I had so many plans for us last night. A walk on the beach, a kiss in the moonlight. And when you called to say you were leaving, I guess I lost it. I lashed out, and the moment those words were out of my mouth, I hated myself." Gabe leaned forward and kissed her lightly. "Can you forgive me?"

"Honestly? I don't think this is about forgiveness," Brooke said, drawing away. "It's about understanding. What you said last night — about me pulling a disappearing act? It showed you don't really know me, even after all this time. I left Harris Strayhorn because, ultimately, I wasn't ready to be married. I've admitted that was wrong. I don't regret canceling the wedding, but I do regret the careless way I did that and how deeply I hurt both our families. But I've changed. I have a child now, and he has to be my first priority. If you can't understand that, there's no future for us."

Gabe nodded solemnly. "I get it. Really, I do. That's part of what attracts me to you. Your fierceness. And your intelligence. Can we start over? Can I have that second chance?"

"Mama? Where Fawwah go?"

They both turned. Henry stood in the doorway, naked from the waist down, clutching his stuffed Ninja Turtle. "I pooped," he said solemnly.

"This is my life now, Gabe," Brooke said. "Are you really sure this is what you want?"

58

Brooke walked Gabe out to his car, blinking in the white-hot sunlight. "Any news on probating Josephine's estate?"

"I've filed all the paperwork, and I'm still tracking down all the assets," he said. "It's still amazing to me that she allowed the house to deteriorate to the extent it has, even though she had millions in cash and stocks."

"I think she wanted time to stand still after Preiss died. She only allowed Shug to do the barest minimum maintenance."

"Crazy old bat," he said, shaking his head. He turned the key in the ignition. "So . . . are we good? Can I call you again? I need to head back to Savannah this afternoon, but maybe I could take you to dinner when I'm down here next time on estate business?"

"Let's take it a day at a time," Brooke said. "Lizzie and Felicia and I are worried about C. D. Nobody's seen or heard from him in several days."

"He called me just this morning, demanding to know when he can get his inheritance," Gabe said.

"Did he say where he was calling from? I meant to tell you, we checked his cottage at Shellhaven, and it looks like he hasn't been there in a while. It looked like he'd left in a hurry."

"You broke into the guy's house? Bad idea. C. D. is certifiable. He's paranoid, and he's got a gun. There's no telling what he'd do if he caught you prowling around his house."

"We didn't actually break in. Lizzie found the key. And we weren't prowling. We were conducting a welfare check. Anything could have happened to him."

"And did you find anything interesting?"

"No. Just copies of some old newspaper clippings and things of that nature."

Gabe frowned. "C. D. has a record, Brooke. Mostly petty stuff — public drunkenness, disorderly conduct, and a misdemeanor assault. My point is, until we have the results of that DNA test back, I'm not assuming he actually is Josephine's heir."

"But what about the stuff we found out in Savannah? The photos of Josephine with him at the orphanage? The truck she gave him? He still has it, you know. And if he wasn't her child, why was she so benevolent toward the orphanage and the boy's home?"

"The Bettendorfs believed in philanthropy. Josephine's father built hospital wings, paid for local ball fields and libraries. He endowed university chairs, underwrote all kinds of things. Going through her tax records, I can see that up until her husband died, she gave away hundreds of thousands of dollars every year. That truck could be meaningless in the larger scheme of things."

"Or it could be proof that Josephine felt deeply guilty about abandoning her child," Brooke said stubbornly.

"We'll see," Gabe said. "So Lizzie is still living at Shellhaven?"

"Is there a problem with that?"

"Those cousins don't like the idea of anybody who isn't family living there," Gabe said. "They've called me twice to complain that she's trespassing. I thought Lizzie understood that. Magazine article or no, she has no business digging through Josephine's effects. I hate to be the bad guy here, but she really can't stay there any longer."

"But that's so silly," Brooke protested. "She's not hurting anything."

"Lizzie has no standing in this estate," he said firmly. "Please let her know she needs to go. Or I will."

59

On Monday, Brooke attended a child custody hearing, took a deposition on behalf of a client who'd shattered an ankle after slipping on a newly waxed floor at a fast-food joint near the interstate, and on Tuesday, after a day's worth of negotiating, managed to get all the charges against Brittni Miles dropped. Her feeling of triumph was short-lived.

Farrah called shortly after nine. Brooke could tell from her voice that there was an issue.

"What's up?" she asked.

"Don't hate me, but I need to miss work tomorrow," Farrah said. "My granny's back in the hospital in Jacksonville, and Mom says I need to go with her to visit."

"I'm sorry." Farrah's grandmother's declining health was a source of continued concern for the tight-knit Miles family. "You'll be back to work on Thursday, right?"

"Absolutely."

"Good, because I need to take a run over

to Talisa, and I'm going to need you for Henry in the afternoon."

"I'll be there."

Henry squealed with happiness as soon as she pulled into the parking lot at the library. He loved Wednesday morning story hour.

"Hey, stranger!" Janice, the head librarian, a chunky brunette with a fondness for gaudy jewelry and big hair, approached and gave Brooke a hug. "We haven't seen you in a while. Where's Farrah this morning?"

"Family issues," Brooke said. She watched as Henry ran off toward the cozy book-lined children's room, eagerly taking his place among the chattering semicircle of preschoolers seated around Miss Myra, their beloved octogenarian storyteller.

"Life treating you all right?" Janice asked as Brooke plucked the Atlanta newspaper from the periodical rack.

"I'm good," Brooke said. Seeing the newspaper reminded her of something that had been bothering her. "Janice, have you had an older guy in here a lot lately?"

"Tons," Janice said. "The retirees come in to research their stock picks and read their hometown newspapers online, the unemployed want help writing résumés, and the homeless ones like the air-conditioning and use our bathrooms. Which old guy are you looking for?"

"He's short and wiry, has a gray ponytail, always wears a baseball cap?"

"And smokes those stinky cigarillos? Don't tell me he's a friend of yours."

"No. He's an, um, acquaintance."

"He's a pain in the butt is what he is. He's been researching back issues of the Savannah and Atlanta newspapers, doing all kinds of online searches. He seems to think I'm his personal computer instructor."

"Any idea what he's looking for?" Brooke asked.

"He's very interested in local history. Especially the Bettendorf family. Do you know about them? They owned Talisa Island, and the last remaining member of the family died recently."

"I know them," Brooke said.

"I showed him how to search the local genealogical society databases here and in the next county over. And then we had to order him some books through interlibrary loan. One was an old out-of-print book about Josephine Bettendorf Warrick that she apparently commissioned back in the 1970s. He was incensed that we charged him three dollars for ordering those materials and having them shipped here. Gave me the whole line about being a Vietnam vet and how his tax dollars paid our salaries."

"What kind of books?"

Janice lowered her voice. "I don't mind telling you, because you're a long-time patron, but that man, Mr. Anthony, was obsessed with privacy. To the point of being paranoid. He wanted to make sure we weren't keeping any records of what he was looking at."

"Which was?"

"Hmm. Well, he looked at the county property tax records. I know, because I helped him with that. He printed out some records concerning Talisa. And then he also researched legal records from Glynn and Chatham counties."

"Did he say why he was interested in those counties?"

"I tried not to get too close to him, to tell you the truth," Janice said. "His personal hygiene isn't the best, if you know what I mean. But I think I printed out some tax records for him. And he was looking at civil and criminal dockets for those counties too. I remember because he raised holy you-know-what because we charge ten cents apiece for printouts!"

"Weird," Brooke said.

Janice looked around to make sure she couldn't be overheard. "Pretty sure he was also trying to look for online pornography sites too. We have blocks to keep people from doing that, but a couple of times, when he left before signing off the computer, I saw the record of his Google searches. Yeesh!"

"Anything else you can think of?"

"He was very interested in wills and trusts and that sort of thing. Funny, because he didn't strike me as the kind of person who would stand to inherit anything from anybody."

"Fascinating," Brooke said. "Has he been in here lately? Like in the past week or so?"

"I didn't see him myself, because I was at lunch, but Myra mentioned that he was here last week. She finally had to ask him to quit standing outside the doors smoking those cigars of his, because the other patrons were complaining. Excuse me," Janice said, hurrying off to quiet a table of giggling teenage girls.

60

"Brooke?" Lizzie's voice was crackling with excitement when she called early Thursday morning. "I found something. You need to get over here right away and take a look."

"I was planning on coming this morning. Are you at Shellhaven now?"

"Yeah, I'm here."

"Can you ask Shug to come pick me up? I can be at the marina by nine o'clock."

"He just pulled up with Louette," Lizzie said. "I'll ask him now."

Lizzie met Brooke at the Shellhaven dock, and it struck Brooke that although she'd been on the island only a short time, the change since she'd arrived from California was remarkable. She wore shorts, a white tank top, beat-up sneakers with no shoelaces, and a baseball cap. She held Dweezil in the crook of her elbow.

"My chariot awaits," she announced grandly, pointing at a battered blue VW station wagon.

"Where'd you get the car?" Brooke asked, jumping into the front seat.

Lizzie handed over the cat. "Shug knew a guy who knew a guy. So for the price of a battery and new tires, I am now the proud new owner. I had it barged over Monday."

Brooke looked down at Dweezil, who was butting her hand with her head.

"She would like you to scratch her ears," Lizzie said. "And neck and chin. In that order."

Brooke did as instructed, and the cat purred her approval. As she scratched the cat, she brooded once again about how to tell Lizzie that she was about to be evicted.

"Oh, hey, that's Lionel." Lizzie slowed the car as they approached a young Geechee child. He was barefoot, with a fishing pole propped against one shoulder, lugging a bucketful of fish.

"Lionel, what's happenin'?" Lizzie called, pulling up alongside him.

"Hey, Miss Lizzie. You give me ride?"

"Sure thing. Hop in the back."

He wrenched the back door open and slid the bucket across the seat. The smell of fish filled the car. In an instant, Dweezil leaped onto the backseat and began pawing at the bucket.

Lizzie turned to look at the boy. "Did you catch all those fish?"

"I cotched some, but Dobie, he give me some he had extra."

Lizzie frowned. "Those fish look pretty small, Lionel. They're not really keepers."

"Oh yeah, they keepers. My mama gonna keep 'em and fry 'em for supper tonight."

"Next time, Lionel, they need to be fourteen inches long. Otherwise, you need to throw them back while they're still alive, so they get big enough to make some more fish babies. If the ranger man comes around and finds you with those little fish, you could get into trouble."

Lionel shook his head vigorously, sending his dreadlocks flying. "The ranger man already come 'round today. Dobie, he see him coming, so he give me these fish and tell me go home."

Lizzie rolled her eyes. "Dobie knows better than to keep undersized fish, Lionel," she said. "It's probably better if you don't take any more fish from him."

"But he's my friend," Lionel protested. "He give me money to go to the store to get his smokes and let me keep the change and get me some candy and Cokes."

Lizzie pulled the car to a stop in front of the Oyster Bluff sign. "Okay, pal, this is as far as we go today."

She watched the child trudge away. "Dobie is sort of the town drunk of Oyster Bluff. He ignores all the local game and fish regulations. According to Shug, the Department of Natural Resources ranger regularly issues him tickets, but he tears 'em up and ignores the fines."

"Seems like you've settled in and gotten to know the locals," Brooke said.

"They have a covered-dish supper Sunday nights at the Oyster Bluff community house. Louette invited me." She patted her belly with a rueful grin. "The food is unbelievable. Baked redfish, shrimp pilau, deviled crab. The island's not such a bad place once you get used to the humidity and the gawd-awful bugs," Lizzie said. She slapped at an invisible bug on her forearm and grimaced. "I'll never get used to the damn no-see-um gnats." She glanced over at Brooke, noting her glum expression. "What's wrong? You're not looking too cheery today. How did your date with sugar daddy Gabe go?"

"It started out great, but then I had to cut the night short because of a crisis at home," Brooke said. "The thing is, Gabe wants you out of Shellhaven. Like, right away."

"What's the big hurry?"

"I'm sorry," Brooke said. "I hate to be the bearer of bad news, but the odious Dorcas and Delphine have apparently been kicking up a fuss. They say you're trespassing, and Gabe agrees that you really don't have a right to be going through Josephine's papers."

Lizzie's answering smile was enigmatic.

"Just wait until you see what I uncovered in those papers. You can tell Dorcas and Delphine to take a flying leap."

"Step into my office," Lizzie said as they entered the library.

Brooke set Dweezil on the floor, and the cat immediately leaped onto the windowsill.

Lizzie pointed at a battered green footlocker. "I found this shoved way at the back of the closet in here. The lid was covered in an inch-thick layer of dust and spider eggs. Louette said she's never seen it before, and I'm pretty sure it hadn't been opened in decades."

S. G. Bettendorf — RCAF was stenciled on the side of the trunk, and the lid was unlocked.

Lizzie plopped down on the floor, and Brooke sat down beside her. "This was Gardiner's air force footlocker. I found a letter from the RCAF inside, indicating that it was shipped back here to Shellhaven after he was killed in 1942."

Brooke peered inside the trunk, not knowing what to expect, but it was empty except for a lingering, dank odor.

"I had to throw most of the stuff away," Lizzie said apologetically. "The clothes were moldy and full of silverfish." She turned and retrieved a thin packet of papers.

"Fortunately, these were wrapped in some

kind of oilcloth, so they were pretty well preserved." She handed over a gray cardboard folder.

Inside was a hand-colored studio photograph of a young woman. Her blond shoulder-length hair was parted on the side and swept back from her face. She wore a blue sweater and a sweet smile.

Brooke stared down at the photo, transfixed. "It's Millie, right?" She turned the photo over.

In girlish looping script, the sender had written, *To Gardiner: All my love, Millie.*

"She looks so young," Brooke murmured. "But I don't understand what Gardiner was doing with this."

Lizzie handed over the packet of papers, and a yellowed newspaper page fluttered to the floor. It was from the front page of *The Florida Times-Union,* dated October 10, 1941. BOSTON INDUSTRIALIST STILL MISSING; FOUL PLAY FEARED.

"Read the letters and you'll understand." Lizzie said.

Oct. 29, 1941
Hingham, Mass.

Dear Gardiner:

Thank you for your kind letter of condolence concerning Russell. I'm so torn and confused right now, your letter was a great comfort. Perhaps you're right, and he and I were never meant to be. His poor grandparents are distraught, of course, but your dear father has been wonderful dealing with everything, and I will be forever grateful to him.

Please tell me all about your training. Is it exciting? Fascinating? Terrifying? Things are very quiet here at home with Mother and Grandmama. We never speak of what happened on Talisa, but I believe they feel I'm somehow to blame for Russell, and I fear I will never be able to move past this awful doubt. Maybe I will become an old maid and crochet doilies and shout at small children who ride their bicycles past our house. We read the newspapers every day and listen to the radio for war news, and I can't help but be frightened for you. Please let me hear from you soon.

Your good old friend,
M

Nov. 10, 1941
Hingham, Mass.

Dear Gardiner:

I believe our last letters must have crossed in the mail. I think of you often too and pray constantly for your well-being and safe return home. Of course I would love to see you when you are back in the States on leave at the end of the month, but are you certain you wouldn't rather spend your precious time with your family? I know Jo would be so disappointed not to see you. We had lunch together last week, and she spoke of you constantly. We had a fine time gossiping. Did you know she is doing volunteer work with the Red Cross? And Ruth has a new beau. He is from Chicago and very dashing. Not nearly as dashing as you, though, in your splendid RCAF uniform, so I do thank you for the photo, which I have hidden in my Bible, because Mother has become such a terrible snoop. She quizzes me constantly about who I am seeing and speaking to on the telephone. She has no idea of our friendship, because I am the one who brings in the mail every day, and I keep an eagle eye out for letters from my favorite airman. Speaking of the mail, must stop now before the postman arrives.

Fondly,
M

Brooke sighed. "Wouldn't you just love to read the letters Gardiner wrote to Millie?"

"I would. And I looked for his letters but didn't find any," Lizzie reported. "They weren't in the trunk, which makes sense."

WESTERN UNION: DEAREST G: CONFIRM I WILL BE ON TRAIN FROM BOSTON, ARRIVING GRAND CENTRAL STATION AT 12:10 P.M. NOV. 27. UNTIL THEN, M.

Nov. 30, 1941
Hingham, Mass.

Darling Gardiner

I know it's terribly selfish of me, but I was so very glad to have had you all to myself last weekend in New York. I never dared to dream in all the years we have known each other, since I was a funny-looking little kid pestering you for a ride in your car, that you would feel the same way about me as I do about you. My darling, I cannot believe that we wasted so much time pretending otherwise. But now that we are older and wiser, I don't intend to let a moment go by without telling you that I love you, have always, will always. The trip home was fine, but the train was awfully crowded and overheated. You asked me what I told my mother about my trip, and I am ashamed to report that I told her I was meeting Ruth in the city for some shopping. I did take Ruth into my confidence about our feelings for one another. First, because I simply had to share my happiness with someone, and second, in case Mother checks up, Ruth will cover for me. Unfortunately, I don't think it's wise to let Josephine know just yet about our relationship. I love Jo so, but you of all people know how prickly she can be and how jealous and protective she is of her beloved big brother. Gardiner. There are so many things I regret in my life — Russell and so on — but the hours I spent in your arms last weekend are something I will never forget or regret.

Your most loving M

Dec. 11, 1941
Hingham, Mass.

Darling G:

Well, it's war. We all listened to President Roosevelt on the radio this week, and afterward, I hid in my bedroom with a pillow over my head while I had a good long cry. I try not to worry about you, but since your training has ended and you'll be flying missions soon, that is impossible. So whenever I feel a black mood coming on, I pick up my knitting needles. Yes, your girl is knitting, and the results are ghastly. Which you will see for yourself — as soon as Grandmama manages to teach me how to cast off. The war is all we talk about and think about now. Ruth's beau has signed up and shipped off to Camp Pendleton in California.

Maybe now that the United States has joined the fight, we will be that much closer to beating the Germans and the Japs. All I know is that I live for the day when we will be together next. Is there any chance for New York again? Maybe at Christmas? You did mention that you might get leave again before you receive your orders, so I live in hope and am already making up a fine whopper of a tale to tell Mother. In the meantime, I am enclosing something to keep you warm in my stead.

Your loving, lousy knitter,
M

Brooke looked up, and Lizzie thrust a bulky woolen bundle at her. "Here."

It was a gray woolen scarf, knobby, full of dropped stitches, knots, and holes, but Brooke held it to her nose and inhaled. The scarf had retained the scents of cigarette smoke and camphor.

"Millie knitted this," Brooke said wonderingly, stroking the coarse woolen fabric. "Over seventy years ago." She sighed and looked down at the diminishing stack of letters in her lap. "This is so amazing and unexpected. But I feel like such a voyeur, reading my grandmother's love letters."

"I know," Lizzie said, nodding sympathetically. "Keep going anyway."

Jan. 8, 1942
Hingham, Mass.

Darling G:

Christmas came and went without you, and I was in a terrible, foul black mood. Please forgive my selfishness. You warned me that it was unlikely you could get away again, so this is all my fault. Can you forgive me for not writing sooner and sending you buckets of love and cheer? I did receive your sweet gifts. We all loved the maple syrup, which was such a treat with all the sugar rationing now. And the cashmere sweater was much too extravagant, and a totally improper gift from a gentleman to a spinster such as myself, which made me love it — and you — that much more. We actually spent Christmas Day with Jo and your papa at the house in Boston. There was a ham sent up from Talisa and oysters and as much jollity as we could muster under the circumstances. I believe Mr. Samuel has finally come around to agree with your views on the war, and at any rate, he and Jo are so terribly proud of their royal airman. I know you can't tell me much about your orders or where you're being sent, but I pray every moment that God will keep and protect you until we are together again.

Your loving, bratty M

Brooke's eyes filled with tears as she tucked the letter back into its envelope. "I want my mom to read these letters. This is a side of Millie I don't think either of us ever saw. I know I didn't. Even despite the war, she seems so young and alive and joyful and frank and funny in these." She found a tissue and dabbed at her eyes. "This is so unbelievably poignant, knowing Gardiner actually didn't make it back to Millie." She sniffed.

"From the documents I found with the footlocker, Gardiner's Spitfire was shot down by the Luftwaffe while he was on a bombing raid in northern France at the end of January '42," Lizzie said. "He'd just strafed a railway station in Boulogne and was headed back to base when his plane was hit."

Lizzie passed a hand over her own glittering eyes. "I researched it, you know? Online? These kind of RAF missions were called 'Rhubarb Raids.' They were basically just a nuisance to distract the Germans and keep them from concentrating on fighting on the western border. I think Gardiner and the men in his squadron were considered collateral damage."

"Fuckers," Brooke whispered.

"There's one more letter from Millie," Lizzie said hesitantly, holding it in her outstretched hand. "And it's what Grandma Ruth would have called a doozy."

61

Feb. 21, 1942
Hingham, Mass.

Darling Gardiner:

It's nearly midnight here at home. We've had so much snow this month, the drifts have nearly covered the dining room windows. Grandmama has had the flu, and now Mother has a fever too, but the weather has been so terrible the doctor can't get here to check on them. Right now, I am tucked into bed under my quilt. I have all your beautiful letters saved in the now empty chocolate box you gave me in New York. Nights like this, when I am lonely and afraid, I read and reread them, and your sweet words of love give me strength. I'm praying that I'll receive one of your letters any day now. It's been a month, and I miss you so terribly, my darling. I follow the war news and believe your squadron must be in England by now, though I know the censors won't allow you to say more. The thing is, darling, I have some news of my own that I'm afraid can't wait. I'm pregnant! By my calculations, the baby is due in August. I finally saw a doctor in the city this week, and he confirmed my suspicions.

I am so terribly sorry to bring you this news now, but I really don't know what else to do. We talked about marriage in New York, and I know I was the one who was afraid of creating a scandal by marrying so soon after Russell, but now I realize just how foolish I was. Oh, if only we had married in November, and I could call you my husband and announce this news to the world and hold my head high.

Of course, I dare not tell Mother. Do you know, she still seems to be mourning Russell? So far, I think my secret is safe. I've barely gained any weight, and aside from a little bit of morning queasiness, I feel fine. I did confide again in Ruth, and she has been my rock. She suggests that if you can somehow get emergency leave to come home, we could have a quick wedding. Eyebrows might be raised, and tongues would be wagged, and months would be counted, but that is the least of my concerns right now. But we both agree Jo cannot hear about the baby until after we are married and you have made a "respectable woman" of me. You know your sister can be terribly old-fashioned.

Write to me soon, darling Gardiner, and tell me what to do. I love and miss you with all my heart, but the thought that I will soon hold our own sweet baby in my arms has me giddy with excitement. And terror. Do you know, I've never held a newborn or changed a diaper?

Your expectant M

Brooke read the letter a second time and again a third time. She heard the loud ticking of the grandfather clock in the corner and the whir of the box fan in the window, and she felt the slow slide of sweat trickling down her back. Finally, she looked up at Lizzie, who was watching her with open curiosity.

"My God," Brooke said finally. "Millie was pregnant with my mother. And Gardiner was my mom's father. Not Pops. Gardiner."

"That's what it looks like to me," Lizzie said. "Gardiner Bettendorf was your grandfather. Which means that Josephine was your great-aunt."

Brooke's hand trembled as she handed the letter back to Lizzie. "I've got to talk to my mother."

"Agreed," Lizzie said. "And then you'd better call Gabe too."

"Gabe?"

"Uh, duh. If Gardiner was Marie's father

and your grandfather, unless I'm sadly mistaken, that makes the two of you Josephine's closest family. Her heirs."

Brooke let that sink in for a moment, especially in light of what they'd learned during their visit to the children's home in Savannah.

"Don't count out C. D. yet," Brooke cautioned. "If he really is Josephine's long-lost son, he'll be calling all the shots around here."

"And he'd be your mom's cousin."

"Eeeewww," they said in unison.

Brooke flopped backward onto the carpet and stared up at the ceiling, whose plaster was water-stained and flaking. "This whole thing is too weird to be true."

"I know. It's gonna make a great story. And just think! You'll have every right to tell Dorcas and Delphine to kiss your grits."

"Kiss my grits?" Brooke said. "Now I know you really have gone native."

62

Brooke and her mother sat in the small room her parents had added to the back of the 1920s-era Ardsley Park home. Marie had transformed the former den into a cozy sunroom, painting the dark pine paneling, ripping down the drapes, and installing a pair of flowered chintz love seats, wicker armchairs, and huge baskets of ferns and pots of pink geraniums.

"I fixed us an early supper," Marie said. There was a large club salad with wedges of juicy red tomatoes, hard-boiled eggs, sliced, poached chicken breasts, and bacon bits. She served Brooke a plate and handed her a linen napkin rolled around the flatware.

Marie had never flagged in keeping up the standards Millie had instilled in her. Bone china, linen napkins, and always the good silver. The only time Brooke could ever remember eating off paper plates was when the family went on beach picnics.

"Okay," Marie said. "You've got me on pins

and needles. What's so important that you had to drop everything and drive up here today? Is it something about Josephine? Have the DNA results come back on C. D.?"

Brooke sipped her iced tea. "Yes, it's definitely about Josephine. But this isn't about C. D., Mom. It's about you. And Millie. And Gardiner."

"Oh yes," Marie said. "The pilot. He was killed in the war, right?"

"That's right." Brooke handed her mother the packet of letters. She'd had Farrah make photocopies of everything before leaving the office, but she wanted Marie to read the originals.

"Before I forget, your dad wants you to call him."

"Why? What does he want?"

"He'd like to speak to you. Could you just do me a favor and call him, please?"

"No." Brooke abruptly set her glass down on the table. "I'm not calling him. He can call me if it's that important."

Marie handed the letters back. "I'm not looking at these until you call your father."

"Mom! This is really important. It's why I drove all the way up here today."

Her mother folded her arms across her chest. "What your dad has to say to you is important too. So I'd say we're at a stalemate."

"Okay, fine. You read the letters while I call Dad."

"Good idea." Marie picked up the first letter and adjusted her reading glasses.

Brooke was too jittery to sit and watch her mother read Millie's letters to Gardiner Bettendorf anyway. She walked slowly up the stairs and without really thinking about it pushed open the door to her old bedroom.

It was a small room, with a low, sloping ceiling and pink-and-green-striped wallpaper, last decorated when Brooke turned fourteen. Marie hadn't gotten around to redecorating it yet, for which Brooke was thankful.

She sat on the white-painted canopy bed and scrolled through her contacts until she found Gordon Trappnell's cell number. She checked the time. Not yet five. With luck, he'd still be at his office and out of earshot of Patricia, his second wife.

Gordon and Patricia had been married for five years now, but Brooke still refused to refer to her as her stepmother. Once, Patricia and her first husband had been close friends with Gordon and Marie. They'd been members of a neighborhood supper club, and Patricia had been part of Marie's book club. But the divorces had shattered both those groups, not to mention Brooke's own fondest notions about her parents' "perfect marriage."

She tapped his number, silently hoping he

wouldn't pick up. But he did, on the first ring.

"Brooke? Is that you?"

"It's me, Dad. Mom said you wanted to talk to me. What's up?"

"Oh. Well . . ." Her father seemed to be at a momentary loss for words. "How are you? How's that boy of yours?"

Fifteen seconds. She was only fifteen seconds into a call with her father and already doing a slow burn.

"His name is Henry, Dad. H-E-N-R-Y. And he's fine."

"I know his name, Brooke. Your mom keeps me up to date on everything. Is his arm healing? Maybe next time you come up, we could get together. I'd really like to see him."

An acid, sarcastic response was on the tip of her tongue, but she chose to let the moment pass. "That would be nice. His arm is totally healed. I'll see what I can do about a get-together. In the meantime, what's so important that you needed to talk to me about?"

"Marie tells me you've started seeing Gabe Wynant. Actually dating?"

"Don't start on me about the age difference, Dad," Brooke warned. "We've seen each other socially a couple of times. It's no big deal, and besides, we've known each other for years."

"Actually, you don't really know him at all," Gordon said. "This isn't about that, although it's ridiculous for a man his age —"

"Whoa! I'm thirty-four years old, you know. A little past the age when I want dating advice from my daddy."

"Listen to me, damn it! Patricia says Gabe is a charlatan —"

"Okay, just stop right there. I'm not going to listen to your new wife's character assassination of a man I've known and admired for the past decade."

"If you'd just let me finish," Gordon said.

"Nope. Not interested. Nice try. Bye, Dad."

Brooke disconnected, still fuming. She stared at the assortment of framed photos on her old white-painted dresser, Brooke laughing into the camera with her best friend, Holly, on the beach at Tybee Island. There was Brooke in her cap and gown after her graduation from Savannah Country Day. She picked up the oldest photo, a three-generation snapshot of her grandmother Millie seated on the sofa next to an impossibly young-looking Marie, who held an eighteen-month-old Brooke in a frilly white Easter dress.

Millie was gazing adoringly at the baby, and Marie was beaming proudly.

Brooke's memories of Millie, her granny, were hazy now. She remembered a crystal lidded dish, always placed on the coffee table and filled with pink jelly beans for her visiting granddaughter. She remembered stacks of library books and record albums, mostly classical music, that Granny played on a bulky turntable in what she called her "hi-fi cabinet."

She took the photograph, left the bedroom, and walked slowly downstairs, where her mother was still seated in the sunroom.

"Mom?"

Her mother's beautifully composed face was in ruins. She stared numbly at the letters. "Where did you find these?"

"Lizzie found them. In Gardiner's footlocker, which was shoved way in the back of a closet in the library at Shellhaven. The military shipped it there to Josephine after he was killed."

Marie scowled. "That horrible, horrible woman."

"Who? Josephine?"

"Yes." Marie tossed the stack onto the table. "She read these letters, then hid them. She knew Mama was in love with Gardiner, was having — I mean, had — his child. Mama was her oldest, dearest friend. And Josephine just cut her out of her life. No wonder she wanted to make amends with us."

"I've been thinking about that," Brooke said. "Maybe that's why Josephine quit talking to Ruth too — because she knew Granny had confided in Ruth but not in her. Of course Josephine read all the letters. She must have been furious at her best friends."

"Why? Why, after Pops died, didn't she

reach out to Mama? The secret wouldn't have mattered so much then, not between the two of them, anyway."

"I don't know," Brooke admitted. "There's so much I didn't understand about Josephine. After Preiss died, she was essentially alone for the next forty years or so. All those years, she had no family, and she isolated herself from her oldest, closest friends. But she did have family — she had us, and we were what? An hour and a half away, in Savannah? A phone call, that's all it would have taken. Instead, she waited until she knew she was dying."

"Mama never said a word," Marie said, twisting and untwisting the napkin she held in her hands.

Brooke sat down in the chair opposite her mother's and gripped her hands in hers.

"Do you think Pops knew?" It was a question that had haunted Brooke since she'd read Millie's last letter to Gardiner.

"He must have, but he certainly never let on to me," Marie said, attempting a smile. She dabbed at her eyes with the napkin. "Pops was my father," she said finally. "He was! He was the most patient, most loving and gentle man in the world."

"I can't believe Granny kept this a secret, all these years. And none of us had any idea."

"I can," Marie said. "Looking back now, I can understand why she was so private, and self-contained. I always thought it was just that famous New England reserve."

"It must have been awful for Millie, keeping that secret. Pregnant and unmarried, knowing it would cause a scandal, wondering if Gardiner would come home from war to marry her. And then having to grieve him all alone," Brooke said.

"I'm glad Josephine didn't reach out to us," Marie said. "I couldn't have forgiven her for the way she treated my mother. She didn't deserve to call us her family."

Marie jumped to her feet and went into the kitchen. When she came back, she had an open bottle of wine and two glasses. She poured a glass and offered it to Brooke.

"No, thanks. I've got to drive home, remember?"

"Right." Marie took a long drink of the wine.

"These letters change everything, you know. You're Josephine's niece, her closest relative and her heir, unless we find out that C. D. actually was her son."

"I don't need Josephine Warrick's money." Marie's voice dripped scorn. "I had a career and saved my money, your father was generous with the divorce settlement, and I've done well with my investments. I thought it was a nice gesture when she reached out to us. I thought I'd be indulging her by going over to Talisa to meet her. And yes, I wanted you to have whatever bequest she wanted to give you. But knowing what we know now?" She drained the wineglass. "I'd be willing to *give* that damn island and the house to the state just to spite Josephine."

"Who are you kidding?" Brooke said. "You're the least spiteful woman I know. Anyway, are you telling me you're not even just a little bit curious about Josephine's estate? Don't you want to know what it's worth? Call me a mercenary little money-grubber, but I am. I've been wondering ever since I first set foot in Shellhaven."

"I feel like I'm suddenly living in some weird parallel universe. All of a sudden, I'm not who I thought I was. I can't even begin to process this. Anyway, what if this is all some kind of a mistake? And we're jumping to conclusions?" Marie asked.

Brooke pointed to the letters. "Do you think they're fake? Does that look like Granny's handwriting?"

With a fingertip, Marie traced the elegant slanting script on a brittle envelope.

"It's Mama's handwriting," she said slowly. "And the voice in these letters, it's hers. I can hear her so clearly as I read them. She used to write me letters like these when I was away at college. I still have them, you know. Packed away somewhere in the attic. I even have a few letters Pops sent me when I was away at summer camp. He knew I was homesick, so he'd draw these funny little cartoons of my cat, Mrs. Whiskers, with the silliest balloon captions."

She sniffed and dabbed at her eyes again. "I wish you'd known Pops, Brooke. I wish he'd known you. And Henry, of course."

"I wish it too." Brooke stood up. "I'd better hit the road."

Reluctantly, Marie handed her the letters. "You'll need to give these to Gabe, right?"

"Yes. I had Farrah make copies of everything for you, but he'll want the originals," Brooke said. "And I wouldn't be surprised if the cousins, once they hear this news, don't insist on getting your DNA compared to Josephine's."

Marie shuddered. "Does that mean needles? You know how I feel about blood. And needles."

"I think it's just a matter of something simple. Like a cheek swab," Brooke said.

They walked toward the front door.

"Did you talk to your dad?" Marie asked.

Brooke tensed. "Briefly."

"Gordon wouldn't tell me what he wanted to discuss. From the look on your face, I'm guessing it didn't go well."

"You could say that. He doesn't like the idea of me dating Gabe. I wish you hadn't told him I was."

"I didn't think it was classified information. Did Dad have a specific objection, or was it just the age thing?"

"Patricia has some malicious gossip about Gabe that she's just dying to spread, but I shut him down before he could get started."

"Maybe you should have listened," Marie said. "Gordon is many things, but a gossip isn't one of them."

"I've known Gabe for years. I think I know him a lot better than Patricia does," Brooke said.

Marie kissed her daughter on the cheek. "Sometimes the people we think we know the best are the ones with secrets we can't even fathom. Drive carefully, okay?"

63

On Friday morning, Brooke's cell phone buzzed to signal an incoming text. It was from a number she didn't immediately recognize. It was a screenshot of a court document. She squinted as she read the tiny print. It was a copy of a Chatham County property tax lien against Gabe W. Wynant, in the amount of $90,000, on behalf of KPW Roofing Inc.

Beneath the screenshot was the text message:

> Heard you've been looking for me. Your boyfriend Gabe is a phony. If you want to know what I know, come over to island and we'll talk.

Now she knew the number. It belonged to C. D. She was relieved that he was apparently alive and well but annoyed at his reference to Gabe as her boyfriend. And what was this about a lien?

Okay, when and where?

My friend Ramona has a boat tied up at the municipal pier. It's called *Foxxy Lady.* She's waiting. I'll pick you up at the Talisa dock. Come now, okay?

She hesitated, wondering why she felt uneasy about responding to a text from the old man. He was harmless, wasn't he? But where had he been hiding, and why was he reaching out to her now? Her thumbs flew over the phone's keyboard.

Waiting on my assistant to arrive at office. Can't leave 'til then.

She glanced at the clock on the office wall. Farrah was thirty minutes overdue. So this was what the old man had been furtively researching in the library databases. The real estate lien must have been the result of a clerical error. Gabe's town house in Savannah was on West Jones Street, one of the most beautiful streets in the downtown historic district. It was easily a $2 million property. She frowned. What was C. D. up to?

The office door opened, and Farrah breezed in, her cell phone wedged between her shoulder and left ear as she sipped from a huge Styrofoam Slurpee cup. Brooke fixed her with a disapproving stare. "Gotta go," Farrah told her caller. "My boss is giving me the death stare."

The girl set her backpack and Slurpee on her desk. "Sorry about that. What's up?"

"You're late," Brooke said. She picked up her phone and texted C. D., and she reached for her pocketbook.

Leaving now.

His return text was almost immediate.

Come alone and don't tell nobody.

"I've got to go," she told Farrah. But the idea of a secret meeting with this paranoid old man was making *her* feel paranoid.

"Go where?" Farrah asked, sifting through the stack of papers piled atop her desk.

"I'm meeting C. D. over on Talisa." Brooke quickly filled her assistant in on her mission. "It's probably bogus, but he claims to have some damaging information about Gabe. Do me a favor, will you? Just in case, take a look at the online tax records for Chatham County. See what you can find in the way of tax liens." Another thought occurred to her. "While you're at it, check the plaintiff and defendant indexes and see if Gabe has been party to any recent civil actions."

Farrah nodded as she scrawled notes to herself. "How far back should I look?"

"Maybe the past three years? And while you're at it, check the Glynn County records too. I can't remember the exact address, but his house on Sea Island is on Blue Heron Street. It might be listed under Sunny Wynant."

"Who's she?"

"His wife. She died two years ago."

"For real? I mean, he drives a Porsche."

"It's called due diligence," Brooke said. She fixed her assistant with what Farrah called her death stare again. "This is all highly confidential stuff. A man's reputation is at stake. If anybody asks, just tell them I had an appointment this afternoon. Not a word about my going over to the island or who I'm meeting with. Right? I'm not sure how long I'll be over there, so can you pick Henry up from day care if I'm not back by 2:30?"

"Sure thing."

"And Farrah? If you're late picking Henry up? That's a firing offense."

C. D.'s friend Ramona had jet-black hair that fell nearly to her waist. She wore flowered board shorts and a neon-orange bikini top that displayed a pair of saggy sixtysomething-year-old breasts. "All set?" she asked after she'd helped Brooke onto the eighteen-foot *Foxxy Lady.*

Brooke nodded, and Ramona backed the boat away from the slip.

"You're a friend of C. D.'s?" Brooke asked. "Have you known him a long time?"

Ramona's smile was enigmatic. "Been knowing him off and on for a while. More off than on, but since last week, I guess you'd say we're on again."

"Has he told you what all the secrecy is about?" Brooke asked.

"He *says* he's fixin' to come into an inheritance — which, knowing C. D., is a lot of crap. He also says I should keep my mouth shut about what I know, so that's what I been doing." Ramona turned her back to Brooke, and a moment later the boat was flattening out, skimming across the calm waters of the river with Talisa straight ahead.

C. D. was seated on a black motorbike at the edge of the Shellhaven dock. He raised a hand in greeting to Ramona, who returned the salute. Lionel, the little Geechee boy who'd been sitting on the dock, waved too.

As Brooke walked toward C. D., she heard the boat's engine start and turned to see the *Foxxy Lady* pull away from the dock.

"Get on," C. D. said in lieu of a greeting.

"No helmet?" Brooke asked nervously, straddling the bike and gingerly wrapping her arms around the old man's midsection. She noted the leather holster clipped to the waist of his shorts.

"We ain't goin' that far," he said. "You

didn't tell nobody you were comin', right?"

"Right," she lied.

He steered away from Shellhaven, turning in the opposite direction. The small bike's engine labored beneath the weight of two riders. Bits of rock and crushed oyster shell sprayed her ankles and calves as they rode along, and she kept her lips clamped together and eyes squeezed shut against the stirred-up sand and grit.

The bike finally slowed after they'd been riding for ten minutes. She looked up when she heard the waves pounding ashore and saw the old lighthouse looming in front of them.

"We're here," C. D. said.

She was grateful to hop off the bike and have both feet on the ground again. He pushed the bike off the roadway, leaning it against the abbreviated porch of a small wooden edifice that Brooke realized must be the lighthouse keeper's cottage, the same one Josephine, Millie, Ruth, and Varina had stayed in the night before discovering Russell Strickland's body.

Was this where C. D. had been hiding out?

Instead of entering the cottage, C. D. turned and walked toward the lighthouse itself.

"In here," he said, pushing against the heavy wooden door, which opened inward on long-disused hinges. An open padlock hung from a rusty hasp screwed into the rotting wooden doorframe.

"Here? In the lighthouse?" Brooke peered uneasily inside. The landing in front of her was narrow, maybe six feet wide, and green-painted wooden stairs spiraled up the exposed brick column. Dust motes swirled in the shaft of sunlight pouring down from the top.

"You got a better place?" He started up the stairs, and she was surprised at how nimble he was. She stood, rooted in the doorway, already regretting having come this far. She saw now that C. D. Anthony wasn't just a harmless, aging eccentric. He was paranoid, and he was armed.

C. D. read her expression. "Come on, now. You think I'm gonna hurt you? I swear, that ain't what this is about."

"What is this about? Why can't we just talk down here?" Brooke hoped her voice sounded steadier than she felt.

"I like it up top." He jerked his chin upward. "You got a 360-degree view up there. I can see anybody coming or going. See the whole island. That's why I chose it. Anyway, I got my dossier up there. That's what I want you to see."

He started up the stairs again, calling over his shoulder. His high, reedy voice echoed off the curving walls. "Your friend Gabe? He ain't what you think he is, and I can prove it. I know you don't believe me, but ain't you curious?"

She was, damn it. Almost against her will, she began to climb, higher and higher. Once, halfway up, she stopped to catch her breath. She made the mistake of looking down and was seized by a sudden wave of terror. The stairs spun crazily beneath her feet, and she felt herself about to pitch backward. Panic-stricken, Brooke clawed at the brick wall, trying to gain a handhold. Bile rose in her throat, and she felt a crushing weight on her chest. She knelt and gripped the wooden stair risers at waist level.

"You coming?" C. D.'s disembodied voice floated from above.

"I can't do this!" Brooke cried when she could catch her breath. "I'm dizzy. I'm afraid of falling!"

"Happens all the time. Don't look down. Just keep coming."

Hot tears streamed down her cheeks. She managed to stand upright. She took a step. Paused, took a breath then took another step, and then another.

C. D. leaned casually against the glass-enclosed turret. "Took you long enough," he said when Brooke finally crawled onto the wooden landing. Her hands and knees were blackened from the gritty stairs, and she was sick and scared and bathed in her own sweat.

"Dizzy," she gasped.

He reached into a Styrofoam cooler and

handed her a bottle of water. "Don't be such a crybaby."

After she'd regained her hard-won composure, she looked around at what must have been the lens room when the lighthouse was still operational. Queasy as she was, even she would admit that the view was, as advertised, spectacular. She understood why Farrah and her friends trespassed here. From 120 feet up, she could see the roof of Shellhaven and its outbuildings, the dock, and the river, and in the far distance, the mainland. The sweep of untouched beach and endless ocean felt calming. When she turned toward the north end of the island, she could see the state's ferry boat churning away from the island.

But the sudden head movement brought on another spasm of anxiety and nausea. She slumped down onto the floor.

"You done sightseeing?"

C. D. had made himself a rat's nest of dirty clothes and a sleeping bag. A backpack was stashed beside a wooden soft drink crate, atop which sat a file folder and a heavy, lethal-looking flashlight.

"Here's what I wanted to show you," he said with a smug smile. "My dossier."

Brooke opened the folder and made a show of leafing through the documents, but trying to read the already blurry printouts made her even queasier.

"What exactly do you want from me, C. D.?" she asked.

"I need your help. Your lawyer buddy Gabe tried to kill me."

Humor him, Brooke thought. *Isn't that what you do with delusional people?*

"I don't understand," she said slowly. "Why would Gabe try to kill you?"

"Because I know stuff about him. Stuff he doesn't want anybody else to know. He tried to kill me once, and he'll try it again unless you help me."

Oh God. C. D.'s paranoia was in full flower. She eyed the holster on his hip. If challenged, would he become violent or unhinged?

"You're saying Gabe actually tried to kill you? When was this?"

"Last week. I don't know the day. I been running and hiding, and I lost track of time."

"Tell me what happened."

"I been calling him a lot to, you know, try to get him to speed up this inheritance thing. Or just float me a loan, you know, until the court or whoever decides that I'm Josephine's son and I'm her heir. I guess it pissed him off, because last week when I called, he said I was full of shit, just some damn drifter who was trying to cash in on a sick old lady. He said he'd done some research and found out some bad stuff about me."

"Like what?" Brooke asked.

"I ain't a damn saint. Never said I was.

Maybe I wrote some bad checks when I was between jobs, and maybe I got in some bar fights and got locked up for public drunkenness for pissin' on somebody's tires."

"Okay," Brooke said soothingly. "Those kinds of things happen. Totally understandable."

"Ticked me off, you know? Some damn lawyer digging up dirt on me. So I decided I'd see what kind of dirt I could dig up on him."

"Is that when you went to the library in St. Ann's?"

"You know about that?" C. D. asked. "They keep records of who all looks up that stuff? Them librarians said they didn't do that."

"I have a confession to make," Brooke said, coloring slightly. "We — that is, Lizzie and Felicia and I — were worried when you just disappeared. So we went over to your cottage, and we found the key where you'd hidden it, and we went in. I'm sorry, C. D., but really, we were worried that you might be sick or something."

"Snooping. Spying on me," C. D. said accusingly. "Big Brother always watching."

"We found some of those papers you printed out from the library, the old newspaper photos and clippings. I was in the library yesterday, taking my son to story hour. I asked the librarians if they knew you, and they told me you'd been doing a lot of your own research and that they'd helped you figure out how to use the computers and access databases."

"You know they charge you for stuff?" C. D. said, indignant. "I mean, that library is paid for with my tax dollars. And hell, I'm a senior citizen and a Vietnam vet. But yeah, that's where I was doing my research. After that crook Gabe dug up his dirt, I figured two could play that game. So I got them library ladies to show me how to look at the clerk's records in Savannah and up there at Sea Island, where he's got that fancy house of his."

Brooke pulled out her phone and pointed at the text message he'd sent her. "Is that where you found this?"

"And there's a bunch more like that too," C. D. said smugly. "He's plastered bad paper all over Savannah. And that place of his up at Sea Island, it's got all kinds of liens on it." He tapped the file folder. "I'm not just talking about tax liens, either. Roofers, electricians, landscapers. Hell, the guy that cleans his swimming pool has a lien on that house."

"Are you sure you've got the right address and the right Gabe Wynant?" Brooke asked. "I've known Gabe for years. We worked in the same law firm. He's a wealthy man with a thriving legal practice. I've been to his house downtown on West Jones Street several times. It's probably worth $2 or $3 million.

The same for the Sea Island house. Gabe is one of the most respected attorneys in Savannah."

"He's a damn crook is what he is. Look at all them small businesses he stiffed."

Brooke said. "Look, C. D., Savannah's still a small, gossipy Southern town. If Gabe were in some kind of financial trouble, there would be rumors, and I'd have heard something."

"How long you been living down here?" C. D. asked.

"Three years," she admitted. "I guess I have kind of cut myself off from the rumor mills."

"You know the guy in the $2,000 suit and Rolex watch that drives a Mercedes and a Porsche," C. D. said. He took off his cap and bent his head down. "Look here."

There was a knot the size of a hen's egg on the back of C. D.'s skull with an angry, jagged red scar running through it. "This is the guy I know."

"Oh my God. Gabe did this to you? When? How?"

"Last week. I called him up and told him I wanted to talk to him about getting an advance on my money, and he just laughed. Said I wasn't getting a dime. So I texted him the same photo I sent you, of those bad check charges, and all of a sudden, his calendar got freed up in a hurry. He said he couldn't get down here until early evening. I was supposed to meet him at seven, but it was closer to eight. He said he'd got tied up in traffic, which I think now was just a lie.

"Anyway, I sat in the boat, had some beers, waiting. Hell, I been waiting my whole life, what's a couple of more hours? He showed up, and it was dark, but I wasn't too worried, because the boat's got running lights, and anyway, I could cross that river blindfolded if I had to.

"He come on the boat, acting kind of nervous, and I offered him one of my beers. We talked a little bit about me getting my money, and he was acting like he actually had the money on him, but he wanted to talk more once we got to the island. I was just about out of the no-wake zone, had my back to him, when out of nowhere, he took that full beer bottle and bashed me on the back of my head. Before I knew it, he'd flung me off the side of my boat."

"You could have been killed," Brooke said.

"He thought he had killed me," C. D. said. "I don't know how, but I never even blacked out. I swam under water until I thought my lungs would explode. He took off and headed back toward the city dock. Me, I managed to make it over to the creek bank. I was bleeding and had a hell of a headache, I'll tell you that. Lucky for me, the tide was coming in. I swam to a dock a little ways away. Climbed up, walked back to town, and got ahold of Ramona. She took me to the emergency room, and they stitched me up. I stayed at her place that night, then I got her to bring me back over to the island. Just wanted to sleep in my own bed and figure out what my next move was, you know?"

"But you didn't stay there," Brooke said. "Louette and Shug checked. We checked. It looked like you'd packed up and left in a hurry."

"I got to the cottage that night, and the lights were on. I could see him, through the window, going through my stuff."

"Who?"

"Wynant. He was real careful not to mess stuff up, but I seen him take those papers, the ones that showed all the bad check charges and liens. I watched him, and after he'd gone, I went in, and like you said, I packed up some stuff, got some food, and got the hell out of Dodge. Come over here and let myself into the lighthouse, and I been staying here ever since."

"I'm glad you reached out to me, but why now? And why hide out at all? Why not go to the sheriff? That's attempted murder, C. D."

"The sheriff? The same one who locked me up for pissin' on his deputy's tires? You think he's gonna believe me over the lawyer with the suits and the watch and the Porsche?"

"But you could show him those same papers you showed me; it's pretty incriminating evidence, C. D. He seems like a reasonable guy to me."

"That's because you're a cute young lawyer lady, not a crusty old bastard like me," C. D. said. He rooted around in his cooler and brought out a sandwich. "Want one? Well, this is my last one, but I got some chips you can have if you're hungry."

"No," she said weakly, fighting another wave of nausea. "God, no."

Her phone, tucked into the pocket of her jeans, pinged softly, startling her, because her cell phone reception on the island was usually so spotty. She reached for it and saw she had an incoming text from Farrah.

G was here. Told him I don't know where u r, but seemed suspicious. FYI.

"Who's that?" C. D. asked, instantly wary.

"It's from my babysitter. C. D., does your phone have cell service up here?"

"Yeah, best reception on the island usually, 'cause we're up so high, but it ain't got no juice now, and I left the charger at my place."

Her own phone indicated she had only one bar, and her battery was running down, but she tapped Farrah's number, praying the call would go through.

"Who you calling?" he demanded.

"My babysitter. I need to tell her to pick up my son from day care, okay?"

"Hey," Farrah said, her words rushing

together. "Brooke, I'm sorry. I was telling Gabe you had an appointment, and just then, Brittni pulled up outside and honked her horn. I went out to talk to her. I swear, I was only gone a minute. But I had all those printouts on top of my desk. I think maybe he saw them."

"Are you sure?"

"No, but he left in a big hurry," Farrah said. "I tried to call you for like, half an hour, but then I remembered you don't have cell service over there, so I tried a text."

C. D. was staring at her intently, his hand resting lightly on the gun on his hip.

"Okay," Brooke said cautiously. "That's fine."

"Huh? You seem kinda weird. Is something wrong? Where exactly are you?"

"Yes," Brooke said pleasantly. "I think that's a great idea. You and Jaxson can pick up Henry. Take him to that place the two of you used to go last summer, with the great view, okay?"

"Huh? Are you talking in code?"

"Come on, wrap it up," C. D. said.

"Yes. Okay, gotta run," Brooke said. "Also, maybe pick me up a bottle of Captain Morgan?"

"What the hell, Brooke?" Farrah said, just as Brooke was disconnecting.

C. D. sighed his annoyance. "Look, I called you because I need help." He looked her square in the face, his voice pleading. "I need you to go to the sheriff with me and tell him I'm telling the truth. Don't let that lawyer get away with what he done to me. Don't let him cheat me out of what I'm due from Josephine."

"All right," Brooke said finally, tucking her phone away. "I'll see what I can do." She stood, but the room seemed to swim beneath her feet again. She swayed slightly, then slumped against the glass.

"Hey, you don't look too good," C. D. said. He took her arm and tried to steady her. They heard a car coming, and he was on instant alert. He picked up the binoculars resting on top of the fruit crate and looked.

"Shit. That's Wynant."

64

C. D. whirled around to confront Brooke. "You lied, damn it. You led him right to me!"

The truck was the ancient turquoise one that belonged to Josephine. She'd noticed it earlier, at the dock, parked with the other vehicles under the shade of a twisted cedar tree. She watched as it pulled up to the grassy area at the foot of the lighthouse. Gabe hopped out and looked around. He darted toward the lighthouse keeper's cottage, trying the locked door and peering in the window, before staring up at the lighthouse. C. D. ducked down onto the floor, and Brooke reflexively followed suit.

"I didn't tell him anything. I swear I didn't," Brooke said. She didn't know whether Gabe's arrival was a rescue mission or not.

"How did he know we were here?" C. D. grabbed the front of Brooke's shirt. "Was that him you just called? I should have known you're in cahoots with him. Lemme see that phone." He took her phone, and stared down at the screen.

Brooke wrenched away from the old man. "Think about it, C. D. I had no way of knowing you were here at the lighthouse. And I have no idea what Gabe is doing here."

C. D. duck-walked away from the window, then stood, his fingers resting nervously on the holster on his hip again. "If you're lying to me . . ."

"I'm not."

They heard the door open below.

C. D. cursed softly. "Forgot to lock the damn door." He stood looking down the stairwell. "Wynant, I seen you down there. You need to not come up here. I already told Brooke what you've been up to. You're done, asshole."

"Brooke?" Gabe yelled. "Are you up there with him? Are you okay? Has he hurt you?"

"I ain't ever hurt a woman in my life," C. D. called. "You're the one that bashed me in the head, threw me into the creek, and left me for dead. But the joke's on you. I'm alive, and I'm fixing to tell the sheriff everything I know."

Gabe's footfalls echoed off the brick walls. They heard his labored breathing, and then he stopped.

"Brooke, whatever he's told you is bullshit. He's been trying to blackmail me. It's true, I had some money problems right after Sunny died. I was out of my head with grief, I had no idea about the kind of money she'd been spending. But that's all it was."

Could that explain the source of Gabe's financial distress? Had C. D. overreacted?

"Yeah, right!" C. D. hollered. "How do you explain what happened on the boat the other night? How'd I get that gash on the back of my head?"

More footsteps, and Gabe stopped again. "He's been trying to blackmail me. Calling me repeatedly. I agreed to meet with him, but once we got on the boat, he started threatening me, waving that gun of his around. He'd been drinking. When I refused to give him any money, he shot at me! He missed, and that's when I hit him with the beer bottle and took off for the dock. He could have killed me."

Brooke glanced over at C. D. He'd admitted to taking potshots at park service rangers, so why wouldn't he have shot at a lawyer he suspected of defrauding him?

"Brooke?" Gabe shouted. "Talk to me. Are you okay? C. D., you just let her go. She's not involved in this. Let her go, and you and I will settle our differences."

She felt C. D.'s fingers dig into the flesh of her upper arm. He released her for a moment, pulling his revolver from the holster.

"I'm fine, Gabe!"

"Shut up, damn you." C. D. jerked her backward. "Don't you know he's a liar?" She flinched as his sour breath sounded hot and low in her ear. "Tell him to get out of here. Get out, and then I'll let you go."

"He says if you go away, he'll let me go," Brooke called.

"He's lying!" Gabe yelled back. "If he means what he says, he'll let you walk down these stairs and leave with me."

Gabe's voice echoed in the stairwell. They heard his footsteps, sensed him coming closer.

"Don't you come up here!" C. D. yelled. His rheumy, red-rimmed eyes darted around the room. His hands shook badly as he tried to slot bullets into the pistol's chamber. Brooke had the sense that he was coming unglued before her eyes, the raw nervous energy sizzling through every cell of his body.

Agonizing seconds passed, each one marked with the sound of Gabe's inexorable upward climb.

Brooke's eyes were riveted on the old man. Right now, he was focused on Gabe, but in his hyper-paranoid state, he might turn the gun on her at any moment. She mentally measured the distance to the stairs, tried to calibrate the trajectory of bullet to human bone and blood — hers, Gabe's, C. D.'s. She had to do something to pause this nightmare, but she felt paralyzed. Finally, she inched away from him, pressing her back against the wall, trying to slide out of his sight line.

In the next second, the footsteps accelerated. Gabe was running. He burst onto the stair landing, a black pistol aimed directly at C. D.'s head. Startled, the old man scrabbled backward, firing wildly, his bullets ricocheting off the ceiling. Gabe leveled the gun, his finger on the trigger.

"No!" Brooke screamed, lunging toward Gabe, who fired.

The gunshot roared, echoing and bouncing off the brick walls, louder than anything Brooke had ever before experienced. She screamed and watched in horror as C. D. dropped his gun and fell to the floor, howling in pain. He writhed on the floor, blood pooling from his shoulder.

"Come on. We've got to get out of here." Gabe grabbed her arm and tugged her toward the stairwell.

Brooke pulled away and knelt beside C. D., whose face was already ashen. "We can't leave him like this." She grabbed a T-shirt from the mound of C. D.'s clothing and clamped it against the shoulder wound, which burbled blood.

"Leave him," Gabe barked. "The bastard tried to kill me twice."

"No. He'll bleed to death. He's a crazy, sick old man. I can't leave him like this." Brooke looked up at Gabe. The warm, caring, courtly barrister had vanished, and in his place was this cold-eyed killer, ready to exact vengeance from anyone who crossed him.

"He killed Josephine," Gabe said calmly. "He would have killed you too if it hadn't been for me. Why do you think he lured you up here? You're what's standing between him and Josephine's money."

"No!" C. D. growled, trying in vain to sit up. "I never."

Brooke pressed down on the wound, and C. D. moaned. She shook her head. "I don't believe that. He could have killed me before you got here. He wouldn't hurt me. He's bleeding badly. You've got to go for help, Gabe. I'll stay here with C. D., but you've got to get help."

Gabe's face as he stood over her was twisted with fury. "I tell you, he's dangerous. And I'm not leaving you here with him. Let's go," he said abruptly, waving the gun at her.

"No," Brooke reached for another shirt to stanch the flow of blood.

"Now, goddamn it!" Gabe slapped her hard with the flat of his hand, so hard her ears were ringing, so hard the band of his thick class ring cut a gash in her cheek. Stunned, she felt the warm trickle of blood down her face. He grabbed her arm and began dragging her toward the stairwell. He stepped off the landing and onto the next step, intent on bending her to his will.

Brooke looked down, and suddenly the endless, dizzying nautilus shell staircase spun beneath her feet. "No!" she screamed as the panic seized her and swallowed her whole. "Leave me alone." She fell to the floor and grasped the iron handrail with both hands.

Gabe grasped her by the ankle, and she instinctively kicked out, catching him square in the gut. His face registered a momentary flash of shock before he toppled backward, down and down and down, the sickening thud of his falling body echoing in the brick stairwell.

Time stopped. She was conscious of crawling to C. D.'s side, of wadding up another shirt, pressing it to his shoulder. The old man was deathly quiet, his breathing shallow.

She reached for her cell phone. She had only half a bar. She tapped the number for the house phone at Shellhaven, but before the call could connect, the phone went dead. She had to go for help before C. D. bled to death. She tried to stand, but the floor swam beneath her feet.

"Brooke! Brooke!" Two distinct women's voices floated up from below. "Are you up there? Are you okay?"

"I'm here," she managed. "We need help."

Their footsteps pounded on the wooden steps, pausing only when they'd reached the lawyer's body, corkscrewed across the stairwell, his head resting at an unnatural angle.

"Oh my God!" Lizzie gasped.

Another moment and they were both on the landing, surveying the carnage before them — the blood, the forgotten pistol, and a barely conscious old man and his makeshift nurse, who was softly weeping.

"Get help," Brooke croaked. "He's been shot, and he's lost a lot of blood."

"The sheriff is on the way," Lizzie said.

Felicia gently pried Brooke's hands from C. D.'s shoulder. "Let me do this," she said. She gingerly lifted the shirt, blanching at the sight. "The bleeding seems to have stopped."

"Gabe," Brooke said, her throat dry. "Is he . . ."

"Dead?"

Lizzie and Felicia exchanged a look that confirmed Brooke's worst fears.

"I killed him," Brooke whispered. "I did this. After he shot C. D., Gabe was trying to get me to leave. But I couldn't leave C. D. And then, I looked down, and the stairs." She shuddered. "Dizzy. I nearly blacked out. I couldn't move. The nausea. He hit me. And then he started to drag me down those stairs. I just couldn't. I could feel myself falling. So I kicked him." She was weeping again. "I kicked him, and he fell backward, down the stairs. I didn't mean to, but I killed him."

"Hush." Felicia wrapped her arms around Brooke. "Don't talk."

They heard cars approaching. Lizzie looked

out the windows. "Sheriff's here. He's got a deputy and Shug with him. I'd better go down there and tell them we need a stretcher, for C. D."

"And a body bag for Gabe Wynant," Felicia said.

"They'll arrest me for murder. I'm going to prison. And Henry. My Henry . . ." Brooke buried her face in her hands.

"You're not going anywhere," Felicia said. "It was self-defense, right, Lizzie?"

Lizzie paused at the stair landing. "That's right." Her voice was matter of fact. "Gabe shot C. D. in cold blood. And he would have shot you too. He had the gun to your head, you were afraid for your life. You kicked at him, and he fell backwards." She nodded at Felicia. "Right?"

"End of story," Felicia agreed.

There was a flurry of activity then. Sheriff Goolsby and his deputy seemed to fill the tiny landing with their male presence. Brooke shrank back against the wall, her knees drawn tightly to her chest, as an EMT and an ambulance, hastily summoned from the state park, arrived to bandage C. D., hook up IV tubes, and transport him out of the lighthouse and to the sheriff's boat waiting at the dock at Shellhaven. Before they left, Brooke allowed them to clean and bandage the gash on her cheek.

"Might need stitches," the burly EMT muttered.

Lizzie and Felicia hovered protectively beside Brooke as she numbly answered the sheriff's questions, while the deputy quietly went about his business photographing the scene and taking notes and measurements.

"She's told you everything she knows," Felicia said after the sheriff asked for the third time why a rich, successful Savannah attorney like Gabe Wynant had ended up dead on Talisa Island.

"She's in shock," Lizzie agreed. "No more questions. You can call her tomorrow if you think of anything else."

They waited until the others had gone. "Okay, the coast is clear," Lizzie said, watching the parade of trucks motoring away from the lighthouse. "Let's go home now, Brooke."

They pulled her to her feet. Brooke took two steps, then froze. "I can't," she gasped. "The stairs . . . dizzy."

"You've got this," Lizzie said firmly. She wound an arm around Brooke's waist. Felicia took Brooke's left arm and placed it across her own shoulders.

"We're just going to take it nice and slow," Felicia said soothingly. "Close your eyes. Take a step when we tell you."

"I'll fall!" Brooke started to tremble. "I'll fall, and I'll pull you down with me."

"You won't," Lizzie said. "We've got you. We won't let you fall. Not ever."

65

The emergency room admitting clerk called her name loudly. "Brooke Trappnell?"

Felicia and Lizzie walked with her to the doors leading to the triage area, where a nurse in purple scrubs stood waiting, a clipboard tucked under her arm. "Sorry. I can't let visitors back there. Family only."

"We're her family," Felicia said.

"Sisters," Lizzie agreed.

The nurse rolled her eyes at the improbability of the statement but showed them back to a curtained-off treatment room. "The doctor will be with you shortly."

Brooke sat on the narrow bed while Felicia leaned against the wall and Lizzie perched on a low rolling stool. Her head was pounding, and the gash on her cheek throbbed. She looked down at herself. Her hands and arms were bruised, her clothes were filthy and blood-spattered. "God, I'm a mess."

"You're alive. That's what counts. You scared the living bejesus out of us, you know,"

Felicia said.

Lizzie nodded solemnly. “Yeah. We heard the shots just as we were pulling up to the lighthouse. We didn’t know if you were dead or alive, or what.”

“How did you even know where I was?”

“It was Farrah. You’d better give that girl a raise,” Felicia said. “After that wacky call from you, she knew something bad was going down over there. I guess you gave her some clue about being at the lighthouse. Where she and Jaxson partied? She called the sheriff, and then she called the house phone at Shell-haven.”

“And I picked up,” Lizzie said. “The poor kid was frantic. She was trying to tell me about Gabe and some tax liens and bad checks, and I didn’t really know what any of it meant, but she convinced me that you were in some kind of trouble.”

The nurse pulled the curtain aside. “You’ve got more company. I’d say this is probably your real family.” She glared at Lizzie and Felicia. “You two will have to leave.”

Marie and Gordon stepped into the already cramped space.

Gordon’s face paled when he saw his bruised and blood-spattered daughter. “Jesus! What did that animal do to you?”

Marie nodded at Lizzie. “Thanks so much for calling to let me know what happened.”

“It looks worse than it really is,” Brooke

said. "The EMT said they'll probably just give me a few stitches. I'm fine, really."

"You two," the nurse said, pointing to Felicia and Lizzie. "Out."

"Can't they stay? Just for a few minutes?" Brooke pleaded.

"The doctor is finishing up with a patient now. When he's ready for you, they'll have to leave," the nurse relented.

"I spoke briefly with somebody in the sheriff's office while we were driving down here," Gordon said. "They wouldn't tell me much. Just that there'd been an incident over on Talisa and that two people were injured. I hope to God Gabe Wynant is the other injured party."

"Gabe is dead," Brooke said quietly.

"Good. Saves me the trouble of doing it myself."

Brooke's head felt like it was in a vise. "I don't understand. Dad, what are you doing here? What's any of this got to do with you?"

"You're my daughter. You were nearly killed today. Why wouldn't I be here?" Gordon said, bristling.

"Your dad called me this morning. He was insistent that I make you listen to the truth about Gabe," Marie said.

"You always assume the worst about me," Gordon said bitterly. "And Patricia. Who was only trying to warn you about that snake —"

"Gordon?" Marie's voice held a warning

note. "Let's not get into the family dynamics. Just tell our daughter what you told me this morning."

"Um, maybe we'd better let you guys have some space," Felicia said.

Lizzie nodded. "We'll go check out the coffee situation in the cafeteria."

The two beat a hasty retreat.

"Gabe Wynant was the executor of Patricia's uncle Robert's estate," Gordon began. "Robert Zehring founded Chatham Community Bank, which got bought out by a bigger bank in Charlotte fifteen years ago. Robert's been dead six or seven years. Patricia's aunt Ellie is in a nursing home, suffering with dementia, so Patricia's been trying to help untangle her finances, but she could never get a straight answer out of Gabe. She started doing some digging and discovered there was some funny business with the trust accounts. We hired a forensic accountant and, long story short, discovered Gabe had been treating Ellie's trust account like it was his personal piggy bank. Hundreds of thousands of dollars had gone missing."

"And that's not the only client he's defrauded, right?" Marie looked at Gordon.

"I've been making quiet inquiries around town," Gordon said. "There are two others that I know of. Gabe was slick, I'll give him that."

Brooke's stomach heaved. She made it into

the adjacent bathroom just in time. Marie was by her side in an instant, holding her hair as Brooke hunched miserably over the commode, then helping her back to the examining table.

The curtain parted, and a white-coated doctor appeared. "Brooke Trappnell? I'm Dr. Schaefer."

"We're her parents," Marie said. "Can we stay?"

The nurse came in, bearing a plastic-covered stainless steel tray.

"Better not to," Schaefer said. "Stitches and all. I'll send for you when we're done here."

He turned to Brooke. "How do you feel?" he asked when they were alone, leaning in to look at her face. "This cut is pretty deep. Does your head hurt?"

"It's killing me," Brooke said.

"Nauseous?"

"Very," she admitted.

He held a small penlight and examined her closer. "Does this light hurt your eyes?"

"Yes." She winced, closed her eyes, and turned away.

"And how did you get these injuries?"

She gave him the condensed version, telling him about the dizziness and panic that seized her as she was climbing the lighthouse stairs, and about falling and hitting her head, and then being struck by Gabe.

He nodded. "Vertigo. That could account

for the nausea, but I think you've probably also got a concussion. We'll get your wound area numbed, then I'll stitch you up. With a concussion, I want somebody to check on you every few hours. Do you have somebody who can stay with you tonight? Your parents or one of your sisters?"

"I think so," Brooke said. Her head hurt too much to correct him about the status of her real and newly adopted family.

"The man I was with, C. D. Anthony? Do you know how he is?" she asked.

"He'll be all right. It was a through-and-through gunshot wound. He's one tough customer. We'll keep him overnight, mostly because of his age and the amount of blood loss, but barring any surprises, we should be able to cut him loose tomorrow."

"Can I see him?" Brooke asked.

"Tomorrow. There's not much to see. He's been sedated. You should go home and get some rest."

Lizzie and Felicia were in animated conversation with Brooke's parents as the nurse wheeled her out to the waiting room.

"Who gets these?" the nurse asked, holding up Brooke's discharge papers.

"I'll take them," Marie said. She looked down at her daughter. "The girls and your dad and I have been talking. You're going to need some quiet time at home, so I'm hoping you'll let me take Henry back to Savannah to my house, at least for the weekend."

"Lizzie and I can hang with you," Felicia said.

"Is that really necessary?" Brooke asked, pressing her fingers to her throbbing temples.

"Yes," Marie said, ushering her out the door. "No arguments."

Henry and Farrah were working on a puzzle when they got home. "Ree!" the child cried, ignoring his mother and flinging himself at Marie's knees. She swung him into the air and spun him around as he laughed in delight. Gordon stood just inside the door, an awkward, silent outsider.

"Omygod, Brooke!" Farrah cried. "I was so worried about you. Gabe showed up to take you to lunch. I told him you were at an appointment, but I knew he didn't believe me."

Brooke gave her a wan smile. "You kinda saved my life today. If you hadn't figured out where I was . . ."

"I knew something was bad wrong when you said me and Jaxson should pick up Henry, but it took me a minute to figure out you were telling me you were at the lighthouse," Farrah said, giggling.

"Hey, buddy," Brooke said as Henry reached for her.

His dark blue eyes widened when he spotted her bruised and bandaged face. "Boo-

boo?" he asked.

"Just a little one," Brooke said, taking him in her arms. "All better now."

Henry kissed his fingertip and touched it to her cheek. He stared and pointed at Gordon. "Who's that?"

Gordon's voice was hoarse. "I'm your grandpop, Henry." He took the child's chubby hand in his and solemnly shook.

"Grandpop is my daddy," Brooke explained. "Just like Ree is my mommy."

"Let me take him," Marie said. "I can tell your head is hurting. I can pack his bag, and then we'll be on our way."

Catching the cue, Lizzie stepped up and took Brooke by the arm. "Come on. Show me to your bedroom."

"Henry, would you like to go stay at Ree's house and sleep in the big bed tonight?" Brooke heard Marie ask just as Lizzie pulled the covers back from her bed and urged her to get some sleep.

66

Every four hours, Lizzie and Felicia took turns shaking Brooke awake, asking the questions outlined in the emergency room discharge instructions. Brooke's cheek still throbbed, and her head still hurt. She was disoriented and sleepy, but the women were relentlessly efficient.

When she awoke on her own, she could see the sun through the slats in the window blinds. Felicia was asleep on the other side of the bed, facedown on a pillow.

She found Lizzie in the kitchen, making coffee. "You're alive!" Lizzie said, pouring her a mug.

"Barely." Brooke sat at the table and sipped her coffee. A moment later, they heard water running in the bathroom, and then Felicia joined them.

"How did you sleep?" she asked.

"Badly," Brooke admitted. "All night long I kept dreaming I was falling down the stairs at the lighthouse. Down and down and down.

And then one of you would wake me up and ask me what day it was."

"Sorry," Felicia said. "Doctor's orders."

"The past twenty-four hours all seem like a bad dream. I still can't believe any of it happened. I can't believe Gabe is dead. That he did those things my dad says he did. None of this makes any sense." Brooke looked from Felicia to Lizzie. "Does it make sense to you?"

"We sat up talking last night after you were asleep," Lizzie said, "trying to piece it all together, but some of it's just a guess, and some of it, let's face it, we might never know."

"We took a look at all the stuff Farrah dug up on Gabe yesterday," Felicia said. "The man was having serious financial problems. There were tax liens on his house in Savannah and at Sea Island. He'd even had some bad check charges, although it looks like those were dismissed once he made restitution."

"Probably that's why he looted his clients' trust accounts. He figured he'd be able to pay back all the money before he was found out," Lizzie said. "But the question is, why?"

"Sunny," Brooke said.

The two women gave her a questioning look.

"His wife. She'd been in and out of rehab for years. That couldn't have been cheap. Gabe told me she would go on spending sprees when she was drinking. He claimed he didn't even know about that Porsche he's been driving until he found it in the garage of the house at Sea Island shortly after she died of liver cancer two years ago."

"Classic," Felicia said. "Blame it on the dead wife."

"He needed money, and he needed it fast," Lizzie went on.

Brooke shook her head. "And when I called him and asked him to meet with Josephine to handle her estate, it must have looked like the perfect opportunity. My God, I've been so stupid and so naive."

"You couldn't have known he was broke," Lizzie said. "He fooled everybody."

"I was *such* a chump," Brooke said. "He charmed me, romanced me, convinced me that he was a lonely widower looking for a second chance at love. I wish you'd seen him at the Cloister in black tie and tux. He was in his element. He basically proposed to me Saturday night. He wanted me to give up my practice here, move back to Savannah, and let him 'take care of' me and Henry. Oh my God! He even hinted that he'd love to have a child with me!"

"But you didn't say yes," Felicia pointed out. "You didn't sleep with him, right?"

Brooke blushed and looked away. "I was tempted. Gabe made it pretty clear he intended to seduce me that night. But thanks to Farrah and her lowlife boyfriend, I cut the evening short and drove back home."

"And that's the only reason you didn't fall for all his smooth talk?" Lizzie asked.

"No. A couple of times, he let the mask slip. He yelled at the valet parking kid and threatened to have him fired. And then, when I called from my car to tell him I was leaving instead of spending the night at his house, he got in a really nasty dig about me running away. Of course, the next morning he showed up here with flowers and croissants and a lame apology. Still, it was an eye-opener."

"Never trust a man who hollers at the help," Felicia said.

"This whole time, he's been angling to get his hands on Josephine's money," Brooke said. "That first time he met with her at Shellhaven? I think Josephine must have told Gabe her secrets. I think she told him that day that Gardiner was my mom's father, and that's why he was suddenly, passionately in love with me — he figured if he married me, he could eventually get his mitts on that money."

"Don't be so hard on yourself," Lizzie said. "We saw the way he looked at you. Like Dweezil when she sees a can of sardines."

"Is that supposed to make Brooke feel better about herself?" Felicia asked.

"You know what I mean. It wasn't only dollar signs he was seeing when he looked at

Brooke. There was some real attraction there."

"I think the attraction was that I was vulnerable. I've been so isolated from family and old friends since I moved down here to St. Ann's." Brooke gave the women a sad smile. "Okay, maybe vulnerable and isolated is a nice way of saying I was horny. It's been more than three years since I had a man in my life."

"Seven years for me, unless you count the drunken one-night stand I had at a wedding two years ago," Lizzie said. She turned to Felicia. "You?"

"Next question?" Felicia said.

Brooke stared down into her coffee. "You know what else I think? I think Gabe killed Josephine."

67

Both the women stared at Brooke in disbelief.

"I thought the cops agreed that it was an accident," Lizzie said. "We all saw her that night. Josephine was groggy from mixing the new pain meds with the wine. She tripped over the dogs, fell, and hit her head on the bathroom floor. Right?"

Felicia chimed in. "Josephine was ninety-nine years old, and she had end-stage cancer. I mean, she would have been dead in a matter of days anyways. Why would Gabe risk murdering her?"

"That's what I was asking myself all night long," Brooke said. "And then it came to me. Josephine was ready to sign a will that would have divided her estate between five people — the three of us, plus my mom and Varina. She also planned to leave pretty generous cash bequests to Shug and Louette. And she planned to deed back the property she owned at Oyster Bluff to the original landowners."

"Which would have all gone into effect if

Gabe had gotten that will witnessed," Felicia said.

"But he didn't get it witnessed when he easily could have. Which meant that when Josephine died, that will was invalid. She died intestate — so that meant her estate would be left to her closest blood relatives," Brooke said.

"Meaning your mom," Lizzie said. "And if you're right, Gabe Wynant was the only person who knew about that connection. And I'm not disagreeing with you, Brooke, but it's still so hard for me to think of Gabe as a murderer."

"Why?" Felicia demanded. "Just because he was an apparently rich, classy-looking white dude?"

"Well, yeah, now that you mention it," Lizzie said.

"I wouldn't have believed it either, if I hadn't seen him try to shoot C. D. at point-blank range. If you'd seen his face . . ." Brooke shuddered. "He meant to kill C. D. And I'm not sure he wouldn't have killed me too . . ."

She left the sentence unfinished, but her friends knew she was still dwelling on the way Brooke's would-be suitor fell to his death. They sat sipping their coffee until Lizzie spoke up.

"I get that Gabe had the perfect motive to kill Josephine, but so did C. D., if you look at it like that."

"Huh?" Felicia said.

"We know C. D. is convinced he's Josephine's son, but the will she dictated didn't include him, so he had just as much motive, maybe even more than Gabe, to kill Josephine. Like revenge. Because as far as he's concerned, she dumped him like a cast-off shoe at an orphanage," Lizzie said.

"Maybe you're right," Felicia conceded. "I mean, what does anybody really know about C. D., besides the fact that he was raised in an orphanage? Don't you think it's an awfully big coincidence that he showed up at Talisa, looking for a job, only six months ago?"

"Stop!" Brooke clutched her head with both hands. "I'm already dazed and disoriented. You two aren't helping matters any."

"You're the one who brought up the topic of murder," Felicia said. "What do you want to do now? Do we just keep our mouths shut about our suspicions?"

Brooke sighed. "Lizzie's right. We don't actually know if Josephine's death was an accident or a homicide. I'm so mixed up right now. Gabe gave me my first job right after law school. He was my mentor and my friend. Something changed in him, and I never saw it. But I keep thinking about what my mom said. 'The people we think we know the best are the ones with secrets we can't even fathom.' "

"Who doesn't have secrets?" Lizzie said. "My grandma Ruth used to say there's a little felon in the best of us."

68

October 1941

Millie peered into the steam-clouded bathroom mirror and gingerly touched the bruises on her neck and chest. Blackish-purple handprints bloomed on her breasts. His handprints.

She'd lain awake all night, pondering her situation. Her bruises would fade as they had in the past, but what of her future with a man like Russell Strickland?

Only one solution occurred to her. She found the packet of razor blades in the medicine cabinet, alongside the Pepsodent, the cotton balls, and the Pond's Cold Cream, all so thoughtfully stocked by the Bettendorfs' housekeeper in anticipation of any need a guest might encounter. With a fingernail, she slit the paper wrapper and held the shining blade up to the light. One deft swipe across her wrist would surely do the trick, wouldn't it? But the mess. How inconsiderate. And who would find her? Josephine? Her own mother? Her grandmother? She could only imagine their horror at finding her in a pool of her own blood. She shook her head. No, it was just too ghastly.

Millie's hand closed on the bottle of sleeping pills she'd pilfered from her mother's pocketbook. Almost a whole bottle. These would do the job nicely. She shook them into the palm of her hand. Tiny pink tablets, as sweet and promising as a first kiss. One swallow. Not nearly as messy. She would take the pills, then climb into the bathtub for a long, lovely nap. But what if the pills didn't work? She could barely choke down baby aspirin. What if she vomited them back up? Or worse yet, what if she woke up, still engaged, still doomed to the life with Russell Strickland that had been so neatly planned for her? She could picture the shock and disappointment on her mother's face.

That wouldn't do either. She frowned and dumped the pills into the sink, turning on the tap to wash them down the drain.

Millie looked back in the mirror again. She was no longer the coed who'd met and flirted and become infatuated with Russell Strickland. That girl disappeared the first night he'd forced himself on her, months ago, in the backseat of his car, taken her in the same violent way he took anything he regarded as his property.

The woman who'd emerged from that car

was someone who had to stay hidden. But she was there, just beneath the innocent veneer Millie presented to the world. She turned away from the mirror quickly, having glimpsed the resolute, rage-fueled visage who came and went in the blink of a long, fluttery eyelash.

She brushed her teeth and combed her hair and returned to her bedroom, where she dressed quickly in dark slacks because there was a chill in the air this morning.

The house was eerily quiet as she tiptoed past the closed bedroom doors of her oldest, dearest friends, Josephine and Ruth. What would they think if they saw this version of Millie? She crept down the stairs and into the big kitchen. Someone had put a pot of coffee on the stove, and she was tempted to pour herself a cup to soothe the throbbing in her temples, but time was of the essence. She must act before the sleeping household awakened.

She slipped out the back door and made her way in the predawn darkness toward the garage. She would have her pick of the Bettendorfs' vehicles. The Packard, the roadster, the truck. All the keys were kept in their ignitions, because who would steal a car on an island? She'd read about carbon monoxide poisoning. A length of garden hose inserted in a tailpipe and then wound into a nearly closed window. Just the trick. No fuss, no muss.

A male voice cut abruptly through the morning stillness. "Millie? What are you doing out here?"

Her stomach roiled at the sound of his voice. Her first instinct was to run and hide as far from here as she could get. But just how far could she get on an island?

69

Mary Balent was a presence in Carter County. According to her website, she was a fifth-generation native and had gone to undergrad and law school at the University of Georgia, which made her what faithful alum referred to as a "Double Dawg." Her law office stood directly across the square from the county courthouse, and since moving to St. Ann's, Brooke had watched her with envy as she skillfully navigated the local legal landscape.

Now, a week after her harrowing experience at the lighthouse and Gabe Wynant's demise, Brooke and Marie sat in Ms. Balent's office, seeking representation as they attempted to untangle Josephine Bettendorf Warrick's estate.

Mary Balent had already read the wartime letters from Millie to Gardiner Bettendorf, which Brooke had dropped off a week earlier, and Marie had submitted a cheek swab for DNA testing to compare with Josephine's hair sample.

"We still don't know the outcome of a DNA sample Gabe sent off, comparing Josephine's DNA to a local man who believes he could be Josephine's son," Brooke explained.

"Really?" Ms. Balent said, intrigued. "It was my understanding that Mrs. Warrick never had children."

"There is a chance that she could have had a son out of wedlock while she was living in Savannah in 1942 and given him up for adoption," Brooke said. "My friends and I did some sleuthing. We found some anecdotal evidence that shows Josephine was interested in a boy who was raised at two different children's homes there, but we didn't find any concrete proof. As far as I know, Josephine never acknowledged having a child, and of course, we have no idea who the father might have been."

"But this man, C. D. Anthony, is convinced that he is Josephine's son. He's the man Gabe tried to kill last week," Marie said. "Brooke saved his life."

"We'll have to have this man retested," Ms. Balent told her. "But in the meantime, I'd say your next-of-kin status to Mrs. Warrick is entirely provable. I can get the paperwork started to have myself appointed administrator of the estate this afternoon, and given the circumstances of the previous administrator's death, that shouldn't be a problem, but it's probably going to take a while to get this mess straightened out. It could take months."

"We understand that," Marie assured her. "My most immediate concern is going forward with my aunt's burial. It's been a month now. Josephine's oldest living friend is ninety-one years old and is still heartbroken over her death. For her sake, at least, we'd like the closure a funeral could provide."

"Have you been in contact with the cousins you mentioned earlier? Do they have any objections to a burial?"

"I called them," Brooke said. "They were pretty shocked — and disappointed to discover that Gardiner Bettendorf had a daughter and that she was Josephine's closest blood relative — but they indicated they don't oppose a funeral."

"I'll see what I can do to expedite that. We'll have to get the body released. Have you talked to the sheriff?"

"That's my next appointment," Brooke said.

Marie spent the next ten minutes filling out legal documents as Mary Balent explained what each one meant.

"You know," she told Brooke, "I served on a couple of different bar association committees with Gabe Wynant over the years. I wouldn't say we were friends, exactly, but I respected his expertise. I have to say, all these revelations coming out of Savannah are sending shock waves through the legal community, even all the way down here in little-bitty Carter County. I hear his former law firm has really taken a hit from this, which is a shame. You worked there, right?"

"Yes. Gabe hired me right out of law school," Brooke said, glancing at the clock. "Mom, while you finish up here, I'd better get over to the sheriff's office."

Ms. Balent gave her an appraising look. "I know the sheriff pretty well. Is there anything I can help with?"

"He says it's just a few more routine questions so he can close out the death report on Gabe," Brooke said. "But if it's anything more than that, I might take you up on your offer."

The Carter County courthouse was a looming brown brick Spanish revival–style two-story building from the early 1920s, but the courthouse annex where the sheriff's office was located was a squat 1970s-era concrete bunker with leaky smoked plate glass windows.

Howard Goolsby offered Brooke a seat in his cluttered office. "How're you feeling? I heard you had a concussion."

"I'm much better, thanks," she said, making an effort to sound and look composed. "You have some questions for me?"

"Just a few," he said, opening a file folder

and leafing through the papers inside. "We took statements from those other two women, Elizabeth and Felicia, who witnessed Mr. Wynant's fall. They both said Mr. Wynant struck you. And you feared for your life?"

"Yes." Brooke crossed and uncrossed her legs. "He'd already shot C. D. Gabe grabbed me and was dragging me toward the stairs, but I couldn't leave C. D. there to bleed to death. When I resisted, grabbing for the handrail, he pointed the gun at me. I thought he would kill me. I kicked him, thinking he might drop the gun, but instead, he fell backward."

"I see," the sheriff said, scribbling in a stenographer's notebook. "Could you tell me again how you came to know Gabe Wynant?"

"Again?"

"Please." The sheriff seemed amiable and relaxed.

"He was my boss when I worked for his law firm in Savannah. As I said in our last interview, Josephine Warrick called me over a month ago and asked me to visit her on Talisa. She first said she wanted me to draft a new will for her, and then said she intended to make me and my mother, as well as three other women, her beneficiaries. I explained that I had no expertise in trusts and wills, plus, I had a conflict, since that will would potentially benefit me and my mother. That's when I reached out to Gabe, because I knew he did a lot of estate planning work."

"So . . . the relationship was strictly professional?"

Brooke felt the flush creeping up her neck. "At first, yes. But recently, Gabe let me know he wanted something more. We had a couple of dates."

"But nothing came of it? Was that your idea or his?"

"Why are you asking me this?" Brooke asked, wishing now that she'd asked Mary Balent to accompany her to this interview.

"Just doing my job. We found your name and number several times in Mr. Wynant's phone log. He'd tried to call you several times the morning he was killed."

"My phone has lousy reception on Talisa."

"Mine too," he said with a conspiratorial smile. "That's when the old two-way radios come in handy, right?"

"I suppose." She looked at the sheriff. "Do you know how he figured out where we were?"

"We think so. We found a fisherman who keeps a boat at the city dock. He said Wynant flagged him down and offered him twenty bucks for a ride over to Talisa. That little Geechee kid Lionel? Hangs around that dock all the time? He said a white-haired fella asked him if he'd seen you and C. D., and Lionel obligingly said he'd seen the two of you riding a motorcycle in the opposite direction of the house.

"Now, back to my questions. Remind me why Mr. Wynant would have tried to kill C. D. Anthony? Not once but twice, according to Mr. Anthony?"

There was a rapping at the glass door.

"Come in," Goolsby barked.

Mary Balent stepped into the office. "Sorry I'm late," she said, nodding at Brooke. "Howard, Ms. Trappnell tells me she's already told you everything she knows about this unfortunate matter. Now, what else do you need from my client?"

Without waiting for an invitation, she dragged a chair from the corner of the room and sat beside Brooke, who found herself momentarily speechless.

"Just tying up some loose ends," Goolsby said. "She's a lawyer, the dead guy's a lawyer, I didn't think we'd need to get any more lawyers involved."

"Just one more," Mary said sweetly.

"I was asking your client why Gabe Wynant seemed so intent on killing Mr. Anthony," the sheriff repeated.

"Did you ask Mr. Anthony that question?" Mary asked.

"I did. This office has had some past dealings with Mr. Anthony, who isn't always the most reliable witness. So now I'm asking her."

"Gabe told me C. D. had been hounding him for money, even trying to blackmail him over some financial irregularities C. D. uncovered. C. D. thought it was just a matter of some bad checks, but I think what he'd unwittingly uncovered was something much more serious — the fact that Gabe was in such bad financial straits he'd started stealing from his clients," Brooke said. "Gabe must have known C. D. would tell me everything and that I'd figure out the rest. That's why Gabe tried to kill C. D. He pretended it was to protect me from C. D., but that was a lie."

"Okay." The sheriff scribbled some more notes. He reached into the top drawer of his desk and held out an envelope in a sealed plastic bag. "We found this in Mr. Wynant's car, which was parked in the lot at the city marina."

"What is it?" Brooke asked.

"Lab results on DNA testing performed on hair samples from C. D. Anthony and Josephine Warrick."

"Which show what?" Brooke asked, not bothering to try to hide her excitement.

"No familial relation," Goolsby said. "No big surprise there. I could have told you that old drunk was no kin to Miss Josephine."

"Could we have a copy of that report, Howard?" Mary asked. "For my client's peace of mind?"

He shrugged. "Don't see why not." He walked to the outer hallway with the envelope. They heard the mechanical whir of a photocopier, and a moment later he was back with the copy of the report, which he handed to Brooke. "Anything else?"

Mary Balent spoke up. "Yes, actually, Howard, we'd appreciate it if you could release Josephine Warrick's body as soon as possible so her family can have a funeral."

Goolsby tapped his pen on the edge of the desk and looked at Brooke. "I understand you've only recently learned that you and your mother are Mrs. Warrick's next of kin?"

"Yes," Brooke said. "It was . . . a shock, to say the least."

He rolled the pen over and over between his fingertips. "You being next of kin, I guess I owe it to you to tell you that we now consider Josephine's death a homicide."

"What did you just say?" Mary Balent asked, leaning forward.

"It was set up to look like an accidental death." Goolsby chuckled. "Hate to say it, but Kendra Younts, that hotshot new coroner we got now, she's the one who made a believer out of me. You know she used to be a homicide detective up in Atlanta, until her granddaddy talked her into coming down here to take over the family funeral parlor business and run for coroner. I was dead-set certain when I saw that poor old soul laid out on that bathroom floor at Shellhaven that it was just an unfortunate accident. But Kendra, she had her suspicions. She took all kinds of photos and measurements of the scene and convinced me not to release the body for burial, even after Gabe Wynant called over here raisin' all kinds of hell about it."

"So it was Gabe who murdered her," Brooke said quietly.

"What makes you think so?" the sheriff asked.

"He had the best motive for wanting her dead. Money. Josephine must have told Gabe that my mom was her immediate next of kin. And as far as we know, he was the last one to see her alive that night when he helped her to bed."

"How did the coroner conclude that Mrs. Warrick's death was a homicide and that Wynant was the murderer?" Mary Balent asked.

"Just a feeling she had. She was looking back over the death scene photos and noticed that when we arrived, Miss Josephine was wearing her eyeglasses."

"I never saw her without her glasses," Brooke said. "She was nearly a hundred."

"But if she'd tripped and fallen, don't you think those glasses would have gone flying off? Probably would have been smashed too. But hers were right there on her face. We fingerprinted those glasses, and found a partial print from Gabe Wynant. Plus, our new coroner determined that she was struck on the side of the head with an unknown object, which caused the fall that killed her. And no, we don't have a murder weapon."

"Not much here that would hold up in court, is there, Howard?" Mary Balent asked.

"I won't argue with you. But it wouldn't have taken much for him to have done it. She weighed all of eighty pounds and was eaten up with cancer, on top of which she had some powerful prescription opioids in her system. And since we can't exactly ask a dead man if he was a murderer, that's the best we're going to get," the sheriff said.

"It's more than enough for me," Brooke said firmly. "I've got a son to raise and a law practice of my own and a funeral to plan. So if you'll excuse me . . ."

70

Brooke had barely settled in at her desk the next day when her cell phone rang. The caller ID said *Younts Mortuary.*

"Miss Trappnell?" The woman's voice had a soft, rural Southern accent, which was different from the harder-edged accents of urban Atlanta, Birmingham, or Charlotte. "This is Kendra Younts from the funeral home. I believe we met over on Talisa, the day of your great-aunt's death."

"Yes, I remember." Brooke took a sip of the coffee she'd just poured.

"I spoke to Howard Goolsby last night, and we've gotten the okay to release Miss Josephine to the family."

"That's great. And by the way, the sheriff told me about your theories about Gabe Wynant. Thank you for your diligence."

"I'm sorry for your loss," Kendra said, sounding properly somber. "The other reason I'm calling is because Miss Josephine has a pre-need plan in place with us."

"Pre-need?" Brooke was drawing a blank.

"Yes. She actually set it up with my granddaddy twenty years ago. All the charges have been prepaid, and of course, we have her instructions."

"Which are?"

"Cremation with remains in our Eternal Slumber Bronzesque urn. Now, that model is no longer in production, of course, but the finish on our new Odyssey urn is very similar. Will that be acceptable?"

"Um, sure," Brooke said. "You should probably ask my mom, just as a technicality, but what the hell, I don't think she'll know the difference."

"And Miss Josephine won't care, will she? Oh, sorry, that's a little funeral home humor. Anyway, I'm afraid that's about the extent of your great-aunt's wishes. The notes in the file say that she opted against a hearse or a funeral procession or reception here at the mortuary, and I see that she already has a headstone and a plot in the family cemetery on the island. It's a fairly barebones plan."

"More funeral home humor?" Brooke asked, chuckling.

"Sorry! Can't help myself. My three-year-old didn't sleep last night, and I'm a little punchy."

"I totally understand. I have a three-year-old myself," Brooke said. "What happens next?"

"We can have the remains ready for you by the end of the week," Kendra said. "And if the family decides they would like a reception or something a little more formal, we would love to accommodate you. Miss Josephine was a much-beloved figure in this community, you know."

"I'll consult with my mother, but my feeling is that she'll want to honor Josephine's wishes," Brooke said. "So just plan on having the remains ready on Friday, please."

Shug picked her up at the municipal marina. It had rained the night before, which lifted the oppressive June heat a little but left the air as thick and humid as a wet wool blanket.

"How are things on the island?" Brooke asked. "Is Varina feeling all right?"

"Varina still gets a little blue, but Felicia just jokes her out of it, and once she takes her over to see how her house is coming along, she's all smiles," Shug reported. "Your mama called to say she's sending a roofing crew over to Shellhaven next week, and Louette hasn't been that happy in months. She says I'm too old to be getting up on rooftops, and I can't disagree."

"Have you seen much of C. D.?"

"He comes around. That shoulder's still bandaged up, but I see him out walking most days. That man's like a cockroach, you know? Can't nothing kill him." Shug cast her a sideways glance. "How about you? You gave us all a scare that day. I saw that blood all over you, and I could have sworn you'd been shot too."

She touched the bandage on her cheekbone. It seemed to be healing, and the headaches had also subsided. "I guess I'm almost as tough as C. D.," she said.

He nodded his approval. "Good to hear."

Lizzie was waiting at the Shellhaven dock, behind the wheel of the blue VW. "You look almost human," she said as Brooke climbed into the car.

"Thanks. I'm feeling better every day. Everything good over here? How's your research on the magazine article coming?"

"I've got enough material for ten articles, or one book. Josephine and Preiss had an amazing life. Quite the partnership. Their correspondence is so sweet. It makes her seem like a real person. Almost. I've even found old records dating back to the plantation days. So what have you been up to?"

"I'm finally ramping up my campaign to stop the state from condemning Josephine's land. I've been reaching out to the county commission and our state representatives, asking for a meeting so I can make my case. Also, we're going to have Josephine's funeral on Saturday."

"I heard. Louette's been in a frenzy, getting

the house spiffed up. And Felicia and Varina are here, getting started on their baking. I get a sugar buzz just walking past the kitchen. Are you really having the service in the African Methodist Episcopal Church at Oyster Bluff?"

"It's what Josephine wanted."

"Is that why you're over here today?"

"Not really. I need to talk to C. D."

"He's keeping kind of a low profile. Has he been pestering you about his inheritance?"

"He's called me once or twice. The thing is, I've got news."

"Do tell," Lizzie said.

"The sheriff found the report on C. D.'s DNA testing in Gabe's car."

Lizzie pulled the VW around to the back of Shellhaven and parked. "And?"

Brooke held out the copy of the report. Lizzie read it carefully.

"As you can see, there's zero evidence of a DNA match with Josephine," Brooke said. "He's going to be devastated."

Lizzie was too busy reading to reply. After a few minutes, she looked up at her friend. "Did you read the whole report?" she asked. "Even the fine print?"

"Not really. Why?"

Lizzie thrust the report at Brooke, stabbing at it with her finger. "Check out this part right there."

Brooke squinted at the print, reading it

once, and then again, and finally a third time.

"Holy shit."

"Right? Are you sure you want to give the whole report to him? Maybe you should just tell him there's no match and leave it at that."

"No. He's got a right to know. He's waited his whole life for this. This report might not have the answers he wanted, but he deserves to know something."

"Do you have to go see C. D. right this minute?" Lizzie asked.

"No. He doesn't even know I'm coming."

"Good. I know Varina's going to want to see you."

71

Felicia was taking a cake from the oven, a dishtowel tied around her waist for an apron and a scarf wrapped turban-style around her short-cropped hair. Varina sat at the kitchen table, chopping pecans. Both the women's faces were shiny with perspiration.

"Oh, Brooke girl!" Varina cried. "Come here and let me see what that rascal did to you."

Brooke and Lizzie sat at the table on either side of Varina, who gingerly touched the bandage on Brooke's cheek. "I've got some salve I want you to start putting on that thing," she said. "You do that every night, and you won't ever have a scar on that pretty face of yours."

Felicia mopped her own face with her apron. "Auntie has become a conjure woman since moving back to Oyster Bluff. You watch out, or she'll bury some chicken bones at midnight and put a spell on your enemies."

Varina took a playful swipe at her great-niece's hand. "This one here thinks because she has a PhD, she's smarter than her elders."

"Varina," Lizzie said, her voice unexpectedly serious. "You know I've been going through Josephine's old papers, working on a magazine article. I found something I don't understand, and I wanted to ask you some questions, if that would be okay."

Felicia shot her friend an inquisitive look, but Lizzie brushed it off.

"I'll try," Varina said cheerfully. "I might be an old, old lady, but I still remember a lot of things. What can I help you with, baby?"

"I found an old letter from the fall of 1942 to Josephine from a Catholic priest in Savannah. His name was Charles Ryan. The letter is sort of a progress report for a baby boy named Charlie. It says the couple who took the baby can't continue to care for him anymore, so he's decided to take the baby to the nuns at St. Joseph's. That was an orphanage in Savannah. It closed a long time ago."

"Oh?" Varina said with interest. "Well, I know Josephine used to give money to those orphans. She had a good heart, and she did a lot of good things, but she didn't want people to find out because then they'd think she was weak or silly." Varina set her knife on the cutting board. "But now, if this is about that crazy C. D. saying Josephine is his mother, you just need to stop with that foolishness. Josephine never had no baby. And I'd know, because I was living with her and working for her back then."

"I believe you," Lizzie said, her voice soothing. "But I think, maybe, the person who had a baby was you. Can that be true, Varina? Were you the one who had a baby?"

72

VARINA

The first year after the war started, Josephine went to my daddy and asked could she take me with her to Savannah so I could go to a real school. Josephine told him I was so smart, I should go to a school in Savannah so I could make something of myself. But the real reason was that I had a big secret I couldn't tell anybody about.

Josephine was the only person in the world who knew. And I only told her because I was scared. And ashamed. So ashamed.

My mama died right after I was born, and I never had any sisters, so there wasn't anybody to explain women's things to me. The first time I had my monthly, when I was thirteen, I thought I was bleeding to death. That's when Josephine sat me down and explained things. She was the one who taught me how to take care of myself when I got my monthly.

Josephine was the only person I'd told about that bad man grabbing me at the party for Millie. And I never would have told her at all, except that night when it happened, afterward, when everybody was asleep or gone, I came creeping up into the house as quiet as I could to try to wash him off me because I couldn't go home and let my daddy and brothers know what that man had done to me. When I came out of the bathroom, Josephine was standing there. And after I told her, she took me upstairs to her bathroom and let me take a hot bath. My beautiful new pink dress was torn and dirty, so she gave me some clean clothes to put on and she took that dress and burned it in the fireplace. And then she drove me home in her daddy's Packard. And I promised not to tell nobody.

And Josephine was the one I went to, right after Christmas that year, when I figured out that I had missed my monthly three times.

"Sweet Jesus!" she said. We went up to her bedroom and she locked the door and she looked at me and said, "Well, Varina. This is my fault. And I feel awful about it, and I will help you the best way I know how, if you trust me." And then we both cried and cried.

And that's how I came to move off the island.

Josephine said the public high school for colored students in Savannah was too crowded and not very good, so she put me in a school called Most Pure Heart of Mary, which had been started by some Catholic nuns from Baltimore who wanted to give colored children in the South a better education.

Oh, I loved that school so much. I got to wear a pretty uniform with a white shirt and a plaid pleated skirt and new black-and-white saddle shoes. We had nuns for teachers, and they were strict, but sometimes they could be kind too. My favorite teacher was Sister Helen, who taught English and social studies.

The best part about that school was getting to learn. Sister loaned me her own books to read, because at that time, colored children were not allowed in the big pretty public library on Bull Street. Because of Sister, I read *The Count of Monte Cristo* and *Gulliver's Travels* and *Little Women* and *Jane Eyre,* which was very sad.

73

Varina's face crumpled, and her dark eyes filled with tears.

"What are you saying?" Felicia asked indignantly, her hands on her great-aunt's shoulders. "Where would you get an idea like that? Tell her, Auntie. Tell her it's not true. In 1942, you were what, fourteen? Just a child."

Varina's hands trembled as they clutched for Felicia's. "Oh, Felicia, honey, I'm sorry. I'm so sorry I never said nothing." She turned and faced her niece. "You think I'm a bad person? Maybe I was. Or maybe you just had to know how it was back then."

Felicia knelt beside her aunt. "Auntie, I'd never think anything bad about you. You're the best, the godliest woman I've ever met. I would never judge you. Never. Do you want to talk about it? You don't have to, you know. It's your secret. Not Lizzie's or mine, and especially not Josephine's."

"Get up off that floor now," Varina chided, sniffling. "I guess maybe it's time to talk about this thing. It's been clawing at my heart all these years. Maybe now's the time to let it out."

She took a deep breath and folded and unfolded her hands. "Lizzie has found out my story. My secret. Josephine told you about Millie's engagement party. And I told you while I was hiding in the bushes, I saw that man, the one Millie was supposed to marry, attack her and paw her. I told you I saw Gardiner and him fighting. But I didn't tell you that after Millie and then Gardiner went back to the house, I was trying to sneak on home, and he caught me."

"Who?" Felicia demanded. "Russell Strickland? What did he do to you, Auntie?"

Varina picked up the knife and began chopping the pecans again. "He dragged me back to the guesthouse, where he was staying. And he . . ."

"He raped you?" Felicia whispered.

The old woman nodded, continuing to chop the pecans until they were less than dust.

74

VARINA

I never was what you'd call a grown-looking girl. "Skinny Minnie" is what the other kids called me. So I kept on going to school at Most Pure Heart of Mary, keeping my secret the whole time. When my belly started to pooch out a little bit in the spring, I moved the buttons on my school uniform, and then moved them again.

The crazy thing is, except for my secret, I was happy as could be. I missed my daddy and brothers and friends on the island, but I loved my new school and getting to learn about the world outside Talisa. In April, at a school assembly, Sister Helen called me up on the stage and gave me a prize for being the best student in her class. It was a little gold statue of Mary, and I got a framed certificate too.

But that afternoon, Sister asked me to stay after school. I thought maybe she had a new book for me to read, but when the other students were gone, Sister closed the classroom door, and when she turned around, she had a real serious look on her face.

I knew she had figured out my secret. I sat at my desk and I folded my hands on the top, just like all the students at Most Pure Heart were taught to do, but my hands were shaking and my mouth was so dry I couldn't swallow, and that secret in my belly was kicking so hard I was sure Sister could see it from where she sat at her own desk. In my head I was saying that Catholic prayer we said every morning, right after we said the Pledge of Allegiance.

Hail Mary, full of grace, the Lord is with thee. Blessed art thou amongst women, and blessed is the fruit of thy womb, Jesus.

"Oh, Varina," she said, and she sighed. Her face was as white as that wimple she wore on her head that covered her hair. "What have you done?"

I didn't say a thing. Just stared at my hands.

Holy Mary, mother of God, pray for us sinners, now and at the hour of our death.

"For several weeks now, I've seen something different about you. I thought maybe you were gaining a little weight, and that was good, because you are such a skinny little thing. But today, on that stage, I realized, you are . . . that is . . ."

I looked up and Sister turned her head, and when she looked back at me, her cheeks were bright pink.

"I had such high hopes for you," Sister said. "And now you are about to throw all of that away because you've been a wicked girl."

What could I do? I couldn't look at her, and I couldn't tell her it wasn't me that was wicked, it was that bad man whose name I would never say.

I felt something wet hit the back of my hand and realized I was crying.

"Does your employer know?" Sister Helen asked, meaning Josephine.

I nodded, but I still couldn't speak. It was like my mouth was full of cotton.

Sister sighed. "Well, I'm afraid you will have to leave this school immediately."

I jerked my head up then. "Leave school?" I whispered. "But graduation isn't until two more months."

"You will not be graduating with your class," Sister said. "And I'm sorry about that, but Mother Superior has rules. We can't let the other girls and boys in this school be exposed to something like this. Most Pure Heart is not a school for fallen girls like you."

"No, Sister," I whispered.

She drummed her fingertips on the top of her desk.

"Is there something you'd like to tell me? Some . . . special circumstance you'd like to tell me about?"

"No, Sister."

"Was it a boy at this school? This is very serious, Varina, because if the boy is a student here, I will see that he leaves this school too."

"No, Sister."

She drummed her fingertips some more. "Would you like to see Father? I realize you are not Catholic, but perhaps a good confession and an Act of Contrition . . ."

I shook my head hard. That priest went around with a mad face all the time. I could never tell him what had happened to me. Besides, I was kicked out of school, so there was nothing more to say.

"May I go, Sister?" I said.

"I suppose." She rummaged around in her desk drawer and brought out a black leather change purse. I'd seen her take that change purse out before, on the sly, when some of the boys and girls who came to school looking hungry and raggedy and didn't have enough money to buy milk in the school lunchroom.

She walked over to me and put one hand on my shoulder as I stood for the last time beside my desk, and she pressed a coin into my hand. "For the streetcar fare," she said.

I wanted to throw that money back at her face. I wanted to scream that I hadn't been wicked and that I wanted to stay in school and read all the books and someday, maybe, be a teacher, like her.

Instead, I said, "Thank you, Sister. I still

have your book. Would it be all right if I brought it back to you tomorrow?" Sister lived at the brick convent attached to the school.

She wrinkled her brow. "What book do you have?"

"It's *Treasure Island,* Sister." I didn't tell her that Mr. Robert Louis Stevenson's book was my favorite one so far, even better than *Jane Eyre.*

She hesitated, looking down at me, and that's when I saw her eyes get all watery. "You keep it, Varina. Keep reading. Keep learning, no matter what."

"I'll try," I whispered.

"Take care of yourself, Varina. And the baby."

75

"And you never told anybody?" Felicia asked.

"He told me he'd kill me if I told anybody what he'd done. And he took my pretty pearl pin that Millie gave me, because he said I'd stolen it," Varina said. "I couldn't go home the way he left me, so I snuck back here, to try to clean up, and that's when Josephine found me. She guessed, just as soon as she saw me, what had happened, and she made me tell her everything."

"That bastard," Felicia said, the color rising in her cheeks. "Raping a child. I wish you had killed him, Auntie. I wish he were still alive so I could kill him for you."

"No need," Varina said. "He's dead and gone. Everybody, all my family, all my friends, they're all gone. Josephine was the last one, and now she's gone too."

76

VARINA

March 1942

After I got kicked out of that school, there wasn't much for me to do. Josephine thought I shouldn't go out, because nice people would see me and figure out I was going to have a baby, so I stayed in her house and I did laundry and some cooking and listened to the war news on the radio.

We didn't really talk much about what would happen next. Just the one time, really.

One night, Josephine came home from a party and she came up to my bedroom on the third floor of that town house her daddy owned. I was reading *Treasure Island* again, thinking about pirates and buried treasure and such.

She knocked on the door and then came in and sat on the little chair. "Varina, we need to talk about what will happen when your baby comes."

"I know that," I said, struggling to sit up in

the bed.

"It's going to be very hard on you, trying to raise a baby as young as you are. And there are going to be people saying terrible things about you, because that baby is going to be half-white," Josephine said. "Your family might not want to take you back once they find out."

"I don't want to go back home," I said, because I'd been thinking a lot about that. "I want to finish high school and then get me a job."

"All right," she said. She looked tired. "We still have a couple of months to figure things out. I know lots of people here, and maybe somebody will be looking for a maid or a live-in babysitter."

The first thing I thought of when she said that was *Jane Eyre.*

I couldn't tell Josephine I didn't want to do the kind of work Geechee ladies on the island did, cooking or cleaning or watching other people's children, because that would make me seem ungrateful for all she'd done for me. I really wanted a real job, like in an office. The nuns taught us what they called vocational skills, and I could type fast as anything.

I didn't tell her I dreamed of going to college and someday maybe being a teacher like Sister Helen. It sounds bad to say this, but I was all mixed up inside. Nothing that had happened to me since that night at the party seemed real to me. Not any of it. Not even after the baby started kicking so hard I woke up in the middle of the night. Not even when I had to go to the bathroom every hour and my back hurt every time I went up and down all those stairs at her house.

It didn't start seeming real to me until that very next day. We were in the kitchen, listening to *The Romance of Helen Trent,* our favorite radio program, and all of a sudden I got this awful cramp in my belly — like a lightning bolt or a live wire. It hurt so bad I doubled over. When I looked down, I saw all this warm water running down my legs.

"Josephine!" I screamed.

77

Felicia buried her head in her arms and wept. Her sobs echoed in the big kitchen.

Varina patted her back and tried to soothe her. "Now, honey, that was a long, long time ago. You don't need to be crying for me. I cried all the tears a long time ago."

"How can you say that?" Tears ran down Felicia's anguished face. "After everything that happened to you?"

"Hush now," Varina said, handing her a paper towel to wipe her eyes. "You're getting yourself all worked up about something that's in the past. You think I do that? Look back at those bad times? No, ma'am. Every morning when I wake up, I think, *Thank you, Lord, for giving me one more day in this beautiful place you made for me.*"

"You amaze me, Varina," Brooke said.

Felicia got up and poured four glasses of iced tea. She brought them back to the table and handed a glass to each woman.

When she sat down again, Felicia took a

deep breath. "What happened to your baby, Auntie Vee?"

Varina's face clouded over. "The baby came too early. I was only seven months along. Josephine got the doctor over to the house as soon as she could, but there wasn't anything he could do. My baby was too little and too weak. Jesus took my baby home. And I never even got to hold him."

Lizzie and Brooke looked away, each hating the burden of the secret that they shared.

"Oh, Auntie, I'm so sorry," Felicia said.

"Don't be. It's like Josephine said — maybe that was just a blessing. You know, I was just a baby myself when all that happened. And I don't know what my daddy or brothers would have said if I'd come home with a baby from a white man. Josephine took real good care of me. I was sick with a fever after I lost the baby, but she got me medicine and looked after me just like I was her own little sister. Then, when I was better, she found me a new school to go to. I finished high school, and I went to business school and learned to take dictation, and then she helped me get a good job in a real office."

"Good old Josephine," Felicia said bitterly.

"You don't realize it now, but that was a real hard thing for a little black girl like me," Varina said proudly. "Back then, not many colored girls in the South worked in offices. I worked at the shipyard in Savannah, and then, after the war, I went down to Jacksonville, where one of my brothers worked, and I got a job at the railroad."

Brooke's throat felt dry. She sipped her iced tea and tried to ignore the laser stare Lizzie was giving her. "Varina," she said finally. "You know Josephine had all these secrets she kept all those years. And that's why she hired me and brought me over here to Talisa. Those secrets were eating away at her. She knew she didn't have long to live, so before she died, she wanted to make things right with the people she'd hurt."

"Josephine always did play things close to the vest," Varina agreed. "When Felicia told me about your mama being Josephine's niece, you could have knocked me over with a feather. I never would have known that sweet Millie had a baby with Mr. Gardiner — and then that baby was your mama!"

"How does Marie feel about Josephine keeping that little tidbit to herself all these years?" Felicia asked.

"She was pretty angry," Brooke said. "But then, Millie kept it a secret too. All these years, my mom had no clue that her pops wasn't her biological father. She's slowly getting used to the idea, but it's going to take some time."

"Didn't Josephine tell you that Millie and Ruth and Varina were her best friends? All that High Tide Club stuff, that was just a bunch of crap," Felicia said.

"Josephine had one more secret she was keeping," Brooke said, looking at Felicia. "Lizzie found it by accident this week as she was going through Josephine's papers looking for material for her magazine article, but it didn't make much sense until yesterday when the sheriff gave me the report on the DNA comparison between Josephine and C. D."

Lizzie nodded. "After I found that letter from the priest, Father Ryan, telling Josephine about that little boy, Charlie, I started to wonder again why Josephine was so concerned about that particular boy and no other child."

Felicia's eyes widened as she realized what was coming. "Oh my God," she whispered. She grasped her great-aunt's hand. "Josephine lied, Auntie. She told you your baby was dead, but that was a lie. She gave the baby away! To an orphanage." She turned to Brooke and Lizzie. "I'm right, aren't I?" she asked. "C. D. isn't Josephine's son. He's hers!"

"What's that?" Varina asked, confused. "You're saying my son is alive? He didn't die? How can that be?" She shook her head violently. "No! Josephine wouldn't have done me that way. She wouldn't hide my child from me for all these years. Let me think he was dead when he wasn't?"

"I'm so sorry, Varina," Brooke said.

"There's no explanation for it, but yes, we think that's exactly what she did. A priest who was the pastor at a black church in Savannah was the go-between. He found a couple, probably in his parish, who took the baby for a few weeks, and then he turned the boy over to a Catholic orphanage, where he stayed until he was six. After that, he went to live at the Good Shepherd Home for Boys."

"And you think my boy, my grown-up son, is C. D.? Living right here on this island, working for Josephine?" Varina asked. "I don't understand."

"That bitch!" Felicia exclaimed. "Playing God with people's lives. How dare she!"

"My baby is alive," Varina said, looking from Lizzie to Felicia. "I can't believe it." She turned pleading eyes to Brooke. "How can you be sure it's him after all these years?"

"The only way we can be really positive is if we tried to DNA match you with C. D. There are so many compelling facts it can't be a coincidence. The DNA report we had done on C. D. showed he had African heritage. C. D. was told he was named after the priest who found him abandoned in his church after Sunday mass. That's the same priest who wrote Josephine to give her an update on the baby. We talked to a nun in Savannah; she's nearly a hundred years old, but she remembers the little boy named Charlie who came to live at St. Joseph's

Children's Home. The nuns gave him the last name of Anthony, for St. Anthony, who is the patron saint of the lost. And the priest who brought him there, he was driving a new Cadillac not long after that. The rumor was that the Cadillac was given to him by that baby's family as a reward for keeping his mouth shut. When Charlie was six, he was sent to the Good Shepherd Home for Boys. We talked to a man who lived in the same cottage at the boy's home. He remembers C. D. from that time."

Brooke reached for her phone and scrolled through her camera roll. She found the photo from Good Shepherd of the boys standing in front of their cottage. She enlarged it and handed it to Varina, tapping the photo of the boy the others had nicknamed Buck. "That's him."

"Oh, my. Oh, my," Varina whispered. "He looks like my brother Omar." She thrust the phone at Felicia. "See? Doesn't he look like a Shaddix?"

"I've never seen a blue-eyed Shaddix before," Felicia snapped. But she examined the photo closer, reluctantly nodding. "He was light enough to pass, wasn't he? You know, I've seen that old man dozens of times since we started staying over here, but I never saw it until now."

Varina could not take her eyes off the photo. "When it was my time, the pains were awful. We knew something was wrong. There was so much blood! When the doctor came, he gave me a shot. And when I woke up, there was no baby. Josephine said the baby was born dead, and the doctor took it away with him. She said it was better that way so I wouldn't be so upset."

"I hope she rots in hell," Felicia said. "I'm glad Gabe killed her. Josephine needed killing. I only wish I'd done it myself." She stalked over to the counter, picked up the cooling cake layers, and dumped them into the trash. "I'll be damned if I'll bake a cake and sit in a church and pretend to be sorry that old bitch is gone." She looked over at Varina. "Come on, Auntie. We need to get you home and give you your meds. I don't think I can stand to be under Josephine's roof for one more minute."

"No, ma'am," Varina said. Her voice was loud and clear.

"Now, Auntie Vee," Felicia started.

"You go along home," Varina said. "You're upset. I'll be along in a little while. Lizzie will bring me home, won't you?"

"Happy to," Lizzie said, earning her a glare from Felicia, who stomped out of the kitchen, slamming the screen door as she went.

"Fetch me those cake layers out of that trash, will you, honey?" Varina said. She pointed in the direction of the door. "That girl has had a temper her whole life. There wasn't no reason for her to throw those cakes out. I'll put some icing on 'em and nobody will know the difference."

Lizzie reached into the trash and rescued the cake layers, which had split in half. She brushed away some stray potato peels and placed them on a plate.

"Are you all right?" Brooke asked as the old woman returned to chopping pecans. "I know you've had an awful shock."

"I'm going to pray about this," Varina said, not looking up. "I don't rightly know what to think." She blinked back tears, and a moment later, her shoulders shook as she sobbed quietly on Brooke's shoulder.

Lizzie slipped from the room. A moment later she was back. Varina had regained her composure. Lizzie put two items on the table in front of her. One was a small prayer card with a color rendering of the Virgin Mary, eyes cast heavenward. The other was a string of mother-of-pearl rosary beads.

"These were with one of the letters the nuns sent Josephine, after she'd paid for a new kitchen and hot water heater at St. Joseph's. I thought you might like to have them."

Varina picked up the rosary, letting the smooth beads slide between her fingertips. She clutched the silver crucifix dangling from the end. "Thank you." She looked up. "Could you take me home now?"

"Of course," Lizzie said.

"I'm going over to visit C. D. in a little bit," Brooke said. "I have to tell him that his DNA didn't match Josephine's. Should I tell him about you?"

Varina wound the string of beads around and around her narrow wrist. "What's he gonna say when he finds out? How's he gonna feel about having a mama who's black and a daddy . . ." Her voice trailed off.

78

"This really sucks," Lizzie said as they trudged toward the chauffeur's cottage.

"Totally. I don't blame Felicia for being outraged. I feel like burning down the house too. I don't see how Josephine was able to live with all the pain she caused all those years," Brooke said.

"I guess, at the end, she thought her money would absolve her of all her sins," Lizzie said.

As they approached the cottage, they spied C. D. on the porch, sitting on a wooden kitchen chair. His right arm was in a sling, and as they grew closer, they smelled the acrid smoke from his cigarillo.

He was awkwardly pawing through the contents of a rusted red metal tackle box with his left hand. "Hey," he said. "Excuse me for not standing up."

"How are you feeling, C. D.?" Brooke asked.

"Still kicking," he said. "How about you?"

"Better. The headaches from the concussion are gone, and my face seems to be healing."

"Glad to hear it." He touched his shoulder. "I did a tour in Vietnam, came home and worked on the docks, and been thrown out of just about every bar on this coast, and this is the first time I've ever been shot. Some folks would say I was overdue." He studied the two women's serious expressions. "You just come over here to check up on me?"

"I brought you something," Brooke said, holding out the envelope. "The sheriff found this in Gabe's car. After the shooting."

"You mean after you killed the son of a bitch? Best day's work you ever did." He took the envelope, glanced at the return address, then handed it back. "Can't open it with my bum arm. It's the DNA report from the lab, right? I reckon you already know what it says."

"I do," Brooke admitted.

"And?"

"There is no DNA match between you and Josephine. I'm sorry, C. D. She wasn't your mother."

He reached for the cigarillo and took a puff, letting the ash drop unnoticed onto his lap. "Well, shit. And that's 100 percent?"

"They say 99 percent in the report, because it's scientifically impossible for anything to be 100 percent," Brooke said.

He looked past them, out at the barn, and

then the green lawn that sloped gently down toward the road to the beach, the landscape dotted with huge moss-draped live oaks.

"I guess you and your mama own all this now. Y'all will be wanting me to move along. Right? I mean, I ain't no good to nobody with my arm like this."

"You can stay put. We've hired a new lawyer — an honest one this time — to handle the estate. You can stay as long as you like."

"Okay." His nod was as close as he'd come to saying thanks. He pulled himself up by his good arm, went into the cottage, and came out holding a bottle of beer. "Open that for me, if you would."

Brooke obliged, and he knocked half the beer back in a single long gulp, setting the bottle on the porch rail and letting out a beery belch.

"Back to being an orphan again. It was nice for a while, you know, letting myself believe I might own a piece of this. I ain't ever really owned anything before, except a truck or a boat, stuff like that."

"I'm truly sorry. I know it's not enough, but my mom wanted you to know she intends to honor all the bequests Josephine made for her employees here on the island."

"How much?"

"Twenty-five thousand. You won't get the money right away, because the estate will be probated, but she'll continue to pay your salary, the same as she will with Louette and Shug."

"Guess that's better than nothing, but why's she paying me to sit on my can on this porch? Docs can't tell me yet how long I'll be laid up."

"Consider it worker's comp," Brooke said. "And before I forget, if you're interested, Josephine's service is Saturday, at 6:30 P.M., at the AME Church."

"I can give you a ride if you want," Lizzie offered.

C. D. finished off the beer and belched again. "I'll let you know how I feel."

"Okay, well, I guess I'll see you around," Brooke said.

They were halfway down the path toward the barn when he suddenly called out. "Why'd she give me that toy truck, then?"

Lizzie raised one eyebrow, then followed Brooke back to the cottage.

"If I wasn't her kid, why'd she give me that truck for Christmas? Why'd she treat me special, over all them other kids? Hold me in her lap and act like I meant something to her?"

Brooke took her time answering the question, walking the tightrope between truth and fiction.

"We think your mother was somebody Josephine cared about. Somebody who was special to her. Which made you special."

"Just not special enough to adopt. Or raise as her own," C. D. said bitterly. "Got it."

79

The Episcopal minister imported for Josephine's funeral looked out at the tightly packed pine pews in the small wood-frame African Methodist Episcopal Church on Talisa Island. Her face gleamed with perspiration, and a fly buzzed persistently around the podium.

She was short and young, in her midthirties, with a cherubic face and a tangle of enviable black curls that touched the collar of her vestments. The Reverend Patricia Templeton admitted that she'd met Josephine Bettendorf Warrick only once, six months earlier, when she'd stopped in at her church on the mainland to ask her to preside over her funeral.

"I say *asked,* but really, it was more of an order," Rev. Templeton said.

"I know that's right," mumbled a woman near the back, loud enough to provoke scattered laughter and rib-poking.

"Miss Josephine explained to me that she

believed in God and believed that he was calling her home, and she said that although she had sinned mightily in her life, she had come to believe the promise of redemption that we, as Christians, cherish," the minister said.

"Hmmph," muttered the same woman. Just as Brooke turned to see who the commentator was, she was astonished to see C. D. slip into the only open seat remaining at the back of the church. He was nearly unrecognizable in a starched white dress shirt and baggy black trousers. He clutched his ever-present ball cap in his good left hand, and his wiry gray hair was slicked back to reveal his balding forehead. He saw Brooke's stare and nodded a greeting.

Brooke and Marie were wedged into the "family pew" at the front of the church, alongside Lizzie and Louette and Shug. Varina sat on the right end of the pew, but Felicia, her great-niece, had declined to attend the service. The room was uncomfortably hot, so the AME church members fanned themselves with the photocopied funeral programs.

They'd deliberately planned an early evening service, hoping the June temperatures would have cooled off by six, but Brooke was certain it must have been at least ninety degrees. She felt her eyelids sag. The church, with its simple whitewashed plank walls and Gothic arched windows, had only a single, barely functioning air-conditioning unit installed in a window near the altar. Large brass vases brimmed with bunches of white gladioli, asparagus ferns, and palmettos lovingly arranged by members of the church's altar guild, and gardenias, which had been wired onto chicken wire–framed crosses, hung at the end of every pew, their overpowering scent filling the air.

All of this, even the menu for the reception to be held afterward at Shellhaven, had been spelled out in a letter that Josephine had entrusted to Louette right after her cancer diagnosis.

Brooke had stressed the need for brevity to the pastor and was thankful when, fifteen minutes later, Marie roused her from a nap with a subtle tap on the arm in time to hear Rev. Templeton intone the final words from the Book of Common Prayer.

They recessed from the church while a joyous version of "Amazing Grace" was played on the AME Church's organ and then they gathered outside, shaking hands and accepting condolences from two dozen islanders, most of them current or former residents of Oyster Bluff, along with a smattering of old friends from the mainland whom Josephine had specifically included as invitees to the funeral.

Marie had rebelled on only one point of Josephine's instructions and invited the cousins,

Dorcas and Delphine, despite Josephine's specific ban.

"They're her family too," Marie had insisted. Still, she'd been relieved when the women begged off, instead sending a huge, hideous arrangement of carnations in the shape of an open Bible.

As they stood in the late-afternoon heat, Brooke was grateful for the light breeze that ruffled the fronds of nearby palmettos. She was even more grateful when, thirty minutes later, Shug pulled Samuel Bettendorf's Packard up to the front of the church.

It had been another of Shug's thoughtful gestures. He'd fine-tuned the old engine, then washed, polished, and buffed the car until it gleamed in the dimming sunshine like a burnished coin. He held the driver's-side door as Marie climbed behind the wheel with Varina in the front passenger seat and Lizzie and Brooke in the back.

The funeral-goers milled around inside the house, helping themselves to the buffet provided by Louette, Varina, and other AME church ladies. Platters of golden fried chicken vied with trays of deviled crab, potato salad, pickled shrimp, baked ham, macaroni and cheese, and sliced tomatoes on the polished dining room table. The sideboard was loaded down with more desserts than Brooke had ever seen in one place. Coconut cake, caramel cake, pound cake, chess pie, lemon meringue pie, pecan pie, brownies, and three different colors and shapes of congealed Jell-O salads. Pitchers of iced tea and lemonade stood on a huntboard alongside an enormous crystal punch bowl that held a vivid red concoction that resembled Hawaiian Punch and lime sherbet.

Lizzie brought a plate of food to Varina, who, as the oldest living member of Oyster Bluff and Josephine's oldest friend, held court in a high-backed chair near the fireplace, then joined Brooke and Marie, who stood near a pair of open windows in a corner, hoping for a bit of cool air.

"I don't know about you, but I could really use a drink," Lizzie told the women. "And I can't wait to get out of this dress. I'm melting!"

"Amen to that," Marie said, fanning herself. "I wanted to have an open bar, but Louette and Varina were appalled at the suggestion. They said Josephine didn't mind drinking, but she wouldn't want to be 'likkerin' up half the island,' as they put it."

"How much longer before everybody clears out?" Brooke asked. She'd smiled and nodded and accepted the sympathy of strangers for what seemed like an eternity. Her feet hurt, and she desperately wanted a cocktail.

"It's nearly eight," Marie said. "But it seems like everybody is just settling in."

Brooke looked out at the sky, which had turned a deep bluish purple. She leaned forward and spotted what she was looking for. "It's a full moon tonight."

Lizzie looked out. "Are you thinking what I'm thinking?"

"There's C. D.," Lizzie said, nodding toward the dining room, where C. D. was clumsily attempting to load a plate with fried chicken.

"I saw him in church," Brooke said. "It's sweet that he made such an effort to dress up for Josephine, especially considering what we know now."

"Uh-oh," Lizzie said as Felicia walked into the dining room. "Look who the cat dragged in." Felicia was dressed up too, in a long, black halter-necked dress. She wore subtle makeup and large gold-hoop earrings. Once again, Brooke was struck by how stunning Felicia was.

She stood for a moment, leaning down to chat with her great-aunt before noticing the other women and walking over to join them.

"My goodness, C. D. really does resemble Varina," Marie muttered. "It's uncanny."

Felicia spotted C. D., who'd found a spot on the sofa and was balancing his plate on his lap. "It looks like he's taking the news in stride. Better than I would." She looked at Brooke. "I'm sorry I lost it and blew my stack at you yesterday."

"It's understandable," Brooke said.

"Here's the thing. Auntie is over it. She was upset when she came home, but this morning, when I got up, she was dressed in her church dress, all ready to go. At 7:30 in the morning! She was sitting in a chair, reading her Bible, clutching a string of rosary beads, of all things. And she proceeded to cite me chapter and verse on forgiveness."

Marie smiled. "I think I've marked some of those same verses in my Bible lately."

"She waited until ten, then she went into Louette's kitchen and fixed a plate of food from all the stuff the church ladies have been cooking, covered it with foil, and then she asked me, sweet as pie, if I would take her to see C. D."

"She what?" Lizzie said.

"She wanted to be the one to tell him. I tried to talk her out of it, but Auntie was not having it. So I took her over to C. D.'s cottage. She told me to wait in the big house, then she went up and knocked on the door, and he peeped out, and she offered him his plate of takeout."

"I would have loved to have heard that conversation," Brooke said.

"Me too. I waited an hour, then I walked back over there, and they were sitting on that teeny little front porch, kind of talking and staring at each other."

"How did C. D. seem?" Marie asked.

"Shell-shocked," Felicia said. "Auntie said he had no idea."

"Did she tell him the whole story? About Russell Strickland and the rape and how they somehow disposed of the body and kept it a secret all these years?" Marie asked.

"Yep," Felicia said. "She spilled it all. Then I took her home, and she had a nap and insisted on going over to her house at Oyster Bluff to check on the progress. And then she fixed two dozen deviled eggs and her famous 7UP Jell-O salad to bring over here. I can't keep up with her, y'all."

"Your aunt is a marvel, Felicia."

"She's my superhero," Felicia agreed. "God, I wish I had a drink."

"Look at that moon tonight," Brooke said. "We need to figure out what time the tide is high."

"I'll go ask C. D.," Lizzie volunteered.

She maneuvered through the crowd, then pulled up a chair and sat down beside the old man. They talked quietly for a moment, then he became visibly agitated, gesturing wildly with his good hand and occasionally pointing at Varina, who was in turn watching him.

"That was a whole lot of conversation just to get a tide report," Brooke said.

"You're not going to believe this," Lizzie said as she rejoined them. "That old goat does not miss a beat. Varina told him about being attacked and raped by Millie's fiancé, but she still won't say his name. That's what he was asking me. I figured the secret's already out, right? So I told him everything I know about Russell Strickland, how he disappeared the day after the party and was never seen again. I told C. D. that Russell's grandparents hired a private detective to come down here from Boston to look for Strickland. C. D. wanted to know all about Strickland's family — where they were from and whether they had money. I told him Josephine said the family was stinking rich and that Russell was an only child. His face lit up like it was the Fourth of July."

Brooke laughed. "He'll be over at the library in St. Ann's before the doors open Monday morning, badgering those poor women to help him track down the Strickland family fortune."

"And why not?" Felicia asked. "If there's any money anywhere, why shouldn't C. D. get it?"

"Did you ever get around to asking C. D. about high tide tonight?" Brooke asked.

"It's at 9:10. We've got forty minutes." She glanced at Marie. "Are you in?"

Marie's smile was impish. "You know, I'm seventy-six years old, and I've never done it in my life."

"No way," Felicia said.

"It's true," Marie insisted. "Let's do it."

"But we can't just leave with all these people here," Brooke said. At least a dozen stragglers seemed to have made themselves at home, lounging on the sofas, leaning in corners, chatting with old friends.

"I'll ask Louette to put away all the food. That'll clear stragglers out," Marie said. "I've got a couple bottles of good white wine in the fridge. I'll pack them up and sneak them out to the car."

"And I'll run upstairs and get some beach towels and a quilt out of the linen closet," Lizzie volunteered. "Felicia, will Varina come with us? Do you think she can manage?"

"I'll help her manage. Going out to Mermaid Beach tonight is just what she needs. I think it's what we all need, after the past few days."

80

Marie eased the Packard off the pavement and as far as she dared drive down the sandy beach overlook before stopping and setting the hand brake.

The ocean spread out before them with the full moon a glowing white orb, spilling silver onto the surface of the deep blue sea.

"Look at all those stars," Marie marveled.

Brooke and the others scrambled out of the backseat, and Felicia hurried around to her great-aunt's side, taking her arm and guiding her carefully through the soft sand.

"This looks like a good spot." Brooke pointed toward a flat stretch of beach just above the high tide line. Lizzie spread the quilt onto the hard-packed sand and unfolded the beach chair she'd brought for Varina.

"Perfect," Marie agreed. She set down the basket she'd brought from the house and slipped out of her shoes, easing herself down onto the quilt beside Brooke, Lizzie, and Felicia.

Brooke uncorked the wine, pouring it into plastic cups that she handed around to the others.

"Auntie Vee?" Felicia held out a cup.

"Oh, no, honey," Varina said.

"Just a sip? To toast the full moon?" Felicia teased.

"All right, a sip."

When everyone had been served, Brooke raised her cup. "Let's drink to Josephine."

Felicia frowned and looked away, muttering something unintelligible.

"Felicia Shaddix, don't you go acting ugly," Varina chided.

"Well, I don't mind toasting Josephine," Lizzie said. "She's the one who brought us all together here on this island. She helped me understand a little about my grandmother Ruth and, indirectly, my messed-up, dysfunctional family." She looked at the other women. "Did I tell you I got my ex to go through the boxes of my grandmother's stuff I've had in storage? He's sending me the rest of her letters and scrapbooks so I can look for more of Ruth's correspondence with Josephine and Millie."

"You've got an ex-husband?" Felicia asked.

"Josephine's not the only one with secrets," Lizzie said with a touch of sadness. "We were together for nine years but never actually married, which might have been our problem."

"Sorry," Felicia said. "I know what that's like."

"Not to mention Josephine seems to have reignited my stagnant writing career," Lizzie said, brightening. "I've never been as productive as I've been since I came to Talisa. I've sold my piece about the High Tide Club ladies to *Vanity Fair,* and I've even started fiddling around with a screenplay. So here's to Josephine."

Brooke tapped her cup against Lizzie's. "She made me take a closer look at my family too. I've gained a new appreciation for my amazing mom, and I'm suddenly on speaking terms again with my dad. More importantly, I've reconnected with my own son's father."

"Does that mean you and Pete . . . ?" Marie asked.

"We'll see," Brooke said. "He's coming back into Savannah tomorrow, and he wants to have a serious talk about the future. Whatever that means."

"Josephine almost got you killed," Felicia reminded Brooke, pointing in the direction of the lighthouse.

"That was my own fault. I fell for Gabe's lies. I wanted easy answers, and he was only too willing to give them. Maybe if I'd listened when my dad tried to warn me about him, none of this would have happened."

Varina took a tiny sip of the wine and made a face. "Why do folks like this stuff? Tastes nasty to me. Josephine was my first friend and my oldest friend." She patted Felicia's shoulder. "I know you can't understand it, but that's a fact."

"Auntie! She stole your child, told you he was dead, then gave him to strangers to raise. It's obscene! She treated you just like those plantation owners treated their slaves right here on this island. It kills me to think about it."

Varina was unfazed by her niece's brutal judgment. "Or maybe she did what she did out of love. I was so young. Had no money, no friends or family in Savannah. No education. How could I raise a child? And maybe I wouldn't have been able to love that baby, knowing how he came into the world. I had nightmares for a long time about that bad man. Sometimes I would wake up, crying and sweating, thinking about him, about what he did to me. Maybe I would have seen his face every time I looked at that baby."

"But she had no right," Brooke said. "That should have been your decision, not hers. And what about C. D.? How different would his life have been if he hadn't been dumped in that orphanage and then shuttled off to a children's home?"

Varina shrugged. "I guess that was God's plan. For him and for me." She looked at Brooke, and her eyes seemed to brighten. "I know it was God's plan that brought me back

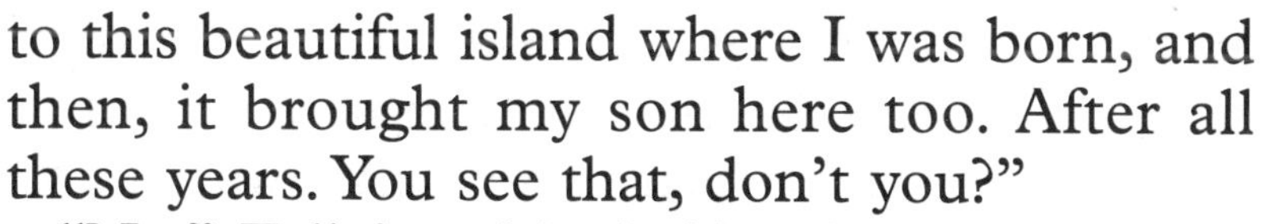

to this beautiful island where I was born, and then, it brought my son here too. After all these years. You see that, don't you?"

"No," Felicia said, shaking her head again. "I don't. I don't see it that way at all."

"Try it this way, then," Varina said. "It's easier to walk around with love in your heart than with hate." She clutched her chest. "I don't want that burden. I let go of all that mess. You need to do that too."

"I'll drink to dear old Aunt Josephine," Marie said. "It's been painful, I'll admit, but finding out that my biological father was Gardiner Bettendorf has been a blessing in disguise. It gives me a new appreciation for Pops, who loved and raised me as his own, and it's deepened my admiration for my mom. I had no idea of the depth of her courage and quiet determination. And her strength. And now . . . all of this." She waved her arm at the landscape around them. "Talisa is such a wonderful opportunity and a challenge, especially for somebody my age. Ever since I found out, I wake up every morning and my head is spinning with plans and ideas for Shellhaven and Talisa." She grinned. "After all those years of being a wife and stay-at-home mother, of being a volunteer and a fund-raiser, I have a project again. And it's big and inspiring and intimidating. I tell you, it's like a youth tonic!"

"What kind of plans do you have?" Felicia

asked, sipping her wine.

"I really want to fulfill Josephine's dream of saving the island and keeping it out of the state's hands, but I'm going to need all of you to get on board."

"Us?" Felicia looked skeptical.

"All of you," Marie said. "Josephine had the right idea."

"But the wrong lawyer," Brooke said. "Which was my fault."

"I'm going to honor her intentions as best I can. I'll create the Talisa Trust, with all of you as partners. First priority is to preserve and update Shellhaven."

"Please tell me that means central air," Lizzie said.

"Central heat and air, a new roof, updated electrical. All new bathrooms and a new kitchen. I've got a contractor coming over Monday to start working on an estimate."

"Does that mean you're moving to Shellhaven?" Lizzie asked.

"Full-time? No. I've got a much better idea. I want to turn Shellhaven into a nonprofit retreat house for writers, painters, musicians. We could offer residencies for creative types to come for, say, two weeks or maybe even a month's stay. That's why all the bedrooms will need new en suite baths. Then, I want to convert the barn into studio spaces, maybe with moveable walls so there could be a central performance space for readings or art exhibits or concerts. I'm not going to live here full-time, but I was thinking maybe you" — she pointed at Lizzie — "might agree to that. I wouldn't want you to give up your writing, now that it's going so well again, but maybe you could live on-site and help vet the writers applying for residency."

"Twist my arm," Lizzie said.

"Mom, that's a genius idea!" Brooke exclaimed. "Why didn't you tell me?"

Marie tapped her skull. "A lot of it's still just up here. But you won't mind, will you? Not inheriting some big old white elephant of a house to clatter around in during your old age?"

"No." Brooke laughed. "And I definitely won't mind missing out on the upkeep or the tax burden."

"What about all of Josephine's cars? She loved those old things," Varina said wistfully.

"I'll have a new garage built, and of course, I'll keep the Packard, but those other cars are too rare and valuable to keep here on the island, where the salt air is so destructive and nobody really drives them. I want to sell them and use the money for something that does real good."

"What kind of good?" Felicia asked.

"I'd like to buy a new, larger capacity boat for the children going over to the mainland for school. Right now, they have to rely on the state-run ferry, which stops running at five on weekdays. This way, they could participate in after-school enrichment programs they miss out on because they don't have a reliable way to get back to the island late in the afternoon."

"I notice you haven't said much about Oyster Bluff in all your grand schemes," Felicia said.

"That's my department," Brooke spoke up. "You all know that Josephine had finally decided to sign over all the deeds for the houses she bought there over the past twenty years or so. I was working on that before she died. It's complicated, but we'll get there."

"Felicia, it sounds like you're still not really on board with any of this," Marie said.

"I don't want to sound ungracious, but it's still hard for me to believe good can come out of all the destructive things that woman did," Felicia said. "I know you mean well, Marie, but do you really believe you can just wave some money around and think that fixes things?"

Marie gave it some thought. "You're right. Money won't fix everything. It will certainly help with things like roofs and plumbing, but I'm under no illusion that I can turn Talisa into some kind of utopia. So I'm going to invest in brick and mortar, but I also want to establish an after-school tutoring program and a college scholarship fund for Geechee children on the island. Maybe that's something you could get involved with. You'd sure be a great role model for them."

"Too many children leave the island and never come back here," Varina said sadly. "You know there's only ten school-age children living at Oyster Bluff right now? When I was coming up, we had our own schoolhouse. Every house had five or six children."

"There are no jobs to keep them here," Felicia reminded her. "Talisa can seem so closed off from civilization. I remember I couldn't wait to get off the island to go to school and drive through a McDonald's and shop at a real mall." She leaned back on her elbows and looked up at the sky with its dazzling array of stars twinkling in the blue velvet sky. "It didn't occur to me that one day I'd choose to come back here just to get away from the fast-food restaurants and the malls and the traffic and pollution. And to be able to look up and see all these stars, so far from the city lights."

"You're a Geechee girl," Varina said fondly. "Ain't nothing you can do about it. You got salt water in your veins, and it pulls you back here just as surely as the moon pulls that tide."

Felicia refilled her wineglass. "Maybe. Oh, hell. You know what? You're right, Marie. It's a start. It'll make a difference."

"We'll make a difference," Brooke said, taking the bottle from Felicia. "All of us."

"Okay, I'll toast to that," Felicia said. She raised her cup, then clicked it against Brooke's, who clicked hers against Lizzie's, who clicked against Marie's glass. Varina touched her glass to Felicia's, completing the circle.

"Here's to the High Tide Club," Felicia said. "Here's to us. And here's to the ones who brought us here."

"To Varina," Felicia said, blowing her great-aunt a kiss.

"And Ruth," Lizzie declared.

"And even Josephine, God forgive her," Marie said, raising her glass.

"But mostly to Millie," Brooke said, tears springing to her eyes.

They all drained their glasses.

81

October 1941

Russell had backed the pickup truck out of the barn. He was dressed in what Millie recognized as his hunting clothes — long-sleeved tan shirt, tan trousers with leather chaps meant to deflect the burrs and brambles of the island's thick undergrowth, and stout boots. He was loading a pair of rifles into the back of the truck.

"I, uh, was looking for you. Where are you going?" she asked.

"Where does it look like I'm going?" He slammed the tailgate up and walked around to the front of the truck. "What do you want?"

She swallowed hard and gave him a demure smile. "About last night. I'm . . . sorry. It's just there were so many people around, and I was afraid Mother might catch us in the act." She giggled innocently.

Russell opened the door of the truck. "Hadn't you better get back in the house?"

"Why don't I go with you?" Millie asked, placing her hand on his arm and giving it a slight squeeze.

"Hunting? Don't be ridiculous. You don't know the first thing about it. You'd probably wet your panties or faint if you heard a gun fired."

She shook her head vigorously. "You're wrong, darling. Papa was a great shot, and he taught me. And we practiced skeet shooting at boarding school."

"Hunting isn't the same as sporting clays," Russell retorted. He looked up at the sky and seemed to consider her request. "It'll be daylight soon. I should be up in a tree stand by now."

"Let me come," she wheedled. "It'll be fun. My first kill."

"All right, you can come along if you like." He gestured at her clothing. "Will you be warm enough? I don't want to hear you whining about the cold, and there's no time to go back to the house to change."

"I'll be fine," Millie assured him. "Anyway, like the song says, I've got my love to keep me warm."

"Get in, then, before I change my mind."

She clapped her hands softly. "I can't wait to show you what a good shot I am."

The old truck bounced and jounced over every rut in the crushed-shell road, jarring

Millie so thoroughly she was sure she could hear her bones rattling. The headlights illuminated a narrow tunnel through the lush greenery.

"Where are we headed?" she asked.

"One of the colored boys showed me Gardiner's tree stand just up the road here," Russell said. He had one hand on the steering wheel, and the other arm was slung carelessly across her shoulders. "There's a big buck — the fellows call him Zeus — an eight-pointer. I was out here early Friday morning and saw him, but before I could get a shot, something spooked him."

"I'm sure you'll get him this morning," Millie said. His fingertips massaged her shoulder, and she cringed inwardly.

"Damn right I will. And I can't wait to see the look on Bettendorf's face when I show up with the carcass of his buck strapped across the hood of his truck."

He whistled tunelessly as they rode through the inky darkness. "How can you tell where we're going?" she asked, peering through the windshield. "There are no road signs, and it's so dark, I'm hopelessly lost."

"It's just up here, where the road forks," Russell said. "If you go to the left, that's the road to the dock; to the right is where we're going." A hundred yards later, he turned the steering wheel sharply to the right, and several hundred yards later, he pulled the truck off the road. The headlights illuminated a path cutting through the tree line.

He cut the engine and jumped out of the cab. Millie joined him as he pulled the first rifle from the truck bed.

"Where —"

He clamped a hand hard across her mouth. "Quiet, goddamn it," he whispered. "You'll spook the damn deer."

She nodded her understanding, and he removed his hand. "Now listen, because I'm not going to explain it again." His voice was a harsh whisper. He pointed at a towering live oak across the meadow. "The stand is in that pine tree just up there by the oak. You can come with me, but you don't say a word, don't move, don't breathe until I give you the nod. Okay?"

"Okay," she whispered.

He sat down on the tailgate and pulled a flask from the inside pocket of his jacket and took a swig.

Picking up the rifle, he jammed three cartridges into the magazine before turning it right-side up again. He yanked the lever down and propped it beside him before taking another swig of bourbon. "See how I did that?"

He demonstrated the aiming process and blabbed endlessly about the trigger and firing. Finally, he handed her the rifle. "Got that?"

Millie took the rifle and cocked it. "Like this?"

"Don't point it at me, goddamn it!" He nearly knocked the rifle from her hands. "Didn't that useless father of yours teach you anything? Never point a loaded weapon at somebody unless you mean to fire it."

She took exactly five steps backward, her heart pounding. The words she heard in her head weren't Russell's but instead, her dear, sweet papa's.

"That's the girl, Millie," he'd said. "Plant your feet wide to absorb the shock of the recoil. Sight it. Hold your breath. Pull down steadily on the trigger."

Russell was tipping the flask up to his lips. His eyes widened in disbelief. Millie held her breath and pulled.

The blast echoed across the field and knocked her onto the ground. Slumbering birds rose up, squawking from the treetops, but Millie was momentarily deafened. She stood up, her ears ringing, knees shaking badly, her hands still trembling.

The minutes ticked away slowly. Finally, she forced herself to walk back to the truck. The single shot knocked Russell onto his back in the bed of the truck. The silver flask, her engagement gift to him, was still clutched in his hands. She picked it up and tucked it into the waistband of her slacks. Somehow, she managed to push his body backward far enough to close the tailgate.

Millie slid behind the wheel of the truck and clutched the steering wheel with both hands, trying to still the waves of nausea and panic.

The first few purplish-pink streaks of sunlight broke over the distant treetops. It was nearly dawn. She had to get back to the house. Finally, when her hands quit shaking, she pulled out the flask and drank the last few swallows of bourbon.

She was searching for the cap when out of the corner of her eye, she saw movement. As she watched, wide-eyed, a buck emerged from the tree line. His rack was so magnificent it seemed like he might topple over from the weight of it. He walked slowly into the emerging daylight, swung his head in the direction of the truck and, for just a moment, seemed to be staring directly at her. Two seconds passed. The buck turned his muzzle upward, alerted to something. Finally, with a swish of his white tail, he bounded back into the tree line, back to safety.

"Goodbye, Zeus," Millie whispered.

Swallowing her fears, Millie gripped the steering wheel to head back to the mansion. Just as she was about to pull onto the main road, she heard a car coming and stopped, just short of the intersection. It was the roadster! She dove for the floor, praying she wouldn't be noticed, and by the time she pulled herself back to a seated position, she saw Josephine's dark hair whipping in the breeze, and Gardiner, upright in the passenger seat, beside his sister.

She felt a deep wave of longing and regret — and something else — as the car passed. And then Millie squared her shoulders and drove back toward Shellhaven. She allowed herself to feel nothing. Except relief.

82

Brooke stood up and kicked off her shoes. She unzipped the sleeveless black sheath dress she'd worn to the funeral and pulled it off over her head. "Who's up for a swim?" she asked.

Lizzie and Felicia jumped to their feet and immediately began to strip.

"Come on, Marie," Lizzie urged. "There's a first time for everything."

"Yeah, Mom," Brooke said, reaching down to help her mother stand.

"Oh, my goodness." Marie giggled. "I'm too old for this nonsense." But she turned around to allow her daughter to unzip her chic black silk dress, then folded it neatly and placed it on top of the basket with the wine bottles.

"I'll just swim in my bra and panties," she said.

"Nuh-uh. No way," Felicia said. "Skinny-dipping means naked."

"As a jaybird," Brooke agreed, tugging at

the back of her mother's bra.

"Y'all going in without me?" Varina struggled to get out of the lawn chair.

"Auntie Vee! Of course we're not going without you." Felicia and Lizzie each took Varina by the arm. She stood, and her fingers fumbled as she tried to work the buttons on her blouse.

"Let me," Felicia said, and a few minutes later, the old lady stood naked and beaming up at the full moon overhead.

By unspoken agreement, the five joined hands and walked slowly toward the waves, pausing as the warm ocean lapped at their ankles, wading farther in until the water was neck-high on the tiny nonagenarian Varina.

"Ooh, this feels so good," Varina squealed. "But don't let go, y'all. You know I can't swim. I'm afraid that tide will pull me clean out to sea, and I'll end up naked in some country where they don't even speak English."

"We've got you," Lizzie promised, clutching Varina by the elbow.

The old woman let the water sweep her off her feet, and for a few minutes she floated, bobbing tranquilly in the gentle waves, until one swept her under and she emerged, sputtering and coughing, then giggling at the sheer absurdity of the situation.

It was nearing midnight as the women, laughing and talking softly, finally made their way back to the Packard.

It took two tries, but finally the engine turned over, and Marie carefully backed the car onto the pavement. They were passing the lighthouse when Lizzie tapped Varina on the arm.

"Varina, do you ever think about that night? The night y'all skinny-dipped and then slept at the lighthouse keeper's cottage?"

"Hmm?" Varina yawned. "Sometimes I do. Other times it seems like everything that happened that night and the next day was all a dream, it was so long ago. I miss my old friends Ruth and Millie. And now Josephine. Can't hardly believe I'm the last one here."

Lizzie gave her a conspiratorial look. "Since everybody else is dead now, it wouldn't hurt, would it, if you told us where Russell Strickland is? I mean, it would make such a powerful ending to my magazine story if we knew."

"Hush!" Felicia said fiercely. "She doesn't want to think about that. Or talk about it."

"It's all right, honey," Varina said. "I don't reckon it matters anymore. Maybe it would give C. D. peace to know it."

"You really don't have to tell us," Marie assured her.

"No. I think it will be like finally owning my own story," Varina said. "Go on down the road here a little ways, Marie, then turn like you're going to the dock. When you come to the two oaks that look like they've grown together, right before the road to the dock, you take a right at that fork, and you keep going until you see the creek running in front of you."

Marie drove slowly, following Varina's directions until the pavement ran out, and they were on a narrow shell road that grew narrower still, and darker, with the thick oak canopy overhead nearly blocking out the moonlight.

Varina peered into the inky night. "I hadn't been back here since that night. We all swore we'd never come near here again."

"It's okay," Marie assured her. "You don't have to do this. I'll back out of here, and we'll go on back to the house."

"No," Varina said stubbornly. "It's right up here. See that break in the trees? Stop there."

Marie cut the engine but left the headlights on. The warm night air folded in on them like a blanket. They heard the insistent thrum of cicadas and the croaks of tree frogs. From somewhere overhead, a pair of owls hooted from the tops of opposing trees.

A swarm of stinging gnats descended upon them, and soon the women were frantically slapping and trying to wave them away.

"This is the place," Varina said solemnly. She opened the car door and stepped out, clinging to the side of the car for balance. The others followed suit, with Felicia taking her great-aunt's arm.

"Just a little ways up here," Varina said. Her steps quickened, and in two minutes they stood in a clearing dominated by an imposing oyster shell mound.

"This is where we put him," Varina said. "Nobody else on the island would come back here. It's an Indian mound, you see."

"Geechees are superstitious about Indian things," Felicia whispered. "When I was a kid, we used to dare each other to come back here, but nobody ever would because it was supposed to be haunted."

Varina stared at the shell mound, then turned her back to it. "No," she said firmly. "Not haunted. Not anymore." She turned to Marie. "I'm ready to go home now, please."

83

Kavanaugh Park was a lush, green enclave of oaks, magnolias, and head-high azaleas a short walk from Brooke's childhood home in Ardsley Park. She'd dropped Henry off at Marie's house, then bought a picnic lunch at Back in the Day, a nearby bakery and restaurant. Now she sat on a bench under the shade of an oak tree and checked her phone for the tenth time in as many minutes.

He was late. She'd texted Pete earlier in the week, asking him to meet her in the park where she and the neighborhood kids had romped and played as children. It was the same park Marie liked to walk to, back in the days when Henry agreed to sit placidly in a stroller, something he rarely agreed to these days.

Would Pete show up? His return text had been a terse, three-word reply.

See U there.

Her stomach was in knots, her pulse racing. She'd dressed with care that morning, trying to look casual but pretty, sexy but not desperate. It was hot. Of course it was hot. This was June in Savannah. She could feel her mascara already starting to run, and the concealer she'd painstakingly applied to the still-healing scar on her cheek was melting. What had she been thinking when she'd planned this ridiculous affair? She should have met him in a restaurant, or better yet, a bar, where she could have soothed her nerves with a drink. She found a paper napkin and blotted her face with it, then glanced at her phone again. He was ten minutes late. Maybe he'd had problems calling a cab from the airport. Or maybe he was having second thoughts and had caught an earlier flight back to Alaska. If he was having second thoughts, so was she.

She twisted the platinum-and-diamond ring on her right ring finger. Marie had found it in a box of jewelry in Josephine's room and insisted she take it. "If you and Pete don't get together, you can at least wear it on your left hand and tell people you used to be married."

"Ha-ha, Mom. Good one," Brooke had said. But the ring was stunning, and let's face it, nobody else had offered her a diamond ring lately.

Where the hell was Pete? Why hadn't he called? Her cell phone hadn't rung. Really, it was so thoughtless. Hashtag rude. She clutched the bag and decided she would leave. It would serve him right. Maybe she wouldn't tell him he had a son. Maybe he didn't deserve a child as wonderful as Henry.

She saw a yellow cab pass by on Forty-fifth Street, slow down, then drive past. A few minutes later, the car was back. It rolled slowly past, then stopped again. The back door opened, and Pete climbed out. Brooke jumped up and waved as the cab sped away.

The Grizzly Adams beard was gone, and his straight, square jaw was back. Her pulse did funny things as he drew closer. He'd gotten sunburned in Florida. His smile seemed self-conscious. Well, maybe hers was too.

"Hey!" he said, reaching the bench.

"Hey," she said, leaning in to kiss his cheek. He drew back a moment as though he were startled.

Bad idea, bad idea, bad idea. The kiss made her look anxious or desperate. Or both.

"Let's sit," she said finally. "How was the conference?"

"Great," Pete said. "Our paper was a huge success, and it's been accepted by a pretty prestigious journal."

"And the job interviews? How did they go?" Oh God. She sounded like his mother. Next thing you knew she'd be asking if he'd been eating vegetables and flossing.

He nodded. "They went better than I'd

expected. The wildlife foundation position would be a perfect fit for me. I'd be based on the Georgia coast, but they'd want me to travel as far south as Amelia Island, Florida, and as far north as Daufuskie, in South Carolina. Pay's good, and they're establishing a relationship with the University of Georgia Marine Institute, so I'd have access to lab facilities."

"That does sound nice," Brooke said, trying to sound noncommittal.

"I'm not the only applicant, but I'd say there's an 85 percent chance I'll get an offer."

"You said there was another position too?"

"Yeah. It's with the U.S. Fish and Wildlife Service, and that one would be based out west, in the Sierras. I could continue my work on migration patterns, which would be sweet. The guy who interviewed me told me in confidence that I'm pretty much their number-one choice."

"Is there a downside to that one?" Brooke asked.

"I'm worried about the political situation," Pete admitted. "Conservation isn't exactly a big priority with the current administration. If there are layoffs or budget cuts, I'd be the first one to be let go."

Brooke tried to clandestinely wipe her sweaty palms with the crumpled paper napkin she still clutched in her fist. "So," she said cheerfully, "would you want to go back out west?"

Pete's gaze was level and direct. "That would depend on where I stand with you, Brooke. I mean, I've been thinking about this ever since I saw you last week. I still have no idea how you feel about us. I mean, give me a clue here, will you?"

He looked down at her hands and frowned. He gestured toward her hand. "What the hell? Is that an engagement ring? You got engaged since I last saw you?"

"No! I mean, no, it's not an engagement ring. It's a gift from my mom, who just inherited it, which is another long story."

She took a deep breath and reached into her pocket. She handed him a color photo of Henry as an infant, his hair downy, eyelashes thick and lush.

"This is Henry at six months, right after he started sitting up. I named him that after my grandfather, my mom's father, who we called Pops. He died before I was born. You want to know something funny? Last week, I found out that Granny had a secret affair with her best friend's older brother. His name was Gardiner Bettendorf. It was at the very beginning of the war. She'd been in love with him most of her life but never dared let anybody know. They had a one-night stand, and then his plane was shot down over France."

Pete looked puzzled.

"Granny got pregnant that night. But by the time her letter arrived, telling Gardiner he was going to be a father, he was already dead. Being an unwed mother back then, in her social circles, would have been unthinkable. So she married another man, Henry Updegraff, my pops."

He was still looking deeply confused.

"Here," she said, thrusting the bag at him. "I brought us lunch. Have a sandwich. They make these amazing sandwiches at Back in the Day. From their own bread. There are cookies too." She was babbling, and she knew it.

He unwrapped a sandwich and took a bite, chewing slowly. "Why are you telling me all this? I mean, it's interesting, but what's it got to do with us?"

"Take a good look at that picture of Henry, please. Tell me what you see."

"I'm not sure. I mean, I guess he looks like you. He has your lips."

She sighed. "And he has his father's eyes. And nose. And jaw. Henry's yours, Pete. He's your son."

Pete's sandwich dropped onto the bag on his lap. "You said the other day it was some guy who wasn't in your life anymore."

"Which was true. I let you slip out of my life, Pete. You were so far away, and things were so new and raw between us. You were so excited about your work in Alaska, I told myself I couldn't ask you to give that up and come back here. You said it yourself, remember? A once-in-a-lifetime opportunity. I thought you would have resented the baby and resented me."

"No!" Pete said. "Goddamn it! You had my baby and you didn't even tell me?"

Brooke bit her lip. "I know now how wrong I was. You had a right to know. And you have a right to know your son now, if that's what you want."

Pete's eyes narrowed. His voice was hoarse, choky. "You mean you didn't want me to come back when you found out about the baby, isn't that it? I would have come back. I would have been here for you, no question. Don't you know that about me? Do you think so little of me that I would resent you or our child?"

"It's not you that I think so little of, it's me," Brooke said, looking away. "When I figured out I was pregnant, I wouldn't allow myself to believe that you would want me. Who would? I was a mess. And now I am a mess with baggage. A kid."

Pete stared down at the photo of Henry.

"I'm telling you about him now, Pete, because I finally realize what a horrible thing I did. I hope it's not too late. Henry needs a father. He deserves a family, whatever that means."

She reached out and touched the hand

holding the photo. "I'm so sorry I screwed this up. Seeing you now, all my careful reasoning doesn't hold up. It never did."

Pete got up and slammed the bag lunch into the trash. He whirled around to face her. "So what am I supposed to do with this information? You spring this on me out of nowhere. 'Hey, guess what? You've got a three-year-old son.' What the hell, Brooke?"

"You do whatever you want with this information," she said, her voice strained. "I can't say I'm sorry enough, I know. But I couldn't keep this secret any longer. It should never have been a secret."

He paced back and forth in front of the bench, staring down at the photo of Henry. "What time is it?"

"Quarter to one," she said.

"I gotta go," he said abruptly. "My flight's gonna leave soon. You think I can catch a cab or an Uber or something from here?"

"I'll drive you," Brooke said. "My car's parked at my mom's house, right around the corner."

He kept staring down at the photo of Henry on the short walk to Marie's house. "My son," he said, his voice full of wonder. "Who is he? I mean, I saw him at the airport, for what, thirty minutes, and he wouldn't even look at me for most of that time. Maybe you could catch me up on the first three years of his life. What's he like?"

"He's a funny little guy," she said, ignoring the sarcasm. "He walked at exactly nine months. I thought he'd never sleep through the night. He loves to be read to. He has a favorite cartoon, this heinous Canadian kid, Caillou. He adores Caillou. He's crazy smart, Pete. He asks a million questions. He's a climber. He broke his arm climbing on a jungle gym in the spring. He's almost potty trained, but I think he gets a subversive thrill from pooping in his pants at the most inappropriate times. Please talk to me," she pleaded. "Tell me how to fix this. Tell me what to say."

He gave her a long, steady look. "If you don't already know what to say, then it's goodbye." He started to walk away, his long legs eating up concrete. He stopped suddenly and turned to her. "I'd like to keep the picture of our son, if that's okay."

"You're really going back to Alaska without seeing him?" she asked.

He stopped walking.

"Henry's at my mom's house. Right up there." She pointed at the two-story brick house two doors down from where they were standing.

"What if I want to do more than just see him occasionally?" Pete asked, his jaw still set in anger.

Brooke held her breath for a moment,

wondering what that meant. “Are you talking about some kind of joint custody thing?”

Pete shrugged. “Maybe. I mean, I just learned I have a son five minutes ago. It’s gonna take time to figure this out.”

“Whatever you want,” Brooke said softly. “Henry needs a dad. He needs you in his life. I know that now. But I guess how that happens is up to you.”

They were standing on the front porch at Marie’s house. Brooke’s hand was on the doorknob. “Are you seriously thinking of taking the job out west?” She was holding her breath, waiting for him to say something, when the door opened.

“Hey,” Marie said, looking from her daughter to Pete. “I thought I heard voices out here.”

Brooke exhaled slowly. “Mom, this is . . . Henry’s dad. Pete, this is my mom, Marie.”

Marie smiled and held out her hand. “So good to finally meet you, Henry’s dad. FYI, Henry’s up from his nap. Do you two want to come inside?”

“Nice to meet you too,” Pete said, shaking her hand. “Could we, uh, have a minute or two in private?”

Marie closed the door softly, and Brooke felt herself sag against the frame. She realized with a start that this was the same doorstep where she’d gotten her first goodnight kiss after her first car date, at fifteen.

"Tell me what you want, Brooke," Pete said, looking directly into her eyes. "And don't make it just about Henry. Do you want me to stay?" He traced the scar on her cheek with a fingertip. "What happened here?"

"Another long story," Brooke said. "Resulting from a near-fatal lack of good judgment. Could you please repeat that last question?"

"Do. You. Want. Me. To. Stay?"

This time she was ready with an answer. "Yeah," she said softly. "Yeah, I think it would be good if you could stick around to see what happens next. Do you think maybe you could kiss me now? Like, for old times' sake?"

He put a hand on either side of her face and did as she asked, kissing her with a sweet intensity that left her aching for everything she'd missed.

"Okay," he said finally. "I'll move to the coast. We'll figure us out. And the dad thing."

"I hope you know what you're getting yourself into," Brooke said.

The door opened a crack, and they hastily pulled apart. Henry stepped onto the porch, dressed in his favorite SpongeBob T-shirt and a sagging pair of pull-ups. "I pooped," he announced proudly.

Brooke scooped up her son and handed him over to Pete. "About that dad thing . . ."

Epilogue

October 2018

Moonlight dappled the water, and a stiff wind rattled the fronds of palm trees and swirled sand around the ankles of the five women standing at the water's edge.

Felicia tightened the blanket draped around her elderly aunt's shoulders. It had been an unusually chilly October on Talisa, with temperatures dipping into the forties and high winds buffeting the fragile dunes.

"Are you warm enough, Auntie?" she asked.

"There's an extra blanket in the back of the Packard," Lizzie offered.

"Don't y'all be fussin' over me now," Varina said. "I've lived this long, and I haven't frozen or blown away yet."

"Well, I for one am chilled to the bone," Marie said with an exaggerated shiver. "I know we agreed to do this every time we're together on a full moon, but nobody said anything about getting frostbite in the process."

Brooke gestured at the quilt, beach chairs, and picnic basket they'd set up a few yards away. "Don't be such a whiny baby, Mom. We've got hot toddies in the thermoses and plenty of beach towels."

"And what about that fire I built?" Lizzie asked. She'd spent hours digging a pit in the sand and circling it with bricks left over from the latest island restoration project. They'd hauled down a load of wood in the beach cart, and now the flames leaped high into the frigid night air, crackling and sending up showers of sparks.

"I think we should wait until the weather warms up again in the spring," Marie said. "After all, we didn't swim last month when you had court in Brunswick, Brooke, and it seems to me that Felicia was off island in August, visiting her new beau."

"No, ma'am," Varina said firmly. "Y'all know what today's date is?"

"It's October 21," Felicia said.

"Same exact date as the first time, the night after Millie's engagement party," Varina said solemnly. She pointed up at the star-shattered night. "You know what that is? It's a hunter moon, just like that night it all started. We only get one of those a year. Might be the last one I ever see."

"Don't talk like that," Felicia said.

"It's the truth. I'm ninety-one. Nobody in my family ever lived this long. I could go tonight or tomorrow, and I'm at peace with that," Varina said.

"Why is this so important to you, Varina?" Lizzie asked. "I can't believe you don't want to forget this date and everything associated with it. What happened to you —"

"Is in the past. And that's why I cast that ugliness out of my heart. I'm not letting it fester there like a poison-filled boil," Varina said. She grasped Lizzie's hand tightly and gazed out at the moon in wonder. "You know I wouldn't ever say that man's name after that night. I couldn't. But when I woke up to this sunny morning and realized what today is, it struck me from out of nowhere. I can't hate him no more. He is long dead, cold and in the grave, and I am alive and more blessed than I deserve. I got me a son I never even knew about. I got my own little home right here on this island, got family and friends . . ."

Marie nodded and grasped her daughter's hand. Wordlessly, Brooke reached for Felicia's hand.

"His name was Russell Strickland," Varina said. She repeated the name, enunciating and pausing between each syllable. "Russ. Sell. Strick. Land."

Without prompting, the women repeated the name.

"Russell Strickland is powerless over me," Varina said. She shrugged out of the blanket and took one tentative step into the water, and then another, letting out an involuntary yip of shock as the cold water reached her knees and then waist. She turned once, looking over her shoulder at the four women, standing naked on the shore.

"Y'all coming?"

ABOUT THE AUTHOR

Mary Kay Andrews is the *New York Times* bestselling author of *The Beach House Cookbook, The Weekenders, Beach Town, Save the Date, Ladies' Night, Christmas Bliss, Spring Fever, Summer Rental, The Fixer Upper, Deep Dish, Blue Christmas, Savannah Breeze, Hissy Fit, Little Bitty Lies,* and *Savannah Blues.* A former journalist for *The Atlanta Journal-Constitution*, she lives in Atlanta, Georgia.

The employees of Thorndike Press hope you have enjoyed this Large Print book. All our Thorndike, Wheeler, and Kennebec Large Print titles are designed for easy reading, and all our books are made to last. Other Thorndike Press Large Print books are available at your library, through selected bookstores, or directly from us.

For information about titles, please call:
(800) 223-1244

or visit our website at:
gale.com/thorndike

To share your comments, please write:
Publisher
Thorndike Press
10 Water St., Suite 310
Waterville, ME 04901